John R. Wright

LA GRULLA

DRYLAND PUBLISHING LLC
Mancos, CO

DRYLAND PUBLISHING LLC
35722 ROAD J.8
Mancos, CO 81328
www.drylandpublishing.com

Wright, John R., 1948-   /La Grulla
p. cm.
ISBN 978-0-9912659-0-9 (Paperback)
1. Western—Fiction 2. Romance—Fiction 3. Friendship—
Fiction
I. Title

For Thomas R. Wright, splendid horseman and devoted
father

LA GRULLA

Grulla is pronounced **grew**•yah, a Spanish word that can refer to a type of Spanish-bred horse that shares its blue-grey color with the sandhill crane.

•   •   •   •

In the fall of the year, in a small, New Mexico town, Jeff Cameron paid twenty dollars for a mouse-colored mare. This is their story.

ONE

THE SUN is just up, and it is a cold morning. There is thin light, but enough to see the vaquero beating his horse. She is beautiful, and he is lashing her with a quirt. It has tails of rawhide, and she screams, swinging at the end of the rope that ties her to the hitch rack. She crashes into the rail, going down heavily. And still he beats her, as though she has wronged him.

•   •   •   •

HE CAME in on the wagon road from the south, a tall young Anglo on a buckskin gelding, with a little red mule carrying his outfit packed under a diamond hitch. They have been long on the trail and need a rest. His name is Jeff Cameron. For days he has dreamed of a hot bath, a barbershop shave, a beefsteak, and a drink of whiskey. And later, a bed with clean sheets, up off the ground, out of the wind and wood smoke. He was on the road early, anxious to find it.

Through the last stretch of low sage and *piñón* he rode, into the old town of Taos, New Mexico Territory, in the shadow of the ancient Tiwa pueblo. Ahead lay a rutted, dirt street bordered by dust-colored adobe houses, with crude pens for goats, chickens, and hogs, some of which wandered loose in the street.

He stopped his horse to roll a cigarette. There was a hotel in sight, a *cantina*, and a *café*. A barber pole reminded him of that shave. In the street, a couple of Banty roosters with hackles raised, braced for combat, and a ladder-ribbed dog gnawed on a frozen goat head.

He shook tobacco from his pouch onto the creased paper, rolled it, sealed it with a swipe of his tongue, and placed it in his mouth. As he reached for a match, he heard cries of an animal in agony. He rode toward the sound.

Jeff saw a man in the outfit of a *vaquero*, with a rawhide quirt looped around his wrist, lashing a horse that swung at the end of a rope tied to a hitch rack. He sat his saddle, shock becoming anger. He saw the horse crash into the rail with enough force to splinter it, and throw itself to the ground. The *vaquero* stepped in with more blows as the animal struggled to regain its feet. A heavy stroke landed across the horse's face.

Cameron spat out the unlit cigarette, dropped the mule's lead rope, and put spurs to the buckskin. The distance between them was barely thirty yards. So absorbed was the horse beater, with his back turned, that the fast approach of the mounted man went unheard over the screams of the horse. Drawing rein, he stepped down from the gelding as they came even with the struggling pair. Still unaware, the *vaquero* raised the loaded quirt to deliver another blow. It never landed.

From behind, Jeff caught the lash in his hand. He jerked it hard, swinging the man around, and with the other fist struck him in the face sharply, twice. Surprised and staggered, the *vaquero* went for a knife in the sash tied around his waist. Jeff beat him to it, and with it he cut the quirt free. He turned it on the man, who went down under the lash. The knife lay in the dirt.

The horse was on its feet now and backed to the end of the rope, wide eyed and still tied to the broken rail, which angled out into the street. Cameron continued quirting the man as he cowered, cursing and crawling, trying to escape the punishment. But there was nowhere to go.

He reversed the quirt in his grip, wrapping the lash tails around his hand, and brought the butt of the quirt down in a final blow. The vaquero took it squarely on the head, dropped facedown into the road, and did not move.

•   •   •   •

JEFF CAMERON stepped back, heaving for breath. He dropped the quirt and looked toward the grey horse. It stood shaking, nostrils flared.

The street was quiet again, and the nervous mule came toward him with mincing steps, holding his head to one side to avoid stepping on the lead rope. Jeff saw him and waited. The man seemed calm now, and the mule allowed its face to be rubbed. "Sorry you had to see that, Jigger. Not a fittin' thing for a shy boy like you." His voice was breathless. The buckskin returned from its run down the street. The reunion was beginning to calm them all. Except for the abused one, still trembling at the end of its rope.

•   •   •   •

"NICELY DONE, *caballero*," said the old man.

Jeff looked up to see the man smiling at him from a rocking chair on the boardwalk. He was seated in front of a saddle shop, a blanket on his lap, braiding rawhide strips into a set of bridle reins. Looking around, Jeff saw no one else. There were, however, faces peering from windows behind curtains pulled aside. Such a violent start to the day had not gone unnoticed.

The younger man said nothing, but moved to stand over the motionless *vaquero*. He bent to one knee and put two fingers against the man's neck, just under an ear.

"Does he live?" asked the man in the rocker. Jeff nodded.

The old man spoke again. "Such a thing I have not seen in all my years. You were *muy furioso* in your righteous anger. An angel of justice. No man ever deserved a beating more than that one." Regarding Jeff out of watery eyes, he continued. "It was a kindness to spare the *caballa*." Jeff stood up and the braider went on. "But I fear you are not done with him. Or he with you." He shook his head.

"This man that you have bested is *muy malo,* a bad one. He calls himself a *vaquero,* but most of his time is in this *cantina.* He lost much at cards last night, drunk and playing wild. Accusing all at the table of cheating him, he started a fight. The offended men beat him senseless. It appears he gambled away his *pistola,* also, or he would have tried to shoot you. He passed the night on the billiard table." The old man paused.

"At best, he is always irritable. When drinking, he is *el Diablo.* The poor *caballa* there, she suffered his wrath. But now, he will look to you. It would probably be wise for you to go on and kill him." The little man smiled now, appreciating his own advice.

Jeff stepped around the motionless form on the ground, and moved toward the boardwalk and the man in the rocking chair. He had collected his breath enough to speak steadily now. "What's an old timer like you doin' up late in a saloon?"

The braider laughed. "Oh, I was long in my blankets and did not witness it. But news in a small town rides a fast horse. I heard about it this morning."

Jeff stopped at the edge of the boardwalk, near the old man. He nodded. "Seems kinda' cold for sitting outside and workin' rawhide, *viejo.*"

The braider grinned and bobbed his head. "I don't mind. In the Yucatan, where I lived as a boy, it was *muy caliente.* Here it is cool much of the year, and dryer, as well. I prefer it."

Jeff regarded him a moment, then looked at the blue-grey horse. It was a mare. He made a decision, dug down in his pants pocket and retrieved gold coins in the amount of twenty dollars. It was a high price for a horse.

"The mare, she goes with me. That son of a bitch'll never hit her again. Can I trust you to give him this money when he comes around?"

The little man smiled wider and put out a weathered hand. "*Si, claro.* Why not? What use has one of my years for gold? Wine sits badly on my stomach now, and with women I can do nothing. Not since I was eighty. I will pay him for you."

Jeff dropped the coins into his hand and thanked him. He approached the frightened mare. With a low voice and a gentle touch, he calmed her enough to remove the saddle and the severe ring bit bridle, which he dumped next to their still unconscious owner. He took the halter from the mule and eased it onto her head. Then they were ready to move out, Jeff on the gelding, the jittery mare on the lead in his hand, and Jigger coming along loose, willing to follow. He looked down at the man lying next to the horse gear. "Who is he?"

The old man frowned and spat. "He is Jaime Lucero, self-claimed *vaquero.* Also, card cheat, molester of women, and beater of horses. Everyone calls him Bad Jimmy. You may regret you did not kill him."

. . . .

JEFF CAMERON and his little string filed out of Taos, heading north, a weak sun on their backs. So much for the shave, a bath, and clean sheets. And now he had another horse, which he didn't need. Didn't seem he could leave well enough alone. But how could he ignore what he'd seen? His daddy never would have. And not him, either. No Tennessee man would stomach a thing like that.

. . . .

UP IN THE EVENING he found a sheltering patch of aspens, cut by a little wet weather creek, and bordered by massive old cottonwoods. There was a clear spot of about half an acre, knee deep in frost-cured grass. In short order he had his animals stripped of gear and staked out, and the last of a sack of oats divided among them. The undernourished mare acted as if she'd never seen a *morral* of grain, but after watching the gelding and mule tuck into theirs, she caught on.

Jeff dragged up enough deadfall cottonwood limbs to serve a small fire until bedtime, and got it going. He made a batch of pan bread in his small skillet, rubbed greasy with a chunk of bacon rind, and propped it up in front of the coals. He put on water for coffee. While the bread baked, he chewed antelope jerky and watched for the water to boil. The blackened can had once held peaches, and now was his camp pot. He was at the end of his coffee. Just enough for supper and breakfast. While the brew steeped, he took out the makings and smoked.

The creek was not flowing, but there was water standing under a skim of ice in a few pools. He broke open one of the holes and watered his animals as the last light faded.

Later, he stepped out of the fire glow to relieve himself. Then feeling chilled and tired, he rolled into his blankets, pistol tucked against his leg. Trying to imagine how a woman might feel, he slept.

·   ·   ·   ·

IN THE HOUR before dawn, the mare blew loudly and squealed. Jeff jerked awake to a sitting position, the Colt's Patent revolver in hand. There was enough moonlight to reveal a dark shape moving fast toward him, with a glint of steel.

He had just time to point and shoot. The muzzle flash lit up a shocked face. Momentum carried the attacker past him, the flat of the man's machete slapping Jeff across the chest. He leapt up as if his bed were on fire. The mare had broken her stake rope and he could hear her pounding off through the trees.

He yanked up a handful of rank grass and twisted it into a torch, then went to the fire and blew on the coals. The grass caught instantly, making a sorry light, but it was enough. On his back lay Bad Jimmy Lucero, the horse beater, staring blankly at the stars. There was a .45 caliber hole in his left cheek, just under the eye. Little blood came from there. It was flowing instead from the exit wound, soaking into the sandy ground beneath Lucero's head. Jeff put a hand on the man's chest. There was no heartbeat. "Well, Jimmy," he said, "I guess you're done bein' bad."

•   •   •   •

DAWN FOUND the young cowboy once more talking to the dead. "Seems like that old leather braider knew you well enough." He had dragged Lucero's corpse under a steep cutbank on an outside bend in the creek bed. "Told me I ought to of killed you right then." Jeff avoided making contact with the dead man's eyes. "This makes twice you tried to cut me." He untied the bandana from around his own neck and spread it over the body's ashen face. "Should'a hung on to your shooter." He stood quietly for a minute, looking down on the second man he'd killed in less than six months. It didn't feel good.

Going through Lucero's pockets, he reclaimed the price of the mare. He took nothing else off the dead man, neither his gold rings, the fancy Chihuahua spurs, nor the silver concho belt. He was no grave robber, but it was foolish to bury what was his own money. "Twenty dollars won't help you where you're going."

Then he caved the bank down over him, loosening the dirt with his small camp axe until the corpse was covered. He gathered rocks and brush and put them on the dirt heap. "I don't know why I'm bothering with this. A rotten son of a bitch like you deserves to feed every coyote and magpie in the neighborhood." He urinated on the mound. "That's what I think of you, *muchacho*. Besides, it'll keep critters away for a day or two. Other'n that, you go to hell, sir."

·   ·   ·   ·

AS THE LIGHT increased, he back trailed Bad Jimmy's footprints, looking for his horse. He found a common looking bay gelding, tied to an aspen. He recognized the saddle as the one he'd taken off the mare the previous day. Probably a borrowed or rented horse, he thought. "I don't need another pony, and if I did it wouldn't be you. No offense meant."

He checked the girth and it was tight, no doubt to save Bad Jimmy time for a hasty getaway. Jeff left it snug to prevent the saddle from rolling under the animal's belly as it traveled. He then took off the bridle, hung it over the horn, and tied it down with the saddle strings.

About to give the horse a swat for home, he checked himself and took a handful of mane. The gelding was content to stand quietly. "It comes to me that when you get back, some folks are gonna wonder how come you're not packin' Bad Jimmy." He took off his sweat-blackened hat. "I already got one more animal than I have any business with. And if I take you along, then on top of being a man shooter I'm a horse thief."

After a minute more of thought, he set his hat back on and lifted the Colt from its leather. The horse turned its head toward Jeff and fixed a warm, brown eye on him. It blew out a long breath. Jeff cocked the hammer and the animal's ears swiveled around at the crisp, metallic clicks. "It's you or me, pard," he whispered, placing the muzzle of the gun at the base of one of those ears. The gelding made no move.

Nothing happened for a count of five, and then he swung the gun away and fired into the sand a couple of feet back of the horse's hind legs. The animal sprang ahead and disappeared through the trees. Reloading the empty chamber and returning the gun to its holster, he turned back toward his simple camp. "Never shot a horse that wasn't too old to go on, or broke down too bad to heal."

Putting a handful of small sticks on the coals in the fire ring, he reached for the can of cold coffee. As the twigs began to smoke and then flame, he tried to ignore the voice in his head telling him that the day might come when he'd regret his decision to spare that horse.

•   •   •   •

DESPITE LUCERO'S violent intrusion and the scene that resulted, Jeff Cameron was determined to have his coffee, hot as blazes and accompanied by a well-savored cigarette. As he drained the last swallow until supplies could be bought, the mare walked out of the aspens, giving the fresh mound of dirt a wide pass, white eyed and wary. Seeing the buckskin and the mule hobbled near the fire ring, she joined them.

"Figured you'd show up sooner or later," he said. But she continued to look back toward the new grave, blowing sharply. "You can scent that bastard right through all the dirt, can't you, sis." He rose and moved slowly toward her, letting her smell the back of his hand. "And you sure as hell winded him this morning, didn't you. Let me know it, too. Saved me getting a split skull. I owe you for that."

He stroked her neck and whispered to her until she relaxed enough that he could repair the broken stake rope. Then it was time to break camp.

•   •   •   •

HE WANTED distance between them and the resting place of the former Bad Jimmy. He pushed his animals and by midday they had traveled more than fifteen miles. The country was deeply wooded and he easily found a secure spot to noon.

He built just enough fire to warm his hands and soften a piece of jerky, of which he was tiring. Tomorrow or the next day he'd need to shoot some meat. A fat, dry mule deer doe would do. The thought of pan-fried backstrap made his stomach growl.

The Winchester '76 hung in the saddle scabbard. How many cartridges remained? No more than a dozen. He'd need to buy a couple boxes of .45-75s. As far as that went, he needed other things, as well. Both his shirts were worn and brush snagged, and his jeans were thin in the seat. His two pairs of socks were thin, too, and his long johns had holes in the knees. He'd about ridden plumb out of his clothes, but he'd need to watch his remaining funds.

Gnawing the sinewy, dried meat, he considered the recent addition to his string. The mare stood quietly, tied to a young *piñón,* and not so frightened now. She had formed an attachment to the little red mule. For Jigger's part, he was smitten with her, as all male mules were prone to be with most any mare. The buckskin pretty much ignored her.

As she grazed at the end of the short lead rope, Jeff looked her over. She was built right, with a big hip, deep chest, gracefully arched neck, and a long, sloping shoulder. Straight legged and low hocked, her flat cannon bones tied into clean fetlocks and hard, black feet. Her mane and tail were long and black, and she had a luxurious forelock that hinted at mustang ancestors. Pretty never mattered much to Jeff, but he was taken with this one.

The mare's coat was a smoky shade of blue, similar to the color of a sandhill crane. The Mexicans had a word for it, *grulla.* That's what the *vaqueros* would call her. *La grulla.* There was a black, dorsal stripe down the middle of her back, from the base of her withers to the root of her tail. A shorter, perpendicular stripe spanned her shoulders at the bottom of her mane. *Vaqueros* called it the Sign of the Cross. Her legs were black from the knees and hocks down, and there were faint tiger stripes on her upper forelegs. She was a true line-backed dun.

Jeff recognized these marks as indications of the old Spanish blood. Blood of the first horses brought to the Americas by the Conquistadores. Blood brought to Spain from North Africa by the conquering Moors. Blood of the Arabian. Blood of the Barb. The most ancient, most honored, and most prized blood in the horseman's world.

He knew the signs and he knew that any horse possessed of this breeding, when well fed and in good condition, could boast tremendous endurance. His buckskin had some of that blood, but not as pure a strain as this mare. Jeff knew she would have what the old timers called "bottom," the strength to go and go, hour after hour, day after day, not necessarily at great speed, but steadily, and never quit.

• • • •

AFTER ABOUT FORTY-FIVE minutes of mid-day break, he gathered his stock, mounted the buckskin, and took the trail again. With the mare on the lead rope and the mule loose, bringing up the rear, they headed north. It was a clear afternoon and the air was warm. They made another ten or twelve miles before the sun fell behind the pine tops, and with just enough light remaining for a man to see clearly the front bead of a gun sight, they rode up on a small herd of deer. Half a dozen does and fawns of the year, a spike buck, and a young doe off a little way by herself, with no fawn of her own. At fifty yards they were unafraid of the four-legged trio at the edge of the timber. He hadn't planned on a kill until the next day or even the day after, but an opportunity like this was too good to pass up. Carefully sliding the rifle from its boot, he levered a cartridge quietly into the chamber and took his shot from the saddle. The mare set back at the roar of the big Winchester, but the gun-broke gelding and mule stood their ground. The solitary doe ran thirty feet and piled up nose first.

He made quick work of the carcass, removing the backstraps and tenderloins, as well as boning out the hindquarters for wrapping in a blood-blackened piece of canvas he carried for this purpose. With the meat stowed on the mule, they took the trail for another half hour, making two more miles and stopping to set up camp in darkness.

• • • •

WITH A POUND of rare venison loin in his stomach, a cup of cold branch water in his hand, and a hand rolled cigarette in his mouth, Jeff Cameron considered his future. He estimated the distance covered from Taos at forty to fifty miles. Somewhere ahead was the Colorado line. He was uncertain as to details on how this country laid out. He'd heard of Pagosa Springs on the San Juan River, where it was said that boiling water emerged from the ground at many points, releasing great clouds of steam that smelled of brimstone. He could go there.

He had forty-six gold dollars in his poke. Not a lordly sum, but enough to keep him for a month or even two if he managed carefully. It was handy to have retrieved the twenty dollars from his abrupt purchase of the mare. He was still figuring how he felt about that. He reasoned that the dead man had no need of the gold pieces and, anyhow, Jeff felt his cruelty to the horse justified his loss of the animal with no compensation. Sooner or later, the coyotes would dig him up. And coyotes don't spend gold. Not the four-legged kind, anyway. But he still felt a little like a horse thief. As to the killing, he had no such reservations. Lucero was the second man to go down before his gun and, on both occasions, he'd been under mortal attack.

Feet to the fire, his back against his up turned saddle, he thought about the course of the past year and before. His youth in Texas. His leave taking after his mother's death. The miles on the trail. The riding jobs. The card games. The

Didn't grow no cotton. That goddamned gentlemen's war weren't none of his business. And why the hell did Ma need to spend good money on a gravestone for a man that ain't even down there? A man that rotted away in a damned swamp ten years ago?"

He was raising his voice now, and Carla shoved him hard in the chest. "Well, just git the hell gone if all you can do is talk mean!" She was crying.

Jeff clamped his hat back on his head. "Sorry, sis. It just all seems like such a waste." He turned to walk to the barn and his saddle horse.

•   •   •   •

THEY SOLD OUT for next to nothing. The market was poor that sixth year of post-war reconstruction in west Texas. The half section of scrubby rangeland brought six bits an acre. They sold their small herd of thin cattle at the worst time of year, for little more than the green hides would bring. The wagon and team went on the block, too, and when it was done they had barely four hundred dollars for all of it. Jeff let Carla take most of the money to finance a return to relatives in Tennessee and an attempt at a new life. His share was a hundred dollars cash, a sixteen-year-old gelding wearing a twenty-year-old saddle, and his grandfather's muzzle-loading rifle.

It had taken close to a month to settle the estate, far too grandiose a term for their meager holdings. Jeff put his sister on the eastbound train the day after disposing of the last few items, and then stepped up on the aging sorrel and headed southwest. He had no plan. Distance from hurt was what he wanted. So he rode.

About all he had from his father was a deck of cards and some instruction in the game of poker. But young Jeff was leery of the coarse men at the tables in the towns he passed, so he kept his distance from those tables and held onto his money. He wandered without much purpose, occasionally taking for camp meat one of the stringy, unbranded long-horns running loose in the brush in the days after the war. The Tennessee rifle, brought from the Cumberland Plateau country by his paternal grandfather, was a rather light piece for anything much larger than whitetail deer. While the wild beef out in the breaks grew to great size, he could take down a yearling with a .40 caliber ball below an ear when he held a fine sight. Tough steak and cornmeal, bought for pennies from farmers along his way, were the extent of his fare in his first months of independent life.

Some weeks into his journey he swapped the old horse, the small-bore muzzleloader, and six of his hoarded dollars for a three-year-old buckskin colt, green broke and ungelded. He was a bit sorry to part with the old gun, which had been in the family for many years, but it was of limited use to him and was too long and cumbersome for him to carry horse-back.

With the help of a stout Mexican boy who took two bits for his efforts, Jeff castrated the horse the day he bought it. It was a procedure he had helped his father with several times on his and neighbors' farms. The surgery was relatively simple, accomplished with a sharp pocketknife. Infection was the only risk, and he left the incision unstitched to drain after a dousing of cheap whiskey employed as antiseptic. He walked the animal several times daily for five days to control swelling.

During the period of the colt's recovery, Jeff looked to replace the gun that had gone into the horse trade. He met an out-of-work cowhand who sold him a much worn .44 Henry rim fire and a small quantity of ammunition for the moderate sum of three dollars. It was little improvement over the old muzzleloader, chambering an underpowered car-tridge that was hard to find in the country stores he would encounter along the trail. But it was a repeater, with a high magazine capacity and a suitable length for carrying when mounted.

The buckskin healed quickly, and on the sixth day after the operation Jeff judged him fit to travel. He bought shoes and borrowed tools from the local blacksmith, and shod the colt himself. The first mile on the trail was interesting, what with the colt still somewhat sore and occasionally bucking halfheartedly. But if the young man could do anything at all in life, he could sit a horse. By the third day out, the newly gelded animal stood calmly to be saddled and mounted, and was stopping well and learning the aides from rein and leg.

Over the next months and then years, Jeff Cameron lived the life of an itinerant cowhand, drifting like tumbleweed and taking work as he found it. Down in the Big Bend country, he packed mules for the mines. Later, he helped gather cattle from the brush for the first drives to the east and north. Invariably, he was invited to go along, as he was becoming a top hand, learning to rope from the Mexican cowboys with whom he rode. He could catch a longhorn at a dead run, trip and tie him, or bring a calf to the branding fire like a flopping catfish on a line. But he let the herds trail off without him. He enjoyed the cowboy life, but the thought of long days of endless hours, short sleep, poor grub, and skimpy pay kept him from signing on.

During this time, the buckskin was growing into a top horse. At six years, he stood just under sixteen hands and registered eleven hundred eighty pounds on stockyard scales. For such a large animal, he was quick and athletic, and could carry Jeff for fifty miles or more a day, if asked, and still have more to give. Jeff took pride in him and turned down many an offer of more money than he'd ever seen at one time.

Fall of '81 found him in El Paso, roundup done, his pay drawn, and with no obligations for the winter. He boarded the buckskin and put down an extra ten cents a night for him to bunk in the livery barn loft. He had sixty-four dollars in his cowhide poke and as he rummaged in his war bag for his razor one morning he found the old deck of cards from his father. He shuffled, at first a bit awkwardly for not having touched the cards in months. Half an hour of practice later and he was smoother. He put the cards away.

That night he sat down to a gaming table for the first time since leaving the farm. There had been many a saddle blanket game in cow camps in past times, but this was his first experience on green felt. Here all was quiet and smoky, the patrons comprised of Texas and New Mexico cowboys, Mexican *vaqueros*, freight haulers, miners, and others of no apparent occupation and unknown origin. Of professional gamblers, there were none. He moved to different tables around town. On the morning of the sixth day, he rode out with four hundred thirty-two dollars of new money in his poke on top of the sixty he'd saved from his cowhand pay. He had played carefully and quietly, taking no great sum in any one game and so incurring no one's wrath. He had drunk little and whored not at all. And he left El Paso with the beginnings of the first plan of his young life.

•   •   •   •

JEFF SPENT the winter going back and forth across the border, trading in livestock. He bought cattle in Old Mexico, trailed them across the Rio Grande, and sold them for a modest profit in Texas. From his earnings, he bought three blooded horses—a stallion and two mares—that had been shipped out from the Harding plantation southwest of Nashville, Tennessee. The man who'd ordered the horses had died before their arrival, owing a balance of half the purchase price. Jeff was in the right place at the right time and was able to buy them for something less than the unpaid balance. He sold them to a wealthy *ranchero* across the border in Old Mexico, who had a standing order with him for top quality horseflesh. A tidy profit resulted from this trade. And for a time he owned a swift filly that he raced under a ninety-pound Mexican jockey. Regularly, they won. But the racing game was a nasty business and after two fistfights, which he won, and one near shooting, which he thought he probably would have lost, he sold the filly for a good price and moved on. He saved his money. From time to time, he'd ride into a town where he was unknown and find a card game. As always, he played conservatively, winning, but never too much. His strongest asset was his ability to read men from across the table. He did not believe in luck, particularly. He always was quiet but friendly. He avoided gaining a reputation and found himself welcome at most tables. He continued saving his money.

Around noon on the first day of May, he rode north on the buckskin, a '76 Winchester, caliber .45-75, in a scabbard under his right leg and the small, red john mule on a lead rope following, with his outfit covered by a canvas manty, lashed tight under a diamond hitch. A brand new, pearl-grey Stetson sat on his head. The rifle, mule, and hat had been won in a single card game from one man. A big bellied, loud Texan in his fifties, half drunk and playing foolishly. Jeff, annoyed at the man's behavior and knowing he'd be riding out the next day, applied his skills. He won all the man's money and then the mule, next the rifle, and finally the hat. Jeff left him at the table, bare headed and clambering for yet another hand with his boots at stake. He had determined the boots too big or the Texan likely would have found himself barefoot, as well.

His newly acquired hat was somewhat large, so Jeff stopped at a saddle shop, where the owner added a strip of soft glove leather to the sweatband. Then it fit. With his new hat at a slight, jaunty tilt, he made a picture of confidence and youthful vigor as he set out north. He followed the Pecos River, crossing into New Mexico Territory about forty miles south of Carlsbad.

Two

CAMERON'S PLAN was to buy land. Not just to own it, possess it, or take pride in that possession, but to build a dream upon it. His dream began in boyhood, and shaped up in the same way, each time he reflected on it. It looked like this. He saw a band of mares, standing hock deep in good grass, beside a stream of clear water winding through cottonwood shade. Each mare had a strapping foal at her side. Fillies and colts, bright eyed and twitchy tailed. On nearby high ground in this dreamscape stood a dun stallion, deep chested and short backed, his long forelock lifted in the breeze. He watched intently for any threat to his band. And they all had the lined backs, the crossed shoulders, and the striped forelegs, every one of them. Spanish blood.

He rode north along the west bank of the Pecos, the buckskin stepping out smartly, the mule working a little to keep up. And though they made good progress, he wished for wings to fly over hills and valleys.

He'd heard trail hand talk about the country to the northwest. Stories of the old Spanish town of Albuquerque. It sat in the Rio Grande Valley below the Sandia Peaks. Word was that stock prospered when summered in the mountains and brought down to winter in the valley. Jeff figured to look it over as part of his quest. If he liked what he saw, he'd stop. If it didn't suit, he'd ride on.

Day after beautiful day they drifted north and west, using the fine spring weather to steadily put miles behind them. He found new grass shooting up in the meadows, wildflowers bursting on the banks of creeks and streams, and birds in mating games crisscrossing the skies above him. At times he felt mesmerized by the sway of the saddle, the scent of growing things, and the song and sweeping flight of the birds. The spring sun on his shoulders was like a caress of friendly hands. He began to realize that for the first time since early boyhood, he was happy.

Along the way, he stopped at ranches and in small villages, purchasing grain for his animals and provisions for himself. For relief from his fare of wild meat, he bought chickens and eggs, when available, and bacon and cornmeal. It cost little and he enjoyed, as well, the human contact. He was careful with his money. He had little fear of robbery. He figured his buckskin could outrun any effort to pursue him, though that could mean abandoning his mule. He made defensible night camps and considered himself well armed with the Winchester '76.

There was tension, briefly, the day he rode out of Hondo, New Mexico Territory. He'd stayed the night in the loft of a livery barn, over his stalled animals, after a bath, shave, and a *café* meal. The consequence of a few too many whiskies in a hotel bar, he'd slept in longer than usual and had a late start the next morning. About mid-afternoon, he'd rounded a bend in the trail to see two riders in the way ahead. They were poorly mounted and filthy, and from his distance of roughly seventy-five yards he saw no rifles. Pistols he figured on, somewhere on their persons, out of sight. But from where he sat his horse, he was safely beyond sure handgun range.

For a while, nothing was said and no one gave ground. It was a tense couple of minutes. At last he stepped down from his horse and slid the big '76 out of its boot. Turning the buckskin crossways in the trail, he levered a round into the chamber and rested the rifle in clear view across the saddle. The two riders watched without apparent reaction. Then Jeff brought the crescent-shaped butt plate into the hollow of his shoulder and took a fine bead on the chest of the man to the left. For another half minute, nothing happened. Then, unhurriedly, the two riders turned their horses off the trail and into deep scrub oak, disappearing. No one during that time had spoken a word.

He waited another few minutes and then re-mounted, cradling the Winchester in his arm. He rode into the scrub oak opposite where the other two riders had departed and proceeded with vigilance for a mile or so before returning his rifle to its scabbard and picking his way back to the trail. There was no more trouble.

• • • •

THEY WERE in no particular hurry. Jeff estimated they averaged fifteen miles a day, looking the country over as they went. It changed around them, rising gradually in elevation and hosting more timber. After two weeks, they made camp high in the mountains east of Capitan. There were trout for the taking in the creeks and beaver ponds, and elk in the meadows. Jeff killed a young cow, and jerked and smoked the prime cuts. Taking hooks and line from his kit, cutting a willow pole, and collecting grasshoppers for bait, he filled a sack with cutthroats. These he smoked, as well. The animals rested and fed on the lush mountain grass. Jeff and the buckskin rode leisurely up one drainage and then another. It was fine country, but it was not speaking to him. And his stockman's eye told him it was too high for cattle and horse range. Deep snows would be too much challenge.

After four days, they moved on. In another week the smoked fish were gone and he was tired of jerked elk. At a small *rancho* south of San Acacia, he traded what was left of the elk to a giggling *mamacita* for two laid out hens and a dozen eggs. The *segundo* offered him a job when he noticed the rawhide *reata* tied to the fork of his saddle. In fluent Spanish, Jeff politely declined. They insisted he stay to supper, so he ate with the riders, filling up on good beef, *chile*-fired beans, and freshly baked *tortillas*. He spent a comfortable night under a *ramada*, his animals fed and tethered nearby.

At first light, he declined an offer of breakfast and re-turned to the trail. Accepting too much hospitality could bring an obligation to stay and work it off, and he felt the need to be riding again. So ride he did, turning west into the mountains north of Magdalena. He rode over more good land, but none of it spoke to him or his dream. He was not bothered, however. He felt it was out there for him to discover, the place for him, and when he saw it, he'd know it.

He pushed the pace and arrived at the outskirts of Albu-querque in three days. As he rode into the old Spanish city, he was feeling trail worn. His first thoughts, as always, were to his animals. Once they were comfortable in a decent livery barn, his next move was to a mercantile. Two new shirts, a canvas vest, two pairs of denim jeans, along with underwear and socks, made an armload. He looked with interest at new boots, but decided to wait. At the barbershop he bathed, had his hair cut, and was shaved, keeping the beginnings of a mustache. He dressed in the new clothes, depositing the old ones in a trash barrel. The other shirt, jeans, underwear, and socks he carried in a cardboard box, tied up with string.

Next door to the barber was a gunsmith shop and he stepped inside to the ring of a small bell. He set his purchases down on the far end of a glass-topped display case, in which was arranged a variety of handguns and several knives. Beyond it, hung on the wall, was a rack of long rifles, carbines, and shotguns. From the back room emerged a short, thickset man of about fifty, with spectacles low on the bridge of his nose and a bald head, wiping his hands on a rag blackened with gun grease. "Do something for you, son?"

Jeff looked up from the display of pistols. "You the gun-smith?"

The man pointed to a sign hanging high on the wall, over the door to the back of the building, reading, "Ed Reynolds, Gunsmith. No one admitted in workshop without invitation. This means you!" He grinned, "That'd be me."

Jeff nodded. "I got an old Henry in my outfit down at the livery. It's worn some, but it still shoots all right. But I just picked up a Winchester '76, so I got no use for the Henry now. I thought you might like to buy it off me."

The gunsmith grinned wider. "Forty-four rim fire, right?" Jeff nodded again. "How many shells you got for it?"

Jeff's face went into a slight frown. "About a dozen, I reckon."

Reynolds nodded, "That's more'n I thought you'd have. Those rounds are getting almighty scarce. No punch to them. Why, you got to empty the whole magazine into a jackrabbit to kill it. No one wants them old Henrys these days, not since the '73 and '76 Winchester came out. I don't want one neither. Sorry son."

Jeff nodded again. For the time that the gunsmith had taken to answer, he'd fixed his eye on a revolver in the case before him.

"You got a sidearm, young man?" asked Reynolds.

Jeff looked up and said, "Wish I did."

The gunsmith had observed the object of his potential customer's interest, and so he reached into the case and pulled out the pistol and placed it on a square of soft, tanned buckskin that lay on the glass top. "Colt's Patent revolver, Single Action Army, introduced in '73, .45 caliber, four-and-five-eighths-inch barrel, custom-made, elk horn grips. Throws a two hundred fifty-five grain bullet, pushed along by forty grains of black powder. Packs one hell of a wallop. Also known as the Peacemaker. Aims as natural as pointing your finger. Pert' near new, this one here is. I even got the original gutta percha grips that come on it from the factory. Had about a box of shells through it. Make you a good deal, son. Go on. Pick it up."

Jeff took it in his hand. The balance and fit felt right. He'd shot a few rounds through some of the handguns his fellow cowhands owned, but most of them had been Civil War vintage and none of them filled his hand like this one. It felt alive. The cylinder and barrel were a deep midnight blue, the frame was casehardened, and the horn grips were a rich butter yellow. Jeff thought it the most exquisite piece of hardware he'd ever seen. "How much?"

Reynolds removed his glasses and massaged the red place on the bridge of his nose. "Sells new for fourteen dollars. Being as it's a teeny bit used, you can have it for twelve."

Jeff whistled. He set the hammer on half cock, turned the cylinder, and listened to the satisfying clicks of the mechanism. "I'll trade you my Henry and pay some boot."

The gunsmith got a look on his face as though he'd just smelled something bad. "Done said I got no use for that old smoker, son."

Jeff continued to admire the pistol for another moment and then said "Well," in a faintly disappointed tone, carefully setting the piece down.

Reynolds looked at the cowboy's sagging face, then back at the gun. "Aw, hell," he said, "Bring me that damned old beater of yours and give me ten dollars, and we got a deal. I want all the shells you got for it and I'll throw in a handful of .45s for that Colt."

Jeff was smiling broadly, already digging in a pants pocket for his money. "I gotta go to the livery and get that rifle. I'll leave the pistol here 'til I get back."

Reynolds pushed the gun toward Jeff, butt first, then reached under the counter and produced the factory grips. "Take it with you, son. You got an honest look about you. I'd probably be better off if you never brought that wore out smoke pole back here anyway."

Jeff received the revolver almost reverently. "Thank you, sir. I will be back." Tucking the gun behind his waistband in front and dropping the loose ammunition and spare grips into pockets, he picked up his box of mercantile purchases and turned for the door.

"And, son," said the gunsmith. Jeff looked back. "You just hope and pray that you never have to use it for nothin' worse than puttin' down a crippled horse or stoppin' a mad cow."

•   •   •   •

IN THE NEXT BLOCK was a hotel above a bar and restaurant. After going to the livery barn for the Henry and delivering it to the gunsmith, he took a room, stowed his war bag, Winchester, and new revolver in the closet, locked the door, and went downstairs to eat. It was early evening, before emergence of the supper crowd, so there were empty tables. A very dignified, Spanish-looking man of middle age waited on him, his white shirt crisp and trousers sharply creased. Jeff ordered beefsteak rare, potatoes fried with onions, and beans. When the T-bone arrived, it looked as big as a saddlebag. Apple pie and coffee topped off his meal. A leisurely walk to the livery and back to check on his animals settled his stomach. Two whiskeys at the bar reminded him how tired he was. Climbing the stairs in satisfied weariness, he let himself into the room, drew the shade, and undressed for bed. It was his first night off the ground in quite a while. A long awaited luxury. Loading the Colt, he slid it under the pillow, crawled between clean sheets, and tipped over into a deep well of sleep.

•   •   •   •

AFTER ONE MORE DAY of rest, sightseeing, and steak eating, and another night in the hotel, Jeff inquired as to the location of the stockyards. The hotel desk clerk told him the way, and he walked to the livery barn for his horse. The hostler made small talk with him as he saddled the buckskin. A ten-minute ride brought them to their destination. The buckskin was feeling his oats and Jeff slackened the reins enough to let the big horse burn some energy. They moved at a long but controlled canter and the young man reveled, as before, in the smooth power of his mount.

Once there, he rode at a brisk walk around pens and sheds, up and down alleys, and examined corrals of differing capacities. Some contained cattle of mixed breeds, many colors, and a range of ages. Elsewhere, horses of varying size and quality ate their morning hay. Another shed, built long and low, was packed with sleeping hogs. Finally, Jeff found what he sought. An empty, pole corral with a loafing shed in one corner. Back of it was an unoccupied adobe shack about sixteen feet square, with a stove pipe exiting the roof next to the ridge. As he looked on, he saw a mouse run along the outside wall and skitter under the door.

He had noticed something of an office building on his way in and rode back to it. Stepping off the buckskin, he dropped the reins and crossed the narrow front porch to the entry. Through the partly open door he saw a heavy set, dark-skinned man asleep in a captain's chair, dusty boots propped up on the desk. Jeff knocked and went in. The man jerked awake and for an uncertain moment he seemed on the verge of going over backward. But he righted himself like a harbor buoy, narrow on top and broad below. His feet settled heavily on the floor. "*Heysoos Cristo, hombre*, you nearly scare the sheet out of me!"

Jeff grinned. "Pardon, *señor*. You run this yard?"

The man rose to his feet, straightened to his full five feet seven inches, and spoke with recovered dignity. "*Si, señor.*" He executed a courtly bow, sweeping off a sweat-stained, straw hat. "Perfecto Gomez, at your orders. I am *El Segundo* of this facility."

Jeff kept smiling. "The owner around?"

Gomez shook his head, chins wagging. "Unfortunately, no. He is absent on matters of importance. In his place, I am authorized to conduct business with the public. How may I serve you, *señor*?"

A chair sat on Jeff's side of the desk and he took it. A flustered Gomez spoke a little too late, "Please, sit down, *señor.*"

He resumed his seat as well. Jeff hooked a thumb toward the one, dingy window. "There's a small corral on the east side of the yard and a 'dobe shack behind it. I'd like to rent them."

Gomez wrinkled his brow in concentration. "For how long, may I ask?"

"Let's say a month," he answered.

Gomez pursed his lips in consideration. "Six dollars a month for the corral and water."

Jeff allowed a small frown. "Sounds a little steep."

Gomez shrugged weakly. "I do not set the rates, my friend."

Jeff nodded noncommittally. "How 'bout with the shack thrown in?"

Gomez shook his head apologetically. "I regret to say it is unavailable."

Jeff frowned again. "How come?"

"It is for the night man."

"Looks empty to me."

"Presently, we are without a night man."

"So rent it to me."

"We may engage a night man."

"When did the last one leave?"

Gomez looked sheepish. "Two years ago."

"So you save it for a night man you never replaced?"

Gomez tugged his chin whiskers uncomfortably. After a moment of hesitation, he continued. "Unfortunately, there is a superstition, *señor.*"

"About the shack?"

"*Si.*"

"What sort of superstition?"

"The last night man died in there."

"Murdered? Suicide?"

"No, *señor*. Whiskey."

"So rent it to me. I'm not superstitious and I don't drink much."

Gomez scratched his fleshy jowls. "Perhaps you would like to be the new night man?"

Jeff shook his head. "I don't need a job."

"It is not much of a job."

"What's there to it?"

"You must walk around the yard after dark. Not too much. Only a couple of times. Wear a pistol where it can be seen. Or perhaps carry a rifle. You own such weapons?"

"One of each."

"Excellent. The important thing is for it to be known that an armed man is about the premises after dark. Once the word is out, no bad thing will happen."

"What's the pay?"

Gomez made a sad face. "Unfortunately again, there is no actual money for the night man. You see, there is so little work involved, that it is the opinion of my employer that a place to live rent free is ample compensation."

Jeff made a face of his own. "What about the risk?"

Gomez smiled. "But there is so little, *señor*."

Leaning back in the chair, Jeff looked steadily into the large man's eyes until the latter began to fidget. "Alright, here's my offer," he said. "I'll patrol the yard once at sundown and once again around midnight. And I'll do it ahorseback. I'm not traipsin' all over ten acres in the dark afoot. For that, I get the shack and the corral free. And you'll sell me hay and grain for my stock at your cost. And I want one night off a week. How 'bout it?"

Gomez made a stern face. "Who will watch the yard on your night off?"

Jeff smiled. "Same *hombre* that's done it for the last two years."

Gomez looked puzzled. "But that is no one, *señor.*"

Jeff smiled wider. "Exactly."

Gomez seemed even more confused. Then he blushed under his deep tan. "As you say. Exactly. You are a clever man, my friend. You drive a hard bargain, but it is obvious that the shack and corral are empty, bringing no income to this business. And I suspect that a man such as yourself will soon establish a reputation for being no one to challenge. I am sure no harm will come to this place under your watch. As to a night off, could you make it random, not always the same night?"

Jeff nodded. "Sure."

Gomez smiled and went on. "And as to the feed, I beg you allow me a minimal profit."

Jeff looked calmly into the man's eyes. "How much?"

Perfecto Gomez put on a contrite expression. "For the hay, one dollar on the ton, and for the grain, a half cent on the pound."

His fleshy face was pleading and Jeff thought he could afford this man a small portion of dignity. Leaning forward, he put out his hand. "Fair enough, *amigo.*"

Gomez beamed as he shook vigorously. "*Si.* A good arrangement. *Muy bien. Gracias, señor.*"

Both men stood up and moved toward the door. Jeff turned before stepping outside. "Reckon you could sweep that shack out and pull the mouse nest out of the stove?"

Gomez straightened proudly. "Of a certain, *señor.* I will have my best man see to it promptly."

Jeff grinned. "That'd be fine. I'll get my plunder and my stock from the livery, and be back here before supper time."

He turned and stepped off the porch as Gomez all but saluted.

"*Muy bien, señor*. Everything will be in readiness upon your return."

•   •   •   •

JEFF RODE OUT of the yard congratulating himself on a triumph of economy. He had secured lodgings for all three of them for the cost of feed alone, plus a few hours of his time that could hardly be considered work. Now he could concentrate seriously on his land search.

•   •   •   •

OVER A HEARTY BREAKFAST, he took stock of his finances. He'd gotten into his poke to the tune of about seventy dollars, what with the hotel bill, restaurant meals, bar drinks, livery barn charges, half a ton of hay, and a hundred fifty pounds of grain for the coming month. Added to that was the purchase of new clothes and the fine Colt revolver, as well as trail expenses on the trip up from Texas. Not bad, he thought. But the idea of a month of all outgo and no income sat cross grain to his nature. Riding jobs could be had, but that would mean no time to scout for land. That left cards. He needed to find a game.

•   •   •   •

GOMEZ WAS sweeping out the adobe when Jeff rode up with his gear. Embarrassment crossed his face at the sight of his new tenant. "You are early, *señor*," sputtered Gomez. "My man is absent today on matters of importance. I thought it best to attend to this myself, only to see that it is done properly."

Jeff said thanks. He imagined that as long as Gomez was in charge here, someone would always be "absent on matters of importance." No doubt this yard was, in reality, a one-man operation.

In fact, the shack was very presentable, not even cold ashes in the stove, and he voiced his appreciation. Gomez beamed with the praise. Jeff undid his bedroll and laid it out on the rope-sprung bunk, stowed his war bag in a corner, and started a fire in the stove for coffee. It was warm out, and he opened the door and both windows. Gomez declined the offer of a cup and shuffled back to his office, broom in hand.

Stripping the gear from his animals, Jeff turned them into the corral, checked the water tank, and tossed out hay. Later, as the sun dropped, he brought his cup of coffee along with a cigarette to the corral and hooked his boot heel over the bottom pole. The gelding and mule looked up from their supper. "Well, boys," he said in a low voice, "for a while, anyway, I guess we're home."

• • • •

THE NEXT WEEK saw them establish an agreeable routine. Jeff would rise before first light, feed the stock, boil water for coffee, and fry bacon or *chorizo* and maybe an egg or two, with a usual side of beans and *tortillas*. By the time the sun was above the horizon, he was mounted and gone. He carried biscuit and a chunk of leftover meat from the previous night's supper in a saddlebag and stayed out all day. They traveled the country all around, the tall, young *Americano* on the big buckskin, talking to farmers and ranchers, cowboys and hunters, sheepherders and woodcutters. When he'd seen all the nearby draws and hollows, all he could ride in a day, he'd pack the mule on the morning of his off night as watchman, and stay out an extra day. He saw plenty of country, but none yet spoke to him.

On nights he was in town, he'd try to find an early game so he could be back to the yard for his late rounds. He'd take a turn around the pens on Buck, the Winchester across the saddle fork, and then go to bed. There was no trouble.

He gambled conservatively. As was his habit, he made a circle of the bars and card rooms, never sitting down to any one table two nights running. He was quiet and unremarkable, not wanting to become known. Regularly, he won. Some nights he brought only five dollars away from the game, never more than fifty, and probably averaged ten. Playing three nights a week, he made what a cowhand would draw in a month. In the first two weeks, he had replenished his road stake. He had the money from his El Paso bank wired to a new account at The Stockman's Bank of Albuquerque. He added to it with regular deposits. The four hundred dollars from his poke went into the new account as well, and he seldom carried more than twenty dollars on his person. He lived simply and at the end of that first month his balance was just under two thousand dollars. After one exceptional night at the tables, when the cards seemed to be running his way, he gave in to the opportunity to win big, and next day treated himself to a new pair of boots. He considered the purchase of a black hat that caught his eye, but the pearl-grey Stetson, though sweat stained and dirty by now, was still serviceable. Returning to the gunsmith shop, he bought a used holster and cartridge belt for the pistol.

• • • •

JEFF PAID Gomez for another month's feed. The yard boss was happy for the presence of the serious young man with the big bore rifle. The money was welcome, as well.

It was now the end of June and full on summer. He bought four young tomato plants from the garden of an old, leather-skinned woman living behind the yards and transplanted them on the sunny side of his shack. He had tended tomatoes for his mother and having a few of his own was a pleasure. He worked old, rotten manure from the sheep pens into the dirt around the plants and carried water for them in a bucket from the stock tank. He spoke warmly to them, the plants, in Spanish. They thrived. He enjoyed them with his breakfast, sliced and mixed with eggs fried runny.

Jeff gave himself more time to continue his consideration of land in this northwestern end of New Mexico Territory. It was a big country, and despite his constant riding there was much yet for him to see. He told himself that if nothing had caught his attention by the first of August, he'd head north into Colorado.

• • • •

FOURTH OF JULY wasn't much of a holiday in Albuquerque, what with more Indians, Mexicans, and old land grant Spanish in residence than Americans. But a handful of conspicuously drunk, loud, and obnoxious *gringo* cowboys were doing their best to make up for being outnumbered, waving the stars and stripes and shooting at empty whiskey bottles thrown in the air, hitting few. Jeff decided to seek a quieter corner in the old part of town. He rode over after supper and from the street he heard the sweet sound of a woman singing, accompanied by soft chords from a guitar, coming through the open door of a small *cantina*. Tying his horse at the hitch rail outside, he crossed the boardwalk and went in.

He stopped just inside, both to give his eyes time to adjust to the low light of coal oil lamps and to determine the likelihood of any threat. Such care had served him well on more than one occasion. As vision improved, he looked to the source of the music and his breath caught. Across the smoky room, on a small raised stage, sat what he thought must be the most appealing sight of his young life.

Her voice was low and smoky as the air, and she sang in Spanish, a sad song of lost love. She was small and her sandaled feet peeked from under a black skirt, heels resting on the bottom rung of a barstool. An oil lamp hung above her, casting a mellow light on midnight-dark hair. She raised her eyes from her guitar and they were green.

Jeff had been kicked once, while shoeing a horse, dead center in the chest, over his heart. The feeling that struck him now wasn't much different. Her skin was the color of melted caramel, like on a candy apple at the county fair. Her eyes swept the room as she sang and coming 'round rested on his. He didn't blink. He couldn't breathe.

The best he could do was to stand dumbstruck, like a cigar store Indian, with his face on fire, heart pounding. After a quarter minute, when a couple of patrons turned to see what had the girl's attention, his leaden feet lifted from the floor boards and carried him to an empty stool at the bar. The girl's eyes followed him until he was seated.

His idea had been to find a game, but as long as she played, he sat there, nursing a beer, completely transfixed. When she stopped around midnight, he saw her leave with a tall *gringo* of middle age, dressed in town clothes. Draining his glass, Jeff went home.

• • • •

AUGUST CAME and he bought more feed from Gomez. He still rode the country, but less often. On nights the girl played, he was at the *cantina*, sipping beer and basking under her spell. Most times, she left with the man, the tall, angular fellow in black broadcloth, narrowed eyes set above a thick, sandy-colored mustache.

Jeff made discrete inquiries about the girl. He learned her name was Inez Sullivan, child of a Mexican mother and an expatriate Irish father. Patrick Sullivan was one of a number of disaffected Irish Catholics who deserted the American Army and joined the Mexicans to fight against the United States in its war with Mexico. When the outcome became obvious, he deserted again and made his way north, traveling by night and living off mesquite beans and rabbits. Winding up in New Mexico Territory, he tried his hand at the work the area offered. He married late to a young woman from Guaymas, Mexico, on the east coast of the Sea of Cortez.

Soon, there was a little girl. The mother missed the blue water and salt air, and when the baby was two, she simply disappeared. Sullivan made an effort at fatherhood, but homesickness for the old sod, plus whiskey and belligerence, put an end to him. He was shot dead by a freighter he sometimes drove for, whom he had attacked upon his termination for drunkenness. The girl was twelve years old and on her own. Most of this Jeff learned from the barman at the *cantina* where she sang.

On a night in mid-August, he sat in on a game in one of the saloons patronized primarily by *Americano* ranchers and cowhands. He was playing distractedly, chafing at the wait before he could head over to the *cantina* and hear the girl sing. For a week, he had looked for an opportunity to speak to her. That she was aware of him, he knew. Their eyes met often and he thought he sensed favor in her look. But always the man in black broadcloth showed up and thwarted any move. Jeff met his eyes as well, more than once, and each time he saw menace there.

It was still two hours until her performance when a man appeared at the card table and asked to sit in. Jeff looked up to see a tall fellow in a black, round crowned hat and broadcloth coat. A heavy mustache, trimmed cavalry style, covered his upper lip. Of course, Jeff recognized him. They made eye contact, the standing man smiling flatly. When no one objected, he took an empty chair and arranged paper money and coins in a neat stack on the table in front of him. The deal went 'round and Jeff made an effort to concentrate on his cards, feeling the gaze of the girl's escort.

Gradually, the game changed. Jeff had not won much, nor had he lost much. But each time the deal came to the new man at the table, he got no cards worth having. That he was being cheated, he was sure. How "The Mustache," as he thought of him, was doing it, he hadn't a clue. After losing four straight hands dealt by the new arrival, he stood, picked up his money from the table, and put it in his pocket. The Mustache looked up, smiling.

"Had enough, sonny?" Leaning back comfortably in his chair, his eyes rested on Jeff with unconcealed contempt.

"I'd appreciate it if you'd leave off calling me sonny," Jeff said. "Kind of dirties the memory of my daddy."

The Mustache relinquished his condescending smirk for a moment. "Just a figure of speech friend. No offense meant."

Jeff's look was bland as he said, "I guess a gent like you has a mess of friends. Slick talkers mostly do. Just don't confuse me with none of 'em."

The man frowned. He let his chair come back down, the front legs softly contacting the floor. "You seem a little hot and proddy, son."

Now Jeff's eyes went flat and dead. "I get that way when a game goes out of square. And one more time, I ain't your son nor any kin to you."

The man's eyes changed to match Jeff's. "First off, son is just a figure of speech, like I already said. Fact is, I don't believe I'd care to claim you as no kin to me, neither." The two other card players at the table began to carefully gather their cash and chips. The Mustache went on, "And second, what's out of square about this game? What exactly do you mean? And see you answer cautious."

Jeff kept his hands still. "Alright. I mean, exactly, that the game turned sour, went off plumb, you might say, and it got that way just about the time you sat in."

The Mustache straightened in his chair and, as if on cue, the other two men at the table stood and left as he spoke. "I recommended a cautious answer, friend, but it seems almost as if you're saying you've been cheated. Have I heard you right?"

Jeff took a slow, deep breath and said, "If I have been cheated, it was only when the deal came round to you."

The Mustache stiffened visibly. "Those are deadly words, boy. Now think about how you want to answer this." He let a short pause underline the gravity of his next question. "Are you now calling me a card cheat?"

Jeff's eyes were on the man's hands as he answered. "If I could see how you were doing it, the answer'd be 'Yes.' But I can't. You're damn good."

The Mustache made a slow and deliberate move to unbutton the front of his coat as he said, "You are way out on a dry limb, boy. You'd be better served to do more thinkin' and less talkin', and that is a mortal fact."

Jeff's eyes were blank as he replied. "Well, if you're feelin' froggy, then just hop on." Saying this he backed up slowly, bumping his chair, the wooden feet squeaking on the unvarnished board floor.

Very carefully, The Mustache rose from his seat. At that moment, a steady voice came from behind the bar. "Not in here, gentlemen."

Jeff and his opponent turned their heads just enough to see Big Mike Murphy, the barman, all six foot four and two hundred fifty pounds of him. "And not on my shift." He held a sawed-off, ten gauge shotgun leveled at the two of them, the muzzles seeming as big as rain barrels. Both hammers were at full cock, and his right index finger was snug against the front trigger. "This here cannon ain't loaded with rock salt, boys. Now, Jeff, you get your young ass out of here. And you with the lip whiskers, sit the hell down and put your hands flat on the table. I ain't tellin' neither of you twice."

The Mustache eased back into his chair, his eyes never leaving the cowboy. "See you over at the *cantina*?" he asked.

Jeff's neck and cheeks felt on fire as he said, "Count on it!"

Murphy's voice boomed. "Goddamnit, Jeff, I said git!"

•   •   •   •

THE HORSE sensed his man's anger and was jittery under the saddle as they made their way back to the stockyard. At the shack, Jeff loosened the cinch, slipped off the bridle, dropped it over the horn, and turned the buckskin into the pen with the mule. Inside, he reached for a bottle of whiskey that sat on a windowsill, poured three fingers in a tin coffee cup, and slugged it down. Standing there, feeling the burn descend to his stomach, he held out his right hand at waist level, palm down, fingers spread. It shook. Not violently, but noticeably. His anger had cooled only slightly. He'd never thrown down on a man before. But he'd been close tonight. So close that he thought he wanted it. Wanted to jerk his Colt from his holster, yank back the hammer, point the muzzle square at that son of a bitch's chest, and pull the trigger. See him slammed to the floor, a broad, red rose blossoming across the boiled, white shirt, right over his heart. He'd wanted to kill. Wanted it bad.

Hanging his gun belt on a peg in the wall, he sat down at the small table and poured himself more whiskey, just two fingers this time. He sipped slowly. In a few minutes more, his hands were steady enough that he rolled and lit a cigarette. He took the smoke in deep and let it out a little at a time. When it was finished, he tossed the butt in the stove and rolled another. Halfway through the second smoke, the cup empty again, his shaking had subsided.

Through the window, by the light of the three-quarter moon, he could see his animals in the pen, noses down and whiffling in the dirt for any wisps of hay they might have missed.

The buckskin was still saddled and it occurred to Jeff that he had a choice. Either go and un-tack that horse and then return to the house and fall into bed. Or bridle him again, cinch up, and ride to the *cantina*, as he'd intended all along. He was certain The Mustache would be there. That there'd be more trouble, certain, too. Gunplay, likely. Someone shot or even killed, more likely. He took a last draw on his smoke, stood up, stepped to the stove, and flipped the butt into the firebox. Hitching his jeans a little higher, he reset the hat on his head and moved toward the door. Coming to the peg in the wall, he stopped. Several heartbeats passed as he looked at the revolver hanging there, well fitted to the oiled leather holster, each loop on the belt holding a cartridge, moonlight through the window reflecting off the brass casings. Then he took down the rig, buckled it, and went to his horse.

•   •   •   •

RIDING BACK toward the old part of town, Jeff's mind went to the girl. He'd yet to exchange a single word with her, knew almost nothing about her, beyond the fact that she looked to be about twenty years old, made her living with a guitar and a sweet voice, and left work after each performance with the man who wore a cavalry mustache, a black hat, and a broadcloth coat, and who cheated at cards. All he knew beyond that was he wanted to know more.

At the age of twenty-nine, Jeff'd had less experience with women than many men his age. There had been no time for sweethearts growing up. Too much work on that miserable piece of Texas dirt just to survive, no time for paying attention to girls. And damned few girls to pay attention to. Afterwards, on his own, drifting from one riding job to the next, with scant money and less in the way of prospects, there seemed little to offer a decent woman. More than that, he had no interest in a relationship or the commitment required. Not that his young man's veins didn't course with red blood. He'd hired his small share of cow town whores, when the roundup ended and the boss paid off.

But, on balance, a fulltime woman was never part of the picture. Or, at least, never before. Now, however, he caught himself entertaining just such ideas, and they'd kept his head spinning since that Fourth of July night when he first heard Inez Sullivan sing.

He heard her voice now as he stopped his buckskin in front of the *cantina*. Sitting his saddle, listening to the mellow guitar chords, he looked up and down the boardwalk, seeking a darker shape in the shadows, one that might reveal a tall man with a mustache, gun in hand. Seeing nothing of concern, he swung off his horse, tied the git down rope to the hitch pole, and stepped onto the boardwalk.

As was his habit, he stopped in the doorway and glanced around the room. Again, nothing of concern. The girl was in her customary spot. The usual barman was at his post, wiping glasses. Regular customers sat at their regular tables. Most of the men in the room looked familiar to Jeff. The Mustache was not in sight, but he seldom showed until the girl's last song.

Jeff took his normal stool at the end of the bar, as near the small stage as was possible. Without being asked, the barman drew him a beer. Jeff put a nickel down and took the glass. The foam bubbled and popped in his mustache, and the beer cooled him. It tasted good, and as the girl strummed and sang he relaxed a little.

Inez was pretty as ever as she rendered a sad love song. She glanced his way with recognition in her green eyes and a quick smile that was just for him. He felt kicked in the chest again. He nodded and smiled, lifting his glass just enough for a salute that she alone saw.

For an hour, she played and sang. There was still no sign of The Mustache. Concluding for her break, as the scattered applause died out, she rose from her stool and Jeff made his move. It was several steps to the stage and then he was standing near her for the first time, holding his hat and curling the brim in nervous fingers, ready to say his first words to her. She looked up at him, met his eyes, and his jaw locked.

As he fought his frozen tongue, she smiled and said her first word to him. "Yes?" She continued smiling, a questioning look on her face.

At last, he was able to speak. "Maybe we could sit down at a table?"

She looked around the room nervously. "I don't know. He's going to show up sometime." He was curiously unsurprised that their first conversation was on a topic that seemed to be on both their minds, and they discussed it as though they had known each other for years.

Jeff looked down at her. "I don't care if he does."

She turned her head toward to door. "I do. He won't like it if we're talking."

"That don't worry me neither." He kept smiling down.

"Who are you?" She was looking into his eyes again.

"Nobody. Just a cowboy that thinks you're the prettiest thing he ever saw, with the sweetest voice this side of the angels."

She showed a smile again. "That's nice. But you better go back to the bar. I need to freshen up, and he'll be along."

Jeff frowned. "I told you that don't matter."

Her face went neutral and she backed up a step. "And I heard you. Now go sit down and have another beer. Maybe we can talk again another time."

He put his hat back on. "Count on it."

The girl smiled one last time. "I will."

•   •   •   •

HE DRANK two more beers, Inez sang another hour-long set, and still The Mustache did not appear. When the girl stepped down off the low stage, holding her guitar by the neck in a small hand, he was beside her.

"He's not here," he said.

The girl nodded. "I know. Occasionally, he doesn't come. I never know when."

"How're you gonna get home?"

"I'll walk. It's not far. Just a few blocks."

"Then I'll walk you." It came out a little more forcefully than he intended.

She frowned. "Is that so?"

He was stricken by her tone. "Let me try that again." He swept his hat off and smiled the best he had. "I surely would admire to walk you home, *señorita*, if you'd allow me."

She smiled back, coyly, transforming the frowning face of a moment before. "I don't know you, sir. Are your intentions honorable?" She cocked her head primly.

"Strictly," Jeff answered, taking on a serious air. "My conduct is beyond reproach. Besides that, a lady ought to have an escort on the street after dark. There's plenty of rough folks in this town."

The girl nodded again. "You're right. Some of those rough folks come here to listen to my songs."

"Not all of them, miss, and I believe there's some that'd do you harm."

"I suppose that's true enough."

"Then you'd best let me walk you. I'd be pleased to see that you get home safe."

"Well, since my regular escort seems to be absent, I guess you'd better."

He beamed at her agreement, then frowned at the thought of The Mustache as her guardian. The girl was puzzled by the conflicting looks.

"What's the matter?" she asked.

He regained his smile and put on his hat. "Not a thing. If you're ready, why don't we go?"

She nodded, smiling too. "All right then. Let's."

•   •   •   •

INEZ LIVED four blocks away in a small house behind a larger one occupied by an old Spanish couple. In lieu of rent, she did cooking and cleaning, and the arrangement seemed to suit all concerned. As she and Jeff walked in that direction, they carefully began getting acquainted.

"I still don't know your name," she said, her voice from the dark beside him. She was turning her face to him, the light from a sliver of moon reflecting in her hair. He was aware of her scent and liked it.

"I know yours. It's Inez Sullivan."

"Then, you have the advantage of me."

"Sorry. My name's Cameron. Jeff Cameron."

"Pleased to meet you, Mr. Cameron."

"*Con mucho gusto, señorita.* The pleasure is mine."

"You speak Spanish?"

"Yeah. I guess so. Good enough to get by."

"How did you come by it?"

"Spent a lot of time on the border, southeast of here. Cowboyed with a bunch of Mexican *vaqueros* for a few years. Wanted to talk to them in their own lingo. Once they saw I was interested, they went out of their way to help me learn."

"Your accent is excellent," she said.

Jeff smiled in the dark. "Well, thanks for saying so."

They walked a while without speaking. Directly, he broke the silence. "That fella' that didn't show tonight?"

Inez looked up. "What about him?"

"If you don't mind me asking, what is he to you?"

She went a few steps without reply. "I don't guess I mind. But it's a little complicated."

He nodded. "All right."

She went a little further without saying more, as if deciding something. "I'll tell you this much. I'm not his woman, if that concerns you."

"It don't now, since you said it. Besides, I thought he looked way too old for you."

"How old are you?" she asked.

Jeff answered without hesitation. "Twenty-nine and a little bit."

Inez smiled to herself. "Maybe you're too old for me," she said.

He was taken aback. "Well, how old are you?" he asked.

The girl feigned offense. "A true gentleman would never dare ask a lady such a question."

He retreated quickly. "Easy now. I didn't mean any disrespect."

The girl was merciful. "Oh well, then. It doesn't matter, really. I'm twenty-two next month."

Relief rushed over him. "Well, hell. I mean, heck," he said. "If you're twenty-two, I ain't no way too old for you."

"Too old for what?" she asked.

He was instantly thrust back into a state of anxiety.

"Oh lordy, Miss Sullivan."

"Call me Inez."

"Inez, then. I mean I'm not too old to pay attention to you."

"What sort of attention?" she asked.

He was sweating now. She was enjoying this. "Oh, hell. I mean, heck. I mean, to come see you. Take you to supper. Go out ahorseback together. Maybe a buggy ride and a picnic. That kind of thing. I don't know."

"You want to court me, Mr. Cameron?"

In the dark, where he couldn't see, she smiled.

"Call me Jeff," he said.

"Very well, Jeff. Do you want to come courting?"

He stopped walking and the girl stopped, too, turning to look up at his face, the soft light of the moon showing in her eyes. He swallowed, twice. "I expect I do," he said.

She turned and moved on, and he caught up with her. "I like the idea of that, Mr. Jeff Cameron. But we have a problem."

"What is it?"

"It's not *what*, it's *who*," she answered.

He could guess. "That fella," he growled, "The one you always leave the *cantina* with." It was a statement rather than a question.

The girl nodded as she walked and Jeff could feel her mood change. "It's complicated," she said.

"Then you better tell me more about him," he said, "complicated or not."

• • • •

HUDSON SURRATT had known her father shortly before his death and had shown an interest in the twelve-year-old daughter who was already beginning to take the shape of a woman. He had gone drinking with Sullivan, loaned him money, and played the part of the concerned uncle. But Inez learned that her father's new friend was like no doting relative. That he was a gambler, he made no bones about. Rumors had it that he had killed more than one man in disputes over a card table.

After her father's death, Surratt saw to it that she had food, shelter, and clothes, and that she completed her primary schooling. He paid for her to board with a large Mexican family in town. The father taught her the guitar and the mother to cook. She helped care for the younger children. She learned Spanish. At age eighteen, she left the loud, energetic household in hopes of a little independence and moved in behind the old couple.

Until then, Surratt had refrained from approaching her with more than a benign interest, although she felt his eyes linger on her ripening body. And he allowed her no suitors. He warned off in no uncertain terms any boy who came around showing more than passing attention. Given the gambler's reputation, there soon were no young men brave or ardent enough to face the confrontation. This situation continued to the present. I addition, Surratt, over the past year, had begun to press his own suit. So far, Inez had been able to resist his advances, partly due to her insistence that she was still young and confused regarding the world of adult relationships, and partly because, in some strange, twisted sense, Surratt regarded himself a gentleman as well as her guardian.

"Well," Jeff said when the girl had finished, "All that squares with what I know about him."

Inez seemed surprised at that. Stopping in the lane, she turned to face him.

"You know Surratt?"

He looked down and shook his head. "Don't know him. Know of him. Was in a card game earlier tonight where he sat in. He cheated and I called him on it."

The girl looked fearful. "Are you sure about that?" she asked.

He nodded. "Yeah, I put it to him fairly straight on."

She shook her head. "No, not are you sure you called him on it. Are you sure he cheated?"

He nodded again. "Sure enough. I knew I was being cheated, but I couldn't tell how. He's that good. But I let him know I knew, without coming right out and calling him a card cheat. I left him a little room to back up, but he wanted to gun it out. Hadn't been for that barkeep and his sawed-off L.C. Smith, one of us or maybe both'd have some holes in 'em."

Inez looked pale. "This is serious, Jeff."

"Don't I know it," he said. "I never shot anybody. Don't want to. Don't want to get shot, neither."

She inhaled. "Well, he'd be willing to do it, I don't doubt. I told you he's killed over cards before. I imagine you're not the first to catch him cheating, either."

Jeff smiled down at her. "I expect that's true. Don't worry too much. I been in some tights before."

She shook her head, frowning. "You don't get it. You're not hearing me. He'll kill you. You have to understand that. I've seen him looking at you while I sing. He knows you like me. He can't stand that. There's a mortal coldness in him. I felt it from the first time my father brought him to our house. He hates you, I know. And he'll kill you."

"Well," he replied, "Some men take a sight of killin'." But he didn't feel half as brave as he sounded.

•　　•　　•　　•

THEY STOPPED at her little house, oak trees and a border of tall lilac bushes framing her walkway. An awkward moment ensued as they stood at the entry.

She spoke first. "Thank you for seeing me home, kind sir." She offered a small, right hand.

He took it in both of his, holding it gently. It felt warm and it made his blood run faster. "I sure hope I get to do it again. And soon."

A flat voice came out of the lilacs. "I wouldn't count on that, sonny." The speaker was in total darkness. Jeff instinctively put himself between the girl and the voice, sweeping his coattail back to clear his revolver.

"Don't be stupid, boy. You're covered," said the voice from the shadows. Jeff heard the four sharp clicks a Colt pistol makes when being thumbed back to full cock.

The girl's voice was high and panicky. "Hudson, no! Please!"

Surratt cut her off. "Go inside, Inez."

She didn't move.

"Get in the house," he said, "if you don't want to see this fool boy shot dead right in front of you."

Jeff stood frozen, afraid of starting anything, and he feared for the girl. He felt her leave and then heard the door open and close. For a few heartbeats, neither man moved nor spoke. When the tension was fiddle-string tight, he said, "Well, now what?"

The lilacs parted and Surratt stepped into view. A nickel-plated revolver was in his right hand, the muzzle in line with Jeff's middle. His mouth was grinning, but his eyes were dead. He looked his rival up and down, contempt obvious on his face.

"This is what. You are going to turn around and walk back to that *cantina*, get on that big horse of yours, and ride out of this town in any direction you choose. Savvy?"

Jeff was still as a frozen pond, a cold feeling rising through his torso and squeezing his heart. The look and the intensity of the man across from him told Jeff that he had never been closer to his own death. He chose his next words carefully.

"I guess I got no choice. At least about walking away. You damn sure got the drop on me. I don't know about getting run out of town."

The grin left Surratt's face. "I ought to kill you right now. If it weren't for that girl inside, I'd do it. But you've got her fooled at the moment. She thinks you're something. I know different."

Jeff said nothing.

"Anyway," Surratt continued, "here's the deal. You clear out tonight. You don't do that and next time I see you, you're a dead man. I'll kill you. And nobody will see it done. You got 'til daylight and then I'm going to take a pass around this town. I find you still here, I shoot. No more talk. This right here is the end of talking. Unless you got something to say."

Heat was replacing the iciness Jeff had felt. An itchy, dirty craving to kill this man was rising in him. "That part sounds good, as far as no more talking. You talk too goddamned much."

Surratt took two steps toward Jeff and extended the pistol, pressing the muzzle against his breastbone, over his heart, and making him step back to maintain his balance. "Go! Now! Walk! Or die!"

Jeff stood his ground for two beats. Then he walked.

THREE

THE BUCKSKIN was jumpy as Jeff mounted, feeling his man's anger once again. They traveled back to the stockyards at a high lope. The distance wasn't enough to heat the horse up, and Jeff stripped the gear off and turned Buck into his pen. For the second time that night he went to the bottle on the windowsill, poured a healthy portion into the tin cup, and drank it down. "I've been here before," he said out loud, "and not so long ago." His hands were shaking badly and it took him three tries to roll a cigarette. The shakes weren't from fear, but from a hot rage that pulsed down his arms and into his fingers. Adrenaline surged through him like a burning drug. He itched to take up the revolver and use it on the man named Hudson Surratt. And there was the girl. She was in the middle of this and that was turning out to be a dangerous place to be. Three drinks and two more cigarettes later, he undressed and crawled in his bunk, his head spinning. The last image in his mind as he drifted off was the gaping muzzle of Surratt's Colt and his dead eyes.

• • • •

ALLOWING HIMSELF to be run out of Albuquerque rated no consideration whatsoever. But what he should do next, Jeff didn't know. As his morning coffee brewed, he considered his options. He could fort up at the shack and wait for Surratt to bring the fight. But the gambler was not, in his estimation, the sort to come at him head on. More likely, this man would stay out of sight, shadow his target, hold a position on the periphery until the advantage was all his way, and then strike from ambush. So Jeff figured it was best to take the fight to him. What remained was how, including how to keep the girl safe. As he went about his morning duties, feeding the buckskin and the mule, topping up the water tank, forking manure into a wheelbarrow and dumping it on the pile downwind of the shack, he worked out a plan.

•   •   •   •

LATE THAT NIGHT, he tied his horse behind the feed store, a block from the *cantina*. Sliding the Winchester from its scabbard, he levered a cartridge into the chamber, lowered the hammer to half cock, crossed the street, slipped between two buildings, and entered the alley behind the *cantina*. He could hear the girl's guitar, the notes drifting from the open back door. He closed the distance on cat feet. The kitchen was unoccupied and dark, and he eased his way inside enough for a look into the barroom. Inez was on her stool, her back to him. Surratt was not there. Retreating quietly, he returned to the alley, rounded the corner and came out on the street. He selected a dark place to wait, the recessed doorway of a harness shop, next to the *cantina*.

His plan was simple. He'd turn the tables on the gambler. Jeff would brace him on the boardwalk, before he had a chance to go inside. He'd get the drop on the man and issue an equivalent ultimatum to the one he'd received the night before. If Surratt chose to shoot it out, Inez would be safe inside. He thought his chances good, if it came to shooting. While he wasn't much of a hand with a side arm, with his Winchester he was more than competent. And he had the element of surprise on his side. He was guardedly confident.

He built a smoke, lit it, and cupped it in his palm to hide the glow. Taking a drag, he felt calm. There'd been moments of violence in his life. Some nasty fistfights, and once, in a saloon, a drunken teamster had made the mistake of trying to cut him. That had earned the man a lick on the head with a bung starter that Jeff had snatched up off the bar top. But he'd never killed a man, never even pointed a gun at anyone. This night was likely to change that.

His thoughts were interrupted by the sound of boot heels on the boardwalk. From past the *cantina*, on the opposite side of the entry, he could make out a tall shape in the shadows, approaching his position. Dropping his smoke, Jeff lifted the rifle to waist level and staying in the dark he waited for his enemy. When Surratt emerged into the dim light cast by the open door of the barroom, Jeff pulled back the hammer of the Winchester. The sharp, metallic clack rode over the soft guitar music, and The Mustache stopped, dead still. He stood utterly motionless, as stiff as Jeff had been the night before.

"Evening, gambler. That's a good place for you to stand. Right there in the light. I guess I don't need to tell you you're covered."

Surratt remained rooted like a tree. "No need," he said coolly. "What's the play?"

Jeff moved out to where the light of a window fell on him. "Same deal you offered me. You're done here. And you're through bird dogging Inez."

Surratt turned his head toward the street and spat. Then he looked at Jeff. "This is my fault. I'm old enough to know better, or I ought to be. My gut told me to kill you last night and I should have paid attention."

Jeff nodded. "Maybe so, but it's all the same now. So listen good. Here's how it shakes out. We're going to take a walk to where my horse is tied. Then, I'm going to ride behind you, sorta' herd you, while you walk to wherever you got your horse. When you're mounted, we're going to take a ride out of town. Soon as I think we're far enough that you won't try to walk back, I'm going to put you afoot and lead your horse a couple miles further on and tie him. Then I'll circle back. When you locate your horse again, you're gonna get on him and ride out, away from this town and that girl."

Surratt digested the speech for a few seconds. "Sounds like a mighty ambitious plan," he said. "You know I'll just come back."

Jeff frowned. The man's arrogance was incredible, considering his present position. "Could be, but what you got to think about is this. I'll be riding the ridges for a few days, watching the trails coming this way. I see you, I'll knock you out of the saddle with this .45-75, no warning given. And if you lay out and skulk in later, I'll get you then. You'll never get close to Inez 'cause I'll be with her. And if I ever see you again, anytime, anywhere, why then I'll kill you without a second's hesitation, and not one goddamned word spoken. Now it's me who's talking too much. Unbuckle that gun belt and let it fall."

Surratt's face had gone deep red down into his collar. "Why, you damned smart pup. You think you can buffalo me? Goddamn you!" He was trembling in anger now and his voice rose to a shout. "I've done for more saddle bums like you than I can remember. And if you got plans for Inez, I'll tell you this. I won her over a card table ten years ago from that no account, drunk mick of a father of hers. She's mine, goddamn you," he all but screamed. "I own her!"

Neither man had noticed the abrupt end to the music inside. Surratt's tirade had penetrated the barroom and now brought Inez through the batwing doors in near panic. Her surprise appearance momentarily distracted Jeff and gave Surratt an opening. Consumed with rage and sweeping back the tail of his frock coat, he drew his pistol and began firing wildly. Jeff felt a tug at his collar as a bullet grazed his neck and then a sting on his cheek. His rifle at his hip, he instinctively shot back. The three hundred fifty grain slug hit Surratt just under the breastbone. Jeff worked the lever and fired again as the man folded up like an empty sack. Surratt got off one more round as he fell, but caught the Winchester's second slug square in the Adam's apple. That finished him as he landed on the boards. He was dead before he settled.

Jeff stood peering through the white cloud of powder smoke. The exchange had taken less than five seconds. He looked away from the gambler's corpse, trying to focus his mind. Touching his burning cheek, he felt his fingers sticky with blood.

Aware of the sound of ragged breathing, he turned to the doorway. Inez sat on the boardwalk, her back against the doorframe, legs splayed in front of her, a red stain spreading across her white, cotton blouse. Jeff's rifle clattered to the walk as he stepped to her and knelt at her side. Reaching behind her, he cradled her head. His shock was complete. He could not utter a word. She looked at him without recognition, her eyes becoming blank as a last breath rattled through her windpipe. Then nothing.

He was numb. This was impossible. His brain could not process what was before his eyes. It was all wrong. This couldn't be happening. Had not happened. Please, God, no!

Her blouse was soaked now, the brightest red that Jeff had ever seen. He felt his stomach roll. His hands began to shake and he gripped her shoulders to stop them. He wanted to say something, tell her it was all his fault, that he'd planned it so she wouldn't get hurt. He wanted to say he'd like to walk her home now. He could get nothing out. His breathing was fast and shallow, like an overheated dog.

The girl's face was white now as he felt a hand on his shoulder. It was the barman. Jeff paid him no attention.

"Hey, *amigo* Jeff. You got to ride! You cannot help this *pobrecita*. She is dead." The man's words were a buzzing in Jeff's ears.

Raul Blanco was short but sturdy built, thick through the chest and arms. He took hold of both Jeff's shoulders and shook him hard enough to rattle his teeth. "Sonabitch, Jeff, listen to me. It's time for you to ride. *Ahora*! Now!"

Jeff looked up and Blanco saw he was crying.

•   •   •   •

HE COULD SCARCELY ACCEPT that she was dead. But for his prideful determination to force the matter with Surratt, this lovely girl in his arms, who moments before had been so warm, so alive, would surely still be so. He felt his mind coming apart. He laid her down gently, crawled to the edge of the boardwalk, and vomited onto the street. When he'd emptied his stomach, he heaved dry.

Strong hands grabbed him again and yanked him to his feet. With a damp bar towel, Blanco wiped Jeff's mouth and the blood from his cheek. Jeff stood motionless, staring at his friend's face as through a fog.

"*Amigo* Jeff, you got to hear me. Nobody blames you for this. But that one with the *mustaches grande*, the one you killed, he has friends amongst the other *gringos*. This could be *muy malo* for you, *amigo*. I will say the truth to them for you, how this man drew first, how his wild bullets killed this poor girl. But they don't listen to no Mexican too good. So, you can't wait. You got to go now. Once you are safe, and some time passes, you send word to me, tell me where you are. Then I let you know if you can come back. And I will take care of Inez. That is my promise to you. *Comprendé?*" Jeff nodded vacantly. With no hesitation, Blanco slapped him. "Say you understand!"

Jeff's eyes focused and he said through gritted teeth. "Yes, by God, I understand."

Blanco nodded. "*Bueno.* Now you got to ride, *hombre.*"

•   •   •   •

SO RIDE he did, first going back to the shack and packing up. Passing the office, he noticed a light in the window. He reined in to look through the glass in the door and there sat Gomez, working late at his desk. Jeff leaned from the saddle and knocked on one of the porch posts with the butt of his pistol. The large man looked up and then came around the desk and out the front door. He noticed the packed mule and looked at Jeff, whose red eyes and pale cheeks were a clue to something badly amiss.

"Is all not well with you, *señor*?"

Jeff shook his head, his face a mixture of shame and anger. "No, *amigo*, all's not well." He took a deep breath, went on. "There was trouble tonight, at the *cantina*. A man tried to kill me. I had to shoot him."

Gomez put a serious look on his face, shaking his head and crossing himself. "*Madre de Dios!* Is he dead, *Señor* Jeff, this *hombre* you shot?"

Jeff nodded. "Yeah. Dead as dead gits." For a moment, neither man spoke.

"Well," Gomez offered, "It is no more than he deserves. One cannot go about attempting to kill his fellows without consequences." He nodded profoundly, his chins jiggling.

"I s'pose," Jeff agreed. "But it's worse than just that. An innocent girl died, too, by the other man's bullets."

Gomez crossed himself again. "*Jesu Cristo*, such a sad thing, *señor*. Did you know her?"

Jeff's eyes began to fill. "*Si, amigo*, I knew her." The *segundo* could think of nothing to say, looking into the young man's anguished face. Finally, Jeff broke the silence. "I hope you'll tend my plants, my tomato plants. There's some ripe ones and there'll be more soon, if the weather stays this hot. I hate like hell to leave them. They'll make you some good salsa."

Gomez smiled. "That will be my pleasure. *Muchas gracias.*" The smile left his face. Then as a new thought came to him he said, "*Amigo*, I should return some of your money. Your *caballo* and *mulo* have not eaten all the hay and grain you bought from me."

Jeff shook his head. "No, *hombre*, you keep it. I expect this job's no gold mine for you. Buy something for your wife, your kids."

Gomez was trying to swallow a large lump in his throat. "You will be much missed, *amigo*. I have felt very secure these past months, with you and your weapons here to protect this property."

Jeff smiled down at him. The large man displayed a look of genuine sadness. He leaned from the saddle and offered his hand. Gomez took it firmly.

"Well, I imagine you'll get on fine without me. I never saw a prowler the whole time I was here. I don't believe you really need a night man all that bad."

Gomez nodded. "Perhaps not. But one always needs a friend. Go with God, *amigo*." Jeff released the man's hand, turned the buckskin toward the road and moved off, the little mule following. Gomez blinked and crossed himself again. "*Buena suerte, caballero.*"

FOUR

THEY TRAVELED fast for three days along the east bank of the Rio Grande, skirting the old town of Santa Fe, staying wide to the west of it. He wanted distance between himself and the unthinkable events of his last night in Albuquerque. His mind was all conflict and his heart in anguish. The image of the girl on the boardwalk, her back against the doorframe, soaked in her own blood, and that terrible, last, rattling breath were unbearable. He couldn't shake the sight and sound of it from inside his head. So he rode, keeping the river on his left, letting the big horse choose the path, trusting to the animal's surefooted judgment.

The morning of the fourth day found them in the country south of Española. His plan, such as it was, was to cross the Rio Grande somewhere nearby and begin working his way northwest, along a tributary stream he could not name, and eventually cross into Colorado.

They forded the Rio Grande in the early afternoon, continuing along the west bank of the tributary, until late in the day, when he stopped to make his camp. His chores he did heedlessly. He stripped the gear from his animals, staked them out to graze, and then gathered enough wood to last until bedtime. It was warm and he wouldn't need a fire through the night. Digging in his grub sack he found dry *tortillas* and a hunk of goat cheese. Tasting nothing, he forced the food down. Since the shooting, sleep was hard to find, no more than an few hours at a stretch. His dreams were replays of those terrible moments of his last night in Albuquerque. Unrelentingly, in those narrow hours of sleep, he saw Surratt's gun belch fire, saw him collapse in a lifeless heap. Saw again the girl like a ragdoll, limp against the doorframe, the red blossom spreading over her blouse, her final death rattle in his ears like a curse as he knelt over her. Out of his blankets he'd jerk, sweating like a smithy at his forge, but chilled to the bone.

In mornings, he was exhausted as he slumped over the coffee that he barely had the energy to make. It would be approaching noon before he could muster ambition to saddle up and move on. He wondered if those feelings ever would leave him. He examined his regard for the girl, finding that his hurt and confusion prevented him from making a clear assessment. He didn't know if he'd loved her, because he couldn't exactly say what love was. And, after all, they had such little time with each other. He knew that he'd felt light and fine when with her, thinking that if they had more opportunity, that love might have come. And layered over it all was a sense of tremendous guilt. But only about the girl. Concerning Surratt, he felt nothing but contempt and hatred, no regret.

He rode into the shank of one afternoon, laying out his thoughts for inspection, until the spell was broken by the sound of a cow calling. They had been climbing through timber for several hours, with no indication they were on stock range. Again he heard the cow bawl. As he sat his horse, he heard a calf answer. It sounded distressed and hungry. The cries were coming from ahead, down a slope and apparently behind a screen of willows. He guided the horse that way. The mule followed.

He found an old mother cow mired halfway up her ribs in a spring bog. She had churned the soggy turf in a circle around her, telling the story of her struggle to free herself. A scrawny bull calf bawled nearby on higher, solid ground. He was more than ready for his afternoon ration of milk. The cow was just as ready to serve him, her bag swollen tight. But in their present situation, neither animal could do anything to relieve the other. Jeff rode closer. The cattle observed him dumbly.

It was a bad fix for mother and son. The exhausted cow could not get out under her own power. She was doomed and without her the calf would starve. Jeff's eye for stock told him this in a second. His instinct was to take down his *reata*, rope the old matron by the horns, and try to drag her from her trap. But he knew that a dead pull against a stuck object the size of this cow would most likely snap the braided rawhide. That left for the task the stout, hemp rope he had hitched over the mule's pack. It was more than a half inch in diameter and forty feet in length. He decided it would serve. Stepping off the buckskin, he took a moment to tie the mule to a willow switch and then unhitched the lash rope.

Tying a *honda* in the end of it and shaking out a big loop with a long spoke, Jeff stood at the edge of the bog and roped her by the horns. He didn't want it around her neck because a pull required to free her would likely choke her or break that neck. He took the other end of the rope to his horse, mounted, dallied it to the saddle horn, and by steady pulls, alternated with brief tugs with the rope flipped around her hind quarters, he had the old cow out of the trap and standing shakily on solid ground within a quarter hour. The calf went straight in for a muddy teat, its mother too weak to come to him. After a few minutes, she did manage to turn and lick him.

Jeff re-hitched his mule's load and mounted the gelding. Turning the horse back toward the trail, for the first time he noticed the old man sitting a chunky, bay mare, seeming to have risen from the ground, a Sharps rifle across the saddle-bow and a smile on his face. He was dressed in the style of the old Spanish Dons, with a flat-brimmed, low-crowned sombrero set over a silk scarf tied around his head. A short-waisted, embroidered jacket covered his torso, and heavy, leather *armitas* protected his legs. Low-heeled boots mounted with a pair of large rowelled spurs completed the picture. Jeff kept quiet. After another moment of study, the man spoke.

"I decided to watch you work, *señor*. I could not be sure of your intentions until I saw you release my cow. We have a few cattle stolen now and then." Jeff remained silent. The old man continued, gesturing toward the bog. "That is a bad spot, there. I lose an animal to it every few years. I should cut a ditch and drain it. But I never seem to get to it. There is always *mañana*, no?"

Jeff spoke, keeping his voice calm. "I just figured to get her out, *señor*. Never could stand to see a critter suffer. Hadn't any notion of taking her." He sat very still, being careful to keep his hands motionless.

"I satisfied myself as to that some minutes ago. Otherwise, I might have shot you by now."

Jeff nodded soberly. "Well, thanks for that, anyway."

The man grinned. "Forgive the bad manners, my friend. It is for me to thank you. She surely would have died before morning. And her calf soon after. *Mil gracias, señor*." With courtly style and dignity, the old man swept off his sombrero and made a bow from the saddle.

For the first time since seeing him, Jeff took an easy breath. "Don't mention it. Any stockman would have done the same."

The old *vaquero* replaced his hat and smiled broadly. "And that you have demonstrated yourself to be. You handled that cow just as I would have, taking your time. She is old and weak. This *mamacita* has raised many a strong bull for the *rancho*, but the one before you is probably her last calf. See how small and thin he is. *Pobrecito*."

Jeff nodded in agreement. "Yeah, he's a mite scrawny, sure enough. And I don't reckon her milk's all that rich, or that plentiful."

The old man's face took on a look of sadness. "True enough, my friend. Her best days are behind her. It is a shameful thing to be old and with little value." The man looked as though he was lamenting more than the lost youth of this one old cow.

Jeff said, "That is true, *maestro,* and a sad thing, indeed. But it is also true that with years come wisdom, and skill and experience. Much can be learned from those who have lived much." This he declared in formal Spanish.

The old *vaquero* looked up from his gloomy musings with an expression of astonishment. His face again broke into a broad smile. "My young friend, truly you are a pleasing surprise. Your dress and outfit are those of a *gringo,* as is your skin, your eyes, also. And yet you speak my language as well as my own children. Who are you and where do you ride?"

Jeff flushed slightly, but had no reason not to respond. Already he liked this man. And it was obvious he had been trespassing, although he'd seen neither fence nor posted sign. Despite the fact that he was running from trouble, his instincts said here was a friend. He answered forthrightly, in English. "I'm nobody special, *señor,* just a drifting cowhand, not going much of any place. The name is Jeff Cameron, from Texas." Somehow, revealing this much, to this man, made him feel better. He had a good feeling for the first time since the killings.

The man on the bay mare rode across the distance between them, stopped his horse beside Jeff's, and offered his hand. The younger man took it with no hesitation. They shook firmly.

The *vaquero's* eyes were bright as he spoke once more. "I am Don Arturo Gonzales Archuleta. *A sus ordenes, señor.* This is my family's land. And you are my guest. It is my wish that you ride with me to my *hacienda* now. The hour for the evening meal approaches and I am certain a young man such as you is in possession of a healthy appetite. I am hungry, as well. You have done me a service here today. It would be my honor to show you the hospitality of my home."

The man expected an answer. Jeff gave him one. In formal Spanish, he said, "*Con mucho gusto, Patron.*" And added, "The honor is mine."

•   •   •   •

THEY RODE for two hours at an extended trot, leaving the stream to follow a rutted wagon track. It took them higher into the hills, crossing several low ridges and narrow valleys. It seemed to Jeff fine country for the raising of cattle and horses. Much green grass for this late in the summer, mostly low between the ridges. To Jeff it looked sub-irrigated, including the boggy spring that had trapped the old cow. On both sides of the wagon track along the way ranged healthy cattle. He judged them to be of mixed Mexican and English breeds.

As he had opportunity while they rode, Jeff studied his host. He judged Don Arturo to be in his early sixties. His skin was brown, but Jeff thought that to be more from exposure to the sun than from native blood. He suspected this man was descended from an old Spanish land grant family. His height was some of that evidence. Nearly six feet tall, he had broad shoulders and a slim waist. And despite the years and, no doubt, hard miles, he sat his mare as straight as a young pine. His eyes were black, and he wore a salt and pepper goatee. Altogether, he was a considerable man, and a picture of seasoned dignity.

As they rode, he told Jeff of his family, the *rancho*, and its history. It seemed that this old *caballero* had been without the ear of a ready listener for a while. And the story Jeff heard seemed to confirm what he sensed. The Archuletas had come into the country in the late 1700s, a grant of 230,000 acres having been bestowed upon the original pioneer head of the family, the first Don Arturo, for whom Jeff's host was named. The land was reward for extraordinary service to the crown.

The old man's history lesson continued as they rode, and Jeff found himself fascinated. Years of toil and sacrifice, bloody engagements with hostile natives and bands of outlaws. Then good years of little trouble, no violence, ample spring rains, and heavy winter snows in the mountains to melt and supplement those spring rains for summer growth. The Don's adventures as a young *vaquero*, ranging widely over unspoiled country. The great horses he had owned. Men, good and bad, he had known.

As they topped a ridge, Jeff caught his breath. Below them, at the end of the wagon track, was the *rancho*, a jewel set in a ring of low hills. A creek traversed the middle of the large meadow that provided a setting for the headquarters, barns, out buildings, corrals, pens, and living quarters for the riders and their families. He had never seen such a well laid out, attractive operation. His appreciation of what he saw showed on his face.

The old Don swept a hand out toward the grand scene below. "*El Rancho de los Archuletas.* Welcome to my home, *Señor* Cameron. While you are here, you must think of it as your own." He looked Jeff squarely in the eye, unblinking, as he said the words.

The young cowboy understood the significance of the offer. "It is an honor of which I am entirely unworthy. In return for your generous hospitality, I pledge my service to you for as long as I am your guest." Again, the words were rendered in Spanish.

The two men rode down to the barn, turned the animals over to the stable hand, and made their way toward the low, sprawling stone and timber ranch house. As they walked across the packed earth of the yard, neither was aware they were forming a bond that would last until one of them was dead.

•   •   •   •

DON ARCHULETA lived with his one surviving son, his daughter in law, their two teenage daughters, a spinster sister, and an ancient uncle, whose age none could recall exactly. That he was nearing ninety, everyone was certain. The firstborn son had died in his teens in a scrape with horse thieves. The Don never fully recovered from that loss. His wife had died in the birth of the second son. These were tragedies in his past, that could rise in his mind and contribute to his somber aspect, but on this night his spirits were high. He summoned to Jeff a young houseboy, to see to his needs, and then excused himself to dress for supper.

Jeff was escorted to a bathhouse, provided with soap, towel, and a clean linen shirt, and was left to wash up. He found rolled in the towel a straight razor and, touching his bristly cheek, he accepted the invitation. A copper wash boiler sat on a stone counter, filled with steaming water. Thirty minutes later, scrubbed, scraped, and combed, he appeared back at the house, and was instantly met by the houseboy, who lead him to the dining room.

At Jeff's entry, Don Arturo rose from his heavy, carved chair at the head of the massive trestle table, the rest of the family seated in their places. The chair to his right remained empty. Jeff paused inside the door, not certain how to proceed. The Don extended his hand toward the empty seat. He was dressed in comfortable house clothes. He smiled. "Here is my new friend, *Señor* Jeff Cameron. Jeff, this is my family. Come, sit."

• • • •

THAT NIGHT brought him the first deep sleep since the death of the girl. None of the disturbing dreams that had disrupted his rest before visited him that night. He awoke refreshed and with a good appetite. The Don found him seated on the front porch of the main house, pulling on his boots.

"Good morning, my young friend. I hope you rested well."

Looking up with a smile, he said, "I believe I did. I recall little of it. Best I've slept in many days. I thank you." He stomped down hard to seat his foot into the high-heeled boot.

Don Arturo raised a silencing hand. "No thanks needed. But you are hungry? There is coffee ready, and breakfast is only minutes away."

Jeff stood up. "I could eat that old cow I pulled from the bog yesterday, and her calf, too. Mud and all."

The man beamed. "Let's get you started. And then, if it would suit you, I would like very much to have you ride with me today. I need to look over my range and your company would be most welcome."

Jeff took only a moment to decide. He was aware, as the Don was waiting for his answer, that in this man's presence he'd found his troubles receding. They were by no means forgotten, but were becoming less tormenting. "Don't know what could sound better right now," he responded, "than a good feed and then a long ride."

His host showed a wide smile. "Excellent. If you will accompany me?"

Jeff backed up a step, saying. "Just let me get to the bath-house and wash my face and comb my hair. Then I'll meet you there."

Don Arturo made a diminutive bow. "As you wish, my friend."

•　•　•　•

BREAKFAST DONE, the Don offered Jeff a horse from the ranch *remuda*, thinking that perhaps the buckskin needed a rest. Jeff agreed readily, always interested in a new mount and curious as to the training and quality of a horse from the Don's string. They walked to the stables, where a groom had their horses saddled and ready. Jeff was not used to such service and was in the habit of saddling his own animal. But the groom had done his work properly, the cinch neither too tight nor too loose, the position of his saddle on the strange horse just right. They mounted and rode out of headquarters. The Don had chosen for him a tall, young gelding, very powerful and brimming with energy, but perfectly mannered, nonetheless.

They carried food in their saddlebags and stayed out all day. Moving at a long trot most of the time, they covered close to twenty miles before noon. Jeff marveled at the endurance of the older man. He was born to the saddle, that was plain, and moved in such graceful harmony with his mount that he seemed altogether tireless. Here was a man who had spent more time on the back of a horse than afoot upon the ground. And it showed. Jeff thought he'd never ridden with such a splendid horseman.

His host's mount was near the equal of the man, and a different animal than the one he had ridden the previous day. Instead of the chunky, bay mare, the Don was mounted on a young stallion. Jeff guessed him at five years old. Tall and rangy, he was a mahogany bay with a broad white blaze on his face and two stocking legs. He was light and responsive in the *bosal*, as Jeff would have expected. And Jeff's mount seemed a good match for the stud.

Throughout the morning they climbed, gaining altitude and passing through increasingly dense stands of timber. The trail cut across a number of ridges, and the country was dotted with meadows ranging in size from five to over a hundred acres. Each of these meadows was speckled with cattle.

At mid-day, they stopped on a high bluff that looked down over a large part of the terrain they had ridden since starting out. Tying the horses and loosening cinches, they made their lunch from a variety of dried meats, cheeses, and *tortillas*, packed for them by the house cook. A bottle of wine was supplied, as well.

They were hungry and conversation was scant as they ate. A small herd of elk grazed in a meadow about a half mile below them—cows, calves, and a couple of spike bulls. The air was so clear and still that they could hear the cows calling, reminding Jeff of the mewing of kittens. When they were done eating, the Don produced two thin, black cigars and offered one to Jeff. They sat watching the elk and smoked, the silence between them an easy thing, which neither man seemed anxious to break. Finally, Jeff said, "I've seen a lot of country in the last few years, but nothing to match this."

Don Arturo smiled and nodded his grey head. "It is truly extraordinary, is it not?" Jeff smiled as well, looking out over the endless miles of timber, stone, and grass. "I grew up on this land," the Don said, "and although I have traveled widely and experienced much of this world, I have always been anxious to return. At no time in my life has this place been anything other than fascinating to me." He took a long, last draw on his cigar and rubbed it out against a rock. "As a young man, not yet out of my teens, I would take every opportunity I had when the work was not urgent and roam the farthest reaches of this *rancho*. It was larger then, before we were compelled to sell off some of it." He paused there, as though the fact of the forced sale was still a bitter taste in his mouth. "I would take one of the older *vaqueros* with me, for my father would not allow it otherwise, and we would go out with pack animals for as much as two weeks at a time. We hunted and fished, rode the country, and looked into every corner of our land. In this way, I learned the meadows, streams, and rocky headlands. I learned my range."

Jeff could only nod in envy and appreciation. The Don continued. "After several such expeditions, I was able to draw a series of detailed maps of this property, the first of their kind. My father was proud of me." Then he was quiet for an interval, as if recalling those free days of his youth. "I know this place as well as the palms of my hands. I can ride to any location on it, based on a physical description, with no lost time or wasted effort. It is good to know your place in the world so well." Again he was silent for a time. Jeff was quiet too, his thoughts his own. After more time had passed, Don Arturo looked at him. "Do you yet know your place in this world, Jeff?"

On the face of it, it might have seemed too personal a question for a friend of one day's duration to ask another, but Jeff didn't take it that way. Something about this man fostered trust and he found himself answering candidly and without hesitation. "No, sir. I do not. But I'm looking for it. Every day, I'm looking for it."

•   •   •   •

AS THEY CAME into headquarters that night, Don Arturo took Jeff aside before going in. They sat on a bench, under a *ramada* beside the springhouse, rolled themselves cigarettes, and smoked silently. Jeff waited. The old man seemed to be arranging his words and, putting the first smoke in a vest pocket, he rolled a second one before speaking.

Lighting it, he began. "Jeff. I have not known you long, but I consider myself a good judge of horses and men. I have no doubt that you are a good *hombre*, as we like to say. But I feel an unease in you. I suspect that you have left a bad thing behind you. *Muy malo.* I would not ask you the nature of that thing." He stopped speaking to take a long draw on his cigarette. Jeff waited, apprehensively. At length the Don continued. "This is a young, raw land, and many men encounter difficulties. But a bad experience does not always mean a bad man. In my years, I have learned much of men and horses. That you have ridden far and fast I can see. Forgive me for saying so. And a man on the roads and trails can be easy to find. But employed on a *rancho* the size of this, a man may disappear for as long as he likes." Again he paused to smoke, and again the younger man waited for him to go on. "Now," the Don said, "I am going to make you an offer, and I wish for you to think on it overnight, sleep on it, as you *Americanos* say. Then in the morning, you may tell me your decision."

He paused again, and now Jeff felt that a response of some sort was in order. "Please, go on," he said.

"Jeff," said Don Arturo, "my offer is this. It is my wish that you stay here a while, work with the other riders and with me. I always need another, good *vaquero* and you are more than that, I think. I have watched how you handle your own animals and I believe you are a fine horseman, as well as a good hand with cattle. I have a number of colts and fillies in need of training. I saw to this myself up until a few years ago, but I am getting too slow and crippled to start the young ones. I have a couple of riders tending to that job now, boys in their early twenties, but they are too *macho*, too concerned about whether they appear manly. Too often they are impatient with the young horses, and they do not have your hands."

Jeff nodded quietly, not wanting to interrupt. Don Arturo went on. "I will pay you thirty-five American dollars a month. That is a little more than the usual, but I will expect a little more of you and I feel certain I will get it. You will stay in the big house and my late son's room will be yours. You will take your meals with me and the rest of the family." Jeff made to protest, but the older man cut him off. "Do not tell me that it is too much. It pleases me to make you this offer. And I will make it understood to the rest of the men that you will be expected to do the same work they all do, and just as hard, just as many hours, in as difficult conditions as any they must endure. And they will resent you a little at first, for your room in my house and your seat at my table, until they see how you handle your *caballo*, and the way you throw the *reata*, and the way you sit a pitching colt or filly. All these things you can do well. I know it. And when the men see it, they will know, also, and they will respect you." Don Arturo dropped his cigarette into the sand at his feet, ground it out with his boot sole, and stood up. Jeff rose with him.

"I very much enjoyed our ride today," the Don said. "Now let us dine well, and then go to our beds and rest. In the morning you may tell me your thoughts."

Jeff looked the old man in the eye. He knew what his answer would be. He smiled, "As you wish, *Patron.*"

•   •   •   •

THE DAYS were long, the work was hard, and Jeff relished every minute of it. Each morning they rode out of headquarters as the sun broke over the hills to the east, a good breakfast under their belts. Jeff used the buckskin every fourth day. The rest of the time he rode the young horses assigned to his string. Two colts and one filly, in the beginning. As soon as he had one going well, it was turned over to another rider. On days that he expected serious cow work with a great deal of cutting and roping, he saddled Buck. When working the farther reaches of the property, too far from headquarters to return each night, the men would camp or stay in outlying cabins.

As Don Arturo had predicted, there was some tension with the other riders. One man in particular seemed unable to accept Jeff among the crew. It became apparent halfway into the third week of his stay that the fellow would have to be dealt with. As the problem intensified, the other riders waited for the outcome with anticipation. Jeff considered consulting the Don as to what course to take in the matter, but then recalled that he had been warned of just such a development. He would simply have to handle it. In his customary fashion. Straight on.

Lucio Mendez was a year older than Jeff, two inches taller, and ten pounds heavier. He considered himself an accomplished *vaquero*, which he was, as well a master horseman, which he was not. One of the fillies that Jeff had started had been turned over to Mendez. He made a point of showing off in front of the other riders whenever Jeff was present, running the young horse flat out, stopping her needlessly hard, spinning her over her hocks for no good reason, pulling on her mouth. Jeff understood that the abuse of the horse was intended to be an insult to him, a rebuke in response to the perceived favor from Don Arturo. All the same, it would have to end.

On a warm day in early September, half the crew was busy making a sweep of a big pasture to the north of head-quarters, picking cattle out of the oak brush that had missed being branded the previous spring. At the noon break, Jeff and the rest of the hands sat around the cook fire, mopping up plates of *chile colorado, con frijoles,* rolled up in freshly made *tortillas.* Their attention was drawn to the sound of a rapidly approaching horse. Mendez was coming in for his beef and beans, clattering down a rocky slope too fast, the filly lathered. Sliding her to a stop beside the camp wagon, her head was thrown back and her mouth open wide to escape the pressure of the bit. The *vaquero* swung down, looped her git down rope around the wagon tongue, and walked toward the other men, leaving the filly heaving for air, her cinch still tight, sweat dripping off her belly.

For several days, Jeff had been considering his options, how to handle the building tensions with Mendez. He might do nothing in front of others, wait for a chance to catch him alone and deal with him in private. That likely would settle the matter between the two of them, but it would prove nothing to the rest of the crew. He didn't savor the prospect of convincing all these men, one at a time, that he had a legitimate place among them.

Better, he thought, to have it out for all to see, let the chips fall where they may. Such an opportunity had present-ed itself. By its conclusion, he'd be one of them, or he'd ride on.

Jeff put his plate on the ground, set his coffee cup next to it, and stood up. He walked around the opposite side of the fire from Mendez as the *vaquero* took a plate to the pot and ladled up a portion of the contents. Neither man so much as glanced at the other, but the tension in the air was thick and the rest of the riders watched with keen interest.

Jeff went directly to the sweating filly and slipped the bridle from her head, dropping it over the saddle horn. Next, he undid the cinch. This was a serious breach of range etiquette. No man presumed to lay a hand on the mount of another without first asking permission. The other riders ceased eating. Jeff went on with his work. Mendez noticed the eyes of all present directed toward the wagon and looked that way just as Jeff dumped the *vaquero's* saddle disdainfully in the dirt. Without a word he got a gunnysack out of the bed of the wagon and began rubbing the filly down. Lucio's mouth opened in astonishment. There was no sound in the camp, except for that of soft burlap on wet horsehide. Mendez closed his mouth, set down his plate, and got to his feet. Stepping around the fire, he walked toward the wagon, stopping short of it. His voice was flat as he said, "*Qué pasa, gringo?*"

Jeff turned his head and saw the man, feet planted, looking full of fight. He directed his attention back to the horse and answered in Spanish. Since his arrival, he had spoken to these men in their own language.

"I did not put many hours and hard miles on this fine animal and bring her along with a soft touch only to see her ruined at the coarse hands of a brute." He had not even glanced at Mendez as he delivered his statement. The contempt in his voice was clear.

A clattering came from the fire as the youngest of the riders dropped his fork and plate. All of the men sat still as stone. This was serious. Maybe deadly.

Jeff said, "This *pobrecita* is hot and winded. You should cool her out now and eat later. A good *vaquero* always tends to the needs of his mount before his own. You should know that."

Mendez slowly unbuckled his pistol belt and let it fall to one side, followed by his sash knife. "I think perhaps I would prefer to cool you out, *hijo de la perra.*" He moved toward Jeff two steps and stopped. "Will you face me?"

Looking now, Jeff saw that Mendez had disarmed himself. Dropping the damp burlap and then his own gun belt, moving past the still-winded horse, he was closing the distance between them rapidly as he answered with a wide smile. "With pleasure."

The fight, like most, was brief. Mendez had weight and reach on Jeff, and a right like a mule kick. The Texan was quicker and somewhat the fitter. He concentrated on body blows to the thick middle of the *vaquero*, targeting the solar plexus and the ribs. But he paid for working in close. He took solid punches to the jaw and under both eyes. Time seemed to stop as these men struggled before the others.

A blow that landed on Jeff's left ear dropped him to his knees. He feared being kicked, but Mendez backed away to allow him his feet again. Jeff's next punch took Lucio under the breastbone, knocking the breath out of him, leaving him on all fours. In turn, the cowboy stood aside until his opponent could rise.

They were work-hardened, determined men. But the exertion took its toll, their breathing soon in ragged gasps, their clothes torn and blood spattered. In the end, Jeff's edge in conditioning saw him through. Mendez, weaving on his feet, had briefly lowered his guard. Jeff dropped him one last time with a quick left jab to the mouth, followed by a right cross on the point of the chin. He put everything he had left into it.

The *vaquero* crashed to the ground like a felled tree, a cloud of dust puffing out from under him as he landed heavily on his back. Totally spent, Jeff collapsed next to him. The rest of the crew stood transfixed, having formed a circle around them during the fight.

For another five minutes, the combatants lay in the dirt, fighting for air. Finally Jeff sat up, reached an arm around Lucio's back, and helped him to a sitting position. One of the other riders appeared with water and gave it to Jeff. He supported his opponent's shoulders with one hand while putting the spout of the canteen to the beaten man's bloodied mouth. When Mendez had drunk his fill, Jeff took some for himself. Still no one spoke.

The crew looked on as he took the makings from the pocket of his blood-smeared shirt and rolled a cigarette, offering it to Mendez, who took it without comment. Rolling a second one for himself, he placed it gingerly between his own swelling lips. He lit them both with a wooden match struck across his boot sole. The two tired fighters sat in the dirt and smoked. The rest of the men watched quietly.

At last, Jeff broke the silence. Snubbing the butt of his cigarette in the sand, he turned toward Mendez. "What I did was discourteous. I should have asked your permission before unsaddling your horse. I hope that you will forgive my rudeness."

Mendez took one last draw off his cigarette and buried it in the sand also. He placed a finger carefully against his left cheek and pushed, then spat a tooth out onto the ground. Shaking his head he said, "No, *amigo*, you were correct. The filly was a little hot. I was too concerned with my own stomach. As you said, a good *vaquero* always sees to the needs of his mount first. I think I will walk her now."

They helped each other to their feet, and then the rest of the crew closed in, talking fast, rubbing the shoulders of the two exhausted men, grateful for relief from the days of tension. They laughed and joked. From then on, and for as long as Jeff was among them, there was no further trouble. They treated him with respect, welcomed his opinions, and as time passed looked to him for leadership, and at last regarded him with affection. They were all "*bien amigos.*"

•   •   •   •

IT HAD BECOME the habit of Don Arturo to invite Jeff to the *ramada* beside the springhouse for a smoke after supper. The evening after his fight with Mendez, nothing had been said at table about it, although the family had taken the opportunity to steal furtive glances at the young *Americano's* face, where evidence of the contest was plain for all to see. They were, of course, too polite to mention it. All except for the ancient, doddering uncle who, upon Jeff's entrance into the dining room, looked up and asked no one in particular, "Who is this young man with the swollen *cabeza*?"

Now, as Jeff and the Don enjoyed a cigarette, the topic hung in the air like wood smoke on a windless day. As the old man rolled a second cigarette, he spoke casually. "What does Mendez look like?"

Jeff grinned. It hurt. "You heard about that?" he asked.

Don Arturo chuckled. "The *patron* is supposed to know everything that goes on concerning *el rancho*. This is a quiet place, far from the excitements of cities and towns. *Un combaté* as grand as that one, witnessed by half a dozen men? Do you think I would not hear of it?"

Now Jeff chuckled. That hurt, too. The old Don drew on his smoke, let it out in a long, thin plume, and asked again. "So how does he look? As bad as you, I hope. Preferably worse. I have not seen him."

"I cannot say he looks worse," Jeff answered, "but I believe he feels worse. The cook said he had at least one cracked rib, and I saw him spit out a tooth."

The Don winced. "*Mamacita!*" He scratched his balding head. "It does not profit a man to brace you with his fists does it, *mijo*?"

Jeff put a serious look on his face. "I can't stand to see a horse mistreated. I won't tolerate it."

Don Arturo nodded in agreement. "Do you advise me to dismiss him?"

Jeff shook his head. "No, sir. He's a good hand with cattle. I reckon now he'll be a better horseman." He had lapsed into English.

The old man replied in kind. "Yep, I reckon he will."

Jeff turned and faced the Don to see if he was being mocked. But the old man was gazing toward the east, at the rising moon. There was a smile on his face.

•   •   •   •

IN THE LAST WEEK of October, the weather turned cold and it snowed in the high country. The cattle began wandering down out of the upper pastures, a signal to the Don to order the moving of his herd to winter range in the lower portion of the *rancho*. Crews had been cutting wild hay down there since mid-July. It had been learned years ago, through hard experience, that a deep snow could bury the sun-cured grass to a depth beyond the reach of the cattle. Profits for the family would then perish, along with the animals. But with fenced-in stackyards, strung out at regular intervals along the length of the lower meadows, and men stationed in line shacks to toss the hay throughout the bitter weather, the beef came out of winter in good shape.

At the end of the first week of November, the marketable cattle had been sold and the holdovers were safe in the bottom pastures. The *rancho* had been buttoned up for the season. Some of the year 'round men were bringing in more wood for the stoves and fireplaces, and others took on the task of tack repair and harness mending. Still others were assigned to the carpenter, assisting him in maintenance and modifications to some of the buildings. Jeff was working young horses on clear days. But the nights were getting longer and it was too quiet in the big house. He was becoming restless.

For a few days more, he occupied himself with an elk hunt. All the hands looked forward to the results, welcoming a change from beef and mutton. He killed two cows and a bull, the heavy rifle doing its work neatly. He packed the meat out with the help of Mendez, who, after they settled their dispute with fists, had become his closest friend among the riders. Once the skinned quarters were hanging in the cool room, he felt the itch to move on even more strongly. That night, over their now customary, after supper smoke, he set about revealing his feelings to the Don. He went through three cigarettes, working up his nerve. His anxiety was not lost on the old man.

"You are smoking *mucho*," observed Don Arturo. "What troubles you?"

Jeff frowned. "There is no way but to say it. I must travel on, *Patron*." This would hurt, he knew.

Archuleta frowned. "I have sensed a change in you. A restlessness. I had hoped I was mistaken, that what I felt were the naggings of an old man's mind. But now you have said it and that makes it so." He stared down at the cigarette in his fingers, hanging between his knees. Finally he dropped it, rubbing it out with the toe of his boot.

Jeff spoke. "I have never been treated better anywhere. I could stay here and work for you from now on and be happy, if I didn't have a reason to go."

The Don looked over at him. "If it is not out of place to ask, what is that reason?"

Jeff nodded and said, "I want a place of my own, a place like this. Not so big and grand, but mine. And as wonderful as it is to live and work here, as long as I stay, I won't get anywhere toward finding land for a ranch that I build."

Don Arturo held his hands out, palms up. "But, *mijo*, this place will be yours, is yours. Surely, you see that my younger son has no interest in the running of this operation. He is a poor horseman and does no work. This you know. You have seen it. He is more content to take his wife and my grand-daughters to Santa Fe, or Denver, or as far away as San Francisco, or even the City of Mexico, and for what? To stay in fine hotels, eat in the best restaurants, attend grand entertainments, and go to the most expensive tailors to have clothes of the current fashion made for them all. And who do you suppose pays for it? I do. This *rancho* does. All the hardworking people who live here and depend on this place for their very lives. They pay also."

He had gotten a little overwrought and made an effort to compose himself. "Forgive me, Jeff. The frustrations I feel over my remaining son are not your concern."

Jeff put a hand on the old man's shoulder. "That is not so, *Patron*. I understand and I see. And I care for you, this place, and the people on it. But if I stay, sooner or later it will cause problems, because I will want my share and that cannot be. No matter how much you wish I were your son, and no matter how much I wish it, also, he is your blood. There is no changing that. The best I could ever expect would be to rise to the position of *El Segundo*. That is not my plan."

Don Arturo gazed into Jeff's face for a moment, then sighed. "Of course, you are right. A man of your quality and talents would want a place of his own. A place built with his two hands. Even I am not such a man. I was born on this land, as was my father, and his father before him. The blood and sweat of many fathers is soaked into this soil. They claimed the range, built the *hacienda*, fought the weather, *los indios*, and *los banditos*. I am but a steward, but I have done my best. And when I am gone, what becomes of this *rancho*, this land, and these people?"

He leaned over and rubbed his face with callused hands. For a moment, Jeff thought he was crying. Presently, the Don spoke again. "You must go and I wish for you everything good. Only remember that you have a home here, as long as I am alive. Come back if you do not find a place that suits you better. Bring a woman. Have your family here. A good portion of this land will be yours, I promise. I shall have it written so in my will."

And then he *was* crying. Silent, salty tears flowed down the sunburned cheeks, the black eyes turning red. He reached out to the younger man and the two of them embraced, *un abrazo,* as father and son.

Jeff rode out the next morning.

FIVE

The present. November 22nd, 1882. After midnight.

THE MOUNTAIN AIR, chilled and real, had a sobering effect on Jeff, bringing his thoughts back to the moment. Enough of idle remembrance—of wanderings since leaving Texas eleven years before, of adventures on the cattle trails, the killing of Surratt and the terrible consequence to Inez, and most recently of these months riding for *El Rancho de los Archuletas*. All that was past and done.

And enough of riding blind, letting the buckskin choose the way. Time now to make a plan and to set about it with intention. As man and boy, he had often been decisive. Time to be so again.

Banking more wood on the fire against the cold night, he rolled up in his blankets to sleep. In the morning he would point the buckskin north once again, the blue mare and the red mule coming along. He didn't yet know their destination, but as they traveled, he'd work on his plan.

• • • •

SINCERO MONTOYA stepped through the broad wagon door of the Taos livery barn and saw the old bay gelding he'd rented to Bad Jimmy standing by the corral gate, still saddled and staring through the rails at the water tank. Montoya stripped the horse of the gear and turned it into the pen. The thirsty animal went straight to the tank and began drinking. Forking a ration of hay over the top rail, the old man wondered at the appearance of the horse without the rider. It could be that Lucero was laid out drunk somewhere, had tied the horse none too securely, and the gelding had gotten loose, to find its way home. But that didn't seem likely, as the bridle was hanging from the saddle horn. Perhaps the horse had been turned into a corral and left to rest for a time, only to get out through a gate left carelessly open. That possibility also seemed unlikely in that a man resting his horse would almost surely loosen the cinch, allowing the animal to relax and breath more freely. The cinch had been snug.

All this speculation was giving Montoya a headache. Sooner or later Jimmy would have to come around for his tack. Then the old man could present his bill. It was cold this morning and the stove in his office beckoned. He would think more about these matters later.

• • • •

IN THE EVENING of the third day out from Taos, Jeff rode into Chama, New Mexico Territory. He had skirted the towns of Tres Piedras, Tierra Amarilla, and Brazos, concerned that somehow word had gotten ahead of him about his trouble with Lucero. His animals needed rest, however, and the stiffness in his knees and lower back told him he could use some time out of the saddle. A break was needed by all. And besides, he reasoned, it was unlikely that Bad Jimmy had shared his plan for revenge with anyone. It was, therefore, equally unlikely that the corpse had even been found yet, if it ever would be. He decided he could afford a short layover.

He learned that the Colorado line was little more than a day's ride north. Once over the border, he reckoned he'd be out of the jurisdiction of any New Mexico authorities. Still chafing over having run from an incident of righteous self-defense and, worse, feeling heartbroken all over again for having some responsibility for the death of the girl in Albuquerque, he cast about for a way to take his mind off events of the recent past. He was pleased to discover upon his arrival in Chama that it was fiesta time.

Old men and boys paraded through the streets, carrying religious *banderas* and half life-sized plaster figures on tall poles. Vendors sold icons and effigies from booths along the way. Music from cornets, fiddles, and guitars filled the air, and fireworks added excitement. Town folk danced, dressed in their brightly colored best. Squealing children chased one another among spinning skirts and flying boot heels. An army of barking dogs chased the children. After the quiet solitude of the trail, it was a welcome but nearly overwhelming spectacle.

And the food! Outdoor kitchens were set up and cooking furiously at the four corners of the *Zócalo*. Fragrant smoke billowed from charcoal fires, kindled beneath grills covered with every sort of meat available. Beef, lamb, chicken, pork, kid goat, venison, and elk. And huge pots of *chiles*, *pozolé*, *menudo*, *aroz*, and *frijoles*. Corn in the shuck, soaked in tubs of water overnight and steamed in the coals. *Tortillas*, stacked like towers of giant poker chips, both corn and flour, hand patted and hot off the griddle. Jeff's mouth watered as he contemplated his options.

He saw, heard, and smelled all this from some distance, his animals decidedly skittish of the festive din. Riding back along a trickle of a creek he'd passed on the way in, he picked a likely spot, stripped gear from the stock, staked them on what grass there was, and set off walking in the direction of the party. Encountering two small, brown boys wrestling in the road, he hired them at the rate of two bits each to guard his camp for a while. Standing ramrod straight and with stern, little faces, they promised to defend his possessions at the cost of their very lives, if necessary, or at least to holler as loud as they could. With a wide grin, Jeff paid them half, with a promise of the rest when he returned. After handshakes, the boys set to their task.

It was time to eat, at last. His recent diet of jerky and biscuit had left Jeff eager for fresh meat and real cooking. Making his way to the square, he bought samples from each of the kitchens. Carrying two plates mounded with food, balanced one atop the other in one hand, and a large mug of maize beer in the other, he found a place to sit at the edge of the festivities. Eating slowly and with great pleasure, and taking long draughts of the full-bodied brew, he watched the show.

Two hours later, with three more beers and two *sopapillas* dabbled with honey under his belt, he walked slowly back toward his camp, a satisfied, if over grazed, young man. His two, fierce retainers were paid off and then delighted with a gratuity of another dime each. With earnest thanks and snappy salutes, they left at a run.

Jeff's mouth had a lingering burn from the highly spiced fare. Not trusting the downstream water from a creek so close to town, he took a drink from his canteen. Building a smoke and lighting it with one of the last of his matches, he next checked on the animals. He reminded himself to look for a *tienda* in the morning to pick up a few things so he could be on his way.

The music and fireworks had not diminished when the cowboy crawled into his bedroll near midnight. But a combination of beer, rich food, and fatigue was a powerful sedative. As shrieking rockets burst high overhead, casting down flickering showers of red, yellow, and blue on the surroundings, Jeff Cameron threw a last glance at his animals and, satisfied that all was well, slipped into the sleep of the dead.

• • • •

THERE WAS a patch of thin sunlight along the south wall of the livery barn and Sincero Montoya had carried a straight-backed chair to the relatively warm spot. He sat there after taking his mid-day meal, leaning back against the barn wall, both front legs of the chair off the ground, his feet propped on an inverted bucket, doing his best to soak up what little heat the sun over Taos offered. Now and again he dozed. It was an agreeable way to spend a winter afternoon.

He was awakened by the sound of an approaching horse and pushed up his hat brim to see a rider coming his way. He recognized the man as a *vaquero* who rode for the same *rancho* that occasionally employed Jaimé Lucero. Leaning forward until the front legs of the chair settled into the sand, Montoya rose stiffly and ambled into the path of the horseman. When the rider was within easy earshot, the old man spoke.

"*Que pasa, hombre?*"

"*Nada.*"

"Have you seen Bad Jimmy today?"

"No, *viejo*. I have been riding the north range for a week."

"Will you see him soon?"

"Well, I am going to the *hacienda*. Perhaps I will see him. If he is there."

"Is he likely to be there, do you think?"

The *vaquero* shrugged and picked a grain of sand from the corner of his eye. "*Quien sabe?*"

"Well, if you happen to see him, be so kind as to remind him that he owes me for the rent on the old bay gelding. *Por favor*. And I have his saddle, as well."

"He rented a horse from you?"

"*Si, claro.*"

"*Por qué?* What would he need with one of your horses? He has *la grulla* mare, no?"

"He did not say and I did not ask. He was in a very foul temper, even for him."

"Very well. I will speak to him for you, if he is there. If he is not, I will leave word."

"*Gracias, hombre.*"

"*De nada.*"

•   •   •   •

LEAVING HIS CAMP and heading for town to locate a store, Jeff came upon a number of bodies strewn about as though after a battle. They remained where they fell, rolled in *serapes,* but were neither dead nor wounded. They were partiers from the night before, continuing to sleep off their pleasures, despite the morning chill. Other townsfolk were removing detritus from the fiesta grounds.

Jeff found a store and selected items to replenish his stock of provisions. Wooden matches in waxed boxes, a three-pound sack of Arbuckle's Ariosa Coffee beans, five pounds of flour, some dried *chiles,* a side of bacon, a bag of pinto beans, and a couple of boxes of .45-75 cartridges for the Winchester. With a half dozen sacks of Bull Durham tobacco and rolling papers, the list was complete. An hour later, he had broken camp and was back on the trail.

After a day of unhurried travel, Jeff rode into Pagosa Springs, State of Colorado. On the trip up from Chama, he began to hear the voice of the land. Tall timbered hills, broad meadows, snow shouldered peaks, and clean, clear water. Could it be somewhere in this stretch of country that he would find his place? While in Chama he'd learned of a new army post, Fort Lewis, above the also new railroad town of Durango, west of his current location. A possible market for beef and horses. He felt his outlook brightening.

The San Juan River ran through Pagosa Springs in riffles and deep holes. Plumes of steam rose at many points where runnels of scalding water cut trenches through the snow packed banks and emptied into the icy stream. The smell of sulfur was strong on the breeze. Large, deep pools could be seen in the meadows bordering the river, steam rising from them, as well. These were the famous hot springs that gave this place its name.

Every town had a livery barn and Pagosa's was easy to find. Jeff argued with himself over the expense of a ration of grain and a night's shelter for his animals. His road stake was dwindling and what was left of his nest egg remained in his

Albuquerque bank, pending the settlement of his current, fugitive status. But he'd ridden hard over a rough trail and his little string deserved a good feed and a night out of the wind.

After caring for the stock, he wandered the town in the gathering dusk. A newly constructed hotel boasted fine dining, but he opted for *tortillas, frijoles con carnitas,* and a cup of coffee, served in a small *cantina* near the river. He sat by a window and ate with gusto, watching the sulfurous billows rising from the hot pools, backlit by the setting sun. The food was good and the coffee better, and the price was right.

In a short scout around to settle his meal, he concluded that opportunities with cards would be limited. The hotel bar had four tables and the *cantina* where he'd taken his supper had but one. Feeling the hard miles, he returned to the barn for a night in the hayloft, no extra charge.

Next morning he was up early. It was cold and he lingered close to the stove in the liveryman's office. He'd paid for another day for his stock, telling his host he'd see to the animals' feeding himself, and he was told to have at it. That done, he stepped out to hunt his own breakfast. The nearby peaks pushed close to fourteen thousand feet and the sun had not yet cleared their tops.

Seeking a change from Spanish cuisine, he followed his nose to a small false front building, the aroma of coffee and bacon having drawn him there. A front window was open a few inches, releasing its vapors onto the street. The sign over the door read Brakefield's Eatery.

Stepping inside, he found the smell even more tantalizing and he saw a man behind a counter to the rear of the room. The dining area had space enough for only six small tables. He headed toward the counter and the man looked up and nodded.

Jeff grinned. "You know you're cheating, don't you?" The grin stayed on his face as he said it.

"How's that?" The man seemed more puzzled than irritated.

Jeff continued. "Cracking that window to let the smell out on the street. It's more than a body can stand."

Now the other grinned. "I guess it worked on you, didn't it?"

The cowboy bobbed his head. "Sure did." His mouth watered and his stomach growled like a bear.

"Well, the menu's none too extensive," said the proprietor, "but how does bacon, eggs, fried potatoes, and griddlecakes sound?"

"Like pure heaven," Jeff answered.

The man turned back toward the stove. "Sit down here at the counter so I don't have to yell at you. Coffee's just now ready. You're my first victim of the day."

Jeff took a seat as instructed.

The man said, "That bacon you smelled was gonna be for my breakfast, but drawn up as you look, I'll sell you this first batch and get mine next."

"That's right generous. I appreciate it."

Coming back to the counter with coffee pot and cup, the cook poured a scalding draught for Jeff. Upon closer inspection, he realized that he was looking at the smallest man he'd ever seen. Not aware he was staring, he was surprised when the man spoke.

"I'm four foot eleven in my stocking feet. Stopped growing when I was twelve. My folks were normal sized. Doctors couldn't figure it." All this was said without resentment.

"Didn't mean to gape," replied a red-faced Jeff.

"Give it not a thought." The man returned to the stove, seeming to grow taller.

"You look regular size back there," Jeff observed.

The small man turned his head and smiled. "Lean over the counter top and take a look."

Jeff did so and saw a built-up walkway in front of the stove.

"Gives me another foot. If the world don't suit you, modify it to your needs, I say." His speech was brisk and crisp, and Jeff couldn't place the accent. But it would never do to directly inquire as to a man's origins. The subject had to be approached obliquely. He took a careful sip of the still-hot coffee before speaking again.

"Lived here for a while?" Now the man could reveal facts about himself. Or not. His choice.

"About a year," the little cook answered. "Came out from Vermont, for the silver mining. Spent six months over west of here, up in the La Platas, skinning my knuckles and breaking my back. Figured out the real money was in feeding the public. Working men. Ranchers. Miners. Loggers. Freighters. Railroaders. Soldiers, too, before the fort moved over to the Animas Valley. And cowboys in town for a night off. Single men, sick of their own cooking. Maybe that last category fits you. Now sit back down. Your grub is ready."

Conversation died as Jeff eagerly applied himself to the platter set before him. Four thick strips of smoked bacon, half a dozen pancakes, a heap of fried potatoes, and three eggs over easy, sitting atop it all. He found it superb. He was especially impressed with the pancakes and said so. His host smiled. "They're sourdough. Kept that starter alive all the way from Vermont. And it's the syrup. Real maple. Have it shipped from home. There is simply nothing in all the world like real maple syrup on sourdough hot cakes." Jeff nodded vigorously, his mouth too full to speak.

When he had paid the bill and was about to go, the little man put out his hand. Jeff took it and was surprised at the strength of the grip. There were calluses, as well. "James Brakefield. Friends call me Shortstack. Or else just Stack, for short." Here he laughed at his own small joke. Jeff chuckled politely. "Anyway, I feel safe saying that I make the best damned griddle cakes in the entire state of Colorado."

Jeff nodded. "The best I've had anywhere, anytime. And my name's Jeff Cameron, from Texas, Old Mexico, New Mexico, and now here. I believe I could fatten in a place like this."

Brakefield smiled. "Well, you'll have to come back. Tomorrow morning it's sausage with sage. Make it myself. A blend of pork, venison, and a little beef tallow. But come early. Folks like it. I open at six and I sell out by seven thirty or eight. I do supper also. No dinner. That time's for cleanup and my nap. Nothing like a good nap."

•   •   •   •

SINCERO MONTOYA was pushing an empty wheelbarrow back from the manure pile when he saw a mounted man waiting at the livery barn door. He did not recognize him.

"*Buenos tardes, señor*," he said as he parked the conveyance. The man nodded slightly, the brim of his hat barely dipping. He was dressed as a working *vaquero*, sat a tall, grey gelding, and wore a long barrel pistol in the cross draw position.

"How may I serve you, my friend. Grain for the *caballo*?"

The horseman shook his head. "No, *gracias*," he said in a formal voice. "I am told that you rented a horse to Jaimé Lucero some days ago." It was more statement than question.

Sincero nodded his head. "*Si, señor,* that is correct."

"When, exactly?"

Montoya took off his dusty, black hat and scratched his balding scalp.

"Today is Tuesday, no? It was last Thursday, the twentieth. Five days ago."

The *vaquero* nodded. "Did he say anything of his destination, which direction he meant to go?"

Montoya shook his head gravely. "No, *señor*. Not to me."

Nodding again, the rider said, "I also understand the horse he rented returned the next day, wearing Lucero's saddle, but with no Lucero. Is that true?"

Montoya gave another serious look. "*Si, señor.* It was as you say. Early the next afternoon. His saddle hangs in the barn."

"Did you see Lucero ride away? When he left on the horse he rented here."

"I did."

"Which way?"

"The old north road." Montoya pointed as he spoke. The *vaquero* touched his hat brim, turned his mount with a light rein, and trotted in that direction, saying no more. Montoya watched a few seconds. "Please remind him he owes for the horse," he said weakly.

• • • •

THE SUN was three hands above the eastern peaks as Jeff stepped back into the liveryman's office, his stomach comfortably full of Shortstack's good cooking. The man looked up and nodded, then returned his attention to the newspaper spread out on his desk. Jeff backed up to the woodstove, palms spread behind him. He looked out the dirty window, across the yard, and up the hill to see pine tops motionless in the calm air. The winter sky was such a pure, bright blue that he squinted. It would be a fine day. On his walk back from Shortstack's, he had made up his mind to spend a while in this town. The threat of pursuit seemed remote on this crystal morning. It felt good being here.

"I was wondering if you'd mind me using that round pen out back?"

The man looked up again from his reading, his expression showing mild impatience. "What for?"

"Well, I just bought a green filly the other day. Old enough to call her a mare, really. Anyway, she's had some training but she's been handled rough and I need a good, stout pen to smooth her out in. If you gotta have something extra for it, I expect I can manage."

The man leaned off to one side and spat tobacco juice into a lard can on the floor beside his desk. He wiped his mouth with a stained sleeve. "You going to go on boarding the three head here?"

Jeff nodded. "I figured too."

"Then I guess I'm making enough off you, 'specially since you're tending to 'em yourself. Won't cost me nothin' to let you use that pen. Won't cost you, neither."

Jeff smiled and stepped away from the stove to reach across the desk. They shook hands. "I'm much obliged to you, sir."

The liveryman waved dismissively. "It ain't nothin', son. Now git on out of here so's I can read this damn paper."

Jeff turned on his heel and stepped away from the desk, but the hostler's voice stopped him. "Hang on, son. I notice you got an eye for good horseflesh. I got a fine thoroughbred gelding I picked up for an unpaid board bill. Tall, grey horse, 'bout seventeen hands and fast as all git out. Gambler owned him, went bust and snuck out in the night. I been trainin' him to be a racer. Got a little Mexican kid gallops him four days a week. But I'd sooner sell him. Make you a hell of a deal."

Jeff had to remind himself that he was horse poor already. "Guess I'll have to pass, sir. I got about all the string I can use now."

The old man nodded. "All right, but if you change your mind, I expect he'll still be here."

• • • •

JEFF FED his animals and then spent a couple of hours on tack repair and general equipment maintenance. He oiled all his leather goods lightly, replaced a rotten lace that bound the *latigo* to the front D ring of his saddle, and cleaned his weapons. That done, he took the mule's halter from a peg in a support post and walked down the hallway of the big barn. Stopping at the blue mare's stall, he looked over the door. She was cleaning up the last wisps of her morning hay and, turning her neat little head toward the sound of his approach, she regarded him out of warm, brown eyes. The two of them stood still a moment, each taking in the other.

He couldn't say what was going on between her ears, but he knew what was in his mind. He liked what he saw in this animal. If she turned out to be the kind of horse he suspected she might, he thought he ought to consider a breeding, if he could find the proper stallion to cover her. He hadn't named her as yet, just thought of her as the "Blue Mare." And she was. Blue, as in slate, or tending toward grey, depending on the light.

He had scooped up a handful of oats as he passed the grain bin on the way to her stall. Entering carefully, not wanting to make her feel crowded, he extended the hand with the grain to her and stood still. She took a step toward him and stretched out her neck, getting a whiff of the offering. Liking what she smelled, she lipped the hand, but he kept his fist closed, teasing her, making her desire for the oats stronger than her apprehension of him. Finally, when he could see that she was concentrating on the feed and unafraid, he unclenched, relaxed his fingers, and made a flat palm as she ate. While she was chewing in contentment, he slipped the halter over her nose, snugged it up around her poll, and tied it under her left ear.

"I wish you could talk, sis," he said in a low voice. "I'd like to hear your story. And I expect you got a story to tell. I'd give plenty to get a look at your mama and daddy, too. From the look of you, they were bound to be a pair of true Spanish duns."

She listened attentively as he talked, eyes on him, ears forward, as if she was as eager to understand this quiet man as he was to understand her. "And I'd like to know who started you and how he did it. I hope you got lucky and had a sure enough, old time *amansadore* saddle you the first time, somebody with good hands and a light touch. And I hope that goddamned Bad Jimmy didn't have time to plumb ruin you."

She lifted her head and leaned toward him, her nose close to his face, took in a deep breath, getting his scent. She let it out in a long sigh, and it warmed him. It smelled sweet with oats and hay. Taking her out of the stall, he turned down the aisle and headed toward the rear of the yard and the round pen. She followed, willingly.

The circular corral, also called a round pen, had long been employed by horse breakers and trainers as an indispensable aid in the process of gentling horses and bringing them to the bridle. Jeff had used more than one himself. This one was sixty feet in diameter and seven feet high at the top rail, with about six inches of river sand for good footing. In sand this deep, he thought a man could take the edge off a rowdy colt in short order.

Once inside, he dropped the lead rope, letting her sniff the ground and walk the perimeter of the pen while he went back into the barn for his saddle. She wasn't as round in the barrel as the buckskin, so he grabbed an extra blanket. As he re-entered the pen, he made an unfamiliar profile with the saddle held through the gullet, braced against his leg. She backed away from him, a little unsure. He thought that she probably harbored some unpleasant recollections of past saddlings. Walking to the middle of the circle, he stood the saddle on the forks and draped the blankets over it. Backing to the fence, he squatted on his heels and built a smoke.

The mare watched him settle himself, then moved up carefully to examine the pile of tack. She sniffed the blankets and the leather underneath, and lifted her head to regard him. He continued to squat, drawing smoke in and letting it out. Looking at her looking at him.

He smoked the cigarette down to a short butt, which he buried in the sand. There was a soft curry brush sitting on top of a fence post, and he rose to his feet, got the brush, and approached the mare. Her ears were toward him, her nostrils rounded, but her attitude was one of interest more than fear. He moved to her left side and reached out to let her sniff the back of his hand. She remained relaxed and it was an easy thing to drop the hand enough to take hold of the lead rope. She stood quietly as he reached up with the brush, letting her smell it, as well. The next move was to begin the actual brushing, starting just below the left ear and working down along her neck. This, too, she accepted quietly. Both man and horse were calm as the grooming proceeded.

"You're a sight, girl. I never saw a horse in worse need of a curryin.' And I think you like it?"

She answered with a friendly nicker.

Fifteen minutes later, he had brushed her out from the base of her ears to the root of her tail, and from her top line to the fetlocks. This sort of thing did not need to be done in a hurry and was relaxing to both. The lead rope hung loose to the ground. She had remained calm. Taking a hoof pick from one of the saddlebags, he cleaned her feet. She tried half-heartedly to take one of her hind hooves away from him, but he held on gently, moving with her, and she relaxed again and let him pick it out also. She was shod, but long in need of re-shoeing. He'd see to that later.

The presence of iron shoes indicated that she was more or less broke to ride. She had been saddled and bridled when he first saw her and he suspected that Lucero had been using her as his mount. But there was no way to know how much training or what type she'd had. He hoped again that the heavy hand of Bad Jimmy had not ruined her.

He stepped back and tried to look inside the horse, to get some sense of where she was now, in her mind, as she stood quietly beside him. He tried not to over think it, but just to feel. After a minute more, he went to the gear pile in the center of the pen and picked up one of the blankets. Approaching her calmly but directly, he began to rub her over the neck, back, and hindquarters with it. When she made no protest, he laid it in place to take the saddle. The second blanket he laid atop the first, then gently floated the saddle over them both. She stood rock steady for all this.

He snugged the cinch, tightly enough for him to mount without the rig slipping, but loose enough not to bind her. She was fine with that. Next he casually flipped the lead rope over her neck and tied the end off to the halter ring under her chin. It made a rein he could use to communicate with her head. No bit would be in her mouth. Because they were inside a corral, he had no fear of a runaway. He stroked her neck and combed out her thick forelock with his fingers, then cupped his hands over both her eyes and rubbed gently and rhythmically. She bobbed her head up and down, liking it. She sniffed his face and he blew his breath into a nostril, very gently, and she liked that too.

"All right, sweetie," he said, "let's dance." Taking the shortened loop of rein and a grip of her mane in his left hand, he turned the stirrup, put his left boot in deep, grasped the horn with his right hand, and swung up smoothly. She held still as a statue.

Settling himself into a deep seat, he found the offside stirrup with his right foot. And then simply sat. The blue mare remained quiet, her ears turned, one back toward him, and one to the front. For more than a minute he sat and she stood, him rubbing her neck and rump just behind the saddle, and her letting him. He spoke again.

"Well, honey, I guess it's time we moved." He felt relaxed and confident. She seemed unconcerned beneath him. He squeezed with his legs. Still she stood. All right, he thought.

Just a little more. He touched her lightly with one spur, and she grunted like a pig, bogged her head, humped up in the air, and came down stiff legged, then began sunfishing and spinning. Jeff was slung to the side like a dishrag, coming out of the saddle and landing in the sand heavily on one shoulder and the side of his head. It was the first time in years he'd been bucked off. Three good hops. Damn! She'd suckered him.

He lay still a moment, waiting to see if any of his parts said he was hurt. His eyes were closed and there was dirt in his mouth. The next thing he felt was warm breath in his ear, the one not stuck in the sand. He opened an eye and saw the mare standing above him, head lowered, her velvety muzzle not six inches from his face. Gingerly, he sat up, the mare backing one step. They regarded each other. Jeff spat dirt out of his mouth.

"I guess that was to show me you're a lady not to be taken for granted." He got to his feet, giving himself a moment to steady up. Nothing felt broken nor even much hurt. The shoulder would be stiff tomorrow, but beyond that he reckoned he was fine. Without further delay he took the rein in his hand, got a mane hold, and swung up into the saddle again. The mare stood like statuary.

He found his offside stirrup, settled down in the seat, and made a kissing sound with pursed lips. She moved out at a brisk walk, nice as pie. After two circles around the rail, he kissed again, and he she went into a smooth jog.

There was little bounce to it, almost a single foot, like a southern gaited horse. Another cue put her into the silkiest rocking horse canter he could have asked for. As they loped around the pen, she took the proper lead automatically. A true, old time *amansadore* must have given this girl her first lessons, as he had so fervently hoped. In the rest of their time together, she never offered to buck again.

He asked for a little speed, straightened her out, and let her accelerate for a few strides. Then he sat back and bumped her lightly with the reins. She dropped her hind-quarters, brought her hocks up under herself, and did a sweet little sliding stop in the loose sand. Stepping down he went to her head. Rubbing between her eyes, he said, "You just had to let me know to mind my manners, didn't you, sis? Well, count on it, I will."

• • • •

THE *VAQUERO'S* NAME was Juan Pinto, but he usually was referred to simply as *El Cazador*. The Hunter. After his brief interrogation of Montoya, the liveryman, he left Taos by the north road, put his leggy gelding in a long trot, and tried to imagine Lucero's thoughts as he'd ridden away on the rented horse. His extended absence had been noted at the *rancho*, which gave him employment from time to time. Speculation was brisk as to his disappearance and when the subject of the unpaid rent on the horse came up, it was decided that an effort to locate him would be made.

Of much curiosity was the puzzling question of why Bad Jimmy would want to rent a horse in the first place. His ownership of *la grulla* mare was well known, as was his habitual abuse of her. Some were of the opinion that she had thrown him and run off, and he had taken the rental horse to recover her. Others thought that perhaps he had gambled her away. None of that explained the fact that he himself was nowhere to be seen.

It had been *El Segundo* of the *vaquero* crew who had suggested securing the services of *El Cazador*. His specialty was locating lost cattle and stolen horses. On occasion, he hunted men. When offered the assignment of finding Jaimé Lucero, he had accepted.

• • • •

WITH THE SADDLE OFF, Jeff was brushing the mare again, talking softly to her, her ears swiveling this way and that, but one cocked at him all the time. She was liking it, leaning her head toward him as he worked on the spot below her left ear. Abruptly, her eyes and ears were drawn away.

"A right satisfactory entertainment, indeed!"

Jeff looked over in the direction from which the voice had come. A man leaned against the corral, watching them through the gap between the top two poles. The pen was seven feet high, so that made the stranger at least six feet four. Jeff sized him up to be in his mid-sixties, with a great, white beard and mustache, and a whiskey face with broken veins in his nose and under his eyes. But his spine was straight and his shoulders broad.

A lean and hungry wolf, Shakespeare might have called him. His dress was a mix of stained buckskins and plaid woolens, topped off with an odd sort of cap. When he spoke, he rolled his *r*'s with his tongue on the roof of his mouth and Jeff figured him for a foreigner, though not Spanish. A powder horn and hunting pouch hung from his shoulders, and a big skinning knife was slung from his belt in a beaded scabbard. A heavy muzzle-loading rifle rested in the crook of his left arm. Taken altogether, he was a formidable-looking old man.

"You speaking to me?" Jeff was frowning slightly.

The man grinned to show large, yellow teeth, like a horse's. "Aye, I am that, laddie buck. I thank you for the show."

"What show would that be?"

"The one where that filly tossed you so neatly. Right smartly done, it was."

Jeff might have let irritation edge his words. But he could see that it had all been said in a warm tone and with a smile. So when he spoke, it was mildly. "Are you poking fun, sir?"

"Not a'tall lad, not a'tall. I was quite sincere. The acrobatics were most amusing. And the way you stepped back up manfully and put her through her paces. Why, I couldna' have done better mesel.'"

Jeff still wasn't quite sure whether or not he was being made light of, but having sampled so much trouble lately, he thought better of taking issue. And it wouldn't hurt to know a few folks around here. He walked toward the man, the mare following like a pup. The stranger was loading a nasty-looking pipe as he approached, with equally nasty-looking shag tobacco. Scratching a match on a corral pole, he fired up and produced a voluminous cloud of foul-smelling smoke with apparent satisfaction.

"What sort of hat is that," Jeff asked?

The man grinned the widest yet. "Why, that's me own bonnet, lad."

"I thought only farm women wore bonnets."

He shook his head, laughing heartily. "Not a sun bonnet, a Scot's bonnet. What the men of Scotland wear."

Jeff nodded. "So I expect that makes you a Scotchman?"

The man shook his head. "No, sir. I am a Scot. The term Scotch refairs to a type of whiskey. The finest in all the world, I might add." He rolled the *r*'s grandly.

Jeff nodded once more. "The band around your bonnet's all checkered, different colors."

"Right. That's to signify a man's regiment, if he's a soldier."

"You a soldier?"

"Aye, once. Many years ago. No longer."

"Where's Scotland?"

"North of England, at the top. The crown of the British Isles. Heaven on earth." The man nodded and puffed, a dreamy look on his face. It sounded like he said "airth."

Jeff wondered what the old man was doing in Colorado, if Scotland was heaven. Maybe you had to die to go there. Before he could think of more to say, the Scot spoke again, like he was almost compelled to fill the quiet. "Yeh have the look of a range rider, a drifting cowboy, if I may say so. I've na' seen yeh here aboots before."

This opened the topic of Jeff's personal history, but in that sideways fashion which was the frontier custom. "Rode in yesterday, late. Up from New Mexico."

The stranger nodded and went on puffing. "Your voice speaks of the south. Texas, perhaps." It came out, "pairhaps."

Jeff held the man's eye. "I been there."

The Scot put out his right hand between corral poles. "I am Andrew MacTeague, of Clan MacTeague. Call me Sandy."

Jeff shook. The grip was callused and strong. "I'm Jeff Cameron. Good to meet you."

The man bobbed his head and worked Jeff's hand like pump handle. "Cameron, yeh say? Then yer a Scot yersel', by God! This calls for a drink."

SIX

THE TWO of them sat at a corner table, the only occupants of the room, except for an old drunk with his head down on the bar. It was still early. Jeff sipped sparingly at a glass of beer. MacTeague was on his third whiskey. It seemed to have no effect on him. Jeff had little interest in alcohol at that hour, but was intrigued by this unusual individual.

He spoke of his youth in Scotland. Said he had yellow hair as a boy. Hence, the nickname Sandy. He'd worn it long, tied in back with a piece of woolen yarn.

"The lassies were all near death with envy, that golden were me locks." MacTeague had none of the westerner's taciturnity. He seemed to relish conversation, especially when he was leading it. Jeff heard how he'd left Scotland as the Highlands were stripped of cattle, which were then replaced with sheep. He called them "heather maggots." While young, there was time in the British Army, with a posting to India, and from there to Afghanistan, as part of the British Empire's struggle with Russia in The Great Game, as Rudyard Kipling had called it. Then, done with duty and hearing of gold and adventure to be had in the American fur trade, he sailed for New York and made his way west as a young man of twenty-five, forty years ago. But he'd arrived at the end of the boom, just as beaver hats were going out of fashion, and had not made any real money. It didn't much matter to him.

He had trapped, fought Indians, lived with Indians, hunted big game, gone to Rendezvous, raced ponies, wrestled, gambled, gotten drunk, fist fought with other trappers, and fornicated with Indian women. It had all been great fun.

Staying in the wild country, he had taken an Indian wife, continued trapping for the small income it provided, traded a little, scouted for emigrant parties, and otherwise lived off the bounty of the land. Later, he had hunted buffalo to feed the railroad crews, and finally had shot them for their hides. But he'd hated the work, the sight of the prairie dotted with rotting carcasses. There had been more than one tight brush with roaming bands of warriors, the braves enraged at the wasteful slaughter. By then he'd lost his wife in childbirth. The boy baby had died with its mother.

He'd drifted north, up to Montana, where he'd shot meat for the mining camps in Alder Gulch. There was good money in it, while the game held out. Tiring of the need to range farther and farther to find deer, elk, and bear, he moved on. There were other camps, and he found himself drinking more and more, at first to ease the pain in his aging joints, aggravated by too many hours wading in icy beaver ponds, and then simply because his body craved alcohol. And the winters were brutal.

Hearing of the healing waters in southwest Colorado, he'd wound up in Pagosa. He took the cure, letting the hot springs cook the alcohol from his system and relieve the ache in his knees and hips. Not that he'd given up drinking, but he did moderate his intake, relatively speaking. So now he shot wild meat for the hotels and restaurants. The living was modest but adequate and there was still plenty of game in the hills. All in all, it was a good place for an aging mountain man to run out his string.

"I just wish a man could get a drop of decent Scot's whiskey in this benighted country. This witch's brew here would make adequate lantern fuel, but it's hardly fit for drinkin."

A younger brother had followed him west in '55, married a girl from one of the pioneer Spanish families, and had taken up land to the west, in the Animas River valley, north of Durango. He sold cattle and horses to the army post at Fort Lewis, grew hay for his stock, and sold the excess to local hostlers and to the fort. He grew sufficient garden produce on his bottomland, as well as beef, lamb, pork, poultry, and eggs, to sustain his family, his riders, and the families of his married men. They lived in comfort if not luxury. His name was Robert MacTeague. There was one daughter. The wife had died some years past.

"How come you don't go live with them?" Jeff asked. Sandy had been so forthcoming with his story, it hardly seemed like prying to pose the question.

"What? Go abide with that mon? Oh, I dearly love me wee brother. But it's all thrift and industry with him. He canna' tolerate me free ramblin' ways. Huntin' and fishin' and traipsin' about the country are mortal sins to him, to say nothin' of drinkin'. We suit each other best at somewhat of a remove."

• • • •

JUAN PINTO found Jaimé Lucero, or what the coyotes and the magpies had left of him, at mid-morning on the second day of his search. The dirt that had covered the body was little more than a foot deep, and the scent of decomposing flesh had come drifting up to attract every carrion eater in the area. Despite what the scavengers had done to Lucero, he was easily identified by the ornate Chihuahua spurs that were a familiar part of his outfit. Also, by the distinctive knife that he carried in a red sash, as well as gold rings on his fingers. These items were on the corpse. Pinto took note of this. Whoever had sent Bad Jimmy out of this world, that person had been no thief.

El Cazador urinated on the ground around the corpse to discourage further scavenging, then returned to Montoya's to get a mule. The old liveryman inquired as to Bad Jimmy's condition. Pinto replied dryly that, had Lucero been in good health, he'd be renting a saddle horse rather than a pack animal. Missing the irony, Sincero went to the corral and caught a gentle, old mollie, led her into the barn, and equipped her with a sawbuck saddle and a canvas sheet. Winding a lash rope around the cross bucks, he thought he would be pleased when this business with the troublesome Lucero and his unpaid bill was concluded.

• • • •

"I'LL NO ASK you the state of your finances, lad, but if yer like others of yer breed, yer no a rich mon." Sandy MacTeague puffed his stinking briar as Jeff drew on a hand-rolled cigarette. They sat on a bench in front of the hotel bar, taking advantage of the thin warmth of the sun as they enjoyed their smoke. Jeff was getting used to the Scot's way of talking. He took no offense at Sandy's intrusive estimate of his solvency, or lack thereof.

"Well, I ain't broke, but my poke's getting a little light."

MacTeague nodded, a fatherly expression on his whiskey branded face. After a spate of vigorous puffing, he said, "Then let me offer a bit of local hospitality to you. I've a modest cabin a bit east of town on the way up to Wolf Creek Pass. There's a spare bunk, a good, tight stove, and a stout corral with a bit of a barn. As I recently sold two of my older mules, there's extra fodder and empty stalls. It'd be my pleasure to offer a place out of the elements for you and your animals for a spell. Just 'til you get yourself sorted out, mind."

Jeff grinned. "Likely you just need somebody to tell your tales to, besides that old cat you mentioned." Jeff was surprised at how comfortable he felt around this stranger.

Sandy nodded. "Aye, 'tis true that poor old Bonnie Prince Charlie has heard 'em all twice over, and more. He's a piece o' work, that cat. He'll be happy to make yer acquaintance. And a mite of human company on a howlin' winter night would be a thing I'd welcome, too."

"It sounds all right," Jeff said, "But I'd want to pay my way."

Sandy showed a horse-tooth smile. "And so yeh shall, laddie. I'm getting somewhat low on firewood. There's a patch of blow down pine and aspen not forty yards behind the cabin. I reckon with the help of a braw lad such as yersel', I could fill the wood shed in no time a'tall."

Jeff said, "Yeah, especially if that 'braw lad' did the cuttin' while you did the talkin'."

Sandy pretended outrage. "Och! Yeh villain, yeh. How could yeh speak such wicked slander?" Then he grinned. "It seems you know me ways already. Well, even so, it'd be a fair arrangement for the both of us, I believe."

Jeff grinned, too. "I expect so. Some time off the trail would suit me and my stock just fine. And a big, windy story on a cold winter night might be toll'able."

•   •   •   •

THE CABIN sat beside the west fork of the San Juan in as pretty a spot as Jeff had ever seen. A meadow of seventy-five or eighty acres climbed gradually to a timbered ridge running east and west, high enough to take most of the bite out of any wind from the north. Lots of deadfall pine along the meadow's edge provided ample fuel for the stove. Aspens and cottonwoods bordered the river. Ragged peaks rose up behind.

As for the cabin, calling it modest was generous. Whatever its builder had done for a living, carpentry wasn't it. In Sandy's ownership, however, it had been improved and snugged against the winter's blast. When he and Jeff arrived, Sandy lost no time getting a blaze going in the stove, and soon the space was toasty warm, as he had promised. It was a small structure, cozy, no more than fifteen feet square, with a loft.

Jeff offered to tend to the stock if Sandy would start a pot of coffee. He agreed, and when his new friend returned in twenty minutes, chores done, the smell of cooking filled the single room. He leaned the Winchester in one corner and realized how hungry he was, his mouth watering from the aroma of fried meat and coffee. Sandy turned from the stove, fork in hand.

"How does elk steak, potatoes, and biscuit sound?"

Jeff made for the plank table. "Like the answer to a prayer." Hooking a boot toe under a back rung of one of the two homemade chairs, he drew it out and sat as the old man placed a full plate in front of him.

"Tuck in lad. Plenty more when yer ready."

• • • •

DON ALEJANDRO MIGUEL ESPINOZA sat in a cowhide chair on his wide veranda, smoking a black cigar and reading a novel written in French. It was a mild afternoon without wind. He looked up at the sound of an approaching horse. A lean *vaquero* on a rangy, grey gelding was coming his way, leading a mule draped with a canvas-covered load that hung over both sides of the mule's back. Spurred boots were visible below the tarp on the near side. As the rider approached, Don Alejandro recognized him to be Juan Pinto, *El Cazador*. The man stopped his horse in the lane below the veranda steps. The Don rose from his chair and moved to the railing.

"Is that Lucero?"

"*Si, Patron.*"

"You found him where?"

"A short day's ride north of Taos, in a shallow grave under a cutbank. I was not the first."

"Coyotes?"

"*Si.* And magpies."

Espinoza nodded. "Were you able to determine the manner of his death?"

"One bullet. Through the head."

"Very well. Take him to the chapel. Have the old women prepare him."

"*Si, Patron*. His brothers will want to know." The Don nodded.

"I expect to see them inside a week. They will bring horses to sell."

Don Alejandro reached in his vest pocket and produced an American double eagle. He extended his hand to Pinto, who side passed his horse closer to the porch and received the coin. "*Muchas gracias, jefé*. You are very generous." Touching the brim of his sombrero, he turned his gelding trimly and led the mule off in the direction of the chapel.

The Don frowned. "This is inconvenient." He returned to his chair, relit his cigar, and resumed his novel.

•   •   •   •

EARLY IN THE MORNING, after Jeff's first sleep at Sandy's cabin, the two of them took the Scot's remaining pair of mules and rode further up the west fork of the San Juan. Jeff was on Buck and Sandy was riding a tough-looking, paint gelding. At mid-day they ate cold elk and biscuit. An hour later the Scot killed a spike bull with a neck shot at ninety yards. Jeff praised his shooting. Sandy grinned and set about the butchering. Despite his age and creaky joints, he made short work of the job, assisted by his young helper.

The front quarters went on the smaller of the two mules, the hinds on the big one, covered by the hide. By the time the sun was dropping behind the western pines, the meat was hanging in the barn, wrapped in pieces of an old canvas wagon sheet. Sandy beamed.

"There's ten gold dollars, lad." He slapped a hanging front quarter for emphasis.

"Just for a shoulder?" Jeff was astonished.

"No, me boy. For the whole critter. But that's gude money for a half-day's work. A cowhand has to ride for more than a week to make as much."

Jeff agreed. Looking around, he took in the interior of the barn for the first time in daylight. The loft was nearly full of sweet-smelling hay. A tin-lined wooden box was filled with grain.

Packsaddles, panniers, and various bits and pieces of harness hung from nails in overhead joists. Better built than the cabin, it was an agreeable place that gave a feeling of comfort.

Jeff felt something press against his leg and looked down to see an enormous, grey tomcat peering up at him. He bent and scooped it up, and the animal responded with loud purring as the cowboy scratched its neck.

"Well dam'me," exclaimed Sandy. "Lookee there, will yeh. That cat dislikes everyone and barely tolerates me. Prince Charlie is a harsh judge of character. I've never seen him picked up before. Doesn't even allow me that liberty. Yeh must be an extraordinary mon indeed, by God!"

Jeff let the cat jump to the ground. It darted behind the grain bin to resume mouse patrol. "I get along with critters," he said.

In the cabin later, Sandy fried up a pair of blue grouse he'd taken earlier in the day with thrown sticks. It smelled like Sunday dinner in the tight, little log house.

"Timber chicken. Even dumber than the barnyard variety. Never waste a shot on 'em."

Jeff looked up at the heavy rifle, hung on oak pegs driven in the wall over the door. "How come you tote an old relic like that? You could trade for a Sharps .50 for the price of about four elk."

Sandy turned from his cooking, eyed the gun on the wall, then stared at his guest with a mixture of shock and pity, shaking his shaggy white head. "Are you daft, lad? Part with me dear old smoke pole? Why, I'd as soon lose a leg. That piece is a genuine St. Louis Hawken. I won it at Rendezvous in a wrestling match with one Jim Beckworth. Nearly got a broken arm. With it, I've taken more buffalo, elk, deer, and bear than I could ever count, not to mention a couple of pestiferous red men and one bad Texican. No lad, when the day comes that old Wallace there won't serve me, I'll be done sure enough."

Jeff looked puzzled. "Wallace?"

Sandy smiled. "Aye. The gun is named for William Wallace, hero of Scotland, killer of Englishmen."

The birds were done and the hungry men set to with gusto. Jeff thought it like chicken, indeed, and the white meat was a welcome change from beef and elk. Sandy was a fair camp cook, making more biscuits and a pot of rice with gravy from the pan drippings. In a short time, Jeff had reduced his grouse to clean bones and had put away his share of the rice and gravy and biscuits.

Sandy noticed. "By God, lad, for a rangy pup you surely can make a bait of grub disappear."

Jeff wiped his mouth. "That was damn good, Sandy. Sorry about being a pig. This high country air gives me a hell of an appetite. Guess I better get after that firewood business tomorrow."

The Scot smiled. "That'll be fine. As to your gluttony, any cook likes to see his efforts well received. And besides, it ain't like it was haggis."

Jeff's confusion showed. "What the hell is that, 'haggies?'" he asked.

Sandy's face took on a rhapsodic expression. "Haggis is Scotland's national dish. It's sheep's liver, lungs, and oatmeal, cooked in the stomach of the beast. Food of the gods," he declared.

Jeff grimaced. "Uh, think I'll stick with grouse," he murmured.

● ● ● ●

THE ELK MEAT was bound for the hotel up the block from the livery stable. Sandy and Jeff spent two days after the kill putting up firewood. By that time, after two nights hanging in the barn, the quarters of elk were nearly frozen. On the morning of the third day, after coffee, bacon, and biscuits, the new friends packed the meat on the mules and headed for town.

In an effort to manage his alcohol consumption, Sandy kept no whiskey at the cabin, thus limiting his drinking to visits to Pagosa. He knew his weakness and so far had been able to summon up enough self-control to maintain this routine. So upon delivery of the meat to the hotel kitchen and with payment in hand, he was anxious to get to the barroom, buy drinks, and return some of that money to its previous resting place. He, of course, invited his helper to join him. Though it was early for him, Jeff accepted with thanks and sat nursing a beer as the Scot downed a couple of shots in quick succession. Ordering a third, he set about loading his pipe from a beaded pouch, soon to be filling the air around them with billows of pungent smoke.

There was a card game underway at one of the three tables and Jeff observed the play. Small stakes and little skill by a quartet of hung-over cowhands. If he'd been alone and of a mind, he could have sat in and cleaned them all out in a couple of hours. But he wasn't there to gamble and so he sipped his beer and waited for Sandy to make the next move.

Surprising Jeff, the Scot rose abruptly from his chair, knocked his pipe out in a spittoon, brushed flakes of tobacco and ashes from his plaid woolen shirt, and made for the door.

"Come along lad. Dinner beckons."

Jeff caught him on the boardwalk. "You sick?"

"Sairtainly not. Why would you think that?" Sandy looked at him sideways.

"You didn't have but three whiskies in there. I figure you must be colicky or something."

"Not a'tall lad. But it's crowding noon. If yeh've an appetite, and from what I've seen so far I reckon you must, then I'd like to treat yeh to the best dinner in town."

Jeff smiled. "I can always eat. Where to?"

Sandy pointed up the block with his chin whiskers. "To the boarding house of the fair Widow Peach. Wednesdays it's pork chops, pinto beans, mashed potatoes, cornbread with preserves, and deep dish apple pie."

Jeff swallowed. "Good Lord. That sounds like the sort of cooking I grew up on. Where's this Mrs. Peach from?"

Sandy continued his long-legged stride up the walkway. "She's a transplanted Southron, from the war ravaged state of Georgia, if I'm not mistaken. She sets a grand table and I always attempt to appear for Wednesday dinner."

• • • •

ONE BLOCK over from the main street, away from the river, stood a rambling Victorian style house, two and a half stories with wrap-around, covered porches and gingerbread trim. A white picket fence enclosed upwards of an acre of ground, including a large garden plot now in winter fallow. Upon entering the front parlor, Jeff was assailed with heady aromas drifting from the dining room. Sandy clearly knew his way and led his friend to a seat at a long oak table set for a dozen, already occupied by eight boarders and off-the-street diners, tucking in heartily, with little conversation.

Just as the two of them were taking their chairs, the swinging door from the kitchen swept back to admit a truly stunning woman carrying a heaping platter of batter fried pork chops. She was of middle height, with a full, but not overly abundant figure, honey-colored skin, and strawberry blonde hair. Flushed from the heat of the kitchen, a glow of health and vigor radiated from her.

As any properly raised southern boy would, Jeff rose upon her entry into the room. While he stood there transfixed,
her low-cut dress revealed a tiny bead of sweat tracing a path
from the base of her throat, to disappear into a most appealing cleavage. Noticing the new arrivals, she smiled widely.

"Why, Sandy," she beamed, "I was fixin' to give up on
you." Her voice dripped off her tongue like molasses onto a
buttered biscuit. Jeff guessed her to be in her late thirties.

"Och, no, lass. Nay power on airth could keep me away
on pork chop day." Sweeping off his bonnet, Sandy executed
a bow from the waist.

Mrs. Peach set the platter down and curtsied, all in one
graceful motion. Seeing Jeff she asked, "And who is this
young gentleman?"

He opened his mouth, nothing coming out but air. Sandy
saved him further shame. "It is my honor to name Mr. Jeff
Cameron, horseman extraordinaire, native son of the great
state of Texas, late of New Mexico Territory, and currently
assisting me in my endeavors in the game fields. Jeff, meet
Mrs. Adele Peach."

She extended her hand. "Mr. Cameron."

Jeff took it gingerly. It was surprisingly rough. This lady
made her own living. "Ma'am," he replied, finding his voice.
"Don't put too much stock in that windy introduction of
Sandy's. I'd be obliged if you'd call me Jeff."

She tilted her head a few degrees, smiled, and declared.
"And you must call me Addie. Now, I insist you sit back
down and have your dinner." Jeff still stood, his neck and
ears reddening from her attention.

Every head at the table had looked up. She had been
strictly "Mrs. Peach" to one and all since her arrival in town
four years past. An awkward silence was broken by the Scot.
"Sit down, lad, and fill your trencher, or these hearties will
clean the table before we can get started." This earned him

scowls from other diners, but he laughed it off in his hale fashion.

Jeff's ears were still warm as he took his seat, only to redden deeper. Coming 'round the table, Mrs. Peach leaned toward him to put food on his plate, giving him a dazzling smile and an even more dazzling view down the front of her bodice. The other diners gaped in amazement. This favor of personal service had never been extended to any of them.

On the front porch a half hour later, enjoying a smoke, Jeff and Sandy let out their belts in mild discomfort, but great satisfaction.

"A grand repast, laddie buck." He rolled his *r's* through a haze of pipe smoke.

"You don't say," grinned Jeff. He had put away several pork chops, a great heap of mashed potatoes, a couple of helpings of pinto beans, a large square of corn bread with peach preserves, an ample slice of dried apple pie, and at least a quart of cold buttermilk. It was his first taste of that tart beverage since leaving Texas. All topped off with freshly ground coffee laced with heavy cream. Sandy had held his own at the table as well. He sat and, between belches and puffs on his pipe, picked his teeth with a porcupine quill. At last he spoke.

"The widow fancies you, me boy." He nodded sagely.

Jeff's ears heated up again. "She's just being polite to a stranger." To himself he admitted he'd thought the same.

"Nay, mon. She never serves at table. Something aboot you has piqued her interest."

"Well," Jeff muttered. "She don't hurt much to look at."

Sandy nodded again. "No. That she does not."

• • • •

THREE DAYS after the delivery of the remains of Jaimé Lucero by the stern-faced Juan Pinto, the brothers of the deceased, elder brother Emiliano, called Mano, and the younger brother, Pepé, arrived at Don Alejandro's rancho with twenty head of unbranded horses. Some of them were *mesteños* caught wild, but more were young horses stolen from remote ranges far from the headquarters of their owners. They always offered the Don first pick and he usually selected a few of the best ones. As was customary, they arrived within ten days of the same time twice yearly and, as was also their custom, they turned the animals into the usual corral before approaching the *hacienda*. It was another warm day, and the Don was again seated on the *veranda*, smoking and reading. The brothers stopped their mounts at the foot of the steps, dismounted, and doffed their sombreros. They were silent as the Don rose and stepped to the railing.

"Ah, *buenos tardes, hombres.* I have been expecting you. You have brought some *caballos*?" Mano nodded. Pepé stood silent and rigid.

"*Si, Patron.* Twenty head. Several are of a quality to catch your eye."

"No doubt. You always have a few good ones. However, regrettably, there are other matters to discuss first. Unfortunate matters, I fear. They concern your brother, Jaimé."

•   •   •   •

JEFF FOUND occasional card games over the next weeks, but stakes were small and so were his winnings. His savings continued to dwindle. His assistance to Sandy had been for room and board, only. There would be no riding jobs until spring. A cold snap had made the hunting more difficult. As the snow deepened, they were feeling symptoms of cabin fever.

The two of them decided to see what they could find in town. Winter business was always slower at the boarding house, so the Widow Peach invited them to consider a room at a reduced rate. Aside from his bar bill when in town,

Sandy otherwise handled his earnings frugally and had savings on which to draw. He offered to cover the cost of the room if Jeff would agree to resume helping with the hunting when the weather broke. All parties content with the terms, Jeff and Sandy found themselves installed in short order at Mrs. Peach's boarding house.

Winter business was slow for the liveryman as well and he offered them an attractive price for lodging all their stock. The three mules and three horses made a welcome addition to his barn. He agreed to board Prince Charlie at no charge. "I could stand a good mouser around here," he said.

But Jeff was mildly concerned. He queried Sandy, "Won't The Prince run off?"

The Scot shook his head. "He's a hunter, like mesel'. There's mice enough to keep him well engaged at the barn. And we'll visit with a saucer o' cream and a slice o' deer liver now and again to remind him of his prior allegiance."

After another Wednesday dinner, Mrs. Peach asked Jeff to join her in the kitchen for coffee. Sandy repaired to the hotel bar to smoke his pipe and take a "wee dram," as he liked to say.

Filling their cups, the widow got right to it. She looked him directly in the eye and said, "Jeff, I need a man."

She had his attention with that and he blushed above his neckerchief. "Beg pardon, Ma'am?"

Seeing him squirm and hearing her own words again in her mind, she smiled and replied, "I mean I need a man's help around the place."

Jeff relaxed and nodded, "Yes'um,"

She continued, "I had an older fellow who would come by and split wood for the stoves and what not. He did like his jug, though. Too much, I guess. They found him in a snowdrift last month. Stiff as a poker. Figured he staggered into it late at night, floundered around, and was too drunk to get back on his feet. You may have heard about it."

Jeff shook his head. "Must of been before I got here," he said.

She went on. "Well, he split a fair amount of wood before that. I had insisted he stay well ahead of the demands of the house."

Jeff nodded, seeing where this likely was going and beginning to think about it. She continued. "I have another man who brings me wood in the round, sawn to stove length. I bought fifteen cords from him last fall. My departed helper split about four. So I'm down to one cord now that's stove ready. That's too lean a margin. There's about eleven more cords to split. Don't need that all at once, but at a steady rate to stay well ahead of what it takes to keep this big house warm. Also, there's a cow to milk. You said you were a farm boy in Texas. I believe I recall you mentioning that. So I'm assuming you can milk?"

Jeff grinned. "Did it for my mama growing up."

Mrs. Peach smiled back. "Good. All right, can you paint?"

He went to the cook stove and got more coffee for them both. "Painted a barn once. When I was a young'un."

She smiled, nodding her head approvingly. "I have several rooms I'd like painted before warm weather. Not in a hurry. On that, you could take your time, do a careful job. I've done plenty of painting. I'll show you how I like it."

That took him up short, those last words of hers. They invited his imagination down a risky path.

He got his mind back on business. This was a good deal for him, what she had described. Nevertheless, he had revealed himself, blushing from collar to ears. Hoped she hadn't noticed.

She had. There was little she said that wasn't calculated. He would learn that. She was pleased with this evidence of her effect on him.

She continued, "There's another thing. Last summer, a cowboy staying here lost his stake in a card game and then couldn't pay his rent. I took his three-year-old filly to hold against what he owed. I've heard nothing from him since he went off to fall roundup. I have to assume he's not coming back for the horse. Appears I own her. She's halter broke, is all."

Jeff jumped ahead. He was confident in this territory. "I'd be tickled to get her going for you, Ma'am. Get her saddle broke, gentle."

"Wonderful!" She was beaming. He thought her as warm and attractive a woman as any he'd seen up close. "Sandy says you're good with horses. This one seems well bred. You don't rough break them, I hope?"

He shook his head. "I'll start her easy. Take my time. Got all the rest of the winter. Come good weather, she'll be like a puppy. Broke to a lady's taste."

Mrs. Peach flashed him a dazzling smile. His face felt warm again. He hoped it didn't show.

"Splendid. As a girl, I'd go hunting with my daddy. He kept a pack of deerhounds. We'd fly pell-mell through the woods, following his dogs. It was quite thrilling. I believe I'd like to ride again." Her eyes sparkled as she seemed to be recalling the excitement of the chase.

"Sounds like fun," Jeff replied, trying to keep his mind now on horse business, instead of monkey business.

"Yes, well. Then it's wood splitting, milking, painting, and horse training. No women's work. My Mexican girl and I will handle all that. I'll pay you the same wage as any rider. A dollar a day, a warm room with clean sheets once a week, and all you can eat. You'll take your meals with the boarders. From what I've seen, you seem to like my cooking."

He swallowed, "Oh lordy!"

Mrs. Peach gave him another bright smile. "Then, do we have an agreement?" She offered a hand. It was strong, rough, and warm.

"Yes, Ma'am. You got yourself a man."

She eyed him. "I believe I do. And I wish you'd call me Addie."

His head was swimming. "Yes, Ma'am. I mean, Addie."

. . . .

"HERE'S TO YEH, laddie. Sounds like yeh've found a baird's nest upon the ground." Over a drink in the hotel bar, he'd told Sandy of his arrangement with the Widow Peach. The Scot puffed on his pipe as Jeff shared the details of their conversation.

"But do have a care, son. There's likely to be fringe bene- fits. Intoxicating ones. I can see potential for entanglements." He gave a warning look, one eyebrow raised.

"Such as?" Jeff was uncomfortable with the direction of the conversation.

"Yeh know quite well what I refair to."

Jeff rotated his beer mug in a sweat ring on the table. It was a little embarrassing to realize that the signals he thought he was picking up from his new employer were being picked up by someone else, as well. He shifted in his seat. "Well, I can't say I haven't felt an attraction. Guess I'll see how it goes. Let her call the deal." He took a sip of beer. "But just so you know, I'm not lookin' for anything with any woman. Had a thing happen not long ago. Brought it on myself, I guess. There was a girl in it. A real nice girl. Turned out bad for her. Couldn't have been worse. So I ain't lookin'."

Sandy nodded. Again, frontier custom prevented him from asking for details. "That's wise, lad. She's got eight or ten years on yeh. A lady of experience. And remarkably well presairved, if I may say so. But you've told me something of your ambitions, your dream. Have a care not to be side- tracked. 'Tis a tender trap a woman lays for a mon."

. . . .

JEFF'S NEW SITUATION proved to be both comfortable and challenging. Comfortable in that he had a soft, clean bed up off the ground in a snug, warm room, with work that was good exercise without being too taxing, and plenty of good food to fuel his efforts. The challenge was keeping his mind on that work. Mrs. Peach was a very appealing taskmistress and an almost constant distraction. If it wasn't the sight of her lovely face and exceptional figure, it was the sweet sound of her voice, or the clean and heady fragrance of her scrubbed and lightly scented skin.

The best part was that his response to her charms was beginning to distract his thoughts from the dying girl in the *cantina* doorway. He was experiencing some relief. For months his dreams had been plagued with vivid images of the dark-haired singer with the deep, green eyes, shot down on the boardwalk, her blouse saturated in bright red blood. He knew that his bullets had not killed her. They had come from the barrel of Hudson Surratt's revolver. But he feared never being free of a sense of responsibility for her death. If he had simply stayed home that night, the girl would surely still be alive.

At first, in bed in his new room, he would stare at the high ceiling, trying to imagine his employer younger. But he concluded the fully ripened version he saw each day was superior to any youthful image he could conjure. There was a physical force radiating from this woman, almost constantly, whether in the kitchen glistening with perspiration or elsewhere speckled with paint from redecoration. That force was alluring to him. But he knew he should be warned, as well. "Maybe I ought to take roundance on this one," he told himself.

He was daily put to the test as Mrs. Peach showed no reservations of her own around him. She took occasion to be too close to him, inviting his awareness of her presence. Brushing against his shoulder, his arm, his hip as she stepped by him or reached for something. He thought of the Scot's cat, rubbing up against his legs, and half wondered that the widow didn't purr.

He'd gamely return his focus to his work, suppressing the impulse to directly respond to her provocations, ones that reasonably would distract any normal man his age. What made it doubly difficult was the suspicion that such an impulse, did he act upon it, would not in any way be rebuffed. Such ideas were tempered, however, by his renewed inclination toward discretion. So he held to his work, splitting wood in the cold air of the mornings, and painting walls and woodwork in the afternoons in the rooms she'd indicated. And he began the training of the lady's filly.

A look in her mouth told him she was a three year old. The length of her cannon bones promised good height, and she had a well-developed hip and a broad chest. A gracefully arched neck supported a handsome head. And a long, sloping shoulder suggested the probability of smooth gaits. Straight legs and good feet rounded out the package. Her good disposition seemed equal to her promising looks. She always gave Jeff a nicker of greeting as he approached her stall. She clearly relished the brushings and any other attentions he paid her, and made no objections to the saddle. She never offered to buck. He worked her and the *grulla* mare in the round pen behind the livery barn. They both were developing well.

•   •   •   •

JEFF HAD PRODUCED a tall pile of split wood from the bulk of the eleven cords. Fearing his energies were working him out of a job, he decided he should be giving more time to the filly. Or to the painting. They'd finished the first room and were beginning a second.

He anticipated she would have him paint the whole house, now that she had his help. He liked the work well enough. But he was still uneasy around to her. She was—or she wasn't—enticing him, inviting him. He didn't have the experience to know, exactly. Or to respond confidently, or in kind. He was increasingly uncomfortable and wanted relief from it.

So he began simply leaving the house after supper. This despite his sense that it likely was only a matter of time before he was in some situation of her making that would bring things to a head. Daytimes, he was safe enough staying busy. Nights, however, he felt in over his head, staked out like bait.

He stayed away after dark, visiting with Sandy at the bar or playing cards, without his mind much in the game. Then returned late enough for the house to be quiet before going up to his bed. It was not satisfactory, his new routine. It was costing him sleep, taking a toll on his workday, leaving him tired before its conclusion. Avoidance would not be a long-term solution, he was aware. There was a showdown coming, when she chose and on her terms.

SEVEN

NIGHTS WERE crackling cold the week before Christmas. Jeff had come to the eatery owned by the little man from Vermont. It had become his habit to stop in and visit over coffee as Shortstack finished late supper service and cleaned up. Often, he would take up a broom and idly sweep out the dining room as they talked.

This evening was particularly quiet, with a single customer at a front table when Jeff entered. He made his way toward the kitchen and took a stool at the counter. His feet were cold, his hands, too. His gloves were still back in his room. His small friend reached for the blackened coffee pot and filled a cup for him.

"Right brisk out," he observed.

"That it is, my friend," replied Shortstack. "Pour some of this mud down your neck. You'll thaw fast."

Jeff took the mug and cupped it in his hands. He was comfortable here. Shortstack put down a sugar bowl and a small pitcher of cream. Jeff doctored his coffee and took a careful sip. Satisfied, he said, "Stack, you make about as good a cup of coffee as I've had. What's the secret?"

The little man grinned. "Last thing before I serve a cup, I stick my thumb in."

Jeff grinned back. "Does the trick." He drank more, warming himself from the inside out.

"Hey, sawed off! How 'bout some of that down this way?" The lone customer at the front table held his cup in the air, as if in a toast. He was a large, jowly man with a week's worth of black whiskers and a coat opened to accommodate an oversized belly that strained at the buttons of a dirty shirt.

Jeff didn't know him and figured him for a teamster, stuck in town by the last snowstorm.

Shortstack frowned and called down to him. "Be there directly."

Turning back to his friend he asked, "Do you mean my coffee's superior to Mrs. Peach's?"

Jeff nodded. "Hers is all right, but doesn't measure up to this."

His small friend smiled. "She certainly measures up well in other ways."

He reddened. "I expect there's truth in that."

The customer barked, "Hey, picket pin, I still don't see no hot coffee." He swung a heavy boot onto the table in front of him, the sole of it facing the counter.

Shortstack's scalp tightened. He called across the room. "You need to take that foot off my table, sir."

The teamster called back, "And you need to rattle your trace chains down here with that goddamn coffee pot, runt."

Jeff looked from the customer back to his friend. He figured the snowbound man likely had been drinking all afternoon. Shortstack's face was beet red. Reaching into a cubbyhole under the counter, he produced a five shot, Smith and Wesson .32 caliber revolver. Stepping to one side of Jeff, he extended his right arm like a duelist, thumbed back the hammer, leveled, and fired.

The range was no more than twenty-five feet and the bullet went straight through the sole of the boot, the foot inside it, over the man's shoulder, and lodged in the wall. The teamster hurtled over backward in his chair, howling in shock and pain, holding the foot in both hands.

Shortstack walked the length of the room and leaned over the wounded man, putting the muzzle of the pistol against his bulbous, whiskey-veined nose. That reduced the howling to a whimper. The diminutive cook spoke in a calm, unhurried voice. "There's a doctor keeps a room in the hotel down this block. If he's not too drunk, he'll tend to you. Now you get up and get your rude ass out of here or I'll blow this swelled-up strawberry right off your face."

The shot man blinked once and rolled onto hands and knees, crawled to the door, pulled himself up to his good foot, and hopped out of the eatery, leaving a visible blood trail in his wake.

Shortstack stuck his head outside and yelled at the hobbling figure, "Your supper's on the house. And tell Doc I'll cover your bill." Shutting the door against the cold, he walked back to the counter, reloaded the one empty chamber from a box of cartridges stored underneath, and placed the gun back in its slot.

Jeff's jaw hung slack. Shortstack noticed him staring. He smiled and said, "What?"

The sharp taste of powder smoke was in Jeff's mouth as he answered. "Remind me not to mess with you."

The little man chuckled. "Doubt I'll need to."

· · · ·

MANO AND PEPÉ LUCERO, accompanied by Juan Pinto, returned late in the day to the *estancia* of Don Espinoza after a brief expedition to the creek bed where Bad Jimmy's corpse had been found. Earlier they had visited the small, neatly kept cemetery behind the *rancho* chapel. A fresh mound of earth and a whitewashed cross marked their brother's grave. Mano removed his sombrero and crossed himself, as did the other men.

Pinto spoke. "You may have wanted to see him a last time, but he lay in that wash for several days. And the weather has been warm. He was not presentable." He declined mentioning the coyotes and magpies.

Mano's fingers worked his hat brim. "Where was he last seen alive?"

"At the *cantina de los gringos* in Taos," Juan answered.

Mano nodded. "If you will permit us to stay the night, we will ride with the sun."

Juan nodded. "Don Alejandro welcomes you."

Mano turned to his brother. "Clean your weapons, *hermanito*."

• • • •

THERE WAS frenzied activity at Mrs. Peach's in the last few days before Christmas. Jeff helped Addie and the Mexican housekeeper decorate the parlor and dining room. He strung popcorn on heavy thread for hours. That was his job. The women made wreaths and garlands, and baked heaps of cookies. Wonderful smells filled the house. Carmelita sewed tiny cloth dolls to represent the holy family and assembled a small nativity scene in the parlor, set on a table next to the tree, under which brightly wrapped presents were beginning to collect. The boarding house air was festive.

After supper on Christmas Eve, Jeff was on his way to the front door, dressed for a walk to the hotel bar, when Addie called from the dining room. As he turned, he saw her standing in the doorway to the hall. Yellow lamp light bathed her face and figure. She wore a shimmering green velvet dress, a string of pearls calling attention to its low-cut neckline. There was another green object held in one hand. "Jeff," she asked, with a wide smile, "Help me hang this up." She had screwed a cup hook into the overhead doorjamb. A footstool was beside her. She shoved it out of sight with her heel. "I'm just not tall enough," she said.

Jeff walked over, smiling as he came. He refrained from asking how she'd managed to install the cup hook on her own. She returned his smile twice as bright. "Please take this piece of yarn and tie the mistletoe to the hook." She handed the sprig and the short length of yarn to him.

Looking at them he said, "This here's a piece of sage-brush."

She nodded. "I know, but it's all we've got. We'll just have to pretend its mistletoe."

Knotting the yarn first to the sage sprig and then to the hook, he asked her, "What's mistletoe? Never heard of such."

Her eyes brightened. "It's a Christmas tradition. You hang it in a doorway and then wait for someone to pass through."

Jeff frowned, puzzled. "Then what?"

She took a step closer. They were alone in the hall. "This!"

Then he felt her hands tugging on the collar of his sheep-skin coat, pulling him down to her height. Before he could say anything, her lips were on his, mouth open. He felt her tongue. His head spun, electricity raced through him. And then she was heading off toward the kitchen, humming, leaving him standing unsteadily in her wake.

• • • •

JEFF'S BOOTS crunched in the packed snow as he stepped off the boardwalk in front of the bar. It was cold, crowding zero, and looking across the street toward the river, he could see clouds of sulfurous steam rising from the hot pools.

He stood a moment, built a smoke, and put it absent-mindedly in the corner of his mouth. Taking a match from a vest pocket, he held it under a thumbnail to fire it, but waited. Standing lost in mental images, he stared, unseeing through the steam clouds, remembering the kiss, the taste of the woman, the feel of her tongue touching his, the press of warm, firm breasts against his middle. It had all but over-powered him. He'd blushed and hurried from the house, not even taking time to arm himself.

The game he'd sat in on was slow. Who would be out late on Christmas Eve to play poker? Men without families, apparently. A cowboy in town from a nearby ranch, on an errand for the cook. He was all but broke, and played a safe game. Another young man who worked at the bank, playing nervously, not wanting to be seen in a saloon. Jeff should have cleaned them out. Instead he quickly lost seven dollars and quit. His play was amateurish.

He was distracted. All he could think of was strawberry blonde hair, strong hands on his collar, soft lips, and a sprig of sagebrush hanging over his head.

Feeling the cold through his thin riding boots, he came to and lit the match, held the flame to the cigarette, drew in a lung full of smoke, and blew it out. Well, hell, he thought, standing around in the icy air wouldn't settle anything. Hanging the cigarette in one corner of his mouth and shutting an eye against the curling smoke, he shoved his hands deep in the pockets of his sheepskin and started back toward the house of The Widow Peach. He still didn't know what the hell mistletoe was.

•　•　•　•

UP IN HIS ROOM, he lit the lamp, hung up his coat, took off his shirt, jeans, and long handles, and draped them over the chair. Pulling on his nightshirt, he checked the loads in the Colt. It hung from the bedpost, holstered on the worn cartridge belt. Since the November night in the hills north of Taos and the visit of Bad Jimmy to his camp, seeing to his weapon had become a habit.

Crawling under the covers, he found the foot of the bed toasty from a warming iron wrapped in a towel. Surprised by the unaccustomed luxury, he decided that it must be the doings of his employer. This was a courtesy not extended before. He was curious as to what this might mean. He turned up the wick of the bed lamp and opened a veterinary text he'd found at the livery barn under a pile of harness, covered with dust. Turning to the chapter on horse colic, he settled back into the feather tick and began reading. He'd gotten into the second page when he heard a faint tap at the door. Putting the book down and resting his right hand on the yellowed horn grip of the Colt, he spoke in a calm voice. "Who is it?"

In answer, the door swung open easily and there stood Mrs. Peach in a flannel nightgown, carrying a tray. "Merry Christmas, Jeff," she said, just above a whisper. "Warm milk and cookies." He took his hand off the pistol and sat up, his back against the headboard.

He was tight as a fiddle string. The woman glided across the room as if on casters, setting the tray on the nightstand. Without being asked, she sat on the edge of the bed. Blood roared in his head. He felt his face flush.

"It ain't Christmas yet." He instantly felt stupid for saying such a simpleminded thing. He was a damn fool.

Addie gave him a coquettish smile. "Close to one o'clock, cowboy. Christmas morning." She picked up the warm milk and sipped from it, never taking her eyes off his. Then she held the glass to his lips and he drank.

"That's good," he said.

She took a napkin from over the cookies and blotted the milk from his mustache. "There's nutmeg in it, and honey." She took a cookie and bit into it, and as she chewed, she broke off a piece and fed it to him. Ginger snap. Spicy. It was hard for him to swallow. He could smell her, a mix of soap, warm woman skin, and some sort of scented powder.

"I like you, Jeff. A lot." Soft southern trail off to her words. "You like me, too," she went on. It was a statement with no hint of question in it.

He could not find his voice. His eyes were fixed on the reddish blonde hair, blue eyes, butterscotch skin, and all the rest of her, washed in soft yellow from the lamp. When he finally could speak, he said, "I haven't had milk and cookies since I was a little feller. Mama'd bring 'em to me now and then." To his embarrassment, he felt blood filling him up between his legs.

Addie leaned down and kissed him, slow and deep, then rose up and lifted the gown off over her head. Her breasts in the lamplight looked taut and swollen, almost angry.

"Well," she whispered, resuming her seat, "I'm not your mama." With one hand she turned down the lamp, as the other searched for him under the sheet. Finding what she sought, her eyes widened. "And you're no little feller."

•   •   •   •

COME FULL DAYLIGHT, around the tree with coffee before breakfast, presents were opened. Sandy was there, playing Santa Claus, reading the names off the packages and handing them out. From Addie, Jeff got a pair of fringed, buckskin riding gloves. Along with them, she gave him a dazzling, knowing smile that made him blush to his boot heels.

From the thrifty and practical Sandy, he got a box of cartridges for the Winchester '76. Addie opened Jeff's present to find a silk headscarf. To his further embarrassment, she rose from her chair, moved to where he sat on the couch next to Sandy, and gave him a moist kiss on the cheek. Sandy elbowed him in the ribs as she turned to sit down.

Her gift from the Scot was an embroidered handkerchief. She gave him a slightly less radiant smile and crossed the room again to peck him on the top of the head. His ruddy face went ruddier still, but feigning disappointment, he said, "What? No kiss upon the cheek for the poor, old Highlander?"

She laughed brightly. "Maybe if you were shaved."

Sandy drew himself up in mock indignation. "This tender jaw has na' felt a razor in more than thirty years," he croaked. "Even a kiss from one so bonnie as yersel' wouldna' be worth the sting of stropped steel." Then he laughed. Feelings were warm all around. Jeff was spared further embarrassment by Carmelita's call to breakfast.

•   •   •   •

IN THE WEEKS to come, Addie visited Jeff's room every third night. The only boarder on the second floor was an old Confederate veteran, a man in his sixties who'd lost most of his hearing serving an artillery piece at Gettysburg. That was fortunate, as Addie was a hearty lover, at times giving full-throated voice to her enthusiasms. But it was a big house and the downstairs boarders, being lodged in the far wing, heard nothing.

For Jeff's part, his emotions ranged widely. While he soon found her solicitations as addictive as any drug and missed her warm presence on the in-between nights, he knew he did not love her. And despite the affection she lavished upon him, he never felt that it, either, included love. As their moments together increased in intimacy and experiment, he wondered how a woman could do the things she did to and for him without love in the mix. He thought of asking, but instinct held his tongue. In spite of his puzzlement, he was enjoying it all too much and sensed that the wrong question might kill the fun. And fun it was.

If the other boarders were fooled, Sandy was not. One pleasant afternoon in January during the expected chinook, the thawing, warm wind out of the southwest that came most years during that time, Jeff was working the filly in the wide, center aisle of the livery barn, out of the snow, when he noticed the hunter moving toward him on stiff legs.

"Laddie buck," he hailed as he entered the barn, "Greetings to yeh on this bonnie day."

Jeff stepped off the horse, loosened the cinch, and said, "Howdy, Sandy. They run out of whiskey down the street?"

His friend shook his head. "Needed a stretch of the old pins, lest I become intoxicated."

Jeff laughed out loud. "Become? I thought you got up drunk and went to bed that way."

Sandy straightened, beard bristling, and cast a fierce blue eye at him. "As anyone who knows me will testify, I'm never in me cups much before noon and only when in town. That yeh could say setch a thing, and to him who's been all but a father to yeh, by God."

Jeff chuckled. "All right, daddy, I take it back." He walked the filly to the tack room and began stripping the gear from her. Sandy followed, loading his pipe as he went. Jeff looked back and frowned. "Don't let old Eulis see you light up in here. He'll have you on the end of his pitchfork." He had the horseman's gut fear of barn fires.

Sandy took no offense, gripping the stem of the unlit pipe between yellow teeth. "Calm yersel', lad, I'll no fire up in the barn. Just the holdin' of it gives a bit o' comfort."

They were silent as Jeff unsaddled the horse and then began brushing her down. He felt a current of anxiety coming from his friend and, after letting the filly into her stall and tossing her a forkful of hay, he turned to face Sandy.

"All right, say your piece, father."

The Scot did not return the grin on Jeff's face. Instead, he walked out into the muddy barnyard and lit his pipe, puffing energetically until his head was enveloped in a great, stinking cloud. "It's none o' me business," he began.

Jeff guessed where this was headed. "Well, maybe you ought to keep it to yourself, then."

Sandy looked him in the eye. "Yeh told me to say me piece and that I'll do."

Jeff leaned against the barn wall, took out the makings, and joined the man in a smoke. Dropping the hot match in a puddle, he took a long draw, let it out, and said, "Go on then, let's have it."

Sandy puffed and nodded, knitting shaggy brows. "Was I in yer boots, I expect I'd do likewise." He scratched down in his beard and went on. "There's no a mon alive with a healthy spike under his kilt who could resist that woman. But yeh must know, lad, yer fanning a hot bed o' coals. Flames are bound to follow."

Jeff flicked ash into the mud. "What if I told you nothing was going on between me and her?"

Sandy looked up, taking the pipe from his mouth. "Well, I doubt I'd call yeh a liar to yer face, but yeh'd be one, all the same."

Jeff nodded. "That plain, huh?"

Sandy smiled. "I can smell her on yeh right now, son."

"I wouldn't think you could smell a hot horse turd over that damned pipe."

Sandy removed the fuming briar from his mouth. "Don't evade the topic, lad," he said.

Taking a last drag, Jeff dropped his cigarette into the same puddle that floated the spent match. "It was her idea," he replied weakly. "She made the first move."

Sandy narrowed his eyes. "And I've no doubt she had to hold a gun to yer head."

Jeff frowned, then said, "She's incredible."

Sandy nodded, smiling vaguely and puffing vigorously. "I believe it, lad."

"Thing is, there's no love to it, with her or me."

"Pure pleasure."

"Right."

"No entanglements."

"Yeah."

"No consequences?"

"None," answered Jeff.

"That's where yer dead wrong," the Scot countered.

Jeff turned to see Sandy's level gaze, no humor in it.

"Yeh know, of course, that she is a widow?" Sandy said.

Jeff nodded. "Everybody knows that."

"Well, everyone is na' familiar with the saircumstances of her widowhood."

"I guess I'm fixin' to hear about it now," Jeff said.

Sandy remained serious. "Aye, that yeh are." He went on puffing, and Jeff moved to a position upwind. The hunter launched into his narrative. "Gordon Peach was a hero of the War of Northern Aggression, as he refaired to it, a Major in the Georgia Volunteers. Served with valor and distinction. Minor wounds, many times decorated. Unlike most defeated Confederates, his wealth somehow survived the conflict. His business was banking. When they first arrived in '78, they pairchased the big house where we board. The Major bought into the local bank and they settled into the community. Addie spent her time redecorating. The Major moved up in the management of the bank and all seemed to be going along swimmingly for them."

Sandy cleared his throat, spat in the mud, and continued. "Major Peach was a handsome man, tall and wide shouldered. A fair match for Addie, at least in appearance. Unfortunately, his character turned out to be somewhat lacking. Rumors began to drift around that he was less than faithful to his marriage vows. It turned out that his hunting and fishing trips to Chimney Rock, up on the Piedra River, had an added feature. A pair of fetching German girls, twin sisters, actually, had a cabin out that direction. Their business was entertaining gentlemen. When the Major seldom brought any ducks or trout back from his ventures, Addie began to suspect something untoward. The upshot of it was that she rented a horse and followed him on the last of these expeditions, saw his mare tied outside the twins' cabin, and let herself in to find him in a rather large bed, with both the sisters pleasuring him in a fashion yeh may imagine. Apparently, he was in the saddle even as she stepped through the door, and for his efforts he took two balls in the lower back from her derringer at a range of ten feet. The twins made good their escape as Addie fumbled the job of reloading, she being understandably agitated. She eventually managed to recharge the weapon, and the young ladies were obliged to run naked in the timber for several hours while she hunted them. Unsuccessfully, to the girls' good fortune. In the end, it took the Major the better part of two weeks to die, of peritonitis. A grisly death, I might add. No charges were ever proffered against Addie, as the only witnesses to the incident quit the country right smartly, after a midnight return to the cabin for clothing. And that, my lad, is how our fair friend, the Widow Peach, earned the title."

·   ·   ·   ·

To say that Sandy's tale of the widowing of the Widow stunned Jeff would be no more than accurate. His mouth hung open for the last of the story and now, finding it so, he shut it with a conscious effort. The woman who could make him feel so good also was capable of murder, had murdered, in fact. That was a shock to him.

"Are you certain sure about all this? How did the story get out if she didn't tell it herself?"

Sandy scratched his stringy neck and took the pipe from his mouth. "On their way to more peaceful climes, the sisters stopped at the trading post in Chimney Rock, pairchased a few necessities for the road, and mentioned in passing that a wounded man had appeared at their cabin. By the time the authorities got involved, the twins had disappeared like smoke on a stiff breeze. The Major, in his final days, related the details to the attending physician. Addie, of course, denied it. Folks hereaboots put two and two together but, with the twins departed, nothing could be proved. Truth to tell, Addie by then was respected in town. And most folks had heard the rumors regarding the Major's expeditions and reckoned that he had gotten his comeuppance, even if so harsh the administration and final the outcome. So, on balance, the Widow Peach remains well regarded, if a wee bit feared."

Jeff rolled a second cigarette. He lit it deliberately, took in a lungful, held it a few pensive moments, and let it out in a thin stream. Turning to face Sandy he said, "I guess there's a point to you telling me all this."

Now it was his friend's turn to look astonished. "Dam'me, son, are yeh not warned to have a care with the woman?"

Jeff took another draw, then spoke around the smoke as it left his mouth. "Well, in the first place, I ain't married to her, nor am I going to be. And in the second, she don't even love me."

The Scot shook his head. "I doubt that she loved the Major overmuch, either, knowing her as I've come to. But, lad, do yeh know nothing a'tall of women?"

Not waiting for an answer, he plowed on. "There's a thing called possession, which don't necessarily have a thing to do with love. And what exactly is love, after all?" Jeff took a breath to speak, but Sandy waved him off. "No need to answer. That's what's known as a rhetorical question."

Jeff frowned. "A what?"

Sandy rolled his eyes. "Never mind. My point is this. A woman is a hard critter to track. Whether she loved the Major then or loves yeh now is entirely immaterial. What yeh need to get through that young, thick head of yours is this. She has a tremendous capacity for jealousy and her former husband is dead. And why is he dead? For the simple reason that she shot him, twice, and it by God killed him!" Sandy's voice rose in volume over those last statements and by the end he was towering over Jeff, glaring down from his greater height, his white whiskers fuzzed out like an angry cat, almost shouting. Jeff backed up until he was stopped by the barn wall.

Sandy's tirade had deflated him and, knocking out his pipe, he stepped back inside the barn aisle, taking a seat on a convenient stack of grain bags. Jeff stood outside long enough to butt out his smoke, then came and sat next to the old man. Neither spoke for half a minute.

At last, Sandy turned his hairy face toward his young friend. "My apologies for that rant."

Jeff shook his head. "Don't mention it. I expect I needed to hear it."

They were quiet again for a time, as the power of their friendship smoothed down ruffled feathers. "There's a bit more," Sandy said.

Jeff gritted his teeth. "Let's have it."

"All right, lad. You're not the first young horseman to catch the widow's eye."

•   •   •   •

AS SANDY told it, another cowboy had come through the previous year, a dashing fellow who turned out to have more flash than integrity. A fast, hot fling had ensued, Mrs. Peach treating the young man to many of the same privileges she now was granting Jeff. After a couple of months, she'd tired of him, presented him a bill for room and board, and when he was unable to pay she booted him out, keeping a horse he owned against his financial obligation. Upon hearing this last revelation, Jeff's mouth dropped open again.

"That's the filly I been riding for her, ain't it?"

Sandy nodded. "Sadly so, me boy. Sadly so."

Jeff shook his head. "Well, I will be goddamned!"

Sandy put a hand on Jeff's shoulder and with a small grin said, "Hopefully not, lad."

•   •   •   •

TWO VERY TIRED RIDERS on equally tired horses rode into Taos from the south on a cold, windy afternoon in the first week of December. Foul was the odor from their unwashed clothes and skin. Equally foul was Mano's mood, and his brother was guardedly silent, afraid that a word might bring forth his wrath.

What they most immediately needed was a hot meal and a warm sleep off the ground. But what they most wanted was a drink of something strong and some information. The *cantina de los gringos*, otherwise known to its patrons as the Broken Horn Bar and Billiard Emporium, was a short distance from their entry into town. It was, in fact, the last place the departed Bad Jimmy had slept, knocked out on a pool table.

The trail worn men were grateful to step down and tie up their mounts at the hitch rack in front. Mano pressed his fists into the small of his back, stretching and twisting his torso in an effort to relieve the stiffness. Pepé stood patiently until his older brother was done with his contortions. They crossed the boards to the entry door and went in.

The main room was over warm from the efforts of a big, potbellied stove situated toward the back. Two cowboys, likely out of work for the winter and riding the grub line, were intent on a game of straight pool on the rear table. Three elderly *gringos* sat at a card table in the far corner, close to the wood stove, playing an old man's game. Another white man of middle age, in a dingy, striped shirt and greasy apron stood behind the bar, reading a newspaper with the help of wire rimmed spectacles mounted on the end of his nose. All six looked up as the brothers Lucero entered and shut the door against the wind. None smiled at the sight of two *vaqueros* ragged from the trail.

Straightening up off his elbows, the barman put his glasses in a shirt pocket and folded the paper as the brothers approached the bar. He was thin, with an unhealthy cast to his complexion. He looked as if he had a bad taste in his mouth as he said, "I don't keep no tequila ner mescal in here." The tone was neither welcoming nor unfriendly, just flatly declarative.

Mano put a boot on the wooden foot rail and stared him in the eye until the man glanced away. The horse thief pushed his hat back off his head and let it hang by the stampede string against his back. His black hair was matted down and he looked dangerously fatigued as he said, "Then pour us whiskey, something good."

The barman made no move to comply and said, "Lemme see some money."

Mano dug in vest pocket and produced a number of silver pesos, laying them on the bar top. "You take these?"

"Why not?" the barman replied. He turned for a bottle of Kentucky sour mash and a pair of spotted tumblers, setting all three in front of the men. He picked up several coins and dropped them into a cigar box in a drawer under the bar.

Next he reached for the newspaper, but Mano had a hand on it first. "Pour," he said. The barman started to protest, but the look on his customer's face kept him silent and he did as instructed. The brothers lifted the glasses with a murmured "*Salud*" to each other and sipped slowly. A look of satisfaction crossed both faces.

"*Esta bien*," declared Pepé.

"*Si, claro*," agreed Mano. The barman moved to retrieve the bottle, but Mano raised an index finger. "I will buy the rest."

Nodding, the barman said, "Sure," and swept the remaining coins into his other hand.

"A high price," commented Mano.

The barman shrugged. "Comes all the way from Kentucky. Good stuff costs money." The pesos joined the others in the cigar box.

"That is so. I had no thought that you would be so foolish as to cheat us." Mano's black look drove the barman away to check on his other patrons. The brothers took the bottle to a table near the stove and sat, legs stretched out and boot soles toward the heat.

After twenty minutes of quiet drinking, Mano called to the barman, who had resumed reading his paper. "*Señor*, would you bring one more glass, *por favor*?"

Looking puzzled, the man picked up another tumbler, came 'round the end of the bar and walked to their table. "What's wrong with that one?" He indicated Mano's glass with jerk of his bald head.

Mano forced a smile. "Nothing, my friend. That one is for you, if you would care to join us. You don't seem busy and we would like for you to share some of this 'good stuff' with us." Saying that, he pushed a chair toward the barman with his foot. The man took a look around to see if his customers seemed in need. The old card players had fresh drinks and the pool shooting cowhands had been nursing the same beers for more than half an hour.

He felt safe enough accepting Mano's offer. Sitting down, he said, "Well, I guess one won't kill me."

Mano picked up the bottle and poured the new glass full. As the barman sipped, Mano said, "Late last month, around the twentieth, I think, a man was here to drink and gamble. A man like us. A *vaquero*. He lost much, became very drunk, and started a fight. A bad thing for him, for he was beaten senseless. He was allowed to sleep on the green table there."

The barman nodded. "That'd be Bad Jimmy Lucero. I wasn't working that night, but I recall hearing about it." After another sip of whiskey, he continued. "I opened up next morning and the swamper told me. Took him a while to rouse Jimmy and, God, was he in a foul temper when he did come around. Hung over, beat up, sick to his stomach, and broke." He was smirking as he said it, but Mano did not seem amused. The barman sensed the tension and asked, "How's he doing, anyhow? Haven't seen him since."

Mano straightened in his chair. "Not so good. He is dead. And he was our brother."

The barman's face fell. "The hell you say. Well that's tough news, and I am sorry to hear it. You say he was your brother?"

Mano nodded. "He was murdered not long after leaving here. The same day your man woke him up, or perhaps the next, we think. A rider we know found his body in a wash not far from here. To the north."

The barman worried the sparse forelock on his head. "Well, I'll just be damned. I never knowed that part 'til you just now said it." He shook his head. "I have to be honest with you and say that he and I weren't what you'd call *amigos*, but I am sorry to hear this news. Killed by foul play, you say?"

Mano nodded. "Shot in the face. His horse was stolen as well."

The barman leaned forward. "You mean that mouse-colored mare?"

Mano was suddenly alert. "The same. You know the horse?"

The barman frowned. "I reckon I do. Pretty good pony. He left her tied out there to the hitch rail all night, no feed or water, neither. Was a cold night, too."

The older brother looked hard at him, but nodded. "It is true that Jaimé was harsh with horses. Most of my people have a light hand with a horse, but not our brother." Pepé nodded agreement. Mano topped up all three glasses. "Would you perhaps know anything of the man who stole the mare?"

The barman frowned, shaking his head. "'Til you just told me, I didn't even know Jimmy was killed, let alone his horse was stoled. I got no notion of who done neither."

Mano frowned. "Well, *señor*, someone did both and we will find him. And you have not met any two *vaqueros* such as my brother and me. Also, this conversation never took place. *Comprendé?*"

The barman produced a weak smile. "Sure, *amigo*, whatever you say."

•   •   •   •

JEFF HAD two nights to think on what Sandy had told him before he was due a visit from Mrs. Peach. During those days he'd done his work so as to mostly stay away from her. Either he was outside splitting wood, inside painting, or down at the livery, working the filly. He wasn't sure what he thought about the news that there had been another cowboy in his role the year before, but he knew there was no sense in holding it against the man's horse. Besides, the filly was shaping up nicely and he liked her.

It was more difficult for him to decide how he felt about the woman now. He'd as yet seen none of the jealousy that Sandy had described, but he had no reason to doubt his friend's story. If true, as he assumed it was, it must mean only that he was doing a manful job of meeting her needs, all of them, else he'd have received his walking papers by now.

As far as her willingness to use a gun, that was bothersome. The thought of what the Major had suffered at her hand was more than he wanted to dwell on. So he didn't. He told himself he guessed the philandering son of a bitch had it coming. And that any other decent woman raised in the antebellum south, where duels of honor and rights of revenge were the rule, might have done the same. And he halfway believed it.

By the afternoon of the third day, he had made a resolution to break off the affair before things became even more intense. He made up his mind to tell her after supper, and then ask Sandy if he could stay in the hunting cabin until spring. But the right moment proved elusive and by bedtime the talk had not taken place. And when she came to him later, by lamplight, in his room, and let the nightgown slip to the floor, to stand between him and that lamp, her body backlit in the soft yellow glow, all resolve he had for any such conversation disappeared.

• • • •

A COUPLE OF WEEKS had passed since Jeff sat in on a game. Feeling the need for some sort of distraction from his situation with the widow, he pulled on his sheepskin and hurried the two blocks to the barroom. His feet were cold by the time he arrived. He was reminded that he needed something heavier than the riding boots that served him well enough other times of the year.

Closing the door quickly behind him, he went straight to the woodstove, where he found his friend curled up in a heavy, wool mackinaw, his feet near the hot iron potbelly, nursing a whiskey. The Scot looked over the rim of his glass and his red veined eyes lit up with a smile. Jeff grinned back.

"Evenin' to yeh, laddie," Sandy saluted with raised glass. "Yer just in time to buy me a touch up."

Pulling a chair up next to his friend, Jeff called to the barman as he sat. "Whatever this old badger's havin', Bob, and tequila for me. Bring a saltshaker, too, if you please. And a lime, if you got one."

Bob laughed cynically. "You serious? At this time of year?"

Sandy tossed off the contents of his glass as the barman brought their order. They sat and sipped, making small talk while Jeff's feet warmed. Sandy was first to address serious matters. "Have yeh given any thought to what we discussed in the barn lot the other day?"

Jeff frowned. "Yeah. Plenty. I've looked at her close, tried to see some hint of all that mayhem you described. I don't see no scary signs but, like you said before, what I know about women ain't enough to mention."

MacTeague shifted in the chair, took out his pipe, and loaded it. Jeff waved his hat against the noxious billows that swirled as the old man fired up. Once satisfied the evil smelling blend was well kindled, Sandy responded. "She likes yeh, Jeff, that's plain enough. For now, that is. Yer sairtainly keeping her well served, and I don't blame yeh for taking pleasure in the gifts that come yer way."

The pipe had gone out as he spoke and he paused to re-light it. "However, the day will come, and the closer to spring the closer that day, I think, when yeh'll notice a cooling of her ardor. That'll be a sign to yeh, and before yeh know it, there'll be an incident, contrived by her, I expect, that'll give her reason enough, in her mind, at least, to send yeh packin'. It may be the arrival of a replacement, another dashing young horseman. She seems to prefer the type. Or she may just decide to sweep yeh out with the rest of the spring cleaning. Either way, before the ferst of June, I'll warrant, yeh'll be huntin' a new arrangement."

Jeff had been gazing at the flames in the stove, visible through the slots in the firebox door. The Scot hadn't told him anything new. All Sandy'd said had already occurred to him in those moments when he could find a clear perspective.

He said as much now. "Well, hell, I reckon most of that's come to me already. What don't come to me is what to do about it. Just when I get my insides screwed down tight enough to tell her I'm pulling out, she does something sweet and heads me off. And if that don't do it, then she shows up in my room at bedtime and turns the lamp down. So far, I'm froze." He took some salt, drained his glass, motioned to Bob the barman, and pulled out the makings for a smoke. He'd said more than he'd intended and decided that with a cigarette in his mouth, maybe he'd manage to be quiet.

Sandy had no such notion. "I noticed yeh had a slight hitch in yer gait as yeh came in tonight. Air yeh crippled?"

Jeff looked sheepish. "Hell, no, I ain't crippled. That filly of Addie's spooked at a chicken in the barn aisle yesterday and bounced me off a stall gate. It ain't nothing. And what the hell does me limping have to do with what we been discussing?"

The old man smiled down in his whiskers. "Nothing, unless yer too hurt to ride," he said.

Jeff frowned. "I ain't never been too hurt to ride in my whole life. Why?"

MacTeague sipped at his whiskey, then said, "Well, since yeh ask, I been thinking on paying me baby brother a visit. These old bones tell me we're likely to have a week or so of fair travelin' weather. It's about three days slow ride, what with the snow we've had and the little bit of traffic between here and Durango to pack the road. The stage operates this time of year only when enough folks sign up to make a load and weather permits. Anyway, I thought pairhaps yeh'd like a change of scene, for a time, and I'd favor a spot o' company for the journey."

Jeff sipped his drink and considered. The prospect was interesting. The immediate benefit would be space from his current dilemma and time to think things over at a distance.

"How long would we be gone, altogether?"

Sandy scratched himself. "Oh, figure three days ride each way, taking it easy, and maybe five or six days on Bobby's place, if he and I can stand each other that long. Say two weeks, give or take a day or so."

Jeff asked, "How soon do you want to go?"

Sandy gazed at the ceiling. "I have to ride out to the cabin and check on things. A couple days, I would say." He'd smoked his pipe down to the heel, so he knocked it out in the ash box of the stove and reloaded it. Jeff turned his face away from the smoke that erupted from Sandy's mouth as he put a match to the shag. "When might you be ready, lad?" he asked.

Jeff took his hat off and scratched his head. "Oh, I'd have to talk it over with Addie and spend some time splitting up a big slug of wood for all those damn stoves in that barn of a house. I reckon I could be ready to go after two days working. So, as this is Tuesday, maybe Friday morning."

Sandy nodded. "Aye, it'd take me that long as well. D'yeh think yeh'd care to come along, then?"

Jeff considered a few more moments, then nodded. "I expect so. Might be what I need."

The old man grinned and raised his glass. "Aye, that it might, laddie. That it might."

• • • •

SINCERO MONTOYA tossed another shovelful of dry horse manure into the fire and held his hands close, palms toward the heat. Being in the livery business provided him an ample supply of free fuel, and such a fire threw fair heat without a lot of smoke.

Turning his head to avoid what little smoke there was, he saw two mounted men approaching, looking drawn and dirty, riding a pair of well-bred but jaded horses. They, like the men, looked in bad need of a good feed and a rest.

As the pair drew up in the barn lot, Montoya rose from his squat by the fire and gave them his attention. He'd not seen these two before, but he knew the type. Dressed as *vaqueros*, but with a certain look that said their primary occupation had nothing to do with working cattle, unless you counted stealing them. Their weapons were too fine for the average cowhand and the way those weapons hung in the leather, handy to a quick reach, told the hostler to be very cautious with these two.

"*Buenos tardes, señores*. How may I serve you today?"

Mano swung down stiffly. "Our *caballos* are tired and hungry, as are we. Can you feed and stable them?"

Montoya nodded gravely. "*Claro, señor*. Sweet hay and a good ration of shelled corn. All in a dry stall bedded in fresh straw."

Mano nodded. "*Esta bien*. My *hermanito* and I need to eat. Can you recommend a place with *comida buena*?"

"*Si, señor*. My second cousin, Esmeralda. She has a little *cocina* next to the saddle shop. I take my noon meal there most days. *Comida mas fina. Carnitas, aroz con pollo, chiles caliente, enchiladas, frijoles refritos, carne asada.* Anything you want. *Huevos fresca* in the morning, also, with *chorizo.*"

Mano's eyes lit up. "*Muy bien.* My brother and I will return presently. I would pay extra if we could sleep in your loft, no?"

Montoya drew himself up straight. "It will be my pleasure, *señor.* And of course, there will be no additional charge."

Mano touched the brim of his sombrero. "*Gracias, hombre.* You are very generous. Until then."

He handed the reins to Montoya and started for the street. Pepé did the same, following. Though it was a cold day, Sincero removed his hat and mopped the sweat from his balding head with his bandana.

EIGHT

J EFF HEARD humming outside his door. He rolled over and was hit full in the face by the sun coming through the east window. Mild pain behind his eyes reminded him of events of the night before. One drink with Sandy had become two, then three, and playing cards was forgotten. Before he knew it, he'd downed two-thirds of a bottle of tequila. He'd stumbled to his bed after midnight and slept a drunkard's sleep.

The humming in the hall moved off and he recognized the voice of his landlady, employer, and paramour. Rubbing his chin and feeling stubble, he asked himself again how he'd wound up in this fix. The Scot had warned him. But it was just too easy, too good to pass up. Work that demanded little, good chuck, and steady loving with no strings attached. Or so he'd thought before hearing Sandy's tale of the Major's demise.

Rolling out of bed, he set his hat on his head, pulled on pants and boots, and got into his sheepskin. His bladder was more than full and he managed a trip to the outhouse without meeting anyone in the halls.

Back inside, he made his way toward the kitchen guided by the smell of fresh coffee. He anticipated a confrontation with the widow in her employer role. Unpleasant as this might be, he craved the relief that strong coffee would bring him and, as he was never one to put off the inevitable, he entered the kitchen, took a mug off a shelf, and poured himself a portion. He was taking a first, satisfying sip as Mrs. Peach came in.

She looked good. She always looked good, damn her. She'd been outside for an armload of stove wood and the frosty air had brought color to her cheeks. Seeing Jeff, she got a look on her face that was somewhere between a smile and a frown. "This is your job," she said bluntly.

Jeff gave her an "aw shucks" grin. "Mornin' to you too."

"Well," she went on, somewhat disarmed, "it is. You should have been up and filled the wood box an hour ago." She turned to dump her burden.

He took another sip of the coffee, looking over the rim of his cup. "I know it. I got no excuse. Ran into Sandy last night, sat with him too long, had a little too much 'who hit john,' and got in way late. But like I said, that ain't no excuse, just a reason. And I am sorry you got stuck with my chore." He drained his cup and refilled it, then looked her in the eye. His fessing up, along with the apology, had mollified her to a degree.

She poured herself coffee and sat down at the small table. She pushed back a stray wisp of hair and smiled at him. "You've missed breakfast," she said.

He nodded, trying to look contrite. "Reckon I don't deserve any."

She rolled her eyes in feigned exasperation. "Oh, for heaven's sake," she said, "no martyrdom, please. There're a few leftover biscuits in the warming closet over the wood range, and butter and honey here on the table. Help yourself."

Jeff got up and stepped to the stove and had put two biscuits on a plate when she said, "Sit for a minute." He moved away from the stove, turned a chair around backward, and straddled it. He smiled but kept quiet. She asked, "How are you doing?"

He buttered a biscuit before answering. "Fine," he said.

"No. I mean how are things with you?" The look on her face was serious.

"I don't follow."

"Are you happy?" she asked.

"Sure. I guess."

"You guess?" Her voice had an edge of irritation.

"Well, yeah. Why not?"

"I don't know," she came back, "why not?"

Jeff looked puzzled. "Is this some kind of riddle?"

Addie shook her head. "No, Jeff. I'm just trying to find out how you feel about things."

Setting the biscuit back on the plate he said, "I got no complaints. I've got a winter job, a warm bed, and three squares of real good chuck every day."

Addie's gaze was direct and intense. "And?" she demanded.

Jeff felt uncomfortable and blushed as he answered. "Yeah. And," he acknowledged. "And you. You coming to see me in my room a couple times a week."

She sipped her coffee, never taking her eyes from his face. He squirmed in his chair. "You like that, don't you?" she said. "Those visits, late at night, and what I bring you."

He nodded slowly. "Hell, yes, I like it. What natural man wouldn't?"

She smiled. "None I've ever known."

This sobered him. He set his cup down. "You've known a few, have you?"

Her look was more direct, even a bit cold.

"Yes, I have. A few. Do you care?"

"I don't know. I don't have any right to."

"That's true. You don't," she said.

He built a smoke and put it in his shirt pocket. Smoking was not allowed in the house, but he needed to do something with his hands. Taking a wood match out of the same pocket, he stuck it in his mouth and spoke. "I sure never knew anybody like you."

She rose and stepped to the stove for the coffee pot, topped up their cups, and resumed her seat. "No, I'm sure you haven't. Do you think me odd?"

He shook his head. "No. Not odd. Just different."

She looked at him squarely, inclining her head fetchingly. "In what way?" She was smiling, and he lifted an eyebrow. Here was danger.

"Well, for one thing, you don't make no bones about how well you like a poke."

She frowned. "Crudely put. But yes, I like a good poke, to use your word. And you certainly can provide one when I'm so inclined."

He shrugged off the compliment, saying, "This might seem crude, too, but I can't help noticing, and I guess we been close enough that I'm going to speak my mind." When she said nothing, he went on. "I see you don't seem to be concerned about us making a baby."

She let a cynical smile cross her face. "No," she said, "I'm not the least bit concerned. My inability to conceive is a credit to our shared convenience, and your particular pleasure."

Jeff had no expression as he replied, "And yours."

She looked hard at him, then softened. "It's true that you give me great pleasure. More than most. Perhaps more than any other."

Jeff softened as well. "So why are we arguing?" he asked.

She smiled back warmly. "We aren't. This isn't arguing. This is talking. Folks who share a good poke should talk now and then. Don't you agree?" Reaching across the table, she laid her hand over his.

With his other hand, he took the match from his mouth and examined it, then grinned at her. "I expect so."

•　　•　　•　　•

THAT NIGHT in his bed, after their breathing had slowed, her head on his chest, they talked. Just pillow talk at first, and then he brought up the subject of Sandy's invitation.

She didn't comment for a time and he started to say something more when she answered. "Are you tired of this arrangement? Of us? Of me?" She sat up, the sheet slipping down, the lamplight on her nakedness distracting him. "Well, I want an answer," she said.

He scooted back in the bed, his shoulders against the headboard. "No. I'm not tired of any of it, least of all you." He reached out and smoothed a lock of strawberry blonde hair from her eyes. "I just thought I'd go along, keep Sandy company, look out for him a little bit. He's gittin' kind'a long in the tooth. Wouldn't want him broke down out in the snow."

She paused, and then nodded. "You're right, of course. We don't want any ill fortune to befall our dear, old Scotty."

She lay back down and pulled the covers over her bareness. "As long as your work is done up ahead, I don't mind. A change of scene will do you good and some time apart for us is probably a good idea." She reached up and pulled him down under the sheet with her. "I find I've grown rather dependent on these night time visits. I don't like to count too much on anyone or anything. It could become a weakness. So you go take care of Sandy and have a good time. We'll talk again when you get back." She slipped a hand below the covers, drew her nails slowly across his chest, trailed her fingers down through his belly hair, and then gripped him hard enough to make him flinch. "Do you suppose this gun's still loaded?"

He reached out, smiling, and stroked her hip. "One more round anyway, I reckon."

Throwing a leg over him, as she might mount a horse, she said, "Good. You may fire at will."

• • • •

MANO AND PEPÉ stepped out of the *cocina* with full bellies and toothpicks in their mouths. The liveryman had been right. The food was good, especially the fresh, hot *tortillas*. They had eaten heartily and a short walk was in order. Stepping into the street and turning to pass the saddle shop, they noticed an old and weathered little man in a rocking chair, his lap covered with rawhide splits, fashioning a fancy *bosal*. He looked up from his work and nodded pleasantly as they stood before him.

Mano dipped the brim of his sombrero in acknowledgment and spoke. "*Buenos dias, viejo.*" The old man returned the salutation. Mano smiled. "That is *trabajo mas fina.*"

The braider made a self-deprecating gesture. "Thank you, *señor*. I do the best I know how."

"Do you sit here often?"

"*Si.* If it is not too windy. The air is better out here. At times the odor of leather, oil, and glue is oppressive in the shop."

Mano moved more directly in front of the old man, Pepé on his heels. They leaned against the hitch rack across from his rocker. Mano said, "I suppose you see all things that pass in the street.

The old man shrugged. "Well, I have my attention on my work. I pay little mind to what goes on around me."

"Do you know Jaimé Lucero?" asked Mano.

"To see him only. I have never spoken to him."

"Have you seen him recently?"

"No, *señor*" answered the hunched figure. "It must be a month or more."

Mano rubbed the stubble on his chin. Pepé was looking at the place where the hitch rack had been broken and then repaired with a rawhide bind.

Mano ran his hand across the repair. "What is the purpose of this?" he asked mildly.

The old man's face went neutral. "The rail was broken. I patched it. The owner of this shop intends to replace it."

"How was it broken?" The rawhide braider was beginning to feel interrogated.

"A frightened horse. A man was beating her. She shied into it very hard."

"You saw this happen?" asked Mano.

The old man considered his answer. At last, he said, "*Sí*."

Mano removed his hat and wiped the sweatband with his bandana. "What sort of man would do such a thing?"

"A very angry one."

"Did you know him?" asked Mano.

The braider paused. Then he shrugged again and spoke. "Lucero. The one you spoke of before."

Mano straightened up and removed the toothpick from his mouth. "Is that so? *Maestro*, tell us all you saw. *Por favor*."

NINE

SANDY SAT his horse and puffed on his rank pipe as Jeff daisy chained the tail of the lash rope to his mule's pack. The sun was breaking over the ridge of the livery barn roof and it was cold. But it would warm by noon, as it had for the last couple of days, melting the snow and ice, and leaving the trails and wagon roads muddy.

The Scot coiled the lead rope of his own mule and dropped it over the saddle horn. He watched Jeff snug up the blue mare's cinch. He'd been riding her more and felt she was ready for an extended trip. The buckskin would come along loose, to be pressed into service if the mare seemed to be tiring.

Sandy put a false frown on his face. "Yeh take as long as me old grandmither."

Jeff grinned under his hat brim. "Well, maybe your old granny was a good packer. I like to take the time to do it right. I don't appreciate wrecks on the trail. Neither does ol' Jigger here."

Sandy puffed and nodded. "What did herself say about yer leaving?" he asked.

Jeff looked up. "Oh, not much. Said a little break might do us good."

"Did she now?" Sandy took the pipe from his mouth and spat to one side.

"Yeah," Jeff said. "I'd figured on a fuss. Guess I don't know women."

"As I've said before, lad."

"All right. Don't rub it in."

"Didn't mean to. It's just that yeh don't yet get it. She's lettin' yeh have a chance to miss her, think about her, realize what a good thing yeh have here."

Jeff gathered the reins, put his left foot in the stirrup and swung into the saddle, turning for a look to satisfy himself that the mule's pack was sitting level, and said, "Well, I reckon I'm not stupid. Maybe not the smartest, either, but I know a good thing. And I appreciate her and I told her that."

Sandy leaned over and knocked his pipe out against a stirrup. "I'd guess pairhaps she thinks yeh're a mite too comfortable wi' the situation. I expect she'd like yeh to think yeh're not indispensable." He scratched his red nose and said, with a sly look on his face, "What surprises me is how she has na' shot yeh yet, much less run yeh off."

Jeff ignored him, sitting relaxed on the mare, rolling a cigarette. He lit it, took a long pull, and exhaled. Turning to Sandy, he said, "Are we going anywhere, or we gonna just sit and listen to you beat your gums all day?"

Sandy chuckled. "All right, laddie, enough of my wisdom." He turned his pony out of the barnyard, the mule in tow. Jeff dallied the lead rope of his own mule, swung around behind his friend, and followed him west, a cold sun on their backs.

•   •   •   •

THE OLD MAN continued to braid the rawhide, addressing the brothers as he worked. "And then, as Jaimé lay quietly in the street, the young *gringo* gave me a gold piece for the horse and asked me to give it to Jaimé when he awoke. He said it was the price of the mare, *la grulla*. Said he was buying her, that a man who beat his horse so severely did not deserve to own it. Of course, I did as he asked."

"What did this *gringo* look like?"

"Like all *gringos*," answered the old one.

Mano straightened, his voice becoming as flat as his look. "Do not toy with me, *viejo*. I would know his age, his build, the color of his eyes."

The little man smiled down at the work in his lap. "I don't see so good anymore. Not much farther than this rawhide in my hands."

Mano drew back the tail of his jacket, clearing the grip of his revolver.

The braider looked up, then smiled wider and shook his white fuzzed head. "My young friend, do you suppose one as old as I will be frightened by the sight of your *pistola*? With all my infirmities? The pain in my bladder, my locked bowels, my limp member, and rotten teeth? The ones that remain, that is? Do you really think I fear death? Your bullet would be a kindness, *señor*."

Mano relaxed a little and turned loose of his coat flap. Forcing a conciliatory look on his face, he said, "*Maestro*, the man Jaimé Lucero was our brother. Not the best of men, perhaps, but of our blood, nonetheless. The gringo who took his horse also killed him, probably later that same day or perhaps the next. We would be in your debt if you could describe him more fully, *por favor*."

The little man lay down his work and looked directly at Mano. "I will tell you this much, *hombre*. He was very quick and without hesitation. To subdue your brother was the work of only moments. While I do not mourn the passing of a man such as Jaimé, I am sorry for the pain it has brought you. And because it is the privilege of age, I will offer this advice. Do not confront this man, as your brother did. He paid for the horse, and what he did was right. He is full of honor and empty of fear. If you are so unfortunate as to locate him, you may join your brother."

•   •   •   •

JEFF AND SANDY camped that first night east of Chimney Rock at a place called Aspen Springs. The stock ate oats from feedbags as the men fed the fire, smoked, and sipped coffee laced with whiskey. A supper of elk steak and pan bread sat easy on their stomachs. Sandy had his stocking feet propped on a rock, soles toward the fire. Steam curled up from the damp wool.

Jeff rubbed under his nose. "I swear, I believe your feet smell worse hot than cold"

Sandy puffed a great, noxious cloud. "That's as may be, me boy, but I don't smell 'em and they're warm."

Jeff flipped his cigarette butt into the coals. "I doubt you could smell a hat full of horse shit over that stinkin' pipe. What is that horrible weed you stuff it with?"

Sandy smiled blissfully. "Pure British shag. Imported. Send off to Denver for it. Me one and only extravagance."

Jeff snorted. "What about whiskey?"

Sandy bridled. "Good God, mon! Whiskey's no extravagance. 'Tis the water of life."

Jeff stood and stepped out of the firelight to relieve the pressure in his bladder. Over his shoulder he said, "I wish you'd manage to get downwind. The fumes are killin' me."

Sandy smiled and replied, "The direction of the air currents is the business of the Lord. I cannot be held responsible."

Jeff came out of the dark and sat back down. "Well," he muttered, "I don't guess I ever did anything to aggravate the Lord enough to have him send that smoke over here."

The older man chuckled, puffing vigorously. They were quiet for a time. Sandy shifted from one hip to the other and said, "That mouse-colored mare of yours has come a long way since first I saw her. I'll wager she's gained a hundred pounds."

Jeff took a sip from his cup before replying. "More like a hundred fifty. At least since I first got her. She's shaping up, gonna make a fine mount."

Sandy made no comment, knitting his brow, working up to something. Jeff felt it coming and kept quiet. Finally his friend cleared his throat and spat into the fire. "My instincts suggest to me that there's quite a story behind yer acquisition of that mare. I also think, inasmuch as we are boon companions, that yeh might care to tell it."

Jeff drained his cup and rolled a cigarette, using the time to decide. Oh, hell, he thought. Why not? Might help to get it off my chest. I can certainly trust this man. Lighting his smoke, he said, "Well, if I'm going to tell it, I'd best tell it all."

Sandy smiled warmly. "Take yer time, son. The night is young and I've no other appointments."

So he told it all, starting with his search for land, his arrival in Albuquerque, and his meeting of the girl. He told the terrible story straight through, gaining momentum as he went, including his flight, his anguish over her death, his feelings of responsibility, and then the added problem of the incident with Bad Jimmy in Taos, and later having to kill in self-defense. When done, he felt a combination of guilt and relief.

Sandy tossed more wood on the fire, knocked out his pipe, and refilled it. But then he held it, unlit, and simply stared into the flames. Jeff waited quietly.

At length he spoke. "It's a sad tale, lad. Sad indeed. And it reveals much of yer character. But don't blame yersel' over much. Yer actions were honorable on both occasions, if perhaps impetuous. You are young and the blood runs hot in a young man's veins. At your age, I was much the same. There is violence in my past, as well, and I dislike to recall it. But in this wild country, a man is hard pressed to remain untouched by trouble."

Sandy seemed to have no more to say, and it surprised Jeff when the Scot looked toward the blue mare and changed the subject, as though done with the former topic forever. "Always liked that color in a horse," he observed. "Saw many a buffalo pony marked likewise. The Indians swore by them. Traded for one mesel', back in the spring of '66 it was, if I recall correctly. A tough little stallion. Not the gentlest, but stout and game. Very enduring, almost tireless. Had him when I shot meat for the railroad. Put many a fifty-mile day on him, and him getting to be an old horse by then. Made it to twenty-two and was still going strong when we got lightning struck on a high ridge one summer afternoon. Blew me from the saddle, burnt the soles off me moccasins. Was unhurt otherwise. Killed the horse outright. Burnt up me saddle as well. Damnable shame. Wish I had him now. Night, lad." Without another word he rolled into his blankets and was snoring almost at once.

"Night, yourself," Jeff said. Throwing another armload of wood on the fire, he got into his own bedroll and joined his partner in a deep sleep.

• • • •

NEXT DAY dawned clear and cold, the air quiet. Coffee, bacon, and leftover pan bread made a quick breakfast. A *morral* of grain each satisfied the animals, and all were soon back on the move.

Traffic on the coach road had been light. The stage line operated on a diminished schedule during the winter, based on weather, snow depth, and demand. The afternoon thaw made little streams of the wheel ruts, but there was firmer ground between them. Riders leading pack stock could travel without much inconvenience. Around mid-morning, they met another outfit coming from the west. In the lead was a huge black man in a buffalo coat and bearskin chaps, mounted on a mule the size of a cow moose. Following along were three smaller pack mules, all with heavy-looking loads.

As was customary, the respective travelers stopped just outside certain pistol range to take the measure of each other.

After an interval, Sandy hailed the stranger. "Greetings, sir. Our intentions are peaceable. What of yers?"

The man had what appeared to be a sawed-off, double barrel shotgun hanging from his saddle horn by a leather loop. Both his hands were in plain sight and motionless. He smiled, showing strong-looking, white teeth. "I 'spect I'm friendly, too. Whyn't y'all ride on up and visit?"

Jeff had his Colt slung cross draw, as he typically did when mounted, but he felt no need of it now as he and Sandy moved their horses forward. The black man came ahead, as well, and they all stopped again with six feet between the animals' noses.

Sandy touched a finger to the edge of his bonnet. "I am Andrew MacTeague, of Clan MacTeague, and this handsome lad is Jeff Cameron. Who might I be addressing, sir."

The big man's smile went wider. "My Christian name's Luther, last name Powell, but folks mostly jes' calls me Big'un." After taking a breath, he went on. "If you don't mind me sayin' it, you is the funniest talking white man I ever come acrost." Jeff laughed out loud, looking sideways at Sandy. The Scot's face reddened a bit and Luther Powell's face fell with the thought he'd misspoken. "Oh, Lawd. I sho' meant no offense, suh."

Sandy smiled again. "None taken, sir. I am from Scotland, across the sea, in the States near these forty years, but I fear the brogue of home still lingers on me tongue."

Big'un's smile returned as well. "That's fine, then, Mistuh MacTeague, it truly is. Where y'all took out from, if it ain't impolite to ask it?"

Jeff did not share the prejudice common to his time, having worked with several able, black cowhands down south. He decided he liked this big man with the easy, friendly way about him.

"East of here," said Sandy, "Pagosa Springs. And yersel'?"

Big'un hooked a thumb over his shoulder. "Over on the Pine River. Been cookin' fo' a cow outfit, but they didn't treat me right." A small frown crossed his broad face, soon to be replaced with the smile.

"Now I don't mind cookin', ya' see, and I got my Dutch ovens and skillets and such on that first mule there. But my main trade is black smithin'. Dem other two mules has got some of my smithy tools, the light stuff. The heavy things, like my anvil an' fo'ge, they's coming by freight wagon, oncet I finds a place to do bidness." The confidence in his voice told of the pride he took in his work.

Jeff said, "Well, you ought to do well in Pagosa. There's one horse shoer, but he doesn't do much else in the way of ironwork. And he likes his jug. Half the time he's not even in his shop."

Powell's eyes lit. "I kin make most anything outen' a piece o' metal. I kin make a iron tire an' shrink it to a wheel rim. I kin make door hinges, latches, shackles fo' the runnin' gear on a wagon, an' de' springs, too. I kin even make a iron bed frame fo' yo' missus. An' o'cose, I can shoe hosses and mules. I reckon I could shoe a ox, if somebody ast me to, an' I had me a shed built stout enough to rig a ox hoist."

Sandy smiled broadly. The enthusiasm was contagious. "Then," he said, "yeh should keep busy. Yeh're a hale fellow and well met. If ye'd care to step down off that mammoth of a mule, I'd be proud to offer yeh a dram of whiskey."

Big'un rubbed his chin. "I'd sho' admire to join you, suh, but my mules is packed heavy, an' one drink sometimes calls fo' another, as I reckon you know. I dislikes to make 'em stand around loaded whilst I enjoys myself. I'd best be getting' along. But I thank you kindly."

Sandy urged his horse up next to Powell's mule. "Then a stirrup cup, as it were." He reached inside his mackinaw and produced a pewter flask, unscrewed the cap, and offered it to Powell. "No need to dismount at all. Have a good, healthy pull against the chill o' the mornin'."

Powell still seemed hesitant. "I ain't got no cup."

Sandy pushed the flask forward. "None needed. Take it straight from the spout."

Looking skeptical, the man took a polite drink and handed the whiskey back to Sandy, who, wiping the bottleneck on the sleeve of his coat, turned it up and drank deeply. He passed it to Jeff, who took a modest sip, not having much interest in hard liquor at that hour.

The black man sat his mule with a stunned look on his face. Sandy noticed his puzzlement. "Was the whiskey not to yer likin', sir?"

Powell shook his head vigorously. "Oh no, suh, Mistuh MacTeague. It'uz right fine. But y'all drank right after me, didn't use no cups neither."

Sandy looked him in the eye. "What would we need with a cup?"

Powell seemed more confused than ever. Choosing his words with care he said, "Y'all is the peculiarest white mens. I never seen no white man drink after no nigguh 'thout he have a cup o' a glass. Now I think on it, I don't believe I evuh see no white man drink with no nigguh a'tall, cup or no."

Sandy frowned. "That's an ugly word, sir. I reject it. Yeh're a man are yeh not, Mr. Powell?"

"Well, I 'spect I is," agreed the giant.

Sandy smiled. "Then that's all there is to that."

Jeff grinned. "We need to be moving, Mr. Powell," he said. "Reckon we'll be seeing you around Pagosa when we get back."

Luther "Big'un" Powell smiled his widest yet. "I sho' hope so. Y'all is some fine felluhs."

•   •   •   •

DURANGO WAS a bustling hive of frenetic endeavor. It was new and growing up around the equally new Denver and Rio

Grande Railroad. Sandy wanted to pass on through, eager to rest his saddle weary bones in front of his brother's hearth. Jeff agreed, but made a mental note to return when time and circumstances allowed. With all the activity, he imagined that he might accomplish something with a deck of cards.

The main street was a near hub-deep loblolly of snow and mud. Heavy draft teams struggled to pull loaded wagons through the muck, with those wagons seemingly going all directions at once. Working men of every size, color, and description hurried everywhere, loading or unloading wagons, carrying lumber, sacks of grain, or large wooden crates, the contents of which Jeff could only guess. Other men, either unemployed or off shift, went in and out of hotels, restaurants, bars, and brothels. Some drunk. Some sober. One group stood in a circle in the street, cheering and jeering as two men, one large, one small, fist fought in the mud. The bigger man seemed to be getting the worst of it. Jeff and Sandy rode on.

• • • •

SINCE THE UNFORTUNATE ENCOUNTER with Bad Jimmy, Jeff had given little thought to his goal of finding land. So he was caught a little off guard with his first look at the Animas River and the valley it ran through.

The river, slow and winding in the stretch they now viewed, was up to thirty yards wide in places at low, winter level, with a deep pool at every bend. The valley itself lay between soaring, stone bluffs, with changing shades of red, one atop the other like a layer cake and rising hundreds of feet. Along the river banks and stretching back to the higher ground below the bluffs was a heavy growth of sun-cured grass, laid down now by the weight of the last snow. Giant cottonwoods, growing at the water's edge and now bare of leaves, would provide welcome shade on hot summer days. His stockman's eye saw that here was a fine sort of country for the raising of horses and cattle. Jeff heard the voice of this valley, this place, loud and clear.

He sat the mare and took it all in, listening as the land spoke to him. Sandy was fifty yards beyond before he realized that his partner had stopped. Twisting stiffly in the saddle, he called back. "What's the holdup, laddie?"

Jeff pointed with a sweep of his right hand. "Is that the Animas?"

Sandy nodded. "Aye, that it is."

The blue mare moved ahead on her own, anxious to join the other animals. Jeff let her go and when he was closer, he said, "Is this valley all bought up? I don't see no stock ner buildings down there."

"Well now," Sandy answered, "I couldn't say for sure, but I rather doubt it. Why?"

Jeff's gaze was locked on the scene below. "I'll tell you why. I want a piece of it."

The two friends sat silently for a time, watching the river move slowly between snow-covered banks. Sandy loaded his ubiquitous pipe but did not light it at once. "'Tis a fair country. That it is. And it looks good to yeh, does it?"

Jeff nodded. "Best I ever saw."

Sandy dug in his mackinaw for a match and lit his pipe. Once it was going strong, he took it from his mouth and pointed with it toward the river. "So this valley looks like what yeh've been searching for?"

Jeff smiled and nodded. "Yep. Yonder it is."

The Scot clamped the pipe between yellow teeth and picked up the reins. "Well then, me boy. Let's ride on so we can take a closer look."

TEN

ROBERT MACTEAGUE'S RANCH was another few miles upriver, just beyond where Hermosa Creek joined the Animas. Jeff and Sandy rode into headquarters late in the afternoon of their third day on the road. The cowboy was impressed with what was laid out before him.

The house was two stories, built of native red sandstone and ponderosa pine timbers, low-roofed with a broad veranda all around. It looked big and roomy. Down a slight grade from the house were the outbuildings. The main barn was constructed of the same materials as the house and had space for thirty stalls, at least. The corrals and pens built around it added up to over two acres. A large, fenced garden plot was in winter fallow, dried vines and corn stalks laid down by frost and snow. Sheds for poultry and sheep, bordered by hog pens, rounded out the picture. Several ranch hands moved about, occupied with evening chores. All in all, it appeared to be a well-maintained outfit. A small brigade of dogs announced Sandy and Jeff's arrival.

They stopped their mounts at the bottom of the steps as the heavy oak and iron entry door swung open. A man stepped through it onto the porch and commanded the dogs to be quiet. They obeyed at once. He stood before the riders, hands in the pockets of sturdy, woolen pants stuffed into the tops of heavy leather boots. That he was Sandy's brother was obvious, but a very different version of the breed.

Robert MacTeague was half a head shorter than his older sibling, but half again as broad across the chest and shoulders. His bare head was sparsely haired, but his fierce red beard, salted with grey, more than made up for what the scalp lacked.

There was little apparent welcome in the look on his face or the tone of his voice. "Well now, if it's not the legendary frontiersman, the black sheep of Clan MacTeague, come down from his mountain stronghold to pay the brother a visit. Are you broke again and in need of a layup, or is this a social call?"

Sandy grimaced, "And a pleasure to see yeh, as well, baby brother. Glad yeh're in yer typical good humor. Allow me to name my boon companion, Mister Jeff Cameron, late of New Mexico Territory. Unlike me, he is a sober and industrious fellow, and I brought him along to demonstrate how the quality of my associates has improved."

Jeff stepped down off the blue mare, dropped the reins, walked up to Robert MacTeague and offered his hand, smiling. "Don't judge me by my trail pardner, sir. I'm pleased to meet you."

The barrel chested rancher looked Jeff in the eye for two beats, then took his hand firmly. "In spite of your poor choice of a traveling companion, welcome to my home, Mr. Cameron."

• • • •

THE EVENING MEAL was lavish by rural standards. Leg of lamb, boiled potatoes with carrots and onions, freshly baked bread, and dried apple pie, all prepared to flavorful perfection by an old Mexican woman, assisted by her granddaughter. The only departure from classic Scottish cuisine was the addition of a bit of south of the border spicing. Hot coffee and cold milk provided beverage. To Sandy's mild disappointment but not surprise, nothing stronger was offered.

The food was excellent and Jeff ate with gusto. Sandy was in good appetite, as well, and their host put his rations away with mechanical efficiency.

The cook's granddaughter brought more coffee and the three men leaned back and relaxed. Sandy took out his pipe, but a brief, black look from Robert induced him to return it to his pocket.

"Smoke that foul thing if yeh must," said the brother, "but outside this house."

Sandy frowned. "Later, then. Where is me niece?"

The mention of his daughter improved Robert's disposition. "Margaret rode into Durango, to the saddler, to order one built for that Spanish stallion she bought recently." The mention of a Spanish horse got Jeff's attention.

Sandy turned to his partner. "My niece, Margaret Louisa MacTeague. Robert's only child and the pride of our branch of the clan. You'll meet her later."

Robert turned his attention toward the front window. "On the contrary, I rather think you'll meet her sooner. I believe I see her now. She just rode up." Jeff heard a girl's voice outside as a *vaquero* appeared to take her horse. A moment later she stepped through the front door.

Margaret MacTeague was twenty-two years old and in the bloom of health. Her late mother had been a Spanish beauty, descendant of an old land grant family that had been dispossessed in the aftermath of the war with Mexico. The girl was tall, like her uncle Sandy, had her mother's dark hair, her father's ice blue eyes, and a figure that was all her own. Flushed from her ride in the cool air, her skin was glowing. She was, altogether, the most striking female Jeff had ever seen.

"Uncle Sandy," she squealed and came sweeping around the table to leap upon the grinning man as he rose from his chair. She was fit and athletic looking.

Sandy hugged her tight, then held her at arm's length for inspection. "Lord God, girl, but yeh're a picture, and smellin' like a handful of columbines."

The girl's eyes were alight. "Better than you smell, Uncle. Yeh're all campfire smoke and horse sweat and whiskey, plus that horrible shag tobacco. A right gamey old bull yeh are and I love it all." She threw her arms back around his neck and kissed his wooly cheek.

Jeff could only stare at this amazing package of female vitality. While the skin of her cheeks and throat had a rosy glow upon her entry into the warm house from the cold outdoors, the rest of her that he could see was a golden tan, undoubtedly the result of days out in the open, horseback, and the blood of her mother's people. It made her blue eyes all the more striking. She was a little breathless from her ride and the surprise and excitement of seeing her uncle, and her jacket moved snuggly over the rise and fall of her bosom. He was caught with his eyes there as she turned abruptly to notice him.

"And who is this strapping fellow with his mouth hanging open?" she inquired. Jeff felt the heat move up his neck and into his ears.

Sandy chuckled as the younger man rose to his feet. The beaming uncle introduced him. "This is one Jeff Cameron, Texas stockman, up from New Mexico Territory, and currently an associate of mine in Pagosa Springs. Crack shot with a rifle and a splendid horseman."

The girl looked at him directly with a mixture of welcome, reservation, and amusement. She put out her right hand and said, "A pleasure, Mr. Cameron."

Jeff was mortified to realize that he still held a fork in his own right hand. Putting it down awkwardly, pinging it on the edge of his plate, he took her hand. He was surprised by the strength of her grip. Composing himself with some effort, he said, "The pleasure's mine, ma'am. Pardon my lack of table manners."

She held his eyes and his hand for a moment more, then released, and took off her coat and joined them to take her share of the leftovers. Around a mouthful of lamb she said to the room in general, "Thanks for not eating everything."

Her father gently shook his finger at her. "Yeh know perfectly well when supper is served at this table, young lady. If yeh come up short on rations, yeh've none to blame but yersel." Her response was to grin at him and pin him with a sly wink. He rolled his eyes toward the ceiling and went back to his coffee. But he was smiling.

She ate like the healthy girl she was, with unabashed appetite, but with all the manners that Jeff seemed to lack. The conversation turned to horses, custom built saddles, range conditions, and the anticipation of spring. Jeff spoke little, hung on the girl's every word, and took note of the fact that he felt his stomach trying to float up and out of his mouth.

• • • •

JEFF WAS QUIET as he prepared for bed. He and Sandy were sharing a spare room in the main house. The older man was in his bunk, sipping from his flask. Jeff sat on a chair and pulled off his boots and socks. He was quiet for some moments, a sock in one hand, staring at the far wall.

Sandy finally spoke. "Yeh seem far away, lad."

Jeff blinked. "Oh, yeah. I reckon so."

"I could guess what's on your mind."

"That right?"

"Aye. About five foot nine, hair black as a crow's wing, bonnie blue eyes, skin like butterscotch. Am I far off?"

Jeff slowly turned his head. "Nope. You're right on the mark."

Sandy smiled proudly. "And a good head on her shoulders, as well. Graduated from Swarthmore College in Pennsylvania this last spring. She's truly extraordinary, is she not?"

Jeff returned his gaze the wall, a picture fixed in his mind. He nodded dumbly. "I've never seen anything like her."

His friend smiled wider. "You should have known her mother. That woman had fire. Could ride like a Comanche.

The girl's got all that, plus me brother's energy and sense of the right."

Jeff sighed. "I've never seen anything like her."

Sandy grinned. "You just said that."

"Well," Jeff answered, "I never have."

•   •   •   •

HE SLEPT LITTLE that night, and when he did, he dreamed of a dark-haired girl on a dun-colored horse riding through a thin cloud of mist. He could hear the muffled hoof beats.

At first light, he arose quietly to the rattle of Sandy's snoring, put on his hat, then his socks, pants, and shirt, and carrying his boots in one hand and coat in the other padded down the hall and out of the silent house. On the porch it was cold as he pulled on his boots and shrugged into his heavy sheepskin. The sun was still below the ridge to the east, and his fingers were a bit stiff with the chill as he rolled his first smoke of the day. Leaning over, he dragged a match across the floorboards until it caught, then lit his cigarette, shook the match dead, and flicked it into the dirt. He sat on the bench and smoked for a minute, savoring the taste of the tobacco, trying not to think of the girl. But that very effort, of course, kept her in his mind.

Abruptly he stood up and crossed the yard, heading down the gentle slope toward the barns. A few men were moving about. A sleepy-eyed *vaquero* stood on the porch of the bunkhouse, yawning and scratching his belly through his undershirt. The old Mexican who cooked for the crew stepped out of the cook shack door, tossed a pan of dirty water into the yard, and went back inside. The ranch was coming to life.

As he continued toward the barn, the cook came back out with a blackened coffee pot in one hand and a heavy, crockery mug in the other. He called to Jeff as he passed. "*Señor, café para usted?*"

Jeff stopped. "*Esta fuerte?*"

The cook bobbed his head. "*Si, señor.* It is *muy* strong."

Jeff turned toward the man and smiled.

"*Si, con gusto. Muchas gracias.*" He accepted the cup the old cook offered, took a careful sip. As promised, it was hearty brew. He nodded and smiled again. "*Que bueno! Muchas gracias.*"

The cook smiled. "*De nada, señor.*"

Jeff continued on his way, stopping outside the main horse barn to take a last drag on his cigarette and rub the butt out under his boot heel. Going inside, he was greeted by the good smell of horses, fresh straw, oats, and hay. He loved the smell of a barn. Even the rich, underlying odor of manure was not offensive. It was familiar and earthy. Stepping into a dark corner and making sure he was alone, he relieved his bladder into a pile of old straw.

It was dim in there at this hour and he could not immediately find his animals. Upon their arrival the previous evening, a *vaquero* had taken charge of the stock and seen to their care. Jeff wasn't aware of their location. He stopped and cocked an ear.

"Hey, Jigger. Where are you, son?" In answer, the little red mule let out a short bray from halfway down the aisle. Jeff grinned and headed that way, passing stall after stall occupied by well bred, stock-type horses, all contentedly tucking into their morning ration of grain.

The blue mare was several spaces from the entry door and Jeff found her with her nose buried in a feed bunk filled with oats and barley. The mule was in the next stall, eating his own portion. Next to him was the buckskin. Sandy's paint horse and bay mule were just beyond, similarly occupied.

There is a sense of contentment and serenity that is experienced by horses and mules in the act of eating, and that calm can be communicated to humans who are sensitive to the ways of equines. Jeff leaned against the stall door, sipping his coffee and feeling very tranquil. It was a feeling he often had while watching his stock at their feed.

He was so relaxed that he was unaware of the presence of another person in the barn. So when the girl spoke, it startled him. "A fine-looking animal."

He jerked around to see her a few feet behind him and slopped coffee on his boots. For an instant he feared she had seen him urinating, but decided that she had only just come in. All the same, it embarrassed him, and he gave her his "aw shucks" grin. "Boy howdy, ma'am, you move quiet as any Indian."

She smiled back, strong, even teeth shining in the low light. She was dressed to ride, as a man would dress for a day in the saddle. Brown duck jeans. High-topped, spurred boots. Wool coat and a stained felt hat. "It's a habit I picked up from my Uncle Sandy," she said, "when I was a girl. He'd take me hunting with him. He taught me how to stalk game, use the wind, move only when your target has its attention on something else. Like you just had your full attention on your mare. It was easy."

Jeff laughed, shaking his head. "Well, sometimes I just sort of get lost in the thing, when it's feeding time. It's like, well, I mean to say..."

She finished for him. "Like they're drawing you into a dream of their own."

He turned toward her, his mouth opening in surprise.

"You'll catch flies in this barn if you don't close that mouth." she said.

He clamped it shut, then spoke. "But you know what I mean, what I'm trying to describe."

She smiled so directly his stomach wavered. "Sure, I do," she said. "You think you're the only one can hear what a horse is thinking?"

Jeff just stared at her. Eventually he found his voice again. "Well, I guess I just never heard anybody say it before. But that's just the way it is, like you're inside their heads with 'em."

She grinned at him and said, "Yeah, something like that. Kind'a hard to put into words, huh?"

He nodded dumbly, pinned by her look. They stood for a moment, locked on each other's eyes, and then he blinked, cleared his throat, and turned his attention back to his mare.

Margaret stepped in beside him and looked over the stall door. "Have you had her long?"

His mind raced back over the circumstances of his acquisition of this horse and the related events since that morning in Taos. He had no intention of revealing that story, but he did say, "Got her late in the fall. Bought her from a *vaquero* down in Taos. She was way thin, but I've got her almost up to prime shape."

The girl nodded. "She's a fine-looking animal. How old?"

Jeff scratched his jaw and said, "By the look of her mouth, I'd say about five, no more than six."

Margaret nodded again. "How broke is she?"

He grinned. "She bucked me off once, just to let me know to not take her for granted. I think some old timer started her, probably in the *bosal*, then into the bit with the *bosalito* and the two rein. I've got a Santa Barbara bit that I picked up in Albuquerque. It's got a half-breed mouthpiece with a copper cricket roller. She don't have a high tongue set, so the bar don't crowd her mouth. She seems to like it and she packs it easy. She's real light in it."

The girl was smiling at him when he looked back at her. "Sounds like you know horses," she said.

He smiled too. "Yeah. I know a few."

She tipped her head back and laughed out loud. "A sense of humor, as well."

He nodded. "Why not? Life's hard enough without a laugh, now and then."

She smiled wider and agreed, "How true, Mr. Cameron. How true."

He said, "Jeff's the name. Mr. Cameron was my daddy."

She laughed again. "All right, Jeff. And I'm Maggie. No more of that ma'am rubbish."

He put out his hand. "Deal," he said.

She took it and shook. "Deal."

They stood there, saying nothing, watching the blue mare grinding her oats and barley. The contentment of the feeding animals was contagious. And each was very aware of the proximity of the other.

After a minute or two, Maggie straightened and started down the aisle, pausing to take a halter and lead from a peg in one of the support posts. Moving further along, she stopped at a stall door and looked in, smiling. Turning back toward Jeff, she said, "Come down here and I'll show you something."

He walked to her and looked in over the gate. What he saw sent a small shiver through him. Maggie turned toward him and saw his rather stricken look. "What's wrong, man? You look as if you've seen a ghost."

Jeff shook his head. "No ghost, but I swear I've seen that horse before."

Now she shook her head. "There's no way. He's been on the ranch only a few weeks and, anyhow, you've just arrived. How could it be you've seen him?"

Jeff didn't dare say where, didn't tell her it was the horse from his dream of the past night. That it was the one he'd seen her riding through the mist. With details quite vivid in his mind's eye, he remembered the two of them. She was the dream rider, her long, black hair, streaming behind, lifted on the wind stirred by the running horse. And there stood the dream horse, a red dun stallion. Luxurious mane and tail, lined back, striped forelegs, arched neck. Spanish blood. Horse of the *Conquistadores*. Dream horse. For a dream girl.

•   •   •   •

HE DIDN'T DISCLOSE any of that, of course. She'd think him mad or worse, a fool. "You're right," he said, "Couldn't of seen him. Must of been one like him, I guess."

She reached over the gate and scratched the horse on the neck. "Well, maybe. But I doubt there are many to match him." The stallion turned to face her, blowing out his breath, and she tugged on his long, red forelock.

"No," he agreed, "there's few that'd equal this young fellow." Jeff had composed himself and took a moment then to examine the horse in closer detail. Mustang blood, to be sure, but tall for a mustang. Very clean limbed, good bone and straight legged. Maybe a touch of thoroughbred, or standardbred. But that muscle spoke of something else, perhaps Morgan, enough to account for some mass. And, above all, the marks of Spanish ancestors.

Jeff nodded approvingly. "Looks like a lot of horse. How'd you come by him?"

Maggie faced him and said, "A rider came by last month, a *vaquero*, asking about work. Said he was a horse breaker. Dad didn't like his looks. Said no man who wore great, sharp rowelled spurs with a quirt hanging from his wrist would touch a horse of his."

Jeff could imagine that conversation, the bluntness of Robert MacTeague's declaration to the *vaquero*, the reaction of the man, who, if like most his breed, might take such a statement as an invitation to violence. "I expect that made for some tension," he said.

Maggie grinned. "My father has never been known as other than direct."

Jeff looked at the horse. "And the *vaquero* was riding this dun?"

The girl shook her head. "No, he was riding a chestnut gelding, leading this one." She reached out to scratch the horse on his muscled jaw. "I stepped in before things got out of hand. The man needed money but he didn't want to sell this colt. I recognized the blood in him and I just kept upping the offer. And regardless of what I spent, I consider this animal a bargain."

Jeff nodded appreciatively. "A horse like this would be worth plenty."

Maggie smiled, "You think so?"

He looked serious. "Sure. Look at those markings. He's Spanish through and through, with a little something thrown in to give him that height and muscle. I'd pay plenty for him, was he for sale."

Maggie frowned. "He's not."

Jeff looked her in the eye and smiled. "Never thought he was. Just agreeing with you. About his worth, that is."

The girl blushed faintly. "I'm sorry. Forgive my abruptness. It's just that I like Spanish horses. I get one, I keep it."

Jeff looked back at the young stallion. "I didn't take no offense. I know how you feel. I wouldn't take nothin' for that blue mare of mine. She's got good sense and a world of bottom."

Maggie looked at him. "I've noticed your mare. I like her. I want to talk to you about her."

Jeff smiled. "Sure. Just as long as we understand about what I already said. She's no more for sale than this stallion here."

Maggie smiled wide. "Like *you* told *me*, I never had a thought to try to buy your horse. For that matter, I'd be disappointed in you if you felt otherwise about her."

Jeff smiled equal to hers. "Maggie," he declared, "last thing I want is you disappointed in me."

•   •   •   •

HE STOOD OUTSIDE the barn door, rolling a cigarette and feeling foolish. Why did he have to say such a stupid thing to this girl, just when she seemed to be starting to like him a little? How come he couldn't just nod and smile and keep his damn mouth shut?

He lit the cigarette and took a deep drag, blowing it out slowly and spitting a tiny fleck of tobacco off the end of his tongue. He cursed himself again for the embarrassment that had driven him out of the barn. His face had reddened the instant he'd made the declaration. He'd turned and left the girl standing at the stallion's stall without saying another word.

And what must she think of him now? Damned, dumb, stupid fool! He puffed furiously, continuing to curse himself under his breath.

She came out the door as he was pressing the butt of his smoke down into the mud with the sole of his boot. He couldn't look at her.

"You all right?" Her concern seemed genuine.

He continued to stare down at his feet. "Yeah, I'm fine. Just talk too much sometimes."

She took hold of his coat sleeve and drew him around to face her. A surprised frown was on his face as she spoke. Her look was grave. "Don't ever regret anything you say. If you mean it."

He couldn't have been more stunned. "Your mouth is open again." She was grinning, then got tickled and began laughing. It appeared her mood could change in a moment.

Still uncertain, Jeff felt the heat rising once more in his neck, but before he could do or say another thing, she pulled his sleeve again. "Come on, cowboy. Let's get horseback."

•　•　•　•

As THEY were tacking up the horses in the barn, he noticed the easy way she had around the stallion. He was nice mannered for a stud and paid little attention to the blue mare. She was not in season so he had, of course, no reason to react to her. Jeff liked his markings and thought that maybe here was a suitable mate for his horse. More than that, he liked the way she handled him. That she had grown up around horses was obvious. He was looking forward to seeing her ride.

They were quiet as they worked, but as he slipped the bit into the mare's mouth, he said, "Is he broke?"

She continued her saddling and answered without looking his way. "Green broke. Hasn't offered to buck. Spooks a little at things he's not used too. Not bad, though. Doesn't jump out from under you. He just needs miles and wet saddle blankets."

He smiled at her use of the old cowboy axiom. "Did I hear your dad say you're having a saddle built for him?"

She nodded. "Right. This one I've got on him now is a good fit for him, but not so good for me. The seat's too long and it's not deep enough. The saddler is making a tree with bars like this one, but with less distance between the forks and the cantle, and with a much narrower ground seat. It'll take a couple of months, what with his other work. I'm all pins and needles for it."

He stole a look at her when her attention was on bridling the stallion. Lordy God, he thought. What a girl. Then a loud growling of his stomach brought him back to earth. "You folks believe in breakfast around here?" She gave him a half-peevish look, then dug in the pocket of her coat and came out with a cold *tortilla*. Tossing it to him, she said, "Gnaw on that. We'll have bacon and eggs when we get back. Now let's ride."

•   •   •   •

AND RIDE they did, working their way down toward the river as the sun began to warm the air. The girl led and Jeff admired the way she sat her horse. She'd grown up in the saddle, he knew, and it showed. The young stallion was a little unsure of himself, but the girl radiated confidence and communicated it to the horse through light but firm hands and a relaxed seat. They looked good together. He thought he'd never seen anything that looked so fine as this girl on that horse on this morning.

And he had never seen better-looking country. Spring creeks flowed out of the rocks and wandered down to join the river. Snow was drifted in all the low pockets and on the north-facing slopes, but a lot of ground was exposed and the cattle were able to get at the grass. They also were fed hay cut from the river bottoms, stored in fenced stack yards, and located at intervals in the lower pastures. During periods of deep snow, ranch hands would drive out in sleds pulled by draft teams, load the hay, and scatter it for the cattle and horses. It was an effective system of winter range management and the stock came out in the spring in good shape. All this Maggie explained as they rode along.

The track widened and he urged his mare up next to the girl. The stallion turned and made a move to nip at his horse, but playfully, and the girl reined him straight with a soft word of correction. "Reckon you'll cut him?"

Jeff's question seemed to horrify her. "What? You can't possibly be serious. Geld this animal? With his breeding? And disposition? You have to be joking."

He smiled. "I was. Just wanted to see if that'd get a rise out of you."

She gave him a mock frown. "Well, a question stupid as that one is guaranteed to 'get a rise out of me,' as you put it."

They rode on a short way in silence, until he satisfied himself that she was not truly angry, and he said, "That's good. The part about not gelding him, I mean. 'Cause I'd like you to think about maybe letting him cover this mare."

She kept looking straight ahead, grinning as she answered, "I'm way ahead of you, cowboy. The instant I saw her, that was the first thing I thought of."

He grinned, too, but under his hat brim. "I thought maybe the idea had come to you," he said. "We both like these Spanish-blooded horses and I never saw a better matched pair for a breeding."

Maggie had a serious look on her face as she replied. "I agree. They both carry the dun gene with all the classic markings. The foal would surely be a line-backed buckskin, claybank, red dun, or *grulla*."

Jeff was surprised to hear her use the last term. "You know your Spanish words for the color of these horses."

She turned to look at him. "You mean *grulla*?"

He nodded.

"Well," she said, "I've ridden with our *vaqueros* since I was a little girl and I speak the language fairly well. I spotted your mare for a *grulla* when I first saw her."

He grinned and said, "I've always liked this shade of dun the best. This mare looks slate-blue in the right light."

Maggie eyed the mare with obvious appreciation. "What's her name?"

Jeff looked suddenly puzzled. "Truth to tell, I don't know."

She turned to face him. "You don't know?"

He shook his head. "Nope."

She seemed incredulous. "Nope? You mean you didn't bother to ask the man you bought her from?"

He frowned and said, "Well, under the circumstances, the opportunity didn't come up."

She continued staring at him. "That sounds fairly mysterious. You did buy her, didn't you?"

Jeff squirmed in the saddle. He decided to tell her the smallest part the story. "I paid for her."

Maggie stared harder. "More mystery."

So he went on to tell about that morning in Taos, about the beating of the mare, the confrontation with Bad Jimmy, ending with the leaving of the gold piece with the old, rawhide man.

"Go on," said the girl.

He revealed nothing of the subsequent shooting. "I feel pretty sure the old man gave him the money. So, technically, I guess I can say I bought her. I just wouldn't consider the owner much inclined to sell."

Maggie stopped her horse and sat looking him in the eye, an expression of wonder on her face.

"Now your mouth is open," he observed.

She shut it reflexively, and then said, "You are an uncommon fellow, Jeff Cameron."

He raised an eyebrow. "Is that good or bad?"

She smiled a little. "Good. I think."

A look of relief came to his face. "See, the thing is, I can't stand to see a horse mistreated, or a dog, either. Any sort of animal, far as that goes. They can't do for themselves. Since people tamed 'em from mustangs and wolves, they count on us for everything. And more'n that, it's plain mean. And now I'm talking too much again."

She cocked her head a little to one side and said, "No. Not when you say that sort of thing." She held her eyes on his face. He began to fidget under her direct look.

"Well," she said, finally, reaching over to tug on the *grulla's* forelock, "a girl as pretty as her needs a pretty name."

Jeff nodded. "I expect so." After a few seconds of consideration he said, "How 'bout you name her? I was never any good at thinkin' up stuff."

They sat and smiled at each other until it was a little awkward.

"All right," Maggie said, "she's blue. And grey as well, but in the right light, definitely blue. And, inasmuch as we're on a Scottish estate, or as Scottish as any place in America can be, I would suggest some reference to that." She paused, giving it some more thought. Then, "So, what would you say to Bonnie Blue?"

Jeff grinned broadly. "Now see, that's what a woman is good at, thinkin' up nice things, makin' up pretty names."

She met his smile with a questioning look. "For more than that, I hope. But do you like it?"

He nodded. "Yep. I think it's a great fit. 'Bonnie Blue' she is."

As if in agreement, the blue mare bobbed her head and nickered. They both laughed.

Maggie reached out to stroke her neck. "It appears to be unanimous."

•   •   •   •

THEY WERE among cattle now, heavy cows that would begin calving in March, and a lesser number of steers and open heifers. Jeff's stockman's eye noted the quality and condition of these animals, and he admitted to himself that this was some of the best beef on the hoof he'd ever seen. Maggie stopped her horse and looked out over this bunch, which was only a portion of the total MacTeague herd. Jeff quickly judged some hundred fifty to hundred seventy-five head, scattered over about fifty acres of feed ground, with one of the fenced haystacks in the middle.

The girl turned in the saddle and said, "Well, what do you think?"

He nodded and went on nodding as he answered. "This is about as fine a bunch of winter condition cattle as I guess I ever saw."

She turned back to look over the stock and asked, "What do you notice about these animals, Jeff? Something maybe you haven't seen in other herds."

He stroked his jaw. "Well, right off I notice that most of them are black, or mostly black, with some white on the face or brisket. And they're built blocky, more square than a longhorn, say. They look meatier."

She bobbed her head. "Good eye. You're right. Dad sent back to Scotland for five bulls, purebred, Aberdeen Angus. Four got to the New York docks alive. One died aboard ship. One more died on the train trip across country. That left three. That was five years ago. We've been line breeding some of the second and third generation heifers, the best ones. And we've added four more young bulls to the breeding program, bulls that were calved right here on the place. They're three-quarter Angus. We're getting good results, a better finished carcass, more gain from the feed consumed. You'll get to sample some excellent beef while you're here."

The mention of meat made his stomach growl so loud that she heard it. He was mortified and his face went red.

Maggie laughed. "Well now, sir. Seems my lecture has heightened your appetite. I'll not keep you from your breakfast any longer." With a quick smile she reined the stallion around toward headquarters and eased him into a canter. Jeff watched them move off, and she was so damn smooth on that horse, like she just grew out of the saddle, and the mare fidgeted to follow, so he pitched slack in the reins and felt her ball up under him and surge forward, and as they caught up with the girl, he thought he wouldn't mind chasing her from then on.

ELEVEN

THE OLD MAN returned to his braiding, ignoring the Lucero brothers as though they no longer existed. Mano stared hard at him for a moment more and then stepped back out on the street, turning toward the livery barn.

Pepé caught up. "He knows more, Mano."

The older brother nodded. "*Si, verdad.* But he will not tell it. He would let us kill him first. As he said, he is old and tired of living. But no matter. We know what we need to know."

Pepé gave him a dim look. "What do we know?"

Mano smiled indulgently, "Two things, *hermanito.* The place our brother was found. We have seen it once and, if we return, perhaps we'll find a clue we missed the first time. And we know his killer is a *gringo.*"

Pepé frowned, "That is not much."

Mano smiled, again indulging his brother. "Perhaps it does not seem like much, but it is a start."

Now Pepé smiled, reassured.

Mano headed toward the livery, his brother following. "Now we will nap in the barn, allow the horses to feed and rest. We will rise this evening and eat well again, then go back to bed and get a long sleep. In the morning, we will be well rested, and the *caballos,* too. We will have a good breakfast and then ride for the place where Juan Pinto found Jaimé. We will make a more thorough search. We can expect no trail from there, of course, after all this time. But perhaps we will get a feeling. The next settlements are to the north. That is likely the way our man rode from this place. We will go that way, also. It is an exceptional horse he killed our brother for. An unusual color. Someone will remember *la grulla*, and our man, as well. And we will find him. In time, we will find him. Surely as the earth turns under our feet."

•   •   •   •

A HALF MILE from headquarters, they slowed their horses to a walk. The stallion was blowing hard, as much from excitement as from exertion. The blue mare's breathing returned to near normal in the next couple of hundred yards or so. Jeff's frequent exercise rides on her had begun to improve her condition. She had gained muscle and endurance. In time, she would be a hundred-mile-a-day horse.

Little was said during the time it took to ride on in, or while they unsaddled and stalled the horses. As they exited the barn, the old Mexican woman stepped out the kitchen door and crossed to the pump stand over the house well, filled a huge, blue granite coffee pot, and went back inside.

"Well," said the girl, "our timing is perfect. When Hortencia comes out for more coffee water, the first pot already is in the china service at table. And that means breakfast is ready. Are you still hungry?"

Jeff grinned. "As a bear crawling out of his winter den."

The girl went on ahead, and he washed up at the pump. When he entered the house, she was seated at the dining table, along with her father and Sandy. The air in the room was heavy with the aroma of bacon, eggs, beans, *chiles*, *tortillas*, and coffee.

The talk was sparse until the edge came off appetites. Then the topics were the usual. Cattle, horses, weather, beef prices, the mares likely to foal first, and the progress of the Spanish stallion. Eyes on his plate, Robert MacTeague asked, "How was your ride?" Jeff wasn't quite sure which of them was supposed to answer. He looked across the table at Maggie for a sign.

She smiled and spoke up. "Fine, Da'. And thanks for holding breakfast. We went down into the lower pastures, amongst the heavy cows. Mr. Cameron here has an eye for stock."

Robert lifted his attention from a forkful of eggs and beans to regard Jeff. "Is that so?"

Then every eye and ear was on him. His coffee cup half way to his mouth, he paused to take in the looks of Sandy, Robert, and Maggie. It was obvious that all were awaiting his response with anticipation. He set his cup down, fidgeted a few seconds, then plunged in. "Well, sir," he said, "I don't know how good an eye I got, but anyone who's ever rode through a herd could see the quality of your animals. I traded livestock back and forth across the border for a while, longhorns and *Corriente*-bred cows and steers, as well as a few horses. Mostly thoroughbred type that the *hacendados* want for racin'. They love a horse race."

He paused for breath, and no one else commented. It seemed he had the floor, so he forged ahead. "Anyway, I have to say that I've never seen cows that carried so much flesh this time of year. That speaks well of the wild hay you cut. More'n that, those cows look built to make beef. Square and blocky. Less length and leg. More girth and loin. They're nothin' but meat. And they seem quiet and gentler than Texas or Mexican cattle. I doubt they run much weight off trying to fight being handled. They look like money makers."

And that was it. He'd had his say. Somebody else could pick it up from there. He took up his cup again, sipped, and waited. Robert MacTeague had a faint smile on his face. Wiping his mouth, he said, "That's our aim here. I've spared no expense in an effort to improve the finished carcass of what we sell. I suppose Margaret has told you of my importation of Angus bulls all the way from Scotland. The finest beef breed on earth. And I confess to a certain prejudice in that regard, but it's true. One day the west will be speckled with black cattle. No offense, Mr. Cameron, in case your opinion is otherwise, but I think the era of the Longhorn is done. And before you rise up in defense of the breed, I'll be the first to admit that in wild country, no mother defends her calf more courageously than the Longhorn cow. But the range is shrinking. No more can a man turn out a mob of rank cattle on a hundred thousand acres of open range and expect to prosper. That man, if he wants to succeed, must maintain a thriftier type of animal and husband them more closely. He must rotate pastures, cut and feed hay in winter, and cull inferior animals. We eat beef here, Mr. Cameron, but only from individuals of lesser quality. Don't get me wrong. Their meat is superb. But the finest are sold locally or shipped. And though this is not a wealthy family, we do, by careful management of our enterprise, prosper."

And then it seemed that Sandy's younger brother, like Jeff, had his say. Taking a last sip of his coffee, the burly rancher excused himself and went on to attend the duties of his workday. Turning at the dining room door, he looked at Jeff and said, "And thanks, Mr. Cameron, for those generous comments regarding my animals."

Jeff smiled and shrugged. "Just said what I saw, sir."

•   •   •   •

"DA', A WORD, if you have a moment." Saying that, Maggie rose and left the room in her father's wake. A spate of silence allowed the atmosphere to decompress. Sandy and Jeff were left alone to contemplate each other across the table.

The Scot spoke first. "So, lad. How was your dawn ride?"

Jeff colored slightly, seeing the sly smile on Sandy's bristly face.

"Just fine," he answered, "and you can wipe the shit eatin' grin off that ugly mug of yours."

The mug in question took on a look of mock indignation. "How could you say such a thing, and to one who's taken you in like a lost, wormy pup?"

Jeff's face reddened more. "Don't pull that old song and dance on me. You know what I mean."

Sandy leaned back. "Very well. I take it, then, that yer time with my niece was unpleasant?"

Jeff jerked the napkin from his shirtfront and threw it down on the table irritably. "You know damn well it was pleasant as all get out. Why do you have to bait me like this?"

The old man grinned. "Because I always get such a grand rise out of yeh, lad. Yeh're a constant source of entertainment."

Jeff took a deep breath, making himself relax before going on. Running his hand through unruly hair, he said, "All right. It was a fine ride. Saw some good country and fat cattle. Maggie knows this place and her livestock."

Sandy scratched down in his beard and asked, "Doesn't she sit a horse well? Or didn't you notice?"

Jeff got a dreamy look on his face and said, "Oh, yeah, I noticed. It's like they're just one critter."

Sandy set his coffee cup down after a last sip, clinking it on the saucer and bringing Jeff out of his reverie. "So, what are yer plans for the remainder of the day, lad?"

Dismissing for now the image of Maggie sailing along on her young stallion, Jeff said, "Well, if there's nothing that calls for me to hang around headquarters, I'd like to take Buck out. Bonnie Blue's been out already today and Buck could use a stretch."

Sandy's eyes widened. "I did na' know your mare had a name."

Jeff began to redden again. "Well," he mumbled, "she didn't. Not 'til this morning."

The Scot nodded. "And of a sudden you just pulled a lyrical, poetic handle out of the air, did you?"

"Not exactly," Jeff answered.

A few seconds of silence prompted Sandy to ask, "And?"

After a deep breath pulled in and blown out, Jeff said, "And Maggie asked the mare's name and when I said I hadn't gotten around to naming her she said she ought to have one, and she suggested Bonnie Blue. A good Scottish name she said and I thought it sounded pretty, so that's her name."

Sandy nodded sagely. "A wonder how that girl influences every male around her. Horse, dog, or man."

The sly grin was back and, seeing it, Jeff swore, "Aw, hell." And got up abruptly and went outside.

• • • •

MAGGIE STOOD in the parlor, looking out the front window toward the bunkhouse, where she saw Jeff standing with the buckskin, checking his saddle and making adjustments. Once done with her daily briefing with her father, she had ghosted around the parlor while Jeff and Sandy remained in the dining room talking. Her instinct had been to stand by the door in the hope of catching some of their words.

But proper upbringing and personal honor stopped her from outright eavesdropping. She knew next to nothing of this young man. He'd entered her life only the night before. That didn't prevent her from feeling a growing interest in him.

Her father had put on boots and spurs, gone to the barn for a horse, and ridden off toward Hermosa Creek, leaving her with the suggestion that she might make some entries in the ranch account books. As it had been a request rather than an order, she chose to ignore him. At the moment, she much preferred watching Jeff with his horse.

So intent in her observation was she that she failed to hear her uncle slip into the room on moccasined feet. "He cuts a fine figure ahorseback, does he not?"

She jumped at the sound of Sandy's voice. With reddening cheeks and a withering glare she growled, "Why, you sneaky old man. You creep around as if you're stalking a deer."

He smiled at her patiently. "Not that so much, lass. More that it's yer preoccupation with events outside."

Maggie fairly spit, "I can't imagine what you mean."

Sandy winked at her. "Come now, my dear. Not so coy, if you please. I saw the look on yer face as I came in. I think mayhaps yer smitten."

The girl was reddening further as her temper rose. "That's preposterous. I know nothing about him," she said, only to become angrier at the realization that she had confirmed her uncle's accusation.

The old hunter crossed the room and circled her shoulders with a loving arm. "Calm down, girl. This is your dear old Uncle Sandy."

Maggie demurred only slightly. "I'm sorry, but how can you suppose I've any interest in a man I've known less than a day?"

Sandy tugged at his mustache. "Of course, my dear. Very silly of me to suggest otherwise."

She frowned. "Well, sometimes your sense of humor rubs a bit."

He smiled. "My apologies, dear niece. You're absolutely correct. He's not even yer type."

The girl began to fume again. "And how could you possibly know what my type is?"

He made a conciliatory gesture. "Well, I should rather think someone with more education, greater prospects, pairhaps. A man of property."

Maggie rolled her eyes toward the ceiling. "Oh, do shut up Uncle. You're talking gibberish."

The old man smiled. "Of course, dear. I'm certain he has no interest in you, either."

The girl's eyes narrowed. "And why would you think that? Has he said so?" Instantly, she regretted rising to the bait.

Sandy shook his head. "No, no. Not a'tall."

She glared at him. "But you think so?"

He held his hands up, palms out. "No, dear. I don't think so. What I think is that I talk too much."

She nodded sharply. "You're certainly correct on that account."

Still grinning, Sandy bowed and left the room. She turned back to the window in time to see Jeff gather the reins, step effortlessly into the saddle, and jog Buck out of the stable yard. As she watched the pair leave headquarters, she told herself that her uncle was right on one other account. Jeff Cameron cut a fine figure on a horse.

• • • •

THE SEGUNDO, or ranch foreman, second in authority only to Robert MacTeague, was a tall, lean man of mixed blood. Mexican, Ute, and a dash gringo. The little bit of Caucasian ancestry came from a brief tryst his maternal grandmother had with a mountain man during the days of the free trappers. His mother was Ute, his father a vaquero from Sonora. He spoke fluent Spanish, English, Ute, and a touch of Navajo, the last being the most difficult to manage of them all. His name was Juan Loera and he was a splendid horseman, crack shot with rifle and revolver, could rope a cow or horse any way you wanted, and was a cool head and a competent leader of men.

After having been needled to his limits by Sandy, Jeff had saddled the buckskin with the idea of taking a scout around on his own. The ride before breakfast with Maggie had been more than delightful but just now he thought he had a better chance at some clear thinking if he was alone. And the current situation definitely called for clear thinking. Had he been aware of Maggie's eyes on him from the parlor window, he doubtless would have been even more ill at ease. Having mounted the gelding, he rode to where Loera and the cook were visiting on the porch of the bunkhouse and stepped down.

The cook smiled upon seeing him, but Loera's face showed nothing. Jeff walked to within a long pace of them, holding the reins in his left hand, and reached out to the *segundo* with his right. He spoke formally, "*Buenos dias, Jefé.* We have not yet spoken directly. It's Jeff Cameron, at your orders."

The foreman took his hand, a look of amazement on his face. Jeff's formal greeting and introduction, rendered in flawless Spanish, was nothing less than a shock to him. Loera allowed a modest smile to cross his mouth. "*Con mucho gusto, Señor* Cameron. The honor is mine." Unlike the limp handshake Jeff was used to from many *vaqueros*, Loera's grip was strong and sure.

The *segundo* turned to the still-smiling cook. "Permit me to introduce the evil little *viejo* who spoils all our food. *El cocinero,* Nacho Ramirez."

The cook smiled even wider, shaking hands with Jeff. "Please ignore this monstrous tyrant, who beats the men and wouldn't know a *quesadilla* from a cat turd. I am happy to meet you."

Jeff chuckled at this typically rough banter, traded between two obviously good friends. "The pleasure is mine, *amigos.* If Nacho's cooking is as good as his coffee, I am certain the men are well fed, indeed."

Loera put a mock look of horror on his face. "*Señor,* do you mean to say that you have sampled this poison pusher's foul brew and remain alive to tell the tale?"

Jeff laughed louder and the cook feigned a black look at Loera. "*Amigo* Jeff," he said, "See the abuse to which I must submit. Me, a poor, old, broken-down *vaquero,* who in his day could ride and rope circles around this impudent puppy."

Loera smiled down on the little man with genuine affection. "*Pacienté, tio.* I am still learning."

At length, Jeff was able to get a moment to ask Juan if he could point out a way to ride up onto the rimrock. Taking the cowboy by the elbow, the foreman walked him farther out into the yard, where the view was clear of the roofs of the buildings. Pointing with a callused finger, he said, "*Mira, señor.* There, to the east. You can see the beginning of the switchbacks just there, at the end of that line of cottonwoods. You must ride about a mile upstream. You'll see a trail that is plain. It will take you safely through the boggy spots. Then you will come to a ford, also plain to see. Across the river, the trail resumes. Stay on it and you will find yourself at the base of those switchbacks. It is steep and rocky in places. Can your big horse climb?"

Jeff smiled and nodded. "Like a *macho cabrío.* I think his mother was a nanny goat."

All three men laughed. Loera gave Jeff a friendly pat on the shoulder. "Then ride on, *amigo.*"

•   •   •   •

FROM THE RANCH YARD below to where Jeff now sat his horse was about a thousand feet higher and an hour's worth of scratching and scrambling. The steep, rocky trail was little more than a deer path and drifted with snow in spots. But the eager gelding had bowed his neck and bunched his hindquarters to the task, digging in and chugging like a locomotive.

On gaining the heights, Jeff paused to let his horse blow. And then turned Buck north and rode along the rimrock, viewing the country below.

The Animas wound like a lazy snake from the end of his gaze north toward Molas Pass to as far south as he could see, where it rounded a headland and made its way toward Durango. Bare cottonwoods lined its banks, promising shade for man and beast in summer. Ponds dotted the valley floor, some free of ice, no doubt spring fed. These played host to flocks of wild ducks, discernible in the clear air even from this distance. Sun-cured grass, bent from repeated snows but exposed now in many places, would be green and belly deep to a tall horse in July.

He could easily make out MacTeague headquarters, with the low-roofed ranch house, the main horse barn, and even the ranch hands moving about at their work. The air was so clear that he felt he could almost reach from where he was, pluck a horse from one of the corrals, and hold it in his hand as if it were a child's toy. Taken as a whole, the picture was compelling. And the color of the sky, the particular blue of the Rocky Mountain sky in winter. That sky seemed like something a man could drink and drink, and get hopelessly drunk on, and never get his fill.

Considering his impressions since his arrival, he thought he was becoming sure of one thing. That this very well might be the place he'd been looking for. In addition to the fact that it had all the requirements of a good stock range, the setting was so beautiful as to be near heartbreaking. The red rock cliffs, the green timber, the meandering river, and the grassy bottoms all combined to make a paradise on earth. Jagged, snow-white peaks capped the scene to the north. The river teemed with fish and waterfowl, and the hills with deer and elk. If he could have made it just for himself, it would be exactly this.

For an hour he rode the rim north, taking in everything, until he assumed he was beyond the limits of MacTeague range. Hungry again, he took from his saddlebag a *tortilla* wrapped around a large hunk of cold beef and goat cheese. With his mouth full and chewing with satisfaction, he turned his mount back south and angled away from the rim.

Back from the edge of the bluffs, the mesa top was studded with juniper and gamble oak, and the occasional huge, ponderosa pine. They had covered less than a hundred yards before jumping an enormous mule deer buck. It carried a massive rack of antlers nearly three feet wide rising tall and heavy over its roman-nosed head. It was the biggest deer Jeff had ever seen.

The horse snorted, then leapt ahead to give chase. Jeff gave him his head, but pursuit was useless as the deer quickly was swallowed up in brush too thick for them to follow. Jeff had managed to hang onto his lunch, in spite of the fast pace. He resumed eating and they proceeded south.

Approaching a tall, rocky outcrop, he observed a deep overhang receding into darkness. As he rode closer, he could see at the front a wall of stone work, resembling hand-laid masonry. At the cavern's mouth, he dismounted and dropped the reins.

Inside, he found a square-cornered room about fourteen feet on a side, the well-fitted stones laid up with what appeared to be mud mortar. A rectangular door less than five feet tall and no more than two wide invited a look at the room's interior. Jeff had a feeling of unease. He debated with himself for a moment, then stepped through.

By the light of several, consecutive wooden matches, he saw clay jars, some broken, some intact, a number of woven baskets containing things unidentifiable. And then, in a far corner, a skeleton. It had been disjointed and scattered, undoubtedly by animals. From the skull, Jeff figured this to have been a small person, perhaps no more than a child.

Others would have shared this space, would have been part of this household. Unnerved a bit by the discovery, he glanced tentatively around this room with one more match, and then backed himself out the low doorway and into the open again at the mouth of the alcove.

It was a very old place of human habitation, he understood. Perhaps he was the first to happen onto this scene in a long, long time. A certain sense of respect for these long-gone people came to him. A chill briefly traveled his spine. And it came to him, too, that maybe he had no business in this place. He turned and moved to his horse, a little uneasy after all he'd seen.

And it occurred to him that this country, the river, the valley, and the mesa above that appealed so strongly to him had meant as much to others, many years ago.

• • • •

BACK IN THE SADDLE, he resumed his way south, angling toward the rim. And he thought about the people who lived here now, so long after those who'd laid up those stone walls with so much patience and skill. People he liked and respected. People who seemed to like and respect him. And the fact of them only added to the appeal of this place. As he came out of the timber and caught the view of the valley floor and the river again, he brought Buck to a halt and dismounted, tied him to a scrub oak, and loosened the cinch.

He untied his slicker from behind the cantle and placed it on the ground at the base of a boulder the size of a small cabin. Sitting down with his back against the rock, he rolled a cigarette and lighting it took a deep pull and held the smoke in a few seconds, savoring it. He examined his thoughts.

Was this the place? Had he found it at last? Maybe. Probably. It was not only a stockman's paradise but beautiful as well. Everything his eye fell upon pleased him. The river. The cottonwoods. The grass. The sheltering timber. The lifting palisade of stone. The voice of this valley beckoned him like the song of a lovely girl.

And then, there *was* a girl. The girl. What about her? How did she fit into all this? How was he supposed to feel about someone he'd known less than twenty-four hours? Had his experience with Inez and the Widow Peach taught him nothing about the potential for trouble when it came to relationships with women? Was he one of those men whose good sense departed at the sight of a pretty face? Well, so far. Was he crazy enough to plunge into another fall over a female, with the dead girl hardly cold in her grave and a very much alive landlady waiting to warm his bed?

This much thinking had gotten him through the first cigarette. He rolled and lit another, and returned to his considerations. That he was powerfully attracted to the girl was an undeniable fact. First impressions being what they were, he knew that what had gotten his attention in the beginning was her beauty. The glossy black hair, sky-blue eyes, and robust, young body were a combination that no natural man could ignore. But it was more than that.

There was a radiance, a kind of shining light of vitality that emanated from her. Her entry into a room seemed to brighten it like a beacon. The force of life and health she carried with her had dominated his awareness since she had walked into the dining room the night before. Good Lord. Only the night before? Could she have taken a hold on him so quickly as that?

It was her way with horses, too, how she moved around them, talked to them. And how they seemed to respond to her. And the way she looked when mounted, as if grown from the saddle. How she sat a horse, her balance, the graceful way she moved with the animal, as though together they made one creature. The fluid way she blended with the motion of that young stallion, cantering across the snowy pastures out ahead of him and the blue mare. He admitted to himself that in every measurable way, he had never seen her match or even a close second.

Finally, it was simply the way he felt at the sight of her and when he was around her. As if his insides were churning, his chest constricted, his breathing labored. And then the feeling that these insides were floating away, leaving him hollow as a dry gourd, the shell of him ready to float away, too. Unfamiliar with these symptoms, he failed to understand that he was falling in love. With this girl.

And, again, there was this valley. He'd always counted on knowing when he found his place. And heard its voice. This land was speaking to him, singing to him like a siren to an ancient mariner. And her song said stay with me. Fall into my arms, and I'll make your dreams come true.

• • • •

A SMALL CORPS of crushed cigarette butts lay expired between his boots. The sun was low in the west and the air temperature was going down with it. He was surprised to realize that he had spent a good two hours with his back against this rock. He was hungry now. It seemed this clean mountain air gave him an almost constant appetite. The ride back to headquarters would be faster than the ride up, but it would be cold before he made it in.

He got to his feet a little stiffly and rolled up his slicker, moved to the buckskin and tightened the cinch. After a last look out over the valley, he took his sheepskin from behind the cantle and put it on, and tied the slicker in its place. Unhitching the git down rope from the tree, he looped it around the saddle horn and swung up. The horse stood patiently for the cue, and at the faint pressure from his rider's legs moved out to take the trail for home.

• • • •

BUCK WAS hungry, too, and he chafed a little at the bit, wanting to hurry and shed his saddle, settle into a warm stall, and bury his nose in a forkful of sweet hay and a bucket of oats and barley. Jeff had to draw the slightest pressure into the reins to hold the big horse to a moderate and steady pace. Down the steep trail they went, without misstep.

Jeff let his attention drift to take in the scene below and he marveled again at the natural beauty of this valley, and at the subtle color changes now taking place as the sun dropped farther toward the western rimrock. Out in the meadows, the still-grazing cattle were joined by deer and elk, warily leaving the timber edge to feed in the relative security of the fast approaching darkness. Circling flocks of ducks and geese appeared as if from nowhere, dropping gracefully to light on the open ponds, joining others that welcomed them with frantic quacks and honking, settling in to roost for the night ahead. Accompanying this was the music of coyotes, tuning up tentatively at first, then mingling their voices in joyous, full-throated song.

Jeff closed his eyes, as if in a trance, the dusk dimming toward dark. He rode that way awhile, rocking with the buckskin's now flawless pace, as the coyotes caroled him home.

• • • •

THE YOUNGER of the Lucero brothers awoke to the ratcheting sound of the other's snoring. He thought of shaking the older man, enough to break the rhythm and so stop the dreadful racket, but not enough to wake him. This had worked at times in the past. But once it had not, instead having aroused Mano's irritation and earned the younger brother a bloody nose. So, he chose to lay still in the fragrant hay of the barn loft, warm under the several layers of his serape, saddle blanket, and slicker.

But sleep would not come to him, not just from the distraction of the snoring but from a growing sense of dread, as well. A sense that had begun to gnaw inside him as he recalled the words of the old rawhide braider. His limited powers of reasoning, damaged from a kick in the head by a mule he long ago had tried to shoe to please Mano, reminded himself of the warning the old man had spoken at the end of their interview. Yes, Jaimé was dead. The quick and ruthless *gringo* had killed him. He and Mano were pursuing this *gringo*. And when they finally caught up with him, if he was quicker and more ruthless that they were, he would surely kill the both of them.

Having never seen this man, in his fearful mind grew the image of a monster, one bristling with weapons, guns and knives all about his person. One who lived to kill, who took his toll from all who opposed him. Against whom there was no defense. No way to stalk him unawares, as though he had eyes everywhere. As though he could hear their horses coming. That even now the man they sought was planning their meeting. And that to find him was to die.

• • • •

THE LAST LIGHT of dusk was all but gone when he turned the buckskin into the open barn door. A lantern hung from a hook in a beam, illuminating Sandy in a deerskin shirt, leaning against a post, cold pipe clenched in his teeth. He smiled around the stem. "Well, lad, did yeh see some country?"

Jeff swung down and began stripping gear from the horse. "Yeah, I saw a lot of country. Found a cave with stone laid up like masonry, but real old. Nobody's lived there for a long time."

Sandy nodded. "Right, lad. Maybe hundreds of years. Did you see the skeleton?"

Jeff nodded. "Small, like a little boy. Who was it?"

Sandy shrugged. "No one knows. Some Indian child of a long gone tribe, I suppose. It's all best left alone."

Jeff was seeing it again. "I didn't touch nothin'. Just wanted to get away. Like I didn't belong."

Sandy smiled approvingly. "Good lad. What else?"

"Just rode around lookin'. And then sat down to think," he answered.

"About anything in particular?" his friend asked carefully.

Jeff stalled Buck and tossed him hay before saying, "Oh, just things."

"Just things?" Sandy asked.

"Yeah," Jeff came back. "This and that."

Sandy nodded. "I see. This and that."

Jeff nodded back. "Right," he said. "One thing and another."

Sandy straightened from the post and put the pipe into his tobacco pouch. "Any conclusions?" he asked.

Jeff shook his head. "Not really. Got a lot more studyin' to do before I make up my mind."

The Scot nodded. "About what?" he asked.

"Oh," Jeff said, "you know. This and that."

Sandy abruptly strode past Jeff toward the barn door. "Good Christ, mon," he growled, "let's go get our supper."

TWELVE

A T THE END of their first day out of Taos, a long, hard ride covering over thirty miles, Mano and Pepé Lucero came into the little village of Tres Piedras. They ate and slept. Next morning they interrogated folks they met on the street. No one had seen or heard of a traveling gringo on a mouse-colored mare. At noon they rode on northwest.

• • • •

NACHO RAMIREZ washed his face each morning in a pan of water, heated on the woodstove in the cook shack. As was his habit, upon completing his ablutions, he carried the pan out onto the porch and tossed the dirty water into the yard. On the second morning of Jeff and Sandy's visit, the old cook was doing just that as Jeff stepped out the front door of the main house. Seeing him there, Ramirez went back inside and poured two cups of fresh coffee, then returned to the porch and hailed the young man.

"Hey, *amigo* Jeff. You want some coffee?"

Jeff came down off the porch and walked across the yard. "*Muy negro? Muy fuerte?*"

Nacho bobbed his head and grinned. "*Si*, my young friend. It is very black and strong."

Jeff returned the grin. "Then, hell yes, I'll join you in a cup, *con gusto*." He stepped up onto the cook shack porch, taking the mug from the cook's extended hand. "*Gracias, amigo*." He took a careful sip. As advertised, it was potent stuff. Nacho stood by expectantly. Jeff nodded his approval. "Strong enough to float a number three horse shoe. *Muy bueno*."

The cook smiled. "I am glad it suits you, my friend. All the men like it like this."

Jeff agreed. "I was weaned on strong coffee. Can't stand it any other way."

The two of them stood and drank silently for an interval. It was too cold to sit on the bench there on the porch. Presently, Nacho said, "Come inside, Jeff. These old bones need to be warm."

Once they were comfortably situated within the circle of heat radiating from the stove, Jeff spoke. "You said you were a *vaquero* in the past?"

Ramirez straightened his back and smiled. "*Si*, Jeff. Down in Old Mexico. Many years ago. Even before the *Americanos* invaded my country. The men of our family have always been *vaqueros*. My father rode for one of the missions. He took me up in the saddle with him before I was a year old. I grew up on the back of a *caballo*." He was looking out a window to the south, as if he could see himself as a boy, riding break-neck through the rocks and cactus, chasing the wild Spanish cattle.

Jeff appreciated the look in the old man's eye. "Please go on, *maestro*," he said.

"I lived the *vaquero's* life for many years," said Ramirez. "I had a little family at one time. A sweet wife. *Tres niños*. Two boys and a beautiful baby girl, but they all died of a sickness in the drinking water. It almost killed me as well. My body finally recovered, but my heart was *muerto*. I could no longer stay there, looking at those graves each day. I began to want to be down in the ground next to my little wife and our children. So I decided to go from that place. I caught some good *mesteños*, mustangs as you would call them, about thirty, if I remember. I trailed them up to *Los Estados Unidos* and traded them for three very fine cow ponies. I rode for *ranchos* in *Nuevo México*, Arizona, here in Colorado, and even as far north as Wyoming. But the work was *muy peligroso*. The cattle were wild and the country, too. Much danger and many accidents. Many hurts and broken bones. I was a breaker of horses and some of the horses broke me, also. And cattle that I roped would sometimes turn and attack me and the horses I rode. Longhorn cattle, mother cows, very brave. I have had more than one horse killed under me. It was a rough life, but I loved it. Now I am old, too stiff to ride and rope. So I cook for this crew and I take pleasure in the talk of the young riders, the stories of their deeds, their feats of horsemanship, their amazing ability with the *maguey* rope and the rawhide *reata*. How they boast. And I know that not one of them could have half kept up with me in my prime. I could have roped and ridden circles around the best of them. But that is no matter. They are good boys and the older ones are good men. It is my pleasure to take care of them. I not only cook for them. I doctor them, counsel them, hold onto their pay for them, and even mother them a little. But they are good *hombres*. And I talk too much. Forgive me, *amigo*."

Jeff shook his head. "Not at all, *maestro*. It sounds like a wonderful life."

Ramirez smiled with his mouth, but the eyes were sad. "*Si*, my young friend. A wonderful life for a *vaquero*."

The old cook rose stiffly and put more wood in the stove, then turned and said, "But I wish I had seen my children grow up. I would like to have grown old with my little wife. But one never gets through a life without loss and pain. God has given me much and I am thankful. And I will spend the time that is left to me in caring for these riders. They are my family now."

Jeff didn't know what to say so he said nothing. After a moment of reflection, Nacho brightened. "I cannot seem to close my mouth this morning. Here, *amigo*, give me that cup. We will drink a little more of this *café*, which, as you say, will float a horseshoe."

•   •   •   •

TWO DAYS of steady riding from Tres Piedras brought the Lucero brothers into the town of Chama, New Mexico Territory. It was a cold, quiet afternoon and they spent some time at the business of stabling their tired mounts and securing lodging for the night. Mano had decided that they could afford to rest out of the weather for once. Their money was scarce and so was work at this time of year. But there were ways of obtaining money that had nothing to do with either work or the time of year.

Before taking their evening meal they strolled about, making an effort to put on friendly faces and greeting passersby as they familiarized themselves with the small town. But they were unable to disguise their true nature, and most of those to whom they spoke were more than glad to see them walk on.

Good smells drew them into a dimly lit *cantina* and they sat down at the only empty table in the place, the other half dozen or so being occupied by men eating, drinking, or both. They ordered *carné asada, frijoles refritos,* and a heaping stack of smoking corn *tortillas,* with foaming mugs of the local *cervesa.* Mano kept his ear open to the muted conversation in the room, but picked up nothing helpful.

The waiter took their order for a second mug of beer and upon his return Mano engaged him in a few moments of small talk. Reaching into a pocket of his jacket he produced a waxed wrapper from which he drew three small, black cheroots, one of which he clamped in his teeth, one of which he gave to Pepé, and the last of which he offered to the waiter, who accepted it with thanks, dropping it into a shirt pocket for later. Lighting his and his brother's cigars, Mano spoke. "*Amigo,* my *hermanito* and I are seeking a friend of ours who we think may have come this way some time ago."

The waiter gave him a serious but noncommittal look. Mano went on. "It is a matter of some importance, a family matter. We have news for this man that will be of great benefit to him."

At that moment, his chair was bumped by a small boy moving with a tray to a nearby table to collect dirty dishes. Mano snapped his head around to fix the clumsy child in a cold, withering stare. Glancing over his shoulder to apologize, the boy froze mid-stride, terrified. The gunman responded to the boy's apologetic face with a grim smile. "*No problema, niño.*"

Returning his attention to the waiter he said, "The man we seek is a *gringo*, riding a young mare, not so tall, but well built. She is the color of the crane. *La grulla.*"

The waiter shook his head. "I am sorry, *señor*. I have seen no such *hombre* hereabouts and no such horse."

Mano's face showed disappointment. "That is a shame, *amigo*. The family is very anxious to locate this man. There would perhaps be a reward of money to one who has information as to his whereabouts."

Again the waiter shook his head, a look of his own disappointment on his face. "I would like to help you and, surely, I could use the reward you speak of. But, truly, *señor*, I have no knowledge of any such man or *caballa.*"

Mano was distracted by the clatter of the busboy collecting dishes at the table beside him. Abruptly, he child turned to him and declared, "Pardon, *señor*, but I have seen this man you seek, I think."

Mano turned to face the nervous boy. Forcing a smile again and reaching to place a hand on the thin shoulder, he said, "Then tell me what you saw, *mijo.*"

The boy swallowed and said. "It was during the feast of San Mateo, our fiesta day. My little brother and I were playing down by the creek on the south end of the village. A man came walking up from the grassy place down by the water. He gave us money to watch his camp."

The child had spoken rapidly, made anxious by his proximity to such a menacing man. But the promise of money gave strength to his voice.

Mano lifted his hand from the boy's shoulder to muss his hair paternally. "Now take a deep breath, *muchacho*."

He did as told, trying to calm himself.

"Now tell me more about this man."

The little fellow paused, wiped his nose on his shirtsleeve, and continued. "He was tall with great, wide shoulders, but not a heavy man. Not fat."

Mano nodded encouragingly. This was the first physical description he had heard of the man he hunted. "Was he a *vaquero*? A *Mexicano*?"

The boy shook his head vigorously. "No, *señor*. He was a *gringo*. His hair was the color of sand and he wore a mustache that was darker."

Mano turned his head toward Pepé and smiled. Pepé nodded, smiling, also. "Could you guess his age, *mijo*?"

The boy frowned. After a moment he said, "Not old like you, *señor*."

Mano's face clouded for an instant, then returned to a look of benevolence. "Would you say that he was a grown man?"

The boy nodded. "*Si, claro*. Maybe as old as Bernardo here."

Mano followed the boy's eyes to the face of the waiter. "*Quantos años, amigo*?"

The waiter shifted nervously on his feet. "I am twenty-eight on my next birthday."

Mano turned to the youngster again, "This man who paid you to guard his camp, do you remember his horse?"

The boy bobbed his head. "*Si. Claro*. He had two *caballos* and a little *mulo* to carry his belongings."

Mano moved his hand to the boy's back, rubbing it, trying further to encourage him. "Can you describe the *caballos*?"

The boy bobbed his head. "They were very nice animals. A big gelding, light brown, like the tanned skin of a deer."

"And the other?" Mano asked.

"Oh, *señor, qué bonita*! She was beautiful. Such a long mane, so shiny. And sweet. She ate *tortillas* from my hand."

Mano's scalp drew drumhead tight as he asked, "Do you recall her color?"

The boy smiled in recollection. "*Si, señor*. She was blue, like a shadow, but also a kind of grey, like the fur of a little *raton*. The color you said before. *La grulla*."

THIRTEEN

FOR THE THIRD MORNING in a row, Jeff Cameron sat on a hard bench under the veranda of the main house at MacTeague headquarters, stomping his feet down into the heels of his riding boots. There was cloud cover that had moved in early the previous night and this morning was not so cold as the last two. Rolling his customary first smoke of the day, he thought of how much he wanted to ride with Maggie again, to take advantage of her knowledge of the place and have her guide him over the property. And just to watch her ride.

Lighting his cigarette, he heard the door of the cook shack swing open to reveal Nacho Ramirez, with his customary pan of wash water. The old *cocinero* stepped to the edge of the porch and tossed his burden neatly into the yard, where it joined a growing icy puddle. Jeff sat smoking quietly as the former top hand returned to the warmth of his kitchen. "Don't want to end up like him," he thought. "Busted up too bad to ride. God forbid. Sooner have a horse kill me. Or a mama cow on the fight. Or even get shot dead across a card table. Anything but corralled in some drafty cook shack, slinging beef and beans to a bunch of smelly cowhands."

Flipping the butt of his smoke off the porch, he stood up and went down the steps to where it had landed in the dirt and rubbed it out with his boot sole. He snugged his hat down a little tighter and walked to the barn to check on his stock. Sliding back the big door, he slipped inside and called out, "Mornin', children." Both the horses nickered in unison and Jigger erupted with a short bray. That made him chuckle. Three heads leaned out over stall doors to greet him as he came down the alley. "How's everybody this fine day?" No one answered this time. He went to each animal in turn, scratching heads, and dispensing pieces of cold biscuit from the pocket of his sheepskin. And each in turn took its treat and returned to its grain. "Well," Jeff said with mock hurt feelings, "I guess all I mean to y'all is a tasty handout." Again, no answer was forthcoming.

He had hoped to find Maggie at the barn, but no such luck. He checked the dun stallion's stall, thinking maybe she was out for an early ride. But the horse was there, tucking into his morning ration of oats and barley. After another look at his own animals, he headed back toward the house.

He smelled fresh coffee from the main kitchen. As he bent to wash up in cold pump water, his stomach began growling on cue. It seemed to him loud enough for anyone inside the house to hear. Combing damp hair with his fingers, he went in to breakfast.

Sandy and brother Robert sat across from each other, nursing their first cups of coffee. Neither seemed to have much to say to the other. Both glanced up at Jeff's entrance. Sandy displayed his ready grin and Robert gave him a civil nod of the head. Jeff nodded back. "Morning, gentlemen."

Sandy looked briefly and impishly at Robert as he replied, "My brother no doubt rates that title, though I'd not guarantee he'd apply it to me." Robert took a long slurp of hot coffee and ignored his elder sibling.

Jeff had no sooner taken his seat when Maggie strode purposefully into the room, dressed for the out of doors. He rose from his chair at the sight of her and the brothers looked at him curiously, then rose also. Maggie smiled. "It seems to take a southern gentleman to shame you two old, mossy horns into a proper display of table manners." All three men reddened.

They were spared any further discomfort by the arrival of Hortencia and her granddaughter, both bearing great platters of food. Jeff stepped from his place to seat Maggie and returned to his chair. Bacon, eggs, fried potatoes, and biscuits went 'round the table, along with the ubiquitous stack of steaming *tortillas*. As usual, when people were hungry, conversation was sparse.

The edge coming off appetites, talk increased, with discussions of plans for the day. "Uncle and I are taking the spring wagon and driving into Durango to do some shopping," said Maggie.

Robert sat up straighter. "You were there only two days ago."

Maggie cocked her head at a fetching angle. "Aye, Da', I was. But horseback, for a saddle fitting. I'd no way to carry anything bulky."

Her father moved his shoulders against the back of the chair. "And what bulky items have you in mind, girl?"

She took a sip of coffee before answering. "Always the thrifty Scot, eh, Da'?" Smiling, she went on. "I don't know. Nothing in particular. I just want a day in town with this musty old fossil. Do you mind?"

Robert gave an indulgent smile. "I suppose not, lass."

Sandy puffed up in false indignation, complaining. "Well I mind, by God. I may be many things, but a fossil I am not!"

Maggie shot him a teasing look. "So you'll grant me 'musty,' will you?" He put on an even more offended face, held it for a second, then burst out with a guffaw. "Well, I suppose I canna' deny a certain personal gaminess."

Jeff couldn't help piling on. "I can back him up on that."

Sandy responded, "I dunna recall anyone soliciting your opinion, lad."

Jeff grinned at his bristly friend. "No solicitation required. That was strictly voluntary."

Maggie clapped her hands and laughed. "Thank you, sir, for your support."

Jeff smiled at her. "My pleasure."

Robert turned his attention toward the speaker and cleared his throat. "Jeff, if you've no more pressing engagement today, I'd like you to see some of our operation, and that will require the company of one familiar with the property. I've a young man in my employ from Montana, worked here for three years now. Knows the layout top to bottom."

With that, his breakfast finished, he rose from his chair. "I'll just walk to the bunkhouse and see him before he rides out for the day. Name's Will Gunlock. Splendid horseman. Fine fellow. You'll like him."

Jeff glanced at Maggie, who was looking the other way. Trying not to reveal his disappointment in his voice, he said, "Yes, sir. I expect I will."

•   •   •   •

BUCK SWUNG his head toward the barn door as Jeff floated the saddle up onto his back. Looking for whatever might have the horse's attention, he saw the backlit shape of a lean man coming down the alley toward him. As the figure entered the diffused light coming through the high windows, Jeff took stock of him. Tall, about his own height and with a similar, wide-shouldered build. Same sandy-colored hair, a dark brown mustache. For a moment, it almost seemed he was looking in a mirror. The man was dressed for a day in the saddle. His outfit said "cowboy," from the crease in his dusty black hat to the blunt rowelled spurs on the heels of his high-topped riding boots. At arm's length, he stopped and stuck out his right hand.

"I guess you'd be Jeff Cameron. I'm Will Gunlock. Proud to meet you." A good-natured grin spread across the young man's face as Jeff took the offered hand and shook. The grip was callused and firm, and the eyes didn't flinch. He returned the shake and produced a smile of his own. "Guilty as charged. Cameron it is."

Gunlock nodded eagerly. "Glad to see another pale face on the place. Me and Stogie Wilson is the only two white boys on the payroll. Us and old Joe Barr."

Jeff let his expression cool a little. "That a problem?"

Gunlock grinned wider and shook his head. "Aw, hell no. This is a topnotch crew. All good hands. We even got us a tame Apache. Young fella, a Jicarilla, goes by the name of Johnny Blacktail. Hell of a hand. Can ride anything and could track a cockroach across slick rock. We all get along fine. I even picked up a bunch of *vaquero* lingo since I been here."

Jeff relaxed. "Good," he said. "I speak pretty fair Spanish myself. Helps out lots of times."

Will nodded agreement. "Don't it. I jist wisht they wouldn't talk so fast when they git excited. And they git excited a lot."

Jeff nodded. "Yeah. Funny thing. They say the very same about us."

Will laughed out loud. "I reckon so. Say, we got to ride a big circle today. Boss's orders. Let me catch a pony and git saddled up. Be ready in a jiffy." He turned on his heel and went out the way he came, whistling a tune unknown to Jeff.

•   •   •   •

WILL GUNLOCK was just putting his foot in the stirrup as Jeff rode Buck out of the barn and into the lane between two large, rectangular corrals. Gunlock swung up and found his seat as the bay gelding humped his back and began pitching halfheartedly. After maybe four listless hops he abruptly quit and stood steady as his rider stepped down, then moved out calmly as he was led to the gate. Will was grinning as he said, "He ain't but a four year old. Gits a little cold backed on winter mornin's, but he's comin' along good. Got a lot of bottom to him. Gonna make a top horse."

Jeff nodded in appreciation. He'd noticed that throughout the minor fracas, Gunlock had stayed loose, keeping his hands soft, not using his spurs. Here was a rider after his own heart. Here could be the makings of a friendship.

•　•　•　•

BY NOON they had covered over fifteen miles, stopping now and then for Will to point out features of the range that would further Jeff's understanding. Deep snow kept them from exploring the highest portions of the ranch, but that still left much to see. As they sat alongside the Animas, backs up against the trunk of an enormous cottonwood, eating a saddlebag lunch and watching a small flock of mallards paddling about on the rippled surface of the water before them, Jeff thought again that this was, almost certainly, the country for him. The buckskin and the bay grazed with loosened cinches, bridles hung from saddle horns, lead ropes dragging. In this corner of Colorado, on this afternoon, all was right with the world.

After washing down thick, beef sandwiches with cold, clear river water, they rolled smokes and relaxed, soaking up a brief period of sun between bouts of cloud cover. Jeff trimmed ash off his cigarette against a tree root. "How big you reckon this place is, Will?"

The other rider hung his hat on a cross-legged boot toe and scratched his head. "Hell, Jeff. Who knows? These old timers don't never say, and you dasn't ask 'em. Be like asking how much money they got in the bank, wantin' to know how many acres they have."

Jeff blew out a thin plume of smoke. "I expect that's true. Never thought of it that way."

Will put his hat back on. "I've rode over just about all of it, one time or other, in three years. I ain't much of a real estate man, but if you held my feet to the fire, I'd have to say there's somewhere between fifteen and twenty thousand acres, give or take. Most of it's deeded, I think. Maybe a little leased ground. The Boss has worked hard, built it up over fifteen years. Maybe a little more. But, hell, what do I know? Nobody tells me much."

Jeff stood up and brushed off the seat of his pants. "Me neither. You ready?"

Will rubbed out his smoke against the tree trunk and got to his feet. "Yeah. Let's cinch up."

•   •   •   •

IT WAS full dark when two tired horsemen returned to MacTeague headquarters on two tired horses. The circle they had ridden had approached forty miles. In the barn, after unsaddling and feeding their mounts, Jeff and Will shook hands again. "That was a good ride," Jeff said. "I thank you for sharing what you know."

Will scratched at his neck. "What I know don't go far, but I'm happy to pass it on." Pausing a second, he said, "You gonna stick around awhile?"

Jeff shrugged. "Few days I expect. Sooner or later, Sandy and me got to be headin' back to Pagosa."

"What ya' got goin' on over there? Ridin' job?" Will asked.

"No," Jeff answered. As he thought about it, he didn't find much of an answer. "I'm workin' for a widow woman, owns a boarding house. Split wood, do some paintin', milk a cow. Not much. Just tryin' to kill the winter."

Will nodded, a faintly pained look on his face. "She got a good stove?"

Jeff frowned a little. "Yeah, I reckon it's warm enough. And she's a good cook."

Will sought to retrieve the earlier good feeling. "Well, we can always use a top hand around here. Chuck's tasty and plenty, and there's a deep string of good ponies. You might talk to the boss."

Jeff seemed distracted. "Yeah. I'll think on it."

Will grinned. "Good. Hope ya' do. Now, I'm hungry and I'll bet you are, too. I'm for the cook shack. Night, pard." Without another word he turned and walked down the alley, whistling the same unknown tune.

Jeff smiled as he called after him. "Night yourself, pard."

•   •   •   •

"SEÑOR, you spoke of a reward?" The boy wiped damp palms on his apron, fearful of this hard-looking man, but borrowing courage from his desire for money.

Mano was brought back from images of revenge by the boy's words. "*Si, mijo*, I did. Do you know the direction the *gringo* rode from here?"

The boy nodded. "*Si*. We saw him the next morning, while most of the people of our village slept off their celebrating. He rode up out of the creek bottom, stopped at the *tienda*, and went inside. Not long after, he came out with a few things he had bought, packed his little *mulo*, got on his big horse, and left this place, leading *la grulla*."

Mano took a silver peso from his jacket pocket and flipped it in the air, catching it. "Which way did he ride?"

The boy worked up some moisture on his dry tongue. "*Norté, señor.*"

Mano looked at Pepé and motioned with his chin. "Let's go, *hermano*." Rising from his chair, Mano dug out more money and put five pesos in the hand of the delighted boy and patted his head.

Outside, Pepé looked strangely at his big brother. Mano noticed and said, "*Qué?*"

His younger brother said, "That was a lot of money you gave the little *niño*."

Mano smiled. "I love children. I thought you knew that?"

• • • •

THAT NIGHT at supper, Maggie showed off her purchases from the trip to Durango. A wool coat for her uncle Sandy. A big, cast iron skillet for Hortencia. A pair of elk skin gauntlets for her father. Copper rivets and waxed thread for tack repair.

"And nothing for yourself, lass," her father asked?

The girl blushed lightly and her uncle answered for her. "A few items in the nature of private garments, none of which bears discussion at this table."

Maggie smiled over at him affectionately, but with one eyebrow raised. "Thank you, Uncle Sandy. I think."

Jeff expressed thanks for the meal and rose to leave the table. Robert looked up. "Bide a wee, Jeff. I'd have a word with you." He resumed his seat, a little anxious. Sandy and his niece took their cue and excused themselves. As the dining room door shut behind them, Robert stood up, poured more coffee for Jeff and himself, and suggested they take their cups into his office.

The boss sipped silently, a notable departure from his customary slurp, and then looked across the desk at Jeff. "I had a brief conversation with Will Gunlock before supper. He says the two of you had a good ride."

Jeff nodded. "I thought so."

MacTeague went on. "He says you pay attention. Said you asked a number of intelligent questions. And he said you sit a horse as well as any man he's ridden with."

Jeff nodded again. "I'll have to thank him for the kind words."

Robert had a serious expression as he said, "Wasn't meant as a kindness. More of an evaluation. He thinks you'd likely make a good hand. I respect his judgment. And from what

I've seen so far, I'm inclined to agree with his estimate of you." Jeff saw it coming. Another job offer.

I must have a sign around my neck, he thought, and sure enough, when Robert continued, he said, "I'm offering you a job, a riding job. I want you to concentrate on starting our colts. I have a master horseman working here. An old *vaquero* named Joe Barr. From down south. Santa Barbara, Las Cruces, Santa Ynez. Rode for the Tejon Ranch. Worked all over that country. I've never seen a better hand with a horse. And an Anglo, studied under the best of the *Californio* bridle horse trainers. But he's getting long in the tooth, as it were. A little stiff to be starting colts. But I believe the two of you, working together, he in the role of teacher, you as his apprentice, for lack of a better term, could make great progress with our horse program. That is, if you wouldn't have a problem being answerable to another man. And I'm not saying that you are not an expert horseman in your own right." As if feeling that he was talking too much, MacTeague abruptly went silent.

Jeff felt he needed to give some response. "Well, I haven't said if need a job yet." Robert nodded. "But the chance to learn from a real old time *Californio amansadore* is mighty tempting. I reckon I'm a fair horse hand, but I'm not so dumb not to know that there's plenty I don't know, if that makes any sense."

Robert nodded again. "It makes perfect sense."

Jeff sipped his coffee to give himself time to frame his next words. "I like this country and I like the way this outfit operates. If I can ask, what're the terms?"

Now it was MacTeague who occupied himself with his coffee to buy time. Reverting to the usual slurp, he then set his cup down carefully and looked Jeff in the eye. "I expect a lot from my men, but I pay well for it. If you decide to hire on, I'll want long days and a high degree of dedication from you. But I'm inclined to think that's probably your style already."

Jeff held the man's gaze but showed nothing on his face. Robert continued. "You'll live in the bunkhouse with the rest of the crew, take your meals in the cook shack. I know you like the food up here at this table, but don't despair. Nacho is an excellent cook. I go down and eat with the men as often as I can, without offending Hortencia, which is something one should avoid, I assure you. Also, my foreman tells me you speak Spanish like a first language, so I would expect you to have no trouble with my *vaqueros*. Will Gunlock and Stogie Wilson would be your bunkmates. Will you've met, but not Wilson, I believe."

Jeff shook his head. "No, sir."

Robert made a dismissive gesture. "It's no matter. Wilson is much the same as Gunlock, good natured and hard working. I don't waste time on any other type of man."

He paused for some sort of response from Jeff, who said, "I wouldn't imagine so."

Robert nodded. "So, the pay is thirty-five dollars a month to start. If we're both still happy after ninety days, I'll raise you to forty. Thereafter, there'll be a two dollar a month raise each year. There will also be opportunities to earn bonuses. And after a time, again if all goes well, I'll allow you to run some stock of your own on ranch grass. That's a good deal for a cowboy. If you come to work here, you'll be one of the highest paid men on the place based on your horsemanship skills. I don't expect you to discuss your wage with any of my other employees. Juan Loera will know, as well as Joe Barr. Both of them make more than that, so there'll be no resentments." Jeff nodded, but kept his expression noncommittal. MacTeague took on a fatherly expression.

"I appreciate the fact that you are a young man. There will be a reasonable amount of free time, and Durango is only a short ride on a good horse. But I expect you to behave responsibly when not on duty. You will at all times be a representative of this ranch. Excessive drunkenness, chronic fisticuffs, or any form of dishonesty will result in immediate dismissal. If any of that sounds unfair, speak up now."

Jeff straightened his back. "When I hire on, I ride for the brand. What the boss says goes. Anyway, I got better things to do than fight and carouse."

MacTeague's look was all business as he responded, "Am I to take that as an acceptance, then?"

In the duration of no more than ten seconds, Jeff ran it all through his head. Good country. He wanted a piece of it. Good pay. As good as any riding job he'd had. A little free time, now and then. A chance to get into a game and supplement his income. Good chuck. Always a consideration for a man who liked to eat. A topnotch crew, from what he'd seen so far. A chance to study under a master horseman. And the clincher. Margaret Louisa MacTeague. Magic Maggie. But what about Addie Peach? A lot of fun, but sooner or later, a dead end. He rose part way out of his chair and reached across the table. "You got yourself a rider, Mr. MacTeague."

Robert leaned over and shook vigorously, the first real smile on his face that Jeff had ever seen there. "Good. Good!"

FOURTEEN

PEPÉ DUMPED an armload of dry *piñón* branches next to the fire and sat back down on his saddle blanket. It was another bitterly cold night. Mano was in such foul temper that his little brother had avoided speaking for over an hour. They had ridden out of Chama with high expectations, but ten days of searching the country to the north and west had turned up nothing. No one would admit to having seen a tall young *Americano* with a big buckskin gelding, a smoke-blue mare, and a red mule. It was as though the four of them had disappeared into cold, thin air.

The night they had spent in Chama had brought them close to the end of their road stake. They were now subsisting on the stringy flesh of an old cow elk they had found limping along on a broken leg. It was a wonder that a wolf or a pack of coyotes had not seen her first or they would not even have had that.

"All right," growled Mano, "now that you have brought more wood, throw some on the fire, *estupido!*"

Pepé complied without showing offense. He had long ago learned that it was far better for him to absorb his brother's insults quietly than to respond with resentment. On rare occasions, Mano would even show a bit of contrition, as he did now. "Forgive me, *hermanito*. This cold weather and bad meat has me in an evil mood. I thought that we would have this business finished by now."

Pepé took Mano's apology as his cue to speak freely. "I know, brother. I am sick of this trail as well. I wish the *gringo* would walk into the firelight right now so we could shoot him and be done with it and head back south, out of these cursed, cold mountains."

Mano smiled. Simple minded as Pepé seemed, there were times when he "hit the nail on the head," as the *gringo* cowboys would say.

"Would that it could be that easy, *hermanito.*"

· · · ·

SHORTLY AFTER JEFF left his new employer's office, their business concluded for the moment, Maggie came in with a pot of coffee, her thought having been to refresh the men's cups. On seeing her father alone in the room, her face fell ever so slightly, but not so slightly as to escape his sharp-eyed notice. Holding out his empty cup, he said "Thank you, my dear. How thoughtful," and gave her a smile.

Having filled his cup, the girl seemed momentarily at a loss for words and her father came to her aid. "That guest of ours, young Mr. Cameron?"

He let the question dangle until Maggie, with mild suspicion said, "Yes? What about him?"

He looked her in the eye for a few beats and then answered with another question. "Any thoughts?"

Maggie put a vaguely guarded look on her face. "What are you getting at, Da'? You're being rather obscure."

Her father sipped his coffee, set the cup down, leaned back with his elbows on the chair arms, and tented his fingers. "I just wondered what impressions, if any, you might have of him."

She set the pot down on a newspaper that covered a corner of the desk. Folding her arms, she gave her father a still suspect look. "Well," she began haltingly, "he, uh, seems a decent sort, I suppose. A little roughhewn, perhaps, but regular enough."

Robert nodded. "You've ridden with him, correct?"

She nodded in turn. "I have."

Her father rubbed his chin and asked, "How is he with a horse?"

Now the girl was unable to entirely guard her expression. Warmth came to her eyes as she answered. "Very good, Da'. He's not only excellent in the saddle, but he has a calm, intelligent way with them. It's as if he's able to connect with a horse on some mental level. But that's not quite it. It seems almost like some sort of spiritual bond he has with them."

Her father nodded more vigorously. "Good. Very good. I must say it sounds a bit mysterious, but I trust your judgment. How would you feel about the possibility of his joining the crew here?"

Maggie's eye's widened only a fraction as she said, "You mean you intend to offer him a position?"

Robert colored slightly. "Well, my dear, the fact is that I already have."

She held her breath a moment and then asked, "And?"

The father met the daughter's gaze. "He accepted."

She inhaled and let it out slowly, her face showing nothing. "Well, Da', you engage and dismiss men as need be and seldom ask my opinion one way or another. I find it interesting that you ask it now, but after the fact."

He was at a brief loss for words but finally said, "Well, my girl, you're getting of an age to start sharing in the management of the ranch, make some use of that expensive education, so I thought..."

She finished for him. "So you thought you'd hire him and then ask me how I felt about it, as opposed to the other way around?"

He rolled his eyes. "Oh, for pity's sake lass, I didn't intend for this to become a contest. Have I done such a terrible thing? Is the thought of the lad around here so repulsive?"

Maggie picked up the coffee pot and turned for the door. Answering over her shoulder, so he could not see the bright look on her face, she said, "Actually, Da', not so much."

• • • •

A ROARING BLAZE of mixed *piñón* and gamble oak was throwing waves of heat from the river stone fireplace into the main living room as Jeff went in after his interview with the laird of the estate. He witnessed Sandy surreptitiously smoking his briar, sitting on the hearth, and carefully exhaling the noxious fumes up the chimney flue.

Jeff cleared his throat. The old man was dismayed at having been caught. "By God, sir!" he blurted in exaggerated indignation, "Be so courteous as to make a wee bit o' noise in yer comings and goings aboot this house."

Jeff grinned as he crossed the room to sit in a cowhide chair opposite his momentarily red-faced friend. "You better douse that stinkin' thing before the boss comes out of his office." Sandy gave him a look of irritation as he knocked the embers out of the pipe bowl on the hearthstones, sweeping them into the ashes of the fire with a hand.

Jeff sat quietly as Sandy tucked his pipe away in a pocket of his vest. Presently he took a seat in a deep, leather chair customarily reserved for the laird, as if to exhibit a touch of defiance.

"Well," he spoke with recovering dignity, "you and me baby brother were sequestered in there for some little while. What did he have to say?"

Jeff grinned. "Oh, this and that."

Sandy rolled his eyes. "Lord God, not this again."

Taking a wooden match out of a shirt pocket and putting it between his teeth, Jeff said, "I kinda' think that's his business. And mine."

Sandy narrowed his eyes. "Why you ungrateful pup. After I took in your starvin' carcass and treated you like my own son, you have the cowardly gall to side with Robert against me? That's foul doin's indeed, mon." He delivered the lines like a Shakespearean.

Jeff laughed out loud. "You missed your callin' old friend. With your talent, you could have made a fortune on the stage."

Sandy straightened in the chair. "Enough of bandying words back and forth. As your friend and mentor, I'd think I'm rightly privy to the topic of your interview."

Jeff put his feet up on the hearth. The heat penetrated his thin riding boots. "Oh, hell. He offered me a job."

Sandy leaned forward eagerly, elbows on bony knees. "I rather thought he might." Jeff smiled passively at the old man until the latter fairly burst out, "Well Jayzuss, boy, what did you say?"

Slowly, Jeff removed the match from his mouth and said simply, "I took it."

Sandy sat back and smiled hugely. "That's grand, lad. Just grand. When do you start?"

A puzzled look crossed Jeff's face. "Well," he answered a little foolishly, "we didn't get to that."

The Scot shook his head. "No matter. Time enough for details. The thing is that he offered, and you accepted. Now we have to plan our return to Pagosa to settle your affairs and pack your kit for the move back."

Jeff was feeling too good to be annoyed with his presumptuous supporter, but he did manage a small frown as he said, "*We* gotta do what? Since when are you my business manager?"

Sandy affected a hurt expression. "Just trying to be of service, lad."

Jeff relented quickly. "All right, but just don't try too hard. Besides, I'm in no big lather to leave, unless you think we've worn out our welcome already."

Sandy smiled at the recollection of catching his niece in unguarded moments, studying his young friend. "No, lad, I'm certain your welcome remains secure. The laird of this castle, however, me wee brother, might be inclined otherwise as to an extended duration of mine."

•   •   •   •

JOE BARR sat on the stoop of his tiny cabin, his first cup of coffee of the morning on a stool next to his chair and a rawhide *bosal* with horsehair *mecaté* reins on his lap. His corded hands were at work twisting the headstall out of shape and tangling the reins in knots and snags. An old, bitch dog that looked to be half collie and half hound dozed at his feet, curled up on a saddle blanket. Due to his position as horse master, as well as his years of loyal service to the MacTeagues, he was spared the indignity and lack of privacy that life in the bunkhouse would mean for a man his age. Upon his next birthday he would be sixty-two years old. His wife was long dead. There was a daughter named Jodie, living in southern California. Not counting the dog, he was alone in the world.

He was still lean and tough, but lately pains from some of his old injuries were visiting him with increasing regularity. A colt had flipped over on him five years before and left his lower back especially stiff on cold days. The leg he had broken as a thirty year old, when a cow he'd roped turned back and drove him and his horse over a steep cut bank, hurt to one degree or another most all the time any more. But no one had ever heard him complain about his aches and pains. They were no more than an uncomfortable testimony to the life he had lived and loved, and still loved.

His best friend on the place was the cook, Nacho Ramirez. On the rare occasions when they had free time together, the two aging *vaqueros* would sit drinking coffee and trading stories about the old days. Once in a while, they would permit some of the riders to sit in and listen. The younger men were taken by the tales of these legendary pioneers of the western beef industry, and always begged for more when the old men were tired and done.

This particular morning, he was keeping an eye on the horse barn, waiting for that new kid, what the hell was his name? The one that the Boss's shiftless brother had brought along on his latest visit to lay around, eat ranch beef, and do nothing. Cameron, was it? Something like that. First name Jake? No. Was it Jeff? Yeah, that was it. Jeff Cameron.

The Boss had hired him to be Joe's apprentice, whatever the hell that meant. Said he was to be Joe's helper, but more than that, more like a student, and that Joe was supposed to teach him how to finish a horse in the style of the old time *Californios*. As if he could teach some damn kid in a year or two what it had taken him a lifetime to learn, was still learning. And nobody had offered to teach *him*.

Back down there in Santa Barbara, as a shirttail kid, he had to lay in the brush outside the corrals and spy on those old timers, getting bit by sand fleas and deer flies, and collecting burrs in his britches and under his shirt. Nobody offered to make him their apprentice, either, whatever the hell that meant. And he never would have got his start if old Chico Garza hadn't caught him lying out in the weeds and watching, because that colt Chico was working winded Joe and spooked at him, and gave him away.

The old man had jerked him to his feet and started to whip his ass, then thought better of it. Said "*Muchacho*, how come you to spy on me?"

And Joe said, "I want to learn to make a horse, be a true horseman."

And Chico said, "You think you can learn that from watchin' me?"

Joe said, "Yeah, maybe."

And Chico says, "You want to be a real horseman, then?"

And Joe, he answers, with his bony, little chest out, "Hell, yes! That's what I just said!"

"All right," says Garza. "We'll see."

So for six months, Joe got to feed and water and fork up horseshit and pull tails and pick cockle burrs out of manes. And for another six months he got to trim feet and curry coats and hot walk and brace sore tendons, and fork up more shit, and never got close to getting on a horse. But he watched every move the old man made.

Then, finally, Chico stops him one morning while he's pushing a wheelbarrow full of guess what and says "Kid, in a whole year, you ain't complained once, so I reckon maybe you do want to be a horseman after all."

"Sure as hell!" says Joe.

So Chico grins and says "All right, dump your load and then go take down that lightweight saddle hanging in the barn, the one I put on the colts for their first ride. Then catch that little claybank filly. She's ready. We'll see if you are."

And Joe *was* ready and he worked with that old man ten years, 'til Chico died.

Just then Jeff came out of the barn and Joe called to him. He'd been checking on his stock. Had done it every morning, whether he rode or not. Joe liked that much about him, anyway. Watched him ride out from headquarters a time or two. Sat a horse nice, had to give him that. Will Gunlock, who was no expert but a pretty fair hand, said that Cameron was a sure enough rider. Well, maybe. We'll have to see. He sipped at his coffee.

"Hey, son!" Joe called from the porch, making himself sound agreeable. "Have you got a minute?" Jeff stopped and turned to look. Joe waved him over with the hand that held the coffee cup, slopping a little on the old dog at his feet, which if she noticed didn't seem to mind. "Come on over here a minute." Jeff swung that way and began to cover the thirty yards that separated them.

The dog lifted her head and growled at him listlessly, more a formality than a true warning. "Shut up, Daisy," Joe said mildly. She thumped her tail a few times on the porch boards and then laid her head back down and began to snore.

"What can I do for you, sir," Jeff asked? He had manners. Joe liked that too. Showed respect.

"Drag that chair over here and set," he answered. The kid did as told. "I can't imagine how I got this thing in such a snarl." He gave the bridle to Jeff, who'd been on the verge of offering his hand to shake. "I got that damn arthur ritus so bad, I can't hardly do nothin' anymore. These here knuckles is on fire. See if you can fix this mess for me, son."

It took him about five minutes to untangle the knotted up hackamore. He was patient and didn't get frustrated. Handing it to the old man when done, he said, "Almost seems like somebody went out of their way to do this." Joe didn't comment. "I guess you'd be Mr. Barr," Jeff said.

Joe nodded. "Well, I'm Joe anyway. Or what's left of him."

Jeff offered to shake. "Good to meet you. I'm Jeff Cameron."

Joe took Jeff's hand gingerly. "Easy on them knuckles, son." After that he made a point of ignoring the young cowboy, rubbing the rawhide noseband between his thumbs and gazing out over the valley as if his mind were a thousand miles away.

Finally, Jeff asked, "Can I do anything else for you, Mr. Barr?"

The old man nodded again. "Yeah. Leave off with the 'Mr. Barr' stuff. I'm just Joe."

Jeff stood up. "You bet, Joe. See you around."

Joe Barr looked up and gave him a faint smile. "Sure thing. And thanks for the help."

Down off the porch, Jeff said, "My pleasure, sir."

He watched the kid striding away toward the big house, noting the loose, athletic motion of his gait. "Well, boy," he said to himself, "you passed the first test. Most kids would of got all aggravated with that knotted up hackamore. Not you. You took your time. Didn't get frustrated. Just worked it out with soft, slow hands. Showed me two of the most important things a horseman needs. Patience. And good hands. This might work out all right."

Looking down at the dog he said, "Nice fella. Too bad my Jodie never found nobody like that. Never will, I expect. Talks too much. Laughs too loud."

• • • •

HE WAS HEADING to the main house when he saw Will Gunlock and another rider standing on the porch of the cook shack, hunched in their saddle coats and sipping coffee. Gunlock spotted him at the same time and called out, "Hey, Jeff," and grinned.

He turned that way and crossed the yard. Stepping up on the boards, he shook with Gunlock. "How goes it, Will?"

"Toll'able. Just toll'able. How 'bout you?"

"All right," Jeff answered.

Will turned to the man beside him. "Jeff, meet Stogie Wilson, terror of the four corners country. Stogie, this here is Jeff Cameron."

Wilson smiled as he shook. "Aw, that ain't hardly so. I'm plumb peaceable." The first thing Jeff noticed about the man was the source of his nickname. He had the butt of an unlit cigar protruding about two inches from the corner of his mouth. Otherwise, he seemed unremarkable for the business he was in. Five foot seven or eight inches tall. Thickset, with wide shoulders and a deep chest. Maybe a hundred and seventy-five pounds. Somewhat stockier than average. Early thirties.

A beat up hat that had once been silverbelly but now was sweat stained and filthy sat cocked a little on his head. Shotgun chaps and spurred boots. He stood relaxed and easy, no pretense, just an air about him that said, "This is me, take it or leave it," and giving the impression of quiet competence. Jeff found he liked him immediately.

"So, are you signin' on," Will asked?

Jeff nodded. "Looks like it. Boss made an offer. I took it."

Will bobbed his head and grinned wider. "Good. Now I'll have somebody decent to work with." He punched Wilson lightly on the shoulder as he said it. Without looking around, Wilson gave Gunlock a sideways kick in the shin, but not hard.

Jeff chuckled. "Say, Will," he said, "I been meaning to ask you a little favor. I'll be heading over to Pagosa one of these times to get my plunder. Got some loose ends to tie up over there. Could be a couple weeks gettin' back here. I'm leaving my mare. I'uz hopin' you might get a chance to ride her a time or two."

Will's face lit up. "I'd admire to. I been lookin' her over. She's nice."

Stogie chimed in. "Think on it, Jeff. He don't ride too good."

Gunlock gave him a grim look. "Shut up, Stogie. I can ride anything with hair on it and you damn well know it."

Wilson's eyes sparked with devilment. Without missing a beat he came back with, "That so? Then how 'bout that whore over to Chimney Rock last spring? Remember? The big redhead they call the Buffalo Calf? Looked like she'd dress out about two-forty? As I recall, she bucked you plumb out of the sack. Left you with a foot hung in that brass bed frame and a broke big toe. I guess that was somethin' with hair on it you couldn't ride."

Jeff glanced at Will and then Stogie and burst out laughing, and couldn't stop. Will's face went purple and he made a grab for Stogie, but was too slow. Wilson ducked in the door of the cook shack, Gunlock hot on his heels. As Jeff strolled off, still laughing, he heard crashing inside, accompanied by the voice of Nacho Ramirez, cursing in Spanish at the top of his lungs.

•   •   •   •

"SO," SAID Robert MacTeague, across his desk from his new hire, "How long to conclude your affairs in Pagosa Springs?"

Jeff scratched his bristly jaw. "Well, I reckon about two weeks round trip," he answered, "depending on the weather. I'm honor bound not to leave Mrs. Peach in a tight. But even if I can't find a man right away to pick up my slack, I expect I can put the place in decent enough shape to get her through 'til spring, and still be back here in good time."

MacTeague nodded. "I appreciate the fact that you feel an obligation to do right by your soon to be former employer. Reassures me that once you're working here, you'll do as you said, in your cowboy vernacular, and 'ride for the brand.'" Jeff grinned. He was going to learn some twenty-dollar words from this boss.

"Now," said Robert, reaching into a drawer of his massive oak desk, "Take this." He held out a small, leather poke containing what sounded very much like coins contacting each other.

Jeff lifted his hand, palm upraised. "I don't need anything just now, Mr. MacTeague."

His new employer pressed the bag on him. "Don't be absurd, lad. If you're like most cowhands I've known, you're not made of money."

Jeff reddened faintly. "Well, no. I guess not."

Robert reached across the desk for Jeff's hand, turned it up, and placed the poke in it. "This is not charity. Call it a signing bonus, if that eases your mind. You will certainly incur some expense in relocating here. I feel it only good business practice to assist in that effort. Ensures you'll get here all the quicker, in a good frame of mind to commence your duties, without undue financial stress, don't you know."

Jeff hefted the little bag in his hand. It was heavy. "All right. When you put it that way, it don't sound so bad. And I'm gonna earn it, Mr. MacTeague."

The man threw up both hands. "Oh for God's sake, boy. I detest titles. Call me Robert. Just not in front of the crew. In which case, then, it's Boss."

Jeff smiled. "Okay, Boss," he said. And that was a word that he thought to himself was a title if ever there was one.

He set the bag down on the corner of the desk and tried to figure out how to say what he now wanted to say. The fact was, he didn't want to just rush off to Pagosa and turn around and rush back. There were several reasons for this. To begin with, he liked it here. They'd been at the ranch only a few days, and Sandy was reveling in his niece's company. And she obviously loved her smelly old uncle dearly and spoiled him and doted on him shamelessly.

Another consideration was that in this atmosphere he felt more himself, more the cowboy, more the horseman. Less the boarding house roustabout, the splitter of firewood, the painter of bedrooms, the milker of a dairy cow, and the servant to the biological requirements of his lusty employer. Not the sort of job description a man of his cut and ambitions could rightly stay proud of. Which brought to mind the confrontation that was looming between him and that particular woman.

The thought of one woman turned his mind to another. A younger, darker, and more slender one. One who sat a horse as though she shared the same skeleton, the same flesh and blood. He was nowhere near ready to be gone from her just yet. And as he indulged that thought, MacTeague looked up to see him still standing before his desk. The boss sat back in his captain's chair and looked his new rider in his uncertain eye.

"Was there something else then, Jeff?"

He straightened his spine and said, "Well, sir, I was just thinking...I mean, well..."

MacTeague frowned slightly. "Come now, lad, say what's on your mind. I've other matters to attend."

"All right," he forged ahead after a breath. "I just thought I might start sooner. Like maybe I could ride out a few days with Will and Stogie, see more of the ranch before Sandy and I go back. Kinda' get my feet wet. Then, when I get back, I'll have a leg up on the job. And I'll feel more like I deserve this." Saying that, he picked up the leather poke and hefted it in his hand.

The boss knit his brows for a quarter minute before speaking. Jeff worked hard to keep steady eye contact. At last MacTeague spoke. "And how long do you suppose this 'wetting of the feet' might take?"

"Oh, I reckon four or five days. No more'n a week. And the longer we wait to head back, the closer we are to spring and the better the traveling weather."

Robert nodded. "I'll grant you a certain logic in that. But you don't know what you're asking. This means I have to countenance that wastrel brother of mine all that extra time." He looked mildly stricken.

Jeff risked a faint grin. "He ain't all that bad, is he?"

MacTeague grunted, "You didn't grow up with him. But that's not your concern. I suppose I can put up with him if he can put up with me." Thus decided, he continued, "All right, lad. I think it's a sound idea. You may arrange it with Gunlock and Wilson, on my authority. And I'll speak to Juan Loera. Now, off with you. I've paperwork."

Jeff left the office with a sense of victory. He'd managed to postpone what was almost certain to be an uncomfortable interview with Addie Peach and, more importantly, he could continue his present opportunity to see that much more of the intriguing Maggie.

•   •   •   •

HE WAS COMING down the stairs from his second floor bedroom at MacTeague headquarters, his gear and possibles rolled up and thrown over his shoulder, on his way to the bunkhouse to take his place among the other riders. The aroma wafting up the stairwell from Hortencia's kitchen made his mouth water like a hungry dog's. But this was to be his first day on the crew and he figured it best to take his breakfast with the men.

He was focused and looking forward to the prospect of proving himself in his new position. So focused, in fact, that he failed to notice the dark-haired girl in the upstairs hall, watching him pass on the stair. He was halfway to the bottom when she spoke.

"Jeff," she called tentatively. He stopped and turned, looked back up the way he had come. She was in a cotton wrapper tied close at the throat and her face showed the sleep she'd just left. Her hair was down, still mussed from the pillow, and he caught his breath. She looked so like a little girl, all dreamy and warm and ready to be held, that it was all he could do not to drop his outfit and lunge back up the stairs and take her in his arms.

Instead he said, "Mornin', Maggie," and stood there.

She smiled drowsily and walked further down the hall toward the head of the stairs, padding on bare feet. Putting a hand on the newel post she said, "Looks like you're leaving us. I thought Dad hired you."

He humped a shoulder to adjust his load, then answered. "No, no. I'm not pullin' out. Just moving to the bunkhouse. When'd you hear?"

She cocked her head. "What? That you're working here?"

He nodded. "Yeah. I guess your dad told you?"

She bobbed her head. "He did. Right after you came out of his office, after supper. It was a bit left handed."

Jeff looked puzzled. "How so?"

She smiled again. "He asked my opinion of you. Wanted to know what I thought of you working here. Then told me you were hired. I asked what good was my opinion if you were already on the payroll." She turned quiet, looking Jeff in the eye, waiting for some response.

He shifted his weight, then said, "Your opinion means something to me." He stood and waited.

She turned back toward her bedroom and for a moment he thought she was going to ignore him. Then she stopped and looked at him over her shoulder. "You going to the cook shack for breakfast?"

He nodded. "Figured I ought to."

She shook her head the least bit. "Eat once more with us. I'll be down in a few minutes."

He couldn't stop the grin that took charge of his face. "Sure, Maggie. You bet."

•   •   •   •

JEFF LOOKED over the rim of his coffee cup and across the table at Sandy, regretting it instantly. A string of egg yolk ran from his lower lip into his bristly chin whiskers. Jeff kicked his mentor under the table and pointed to his napkin, which hung from the collar of his buckskin shirt. Sandy missed the hint and blurted, "What in hell are you kicking me for?"

This exclamation, of course, brought him to the attention of the others at the table and in seconds Maggie burst out laughing, to be followed by her father. Sandy turned purple and roared, "What is this, by God!"

From the seat to his left, his niece took her own napkin and wiped his mouth and beard for him. "Just a run of the old egg, Uncle. Nothing to twist your kilt over." Sandy saw the evidence on Maggie's napkin and then jerked at his own with a growl, scrubbing his mouth.

Jeff forced himself to stop laughing, but wiping the grin off his face was beyond his powers of self-control. Sandy scowled at him with a look of menace. "Well," said his young friend, "I expect from now on we gotta hitch a bib up under your lip."

This unhelpful comment brought Sandy's frown upon Jeff all the more intently, and he rose slightly, clutching his breakfast knife like a dagger. His younger brother, still chuckling, raised a hand in a gesture of peace and said, "Compose yourself, Andrew. I'll not have my breakfast table a murder scene like some legendary Highland feud banquet, bathed in blood." Sandy sat back down, still sour.

As tranquility returned, Robert looked toward Jeff and said, "Well, lad, this is an auspicious morning indeed. Your first on the Claymore payroll. I suppose you'll team up with Gunlock and Wilson and begin to absorb some of their knowledge of our operation."

Jeff opened his mouth to agree, but was cut off by the determined voice of the lady of the house. "On the contrary, Da'. I've plans for Mr. Cameron, for today at least." It was most certainly a statement of fact, and bore no semblance to a request.

Robert sat back in his chair as if pushed. "Is that a fact now, lass?"

Maggie bobbed her head with a hint of iron in her eye. "That is correct. Inasmuch as you recently told me that it was time for me to take a greater hand in the running of the ranch, please consider this my first official act." Her father opened and then weakly shut his mouth.

Maggie went on. "The situation is as follows. I want apple pie for desert tonight. That, by itself, is not earthshaking. However, Hortencia informs me that the few apples left in the cellar are shriveled and well below standard for one of her creations. Therefore, I require the services of our new rider to assist me in a trip over to Apricio's orchard for some good ones. We'll take one of the mules and pack at least two bushels, as well as some pears and dried apricots, if he has any." After a brief pause for breath, she smiled her sweetest, most disarming smile at her father and asked, "Questions?"

Robert MacTeague could only shake his head slowly and reply with an agreeable, "No, dear. None a'tall. A fine idea. Apple pie sounds heavenly. And I suppose Jeff can ride out with Will and Stogie tomorrow. That acceptable to you, lad?"

Jeff did his best not to let his face split wide open from ear to ear. Trying to sound nonchalant, he said. "Sure thing. I can always tie in to a big slice of apple pie."

Feeling a little more himself again and left out of the apple pie negotiations so far, Sandy declared louder than need be, "Aye. One of the great things about these United States that no other land on airth can match. Apple pie! I fancy a slice or two mesel', with a chunk o' rat cheese on the side."

Maggie giggled, stood, and raised her coffee cup. "The old rat himself has spoken. It's apple pie by decree!"

·   ·   ·   ·   ·

APRICIO CRUZ lived a mile up Hermosa creek from where the wagon road to Durango crossed it, over a bridge of railroad timbers and ties. The newly laid out Denver and Rio Grande right of way was only a couple of hundred yards to the east. No one knew Cruz's exact age, himself included, but he was believed older than most anyone in that end of the valley and undoubtedly had seen at least eighty winters.

The old Spaniard, for he had been born in Andalusia, had come to this place more than thirty years before, having drifted in as a man of middle age from a mission in California. It was a mystery at first as to why the Utes had not killed him outright when he appeared in their territory so long ago. But he was a mild and friendly man, and troubled no one.

The warriors decided, moreover, that he must be crazy to come into their land alone. Not wanting to offend the spirits who surely must be protecting one such as he, they let him be.

Having brought with him seeds from the mission, he planted an orchard of apples, pears, apricots, and peaches, and later on kept bees, as well. After a number of years, he had fruit to trade with the local tribesmen, and honey, which they relished. One more reason not to molest him. He even took a native wife and treated her kindly. She died birthing their first child, a boy who lived only a few hours longer that day than his mother. The Utes were Apricio's in-laws by then and remained his protectors.

He also tended goats and made cheese, and had a large garden from which he harvested corn, beans, and *chiles*. In the fall, his in-laws saw to it that he had plenty of elk meat and venison, which they were happy to trade for his produce.

As time passed, the Utes steadily were displaced by white settlers and, though Cruz was sad to see the uprooting of his kin by marriage, he was a practical enough survivor to make a point of getting on with the new residents. So when Robert MacTeague staked out his headquarters two miles south under the red sandstone bluffs, the considerate old orchard man and beekeeper was all the more pleased to find in him a good neighbor and a decent man.

Apricio's trees stood bare on that late winter morning when Jeff and Maggie came riding up the creek to buy apples. But he had bushels of them in his deep root cellar, along with dried apricots and home-canned peaches, as well as pears still so plump they seemed to have come off the branch only days before.

The two young folks had left the breakfast table in high spirits, even if somewhat at Sandy's expense. The crusty Scot had skulked from the table after a last laugh about the old rat and his rat cheese, but Maggie and Jeff knew his annoyance would be short lived. It always was. He was sure to be in fine fettle by the time pie graced the table that night.

They rode over the trestle bridge a little before nine o'clock that morning, the hooves of the horses and the mule echoing with a hollow note off the dancing water in the fast moving creek below. Jeff was unexpectedly in rapture, having been plucked from cowboy chores to ride with this girl who now reined her young stallion down off the end of the bridge and onto the trail that turned west to parallel Hermosa creek for another mile, which would bring them to the orchards, hives, and gardens of the old pioneer, Apricio Cruz.

•   •   •   •

JEFF WAS twisted 'round in his saddle to check on the mule and make sure it managed to get off the bridge and on solid ground without mishap. He often thought that the ideal packer would be able to swivel his head completely around, front to back, easily and often so as to keep an eye on his pack string. There was a constant concern about wrecks caused by recalcitrant animals, unbalanced packs, or just plain bad luck. Turning back forward, he was struck again by the captivating sight of the girl on the stallion.

As if she could hear his thoughts, she cocked her chin and spoke over her shoulder. "I hope I didn't disappoint you by overruling Da' this morning. You could be riding the range with Will and Stogie." There was a faint hint of mischief and question in her statement.

Jeff debated with himself as to how candid he should be. He couldn't very well admit yet that he'd rather be where he was now, with her, than any other place on earth. On the other hand, he didn't want her to think that it didn't much matter either way.

Trying to pick his words with care, he said, "I doubt those boys will miss me, and I can catch up with them tomorrow. As for right now, I'm enjoying the scenery." He let that hang in the air. She could take it however she liked. What he couldn't see was the faint blush and smile on her face.

"Well," she said, "I could do this by myself well enough. While I'm no expert packer, I can certainly manage a couple bushels of apples."

There was no inflection in her voice and for a second Jeff thought he had underplayed the thing too much. But he was determined to consider his reply with extreme caution, as he knew very well how talented he was at saying stupid things to this girl. He decided on honesty without mush. "I'm happy to help, Maggie. I like ridin' with you."

That seemed to hit her all right. "Same here," she answered. "And you're learning more of the territory in the process."

They went quiet for a time, and then Jeff could smell wood smoke wafting toward them in the cold air. A minute more and he saw a layered haze above trimmed tree branches a couple of hundred yards ahead. Before he could mention it, Maggie turned her head to him and said, "We're about there. Apricio's cabin is just up ahead, and you can see the tops of the trees in his orchard from here."

The next thing to catch Jeff's attention was the sound of an axe biting into wood. And then they were on the edge of a five-acre clearing and there, next to a small stone and timber house, was a thin old man, splitting rounds of pine with accurate, economical strokes undoubtedly honed from years of practice.

The riders were noticed by an aged, collie type dog that had left her place by the man's side. She trotted out to greet the newcomers with a round of barking that sounded a little like warning, but with no real threat in it.

Maggie put the stallion into a lope and called to the dog. "Hey, Carmelita. Don't you remember me?" The dog's ears went down, and an expression came to her face that could only be called a smile. She began wagging her tail so hard it took the rest of her body with it.

The woodchopper had turned toward them at the dog's first announcement and Jeff thought that if this old timer had a tail of his own, it would be wagging now, too. His smile was broad and his eyes sparkled. Having buried the axe bit in the chopping block, he came to meet his visitors as fast as his stiff legs could bring him.

"Margarita! How sweet of you to come see a tired *viejo.*" Stepping up beside her stirrup, he took her smooth hand in both his wrinkled ones. Maggie leaned down and kissed the top of his head. His smiling face seemed to lose ten years.

"The way that split wood is piling up, you look anything but tired," she said.

"Well, you know, these old bones don't like the cold so much these days. It takes a hot stove to keep this blood circulating." Looking back at Jeff, he asked, "And who is this young man with the wide shoulders?"

Jeff stepped down off the buckskin and made his own introduction in formal Spanish. "I am Jeff Cameron, *maestro.* I just started work for *El Rancho de los MacTeagues.*" Reaching out and taking the old man's thin hand gently, he shook it cordially and said, "*Mucho gusto, señor. A sus ordenes.*"

The man's mouth was open as he looked from Jeff to Maggie. She grinned wide. "Jeff is from Texas. He learned Spanish from the *vaqueros* he worked with there. His accent is very good, no?"

Cruz returned his eyes to Jeff, shaking his head. "He sounds like it is his first language."

Maggie was still smiling as she said, "He is a fine horseman and we are very fortunate to have him on our crew." Jeff looked up at the girl, but she would not meet his eyes.

Cruz sensed the wary care with which the young people treated each other. "Where are my manners? There is a pot of strong coffee on the stove, and I have been experimenting with a new cobbler made with apples and home-canned peaches. Please see to your animals and come inside. I must fill my wood box."

While the old man retrieved an armload of pine splits, Maggie led Jeff and their animals into a small barn, which was occupied by a little brown molly mule and half a dozen goats, housed in dry stalls and eating wild cut hay. The goats were munching something else, as well, which Jeff thought looked like apple peelings.

"Let's unsaddle," Maggie said. "I'd like to make a visit of it. He's a wonderful man and I don't get to see him as often as I should."

Jeff began stripping the gear off the buckskin. "I like him already. It's a tidy little operation he's got here."

"I love him dearly," Maggie began to explain. "He's been like a grandfather to me over the years. He half raised me. I rode here often when I was little. With patience and kindness, he taught me what he knew about gardening and orchard care. And beekeeping. I want fruit trees of my own someday. And hives."

Jeff kept his eyes on his work as he thought to himself, "Peaches and honey, with long, black hair."

•   •   •   •

"AND SO, my young friends," said Cruz, after pouring mugs of steaming, tar-black coffee, "you must submit yourselves to my experimentation." Turning to his small, wood range, he took down potholders from a hook in the wall beside it and removed a deep, iron skillet from the oven. A sweet, hot aroma filled the room as the bent, old man set the dessert on the sill of an open window to cool. Topping up their cups, he sat down in a chair he had made himself to wait for the cobbler to cool enough for Jeff and Maggie to sample it.

As the three made small talk, a lean, black cat appeared, jumped into Jeff's lap, and began purring as she rubbed her face against his leather vest.

"*Gatita!*" exclaimed Cruz, as he made to take a swipe at her.

Jeff sheltered her with his hands and said, "That's all right, *maestro*. I like cats."

The old man scratched his head through his snow-white hair. "And that one likes you, *amigo*. Which is a great puzzlement to me. She showed up here a year ago, shy and wild. Only recently does she come to my bunk at night for a little attention. You must be a wizard for her to take to you so."

Jeff stroked her slowly and gently as she settled into his lap. "No, sir. No black magic. Most critters just know they can trust me."

•   •   •   •

THEY JUDGED the mixed apple and peach cobbler to be superb, and after another hour of more coffee and conversation a deal was struck for two bushels of apples and a big sack of pears and dried apricots. As Jeff packed the mule, Apricio presented Maggie with a gift of two large jars of home-canned peaches and one of honey. She thanked him with a long hug and a kiss on the cheek.

They were standing in the doorway of the cabin and, as he watched Jeff throw a tight box hitch over the mule's load, the little Spaniard took a side glance at Maggie's face. She seemed as captivated by the horseman as the black cat had been. Returning his attention to the packing, he said, "Margarita, it appears your papa has hired himself an exceptional young man."

The girl kept her eyes on Jeff and a half smile crossed her face as she replied. "Aye, grandfather. Hasn't he just."

•   •   •   •

IT WAS with considerable anticipation later in the evening that Robert, Sandy, Maggie, Jeff, and Juan Loera sat amid the remains of a standing rib roast of beef and the appropriate trimmings. All eyes were fixed on the door to Hortencia's kitchen. They leaned forward as one with an intake of breath as the door finally swung open, only to sit back in united disappointment for it was the granddaughter with a tray of coffee service. No one spoke as she poured and then set about clearing the table onto the same tray.

But no sooner had the girl disappeared back through the door than it swung out again to reveal Hortencia herself, a look of triumph on her face, with another tray that bore the biggest, the tallest, and the most stunning apple pie that Jeff had ever seen. It was truly a monumental tribute to the old lady's skill. Smiling with forgivable pride she said, "There eese wan more, eef theese wan don't make eet around the table."

As she bent to set the heavy tray down, Sandy beamed and said, "By God, it's lovely as a haggis," and he rose to his feet and raised his coffee cup. "Huzzah, huzzah," he cheered and in a moment each of the other diners had risen, and all smiled at the old cook and clapped their hands. She was entirely overcome, and with tears welling up in her eyes she covered her face with the tail of her apron and fled back into her kitchen.

• • • •

"WELL THEN, lad," said Robert MacTeague around the last mouthful of his second slice of pie, "I thank you for assisting Maggie in the delivery of the makings of this extraordinary dessert. But tomorrow, it's off with you to endeavors best accomplished from the back of a horse. That is, if my ranch manager here has no further claims upon your time."

Maggie looked up from her pie plate to see her father's eyes on her. After a moment to determine if he was making light, which his steady gaze suggested he was not, she answered. "Thank you, Da'. I'll do my best to live up to that title. And no, I do not require the services of the able Mr. Cameron. For now, anyway." All eyes were on her face as she gave Jeff the warmest smile she dared. And, inasmuch as all those other eyes were on her and not him, he thought he could risk her a small wink in return.

• • • •

JEFF SADDLED Buck with a keen sense of anticipation for his first real day on the job. He joined Will and Stogie after his first breakfast in Nacho's cook shack. A day of firsts. Nacho, who was fond of the new hire, went all out. Scrambled eggs with *chorizo* and *chiles*. Feather light pancakes, which he had learned to make from an old *gringo* cook at a previous place of employment. And coffee strong enough to float a mule shoe.

Out at the barn, Will saddled the same four-year-old bay he'd taken on their last ride together. Stogie's mount was a tall, rangy paint mare, hard as nails and no horse to go to sleep on. Jeff chose the big buckskin. Gunlock was in his usual good spirits as he swung into the saddle. Grinning at Jeff he said, "Take a deep seat, pilgrim. We got a lot of rough country to look at. And some fancy ropin' likely before day is done."

Jeff grinned back. "You gonna beat your gums all mornin' or do you want to ride?"

Stogie laughed out loud, then whooped and spurred his mare. She shot ahead and lined into the lane that led from the corrals to open ground. Will and Jeff fell in behind, and three eager cowboys on three fresh ponies left headquarters at a high lope.

• • • •

THERE ARE winter days when the southwest Colorado sky displays a certain pure shade of blue that is unmatched anywhere else. Jeff, Will, and Stogie rode out on such a day. Sheepskin or wool coats felt good at first, but by mid-morning wool shirts and leather vests were more than sufficient. Coats were tied behind cantles.

Will was in the lead, Stogie next, and Jeff last in line on a trail that wound its way downstream beside the Animas River. A mile south of headquarters, Will reined his bay colt down a worn cut in the riverbank, through skim ice, and into the water. A shallow ford across a wide riffle brought them to the far side. Upon dry ground again, Will stopped his horse and allowed it to paw through old, crusted snow for a bite of grass while he took out the makings and rolled a cigarette. Jeff drew rein beside him and did likewise. Stogie pulled up next to Jeff and took the cigar butt from his mouth and examined it critically.

"Got your money's worth out of that one yet, pard?" Will struck a match off a rusty concho on his chaps and lit up, squinting an eye against the curling smoke.

Stogie shook his head with a grin. "Nope," he said, and bit off and spat out the chewed portion of the cigar and put the remains back into his mouth. Rolling it with his tongue into the corner of his jaw where it normally rested, he commenced gnawing on it with visible satisfaction.

Jeff sat the buckskin and gazed across the valley to the timber and red rocks beyond. He narrowed his eyes to study details, the air so clear he expected he could see a bobcat sitting in a tree from where he sat his saddle, if one were doing so. Will noticed his intent look and asked, "What you got spotted?"

Jeff smiled and said, "Well, over at the foot of those cliffs, up on a pine limb, a chickadee's sittin' with a satisfied look on its face, scratchin' the side of its head with a foot. Its left foot."

Will kept a straight face and played along. "Hen or rooster?"

Jeff tried not to grin. "Can't tell. Put its foot down now."

Stogie took the cigar butt from his mouth and said dryly, "Okay, we all agree it's a nice, clear day. Let's ride."

· · · ·

WILL GESTURED briefly with an arm toward the mouth of a side canyon as he led them away from the river and across snow-matted grass toward the foot of timbered slopes. To neither companion in particular, Jeff asked, "What's the plan?"

Will answered. "Boss wants us to check the canyon yonder. It's protected and this time of year it's usually the best feed on our range. We try to keep the cattle out of there in case we get a late storm and need that grass, but we always seem to miss a few. We'll make a circle of it to see. It's pretty much wide open, so it won't take too long. There's a spring up toward the head end and it makes a little pond in some rocks, and it don't hardly ever freeze. If there's cows in there, they'll likely be close by."

It was a lovely setting. From the mouth of the canyon to the head end was maybe a mile, the walls narrowing gradually as the ground gently gained elevation. And it was wide open, as Will had indicated, with oak brush and aspen only along the base of the rising walls. A faint trail on the west side switched back up to a rocky headland, and Will led them to a point with a view of the bottoms.

Stopping his colt where there was room for the other two horses as well, he dug into his saddle bags and produced a collapsible monocular and snapped it out to full length. Putting it to an eye, he scanned the country below. "Can't see any critters at the moment, 'cept a spike bull elk way up above the spring. No beef cows." Going quiet as he continued looking, Jeff and Stogie were silent as well. At length Will said, "But that don't mean there ain't any to home. We need to ride back into them oaks and aspens and circle all that open ground, see if any Claymore critters is hid out."

Still scanning the terrain, he was about to collapse his spyglass when distant movement caught his eye. Raising it again, pointed toward the spring, he grinned and said, "Well, I'll be dipped. Lookee who just got up out of the rocks from his nap for a drink."

Stogie reached across from his saddle and unceremoniously wrested the monocular from Will's hand. After a few seconds to adjust the eye piece he said, "Sumbitch! If it ain't Old Striper."

Jeff strained his eyes to focus on the spring pool, a half a mile away. At the water's edge, with its head bent to drink, was a bovine of some sort, but without the aid of the glass, he couldn't tell if it was cow, bull, or steer. Stogie handed him the monocular. He distinguished a medium-sized bull, with broad, stiletto pointed horns, and a black and brown, brindled coat.

Its thirst apparently quenched, he saw it return to the rocks, slipping out of view. Jeff closed the glass and returned it to Will. The question was on his lips as Will spoke. "That brindle hide bastard is Old Striper. He showed up about two years ago. Don't know where he hails from, but he's Spanish. *Corriente,* maybe, with some fightin' blood mixed in. He managed to breed a dozen or so of our cows the first spring, and late last winter they dropped some ugly, bad tempered calves. We butchered all of them this last fall for meat. Now that you're getting your grub out of ol' Nacho's kitchen, you'll eat a plenty of it."

Jeff wet his lips and asked, "And you can't catch him?"

Stogie reached back and undid the lace that kept his Winchester in the scabbard. "Ain't tried to catch him. Boss put a bounty on him. First rider brings in his ears gets fifty dollars. But he's cagier than an old mossy horn buck. He's got one of my slugs in his ass. Nobody's got in good enough range for a clean shot."

Will nodded in agreement. "And there he sits a good four hundred yards from any sneakin' up cover. Good as ol' cigar butt here is with that rifle, that's just too long of a poke."

Jeff was hatching a plan in his head as he listened. When Will was done speaking, he said, "Let's catch him and cut him."

Both Will and Stogie turned to look at him as if he had lost his mind. "Do what?" they said together.

Jeff nodded enthusiastically, the grin on his face getting wider as he answered. "I'm from Texas, remember. I cut my teeth on hundreds of these wild, Mexican cattle. Them *vaqueros* down south wouldn't think twice about tacklin' an old devil like that."

Will shook his head. "You're one crazy *hombre*. But just for the sake of conversation, how'd you go about it?"

Jeff took out his makings and started to roll a smoke. "Easy as butterin' a biscuit. He's hid out in the rocks where we can't see him. But he can't see us neither. The wind is coming down the canyon right now and it'll keep on 'til it warms up a little more. If you two ride up above that spring, staying back in the trees 'til you're straight above him, then come out in the open where you catch the wind, that bull will get your scent and come out of there with a head of steam. In the meantime, while y'all are getting in position, me and Buck'll ride straight downwind to the low spot about fifty yards below that rock pile he's layin' in. He'll come baling out of there thinking about you two. When he comes past me he won't be more'n a hundred feet away. Buck can catch him, guaranteed. Then it's just a matter of droppin' a loop over them horns and fishin' the rope back around his hip and trippin' him. At the speed we'll be going, he'll hit so hard it'll knock the wind out of him for sure. I'll just hop down with my handy little piggin' string and tie up his feet. Buck'll keep the rope tight while I'm on the ground, and I'll take my bone handled knife and relieve Old Striper of his *huevos*. Then we'll turn him loose so he can contribute to the scenery, but not the breeding program. I'd like to see a big ol' Mexican steer now and then. It'd make me feel at home."

By the time Jeff had laid out his plan, both his companions were bobbing their heads and grinning like fools. Stogie turned to Jeff as the latter lit his cigarette. "You boys from down there sure know how to have a good time."

Will agreed. "This sounds like pure dee fun."

Jeff blew out smoke and said, "Thing to remember, you two got to keep the pressure on. He's got to have his full attention on you boys, so ride hard and push him like hell."

Stogie drew the Winchester out of its boot and levered a round into the chamber. Carefully letting the hammer down to half cock, he said, "I expect this'll probably work about like you say. But if it don't, then we'll do it my way."

• • • •

IT DID WORK like Jeff said. At first. He got to the low spot undetected, well before Will and Stogie were in position. He sat the buckskin with his *reata* in hand, a big loop tucked under his elbow to drop over the wide horns. The horse was excited and its muscles bunched, having been infected by the excitement communicated through his rider's seat. And for a while, they waited.

Jeff's eyes were focused on the edge of the timber above the spring. Any moment, his friends would appear. Their scent would be carried on the downhill breeze with the result that the bull would leave his refuge and make for timber. And there the tricky part came in. Jeff could not be seen, but he would not be able to see the bull either, not until he rose up with Buck out of the swale.

Timing was everything. If he moved too soon, the bull would break back to the rocky grove surrounding the spring where there was no room to swing a rope. Then it would be Stogie's business. If he didn't move soon enough, the bull would have gained too much ground across the canyon floor and even the fleet buckskin would never catch up, and the bull would make the trees and safety. The only way he could judge the right time would be by ear, hearing the bull charge out from cover.

And that's how it went. Will and Stogie cleared the trees and jogged toward the rocks, and in a little over a minute Jeff heard the sound of hard hooves in a hurry. It sounded like the bull was headed straight toward him, making for the scrub oak on his side of the canyon. And in the end, it was Buck who called it.

The big horse bolted up out of the swale, Jeff making no effort to hold him. Half a dozen long strides brought the pair in view of the running bull and, by God, he was right there, boring straight at them, as planned, and at no more than a hundred feet. Buck turned head on toward the bull and closed the distance like a jousting warhorse of old.

For the briefest moment, Jeff feared a collision of the two great skulls, hurtling into each other like runaway locomotives. But then the bull veered and in a scramble of snow and mud struck out on a new path for shelter in the direction of the timber on the other side of the canyon.

Old Striper never had a chance. The buckskin had half again the stride and speed of the brindle. As Jeff leaned in the saddle and began to spin his loop, he could hear the wild whooping of his friends behind him and out of his view, but coming at a hard run.

The ground was open and sloping slightly, clear of obstacles. Only twenty-five feet now separated the man on the horse and the panicked bull. And then they were there, where they needed to be, Buck putting Jeff in perfect position, just off the bull's left hip and no more than ten feet behind.

Jeff made his throw and the loop fluttered down over the horns like an alighting butterfly. The cowboy jerked just enough slack to tighten the loop, then spurred ahead and laid the rope over the bull's back to drop down behind the right hip. And then he took his dallies and reined Buck sharply to the left, spurring at the same time. The big horse found more speed and the *reata* went tight, twisting the bull's neck to the right and back, jerking his hind legs out from under him.

It was a tremendous wreck. At full speed, the bull cart-wheeled as though he'd been tossed out the door of a rolling freight car. Jeff was just beginning to lift the reins for a sliding stop and a leap down to tie the bull's feet together with the piggin' string gripped between his teeth—when Buck stepped in the badger hole.

An even greater wreck. Down Buck went, head first, launching the cowboy over his neck. The rope flew free. Jeff saw the ground coming and made a futile attempt to turn himself in the air. He hit the earth on his right shoulder and the side of his head, ringing his skull like a gong, and he tumbled and skidded for close to fifteen feet. He was going under and he couldn't stop it and the last thing he was aware of as consciousness left him was the staccato sound of gunshots.

• • • •

HIS HEAD felt the size of the world. And it hurt worse than the wickedest hangover of his life. The left eye opened, and that was the best he could do. The right one was swollen shut. His mouth tasted like nothing he'd ever put in it. The good part was that if he felt as bad as all that, he must not be dead.

• • • •

HE MANAGED to turn his head a little right and then left, and there was light coming through a window, but he couldn't yet tell where he was or what time of day. And then he smiled, and that hurt too, but he didn't care, because he'd found Maggie beside him in a chair, chin on her breast, a book open in her lap, asleep. He leaned forward to lift himself up in the bed and a bolt of pain shot through his head that brought a blinding flash behind his eyes, and he groaned out loud.

Suddenly, hands were on him. Gentle, strong hands, helping to ease him back down, his head on the pillow again. From his good eye he looked into the face that brought a smile back to his mouth. She hung close over him, and he thought how perfect it would be to kiss her if lifting his head and neck hadn't felt so bad. As her fingertips moved across his bruised face, he realized he needed a shave.

And then she smiled and the inside of his head felt illuminated again, but not in pain this time. "Welcome back, cowboy. You've been gone awhile." She sat back down and scooted her chair closer.

"How long have I been out?" He touched his head and felt it bandaged. Coarse gauze and tape.

"Well," she said, "let's see. It happened yesterday a little before noon, as I understand it. And it's now just short of three in the afternoon. So about twenty-seven hours."

He looked puzzled. "How'd I get back here?"

She smiled again. "I guess you could still ride a horse, even if you were dead. Will and Stogie got you up on Buck and rode on either side of you. But they said they hardly had to hold you up. Said you were out cold, but still riding. How's the head?"

He frowned. "Very fat and very painful."

She turned to the bedside table, did something he couldn't see, and turned back with a coffee cup half full of a suspicious-looking, green liquid. She held it out. "Drink it."

"What is it?"

"Something to make your head smaller."

With her help, he brought it to his mouth. It tasted vile. "What in God's name!"

"Indian herb tea. Hortencia made it for you. Tastes bad, huh?" She grinned.

"Worse than I imagine something I won't name tastes."

She chuckled, then frowned. "What you did was incredibly stupid."

He looked into her eyes. They were serious. "I guess," he agreed. "I don't remember any of it after tossin' my loop."

"That's because you have a concussion, or so the doctor thinks."

Now he frowned. "You brought a doctor?"

She straightened up. "Of course. You seemed badly hurt."

"So what happened after I caught that bull? I did catch him, right?"

She nodded. "Oh, yes, you caught him, all right. And tripped him right smartly, according to Will."

"So how come I'm layin' here with a busted head?"

She leaned forward again. "Buck stepped in a badger hole. He went down hard. So did you."

He looked stricken. "Is he? Did Will have to?" He couldn't finish.

Maggie took his hand and smiled. "Relax, cowboy. I told you that you rode him back, remember? That horse seems to have bones of steel. I doubt you could kill him with a rifle. He jumped right up and came back to check on you, according to Will. And that was good, because the bull got up, too. Will can hardly believe it, you laid him down so hard. Anyway, the bull got up mad and came for you, but Buck stood his ground and with teeth and hooves he managed to keep Old Striper off of you until Will and Stogie got there and shot him. According to Will, Stogie worked the lever of his carbine so fast that the bull looked like a cribbage board before he hit the ground. Will emptied his Colt as well."

"Jesus Christ!" Jeff blurted.

Maggie smiled. "Sounds like He might have been there, too. I hear He watches over fools." Jeff was tempted to roll his eyes at that, but kept a straight face instead. He squeezed her hand. And then she seemed tense. Drawing her hand back, she rose from the chair and backed toward the door. "At any rate, you've survived and that great horse of yours, as well. The doctor says you'll need some days off before you can ride again. As for Buck, he's sore but sound. I'll bring your supper later. And Will wants to see you right away."

Jeff had felt her change, her stiffening. "Send him on up," he said.

She turned and reached for the doorknob, and he stopped her with his voice. "Maggie?" She turned with a question in her eyes. He smiled, "Thanks for sittin' with me."

She softened enough to return his smile. "You bet."

• • • •

TEN MINUTES later, Will came in with a coffee pot and two cups. Jeff grinned at the sight of him, which stretched the skinned place on the side of his head that had skidded across the pasture. He winced. Will chuckled and set the pot and cups on the nightstand. As he poured, he said, "You look like one of them East Indian Maharajees with your head all wrapped up in that turbine."

Jeff reached for a cup and growled, "Gimme some of that damn mud."

Will half frowned. "Oooh, the champeen roper from Texas is a little ouchy this afternoon."

Jeff took a sip of the coffee. It was strong and tasted good. He felt a bit better almost instantly. "You'd be a grump ass, too," he said, "if your head was throbbing as bad as mine is."

Will made a mock frown. "Not my fault. I was for shootin' that son of a bitch right off the bat. You was the one had to show us how they done it down in the Lone Star State."

Jeff grinned sheepishly. "I guess what they say about pride goin' before a fall is on the level."

Will nodded. "And a hell of a fall it was. But don't take it out on Buck. I never seen a horse do what he done."

Jeff smiled with gratitude. "That's what Maggie said."

Will took a slurp out of his cup and went on. "I don't know how that bull got up so fast, or even got up a'tall. You bedded him harder than I ever seen it done. Should of killed that dirty scamp. But Buck was up even quicker, and he put himself between you and that bull, and fought like a grizzly."

Jeff said, "He's a good horse."

Will shook his head. "He's a heap more'n that. He's as good a pardner as a man could ever have." He slurped again and continued. "Me and Stogie figured your necks was broke. All three of you, countin' the bull. We was a little behind the action, and if Buck hadn't done what he done, that bull would'a mopped you up for certain sure."

Jeff frowned, not wanting to consider alternate, possible outcomes. At last he said, "I reckon I'm lucky you boys can shoot."

Will shook his head emphatically. "Wadn't me so much. All I had was my Colt and I ain't no expert. Shot it dry and probably only hit him twice. But that damn Stogie, he emptied his Winchester faster than a Gatling Gun. And soon's we satisfied ourselves you wadn't dead, I took a look at that bull. He was layin' on his right side, with eight bullet holes right behind the left shoulder. And brother, they was in a pattern you could cover with a coffee cup. And him shootin' from a runnin' horse, by God!"

Jeff looked a little skeptical. "A coffee cup?"

Will made a throw away gesture. "Well, hell, with a soup bowl, anyway." He picked up the pot and the cups and made for the door, then turned with a big grin on his face. Setting his burden down he dug in his jeans pocket, producing a double eagle and a five-dollar gold piece, which he laid on the nightstand.

Jeff looked at the money and then at his friend. "What's this?"

Will picked up the coffee things again. "It's your share of the bounty. We brought that bull's ears in to the boss."

Jeff seemed puzzled. "But it was fifty bucks and there was three of us."

Will turned the doorknob and said, "The boss was so tickled to get rid of that critter that he added on the extra scratch so we could all have a share. Comes out to twenty-five bucks apiece."

Jeff smiled. "A little bonus."

Will grinned wider, then frowned as he said, "Oh yeah, and then he said tell you roping that bull was, and I quote, 'a profoundly stupid thing to do.'"

Jeff ran his hand over his face gingerly. "Yeah, that seems to be a popular opinion around here."

• • • •

SANDY CAME to the doorway a little later. Jeff had just begun to doze and he considered begging off the visit for now. But the look of honest concern on his friend's face made the younger man relent.

"Come on in, *amigo*. I expect you think I did a stupid thing, too."

Sandy's eyes remained serious. "Not a'tall lad. Just the vigor of youth taking charge. Always a pleasure to show off in the company of friends."

Jeff frowned with his mouth, but his eyes were smiling. "More of your left handed support?"

Sandy shook his head. "No, son, I'm just thankful you weren't hurt worse, or your gallant steed."

Jeff looked out the window toward the barn. "Yeah. He's a better hand than I am."

Sandy changed the subject. "The good doctor tells us you are at least four days out of the saddle."

Jeff nodded. "So I hear."

Sandy said, "I think it would be prudent if I rode into Durango tomorrow to the telegrapher and sent a wire to the Widow Peach, apprising her of recent events."

Jeff agreed. "Same thing's come to me."

When he offered nothing further, Sandy said, "Any special messages?"

Jeff demurred. "No. Just say I'm sorry I'm out of pocket for a little longer, and I'll get back as soon as I can."

Sandy tried to catch his eye, but Jeff evaded the look. "Very well, lad. I'll say were starting back as soon as you can ride. Is that satisfactory?"

Jeff nodded gingerly. "That'll do."

●　●　●　●

LATER CAME the last visitor of the day, this one very welcome. Maggie, with his supper. She sat quietly as he made a meal of beef broth, bread, and cold milk. When he was done and had wiped his mouth on the napkin, she took the tray and set it on the nightstand. Turning back, she looked him in the eye, but her face revealed nothing. After half a minute he had to speak. "Something wrong?"

She leaned back in the chair. "Not really. Just trying to imagine what goes on inside that apparently thick skull of yours."

Her words surprised him. "Well, nothing," he said, "outside of trying to figure out what to do with myself for the rest of my life. How 'bout you?"

"You mean me?" she asked. "What goes on inside my head?"

"Yeah," he replied. "I'd be interested."

She looked up at the ceiling. "I don't know if that is any of your business."

He sounded sober as he said, "It probably ain't."

"So what are we talking about?"

He slowly moved his head left to right. "I don't know. All I know is my head hurts."

She stood up. "I should let you sleep. We're just talking nonsense."

Again he shook his head, carefully. "No, we're not. But I get a notion we're not savvying each other any too well either. And I think it's 'cause this isn't so much about what we're sayin', but maybe what we're feelin.'"

She frowned. After studying his face a moment, she said, "You say the most astounding things sometimes."

He ventured the smallest smile. "I guess I'm like that dog that wanted to be a poker player."

She looked at him quizzically. "What?"

He grinned sheepishly. "That dog. He wanted to be a card sharp, but every time he got a good hand, he couldn't help waggin' his tail."

She frowned again, but then smiled faintly. "I think you may have brain damage."

He slightly nodded. "Maybe so. Sometimes I don't know enough to shut up."

She poured him more herb tea. "Drink this so you can sleep. I'll bring your breakfast in the morning. Something more substantial. Bacon and eggs, maybe."

He nodded. "Sounds good. I think I'll have an appetite."

She backed away. "Well, goodnight then." As she reached for the knob, he sat up some and called her name. She stopped but said nothing.

He fidgeted a few seconds, not quite knowing what to say, how to say it, scared to say anything. "Maggie, I ain't crazy. I've just come a long way on a hard trail to get here. I want to stay."

She looked him in the eye for what seemed like ten years, no way to read her face. Then she gave him a warm, reassuring smile and he felt a relief that surprised him. "That's good," she said. "I think I'd like that. Now get some sleep."

• • • •

BUT IT WAS Hortencia's granddaughter who brought his breakfast the next day, and the noon meal, and his supper as well. His agitation grew and it did the pain in his head no good. "Goddamnit! Not again," he thought. "You've gone and stuck your foot in your mouth all the way to your ass. What was all that about a poker playing dog? What are you trying to do here? Every time this woman comes anywhere near you, you get a case of stupid that you can't control. She must think that lick on the head has made you crazy. Didn't she say as much? Brain damage! And you better hope that's what she does think. If she knew the truth, no telling what she'd think. And the truth is you *are* crazy. Plumb crazy about her. And you can't tell if she likes you or thinks you're ridiculous. What else could she think? You act a fool every time you're together, so a fool must be what she sees. Damn!"

He poured himself a stiff shot of herb tea, ignored the smell, and chugged it. His self-critique became more muddled and shortly he was asleep. He dreamed, and his dreams were wild. And bad.

He saw himself flying along on the buckskin, swinging a huge loop at a Spanish bull the size of a freight wagon, that had hot coals for eyes, red lightening flashing across its hide, and sparks shooting from its horn tips. And he caught it, and it turned and gored the horse, and he was thrown through endless night, only to fall into the bed of the comely Widow Peach, who hung over him, naked, with fangs like a mountain lion, and great swaying breasts that burned where they touched his skin.

So he crossed his arms in front of his face in an effort to defend himself and the Widow disappeared, her place taken by the form of Inez Sullivan, her blouse soaked red, her chest riddled with bullet holes, and her green eyes burning him, blaming him, as her hot blood pumped out, splashing over him, scalding him, drowning him.

• • • •

HE AWOKE next morning scared, the memory of his dream vivid. Surely he was going crazy. Until this time, thoughts of the girl killed in Albuquerque mercifully had been absent since making this trip with Sandy. Now it felt like he was sinking back into the old, guilty anguish.

The appearance in the dream of Addie Peach was equally disturbing. It made him dread the coming confrontation with her all the more. He should saddle the buckskin and lead the blue mare and the mule out in the dark of the coming night, saying nothing to anyone, and simply ride away, taking his problems with him. He could always return to old Don Archuleta's *rancho*, set aside his ambitions for a woman and property of his own, and just ride as one more of the *vaqueros*. A simple life. One without much achievement, perhaps, but also without so much heartache.

And then Maggie came in with a breakfast tray, and the sight of her smile, and it was one of her best, pushed out of his head all thoughts of running.

"I'm sorry I didn't check on you yesterday. I had to go into Durango to the saddle shop. I simply couldn't wait to see how my new saddle is progressing." Setting the tray down, she poured him coffee, then leaned over to tuck a napkin into the collar of his nightshirt.

She smelled wonderful, and the coffee did, too. His spirits rose along with the steam from the offered cup. After a first sip, he said, "Don't apologize. You got more to do than nursemaid me. I heard your daddy call you the ranch manager."

She sat down and crossed her legs. She had on high-topped riding boots and fancy, Mexican spurs. Chuckling, she said, "Don't put too much stock in that statement. I

La Grulla - 271 -

believe there was more than a hint of sarcasm in his award-
ing me that office."

Jeff had been steadily drinking his coffee, and now he
held out his cup for a refill. As she turned for the pot, he said,
"And I hope you don't put too much stock in what I said
night before last. I know it sounded loony. I expect I was a
little rattled from my fall."

She filled his cup and then sat looking at him, her eyes
going through to his insides, or so it felt. She said nothing
and her face showed less. He was on the anxious edge of
saying more when she spoke.

"I've been thinking about that conversation. I'm not sure I
follow all you had to say, and you certainly may have been a
little out of your head. But you said one thing that gives me
pause for thought." She went silent an interval, and he hung
on those words like a drowning man to a thrown rope. But
he dared not speak, so he let his eyes beg her to continue.

At length she said, "It was the part about our communica-
tion being more about what is felt than what is said." She rose
to her feet and stepped toward the door, leaving him more
confused than ever. Turning in the opening, she looked at
him for a moment with that same, penetrating gaze. He felt
pinned to the bed, speechless. Then she smiled. "I'm going
out all day on the Spanish stallion. He's up to it and I have a
lot to think about. I'll try to be back to bring your supper up."

Before he could respond, she was gone. He watched the
door swing slowly back on its hinges, as though her afterim-
age was still there for him to see. "You said it girl. Lots to
think about."

•   •   •   •

HIS HEAD had all but quit throbbing and he no longer
needed the tea. Despite the three cups of coffee he'd taken
with his ham and eggs, he dozed off shortly after eating.

No dreams this time, and when he awoke to a soft knock on the door, his head was clear and his mind untroubled. Sitting up with his back against the headboard, he called out, "Come on in."

It was Sandy, and the look of concern melted from his face as Jeff managed to produce a genuine smile. He came in and sat down beside the bed. The odor of whiskey and pipe tobacco hung about him.

Jeff gave him a wry grin, lifting an eyebrow. "Smells like you found a jug in Durango."

The old man reddened a bit and smiled back. "I did that, lad. Found one, dispatched it, and brought its twin back with me. It's stashed in the barn. You appear to be feeling better."

Jeff nodded. "A bunch. I'm ready to get off of this damn bog of a mattress and put my boots on."

Sandy frowned slightly, shaking his head. "The doctor advised four full days in bed. You've had but three."

Jeff frowned back. "Don't matter. And I'm sick of pissin' in a pot, and being stuck in this sinkhole of a feather bed. I'll be down to breakfast in the mornin' and that's flat." He stared into Sandy's face with undisguised challenge. The Scot knew better than to argue with so resolute a look.

"As you wish, lad. I suppose one with a head of granite such as yours would, of course, recover quickly." He dug in the leather pouch at his waist and produced his empty pipe. Making no move to fill it, he clenched the stem between his teeth.

Jeff frowned. "That damn thing stinks almost as bad cold as lit."

Sandy ignored the remark. "I sent the wire to the Widow, as agreed upon, and waited in town a couple hours for a reply. There was none."

Jeff looked bland as he said, "I reckon that gave you time to polish off that first jug."

Sandy seemed distracted as he answered. "Only half of it. I needed the rest for the ride back." Taking the pipe out of his mouth, he said, "Does it not strike you a touch odd that she had no response to the telegram?"

Jeff rubbed his bristly jaw. "I don't know. I sure can't say what makes her tick. What do you think?"

In his turn, Sandy scratched his beard. Putting the pipe back in place he said, "Can't say for sure. Could mean anything, or nothing at all. I discontinued the effort to read the minds of women thirty years ago."

Jeff shook his head. "I never been any good at it. Not with Ma, ner sis, ner any other woman."

Sandy grinned. "Nor with my lovely niece?"

Jeff winced as a sliver of pain shot through his still-tender head. "Most especially not with your lovely niece. Half the time she looks at me like she could see through to my insides. The other half she don't look at me a'tall. Except for the half when she smiles and talks sweet and packs my grub up here and sits with me."

Sandy grinned wider. "That's three halves in one whole, lad. A mathematical impossibility."

Jeff shook his head. It hurt. "Not with her, it ain't. I don't think anything is beyond that gal."

Sandy sat back and drew on his unlit pipe. It seemed to sooth him. "Well, she is a MacTeague, after all. But I'm inclined to think it's the mix. Her mother was a truly extraordinary woman. A combination of sugar and iron. Could produce either, as the occasion demanded. Was smitten with her mesel'. Met her before me wee brother arrived in these environs. Made a half-hearted attempt, in my lame fashion, to attract her affections. But she was wise beyond her years. Spotted me for the rounder that I was. And then young Robert made his entrance upon the stage. Maggie's mother saw his energy and industriousness at once. Set her charming cap for him. Picked him for a husband and father. And a good pick it was, I must say. Poor sod like me had no chance."

The two of them sat silently for a minute, then Jeff spoke up, almost in a whisper. "Well, hell, I reckon I don't neither. I've ruin't ever chance I had with any girl."

Sandy was instantly serious. "Not with Maggie, you haven't, if a chance is what you want. Not yet, anyway."

Jeff's ears pricked up. "Why? What'd she say?"

Sandy shook his head. "Nothing. Not to me, at least. But I know my girl. I've watched her when you are present. You have her undivided attention, even if you can't tell."

Jeff's mouth hung open, inviting the entrance of any passing fly.

His older friend smiled benevolently. "Close your mouth, lad, lest you find a bird's nest in it."

Jeff did as told. Then he said, "But she seems so changeable."

Sandy nodded. "That's because she's trying to figure out what to make of you. You're like no young man she's ever met. Your horsemanship is very attractive to her, in particular the way you seem to reach them on a mental, almost spiritual level. Her words, not mine. But your recklessness is unsettling to her. One day you are the thoughtful and sensitive horse master. The next, you are a wild and near suicidal adolescent, risking your neck to impress your friends."

Jeff bridled at that. "I wasn't no such thing. I just thought it would be fun. Is she against fun?"

Sandy frowned and shook his head. "No, son. Not within reason. I understand that the enthusiasms of young men can get out of hand, through firsthand experience. Was more than a little reckless mesel' in me youth. But she is a female, subject to different motivations. Your behavior of the other day puzzles her. And with good cause. She is a woman. And

it is my opinion that women are no more adept at compre-
hending the behavior of men, than men are of women."

Jeff's head was splitting now and he looked toward the
nightstand, but the teapot had been removed that morning
by the granddaughter at his own request. He turned his gaze
on Sandy. "So, what the hell am I supposed to do?"

The old man smiled. "Just be yersel', lad. I think she is
trying to make up her mind aboot you. How do you feel
about her?"

Jeff rubbed his eyes. "I figured it was plain by now. I'm
crazy about her."

Sandy stood up to go. "Good! I think everything else will
take care of itself. See you at breakfast then."

• • • •

THERE WAS a small mirror on the washstand under the
window. Jeff took his pocketknife from his jeans pocket and
carefully cut away the bandage from his head. The mirror
showed him the image of a young man in bad need of a
shave, with matted, dirty hair, and a bruised and scabbed
face. He immediately had second thoughts about joining the
family for breakfast.

That left few options. He thought he might sneak over to
Nacho's cook shack and have breakfast with the crew. He
would be welcome. Or, and this seemed like the more
honorable course, he could go to the cook shack and wash
up, shave, and return to breakfast at headquarters, as he had
bragged to Sandy that he would. It was early, barely first
light, and he had ample time for either plan.

His hat was an uncomfortable fit, what with his head
being still swollen, as well as sore. But to step out uncovered
was unthinkable, so he worried it down over his tousled hair,
pulled on boots, and shrugged into his sheepskin, dropping
his razor into a pocket. After a tiptoed descent of the stairs,
he let himself soundlessly out the front door and walked

gingerly across the yard to the domain of *El Cocinero*, Nacho
Ramirez.

He had to dodge a thrown pan of dirty wash water as he
approached the steps. Nacho was a little groggy this early and
had not seen him until the last second. With a flurry of
contrite Spanish, the old cook crabbed down off the porch
and took Jeff by the elbow. "Please forgive me, *mijo*. These
sleepy old eyes did not see you coming. *Como esta*? Are you
recovered from your great fall?"

Jeff nodded and grinned at the worried man. "No harm
done, *maestro*. I wasn't paying attention, either. I've been off
my feet for a few days. They are not used to serving me
quickly."

Nacho led him into the kitchen, seating him carefully at
the long dining table. It was luxuriously warm in the room.
Turning to the stove, he brought a big, black coffee pot and a
heavy, clay mug and poured for his young friend. Jeff took a
grateful sip as Nacho asked, "But are you well, *amigo*? The
story that has gone around the *rancho* is truly amazing."

Jeff nodded carefully. "I'm better. Almost ready to ride
again. And, yeah, it was one hell of a pile up. That brindle
bull, I guess you know. The one with the horns like a Spanish
fighting bull? *El Toro Malo*. He came close to rubbing me
out. My *caballo* saved me. Fought that *hijo de la perra* off 'til
my pards got there and shot him."

Nacho shook his head. "*Mucho buena suerte*. Such good
luck. To have a horse like that. God gives a man one great
horse in a lifetime, if he so chooses. That one must be yours."

Jeff smiled up at the former top hand. "He's a good'un.
And I got another one comin' up that might turn out even
better."

Nacho was more than happy to allow Jeff to wash his hair
and shave in the warmth of the cook shack. It was still early
and no hands had drifted in yet. The water was already hot
and the tender-headed cowboy made short work of his
ablutions.

• • • •

A PINK-FACED and slicked-down Jeff Cameron came into the headquarters dining room just as Maggie appeared from her second floor bedroom. She gave him a bright, unguarded smile, which was instantly replaced by a severe frown. With fists on hips she declared, "What in hell are you doing up? Doctor's orders call for another day at least of bed rest."

Her father looked over his coffee cup with a shocked expression. "Young lady!"

Sandy spoke up before anyone else had a chance. "Jeff tells me he is mortally exhausted with the further prospect of relieving himself in a chamber pot, and being stuck in a sink hole." All eyes swung to the old hunter, who was grinning wickedly. Then Maggie, Robert, and Sandy focused their attention back to the patient in question. It seemed to call for some response.

Jeff fidgeted under their gaze. He said, "Well, I'm feeling pretty good. And don't get me wrong. I'm grateful for the nursin' and care. But that soft, down mattress is killin' me. I need to get horseback." He sat then, before anyone could voice further objection.

Making a boarding house reach for the coffee service, he poured himself a cup, took a long draught, and put a look on his face that defied disagreement. None seemed forthcoming. Maggie took her seat and before any more controversy was possible Hortencia and her granddaughter came in with breakfast. The usual, hearty menu deflected concerns. For the moment.

• • • •

THE FAT MAN in the black suit and overcoat struggled against his bonds, but to no effect. Mano, with a bandana covering his face to his eyes, was counting the contents of a money belt as Pepé was making a thorough search of the buggy the man had been driving.

There was close to six hundred dollars in coin and greenbacks. He whistled at his and his brother's good fortune. The fat man blubbered. "You'll go straight to hell if you don't release me this instant and give me back that money!"

Mano looked up with amusement. "Are you God, *señor*, that you can go about condemning your fellow men?"

"No, of course I am not God. But I am a man *of* God. I am the Reverend Franklin J. Peterborough, an ordained minister in the Baptist Church, and that is the Lord's money!"

Mano grinned. "Then you must also be a *bandito,* like us. You should not steal from the Good Lord, *señor.*"

The Reverend looked as if he might explode, and Mano began to chuckle. The preacher blurted, "No, you imbecile! I stole that money from no one. I mean it is church money. It belongs to the congregation to which I minister. That makes it the Lord's!" He was puffing now.

Mano drew his revolver and pushed the muzzle into the man's fat neck, the front sight disappearing between folds of his chins. Reverend Peterborough drew in his breath and went quiet.

"I speak a little *gringo, señor,* and I think I know what that word "imbecile" means. I don't like it much, and you are not in a very good spot to be making insults to anybody, *comprendé?*" He shoved the pistol.

The Reverend nodded carefully. Mano continued. "My brother and I were raised in the one true faith, so it is little to us what sort of church you work for. And besides, we are bandits and horse thieves. This is how we make our living. Surely you would not deny a fellow sinner a chance to make a living?"

Peterborough began to puff up again. "I am no sinner, sir. I am a man of the cloth."

Mano fingered the lapel of the Reverend's overcoat. "And very fine cloth it is. I think perhaps it is too fine for a true man of God. I think your congregation is right now wondering where their overdressed Reverend is, as well as their money. You think so, Pepé?"

Pepé smiled. "*Si, hermano.*" He came over from the buggy. "He is much too fancy for a man of God. Here is a carpetbag full of fine linen underwear and silk stockings."

Peterborough fairly spat out, "This is outrageous! Those are my personal things!"

Mano holstered his pistol and said mildly, "I tell you what, *Señor* Reverend. You can keep your personal things. And you can have this." He tossed a five-dollar bill into the bag. "Now you have a little money and lots of pretty underwear. Also, be happy I did not shoot you. A man who steals the Lord's money deserves whatever bad thing happens to him." Peterborough slumped against the tree to which he was tied, resigned and deflated.

"Now," continued Mano, "if you work very hard tonight, you will be able to loosen these ropes enough to get free by morning. Maybe even sooner. You will get a little cold I think, but you are *muy gordo*, no?" He poked a finger into the Reverend's stomach. "Men as fat as you can stand a lot of cold. And there is your buggy. We're not even going to steal your horse, and she is a nice mare."

The preacher began to sniffle. Mano signaled Pepé to mount up as he stepped to his own horse. As they reined around to take the road, Mano called back over his shoulder, "*Buenos nochés*, Reverend. The Lord will watch over you. Unless you keep stealing his money."

FIFTEEN

B REAKFAST HAD stayed a quiet affair. The MacTeagues all seemed to sense that the young man with the scabbed face and lumpy head did not need messing with. The meal concluded, they left the table to attend to their respective interests, leaving Jeff to consider his options. In fact, he felt too wobbly to ride. He settled on a day spent grooming his animals, repairing his tack, and cleaning his weapons.

• • • •

AFTER A HEARTY SUPPER of beefsteak, boiled potatoes, dried peas, and a wonderful cobbler made with canned peaches, Jeff excused himself to go out on the veranda for a smoke, as had become his routine during his stay at the MacTeague's.

This time, Maggie followed him. She had wrapped herself in a great, woolen capote of her father's. She stood quietly next to him until he got a cigarette rolled and lit. Then she said, "You're leaving soon, aren't you?" It was more of a statement than a question.

He turned toward her and leaned back against a support post. "Well," he answered, "now that I'm healed up enough to ride again, I need to close out my situation in Pagosa. I got to get my gear, take care of a little business, and ride back and start this job. Round trip should take about ten days, two weeks at most."

She nodded with only mild apparent interest. After another half minute of silence she said, "That's a big circle. Are you taking all your stock?"

He shook his head. "If nobody cares, I'm leaving Bonnie Blue here. No sense her going. All I need for the trip is Buck and Jigger. Will said he'd ride her for me, keep her legged up."

Maggie straightened. "Is that so?"

He caught a slight chill in her tone. In an instant he diagnosed it. "If you get a chance, would you put a couple of rides on her, too? I want her to get all the experience she can, under different hands, as long as it's a top hand doin' the ridin'."

For the first time during the conversation, she seemed to relax. "Are you saying I'm a top hand?"

He held her eye with a serious look. "You bet! About as good as I ever rode with."

She softened and smiled. "I'd love to ride her, Jeff. And I'm flattered you'd ask me. I know how particular you are about your stock."

Now he smiled. "Particular who I ride with, too."

In spite of the cold air, she blushed. Recovering quickly, she asked, "And when do you plan to head for Pagosa?"

He ran a finger under his mustache. "I'm thinking day after tomorrow, if Sandy's ready."

Maggie chuckled. "I imagine he's ready. He and Da' are wearing a touch thin on one another."

He grinned. "Yeah, I bet."

Suddenly the girl's face lit up. "Listen, we've had a few rides, but we've never made a day of it. What would you say to going out tomorrow? On the Spanish horses, your Bonnie Blue and my stallion. We'll have a picnic. Hortencia says it will be nice weather for a few days and she's hardly ever wrong. What do you say?" Her eyes sparkled like sunlight on new snow and he could no more have refused her than he could have jumped flatfooted over the roof of the cook shack.

Resisting the urge to take her in his arms he said, "I expect a warm up ride would do me good, before Sandy and I hit the trail. So, yes'um, I reckon I'd be tickled."

•   •   •   •

HE WAS SADDLING the blue mare when Maggie came into the barn carrying a well-laden canvas bag and a double barrel shotgun. He raised his hands and said, "I'm unarmed, Marshal, and I'll come along peaceable."

She had a bright, lilting laugh. "Fear not, stranger. I've got no paper on you today. I'm after the notorious Jack Slade."

Jeff put his hands down. "Well, you're bound for disappointment then. The vigilantes hanged Slade years ago up in Alder Gulch, Montana Territory. Sorry to spoil your hunt, Ma'am."

She grinned at him. "I thought we might get a grouse or a rabbit to add to the menu for our picnic. And there might be ducks on the river."

Jeff raised an eyebrow. "Can you use that cannon?"

She straightened to her full height. "Certainly. With no sons to take hunting, Da' made a passable wing shot out of his darling daughter. Are you shocked?"

He shook his head. "No, Miss MacTeague. I'm not shocked, ner much surprised. I'm beginning to learn that you're able to do just about whatever you get a notion to."

She cocked her head teasingly. "Do you find me unladylike?"

He smiled the brightest he could. "Anything but, Maggie. Anything but."

•   •   •   •

NEITHER HORSE had been ridden for a few days and they were eager. Jeff and Maggie let them go at a high lope, not a full gallop, but fast enough for the wind to undo the girl's hair pins and cause her long, heavy tresses to stream out behind her. He let her get ahead a little so he could watch her unobserved. Once again he thought that he could ride after this girl from now until the end of his days.

After a half-mile canter, the horses were willing to slow down. At a long trot, the two of them rode upstream along the Animas, going through natural pastures divided by tributary creeks fringed with red willow, cottonwoods, and gamble oak. Maggie showed him the location of two springs that were new to him. She pointed out boggy spots that could be a death trap for cattle in hot weather, as well as locations where salt was put out for the stock. He was learning this range.

At about eleven o'clock they were approaching a wide, slow bend in the river when Maggie stopped her mount and produced a small pair of binoculars from her saddlebag. Raising them to her eyes, she scanned the water. Jeff saw a grin crease her face. "I thought so. Looks like about a dozen mallards down there, in that slack spot, below the riffle."

With his unaided eye, Jeff could just make out at about four hundred yards some moving black specks. Maggie handed him the glass. It took him a few seconds to find them, but then there they were, sharp and clear. Fat, wild ducks, the drakes with bright, bottle-green heads. He turned to the girl and said, "You got a good eye. I never would of seen 'em if you hadn't pointed 'em out."

She smiled. "Thanks, but it's not so much good eyes as knowing where to look. I've found ducks in that hole lots of times." Stepping down, she walked her horse to the nearest scrub oak and tied him. Jeff followed suit. "Here's our strategy," she said, as she drew the long barrel, ten gauge hammer gun from its custom made saddle scabbard. "The wind is from us to them, which is good, because ducks like to take off into the wind." As she offered this bit of knowledge, she dropped two shells into the open breech of the gun.

He was skeptical. "Won't they scent us if they're down-wind?"

She smiled at him. "Ducks don't seem to have much of a sense of smell. So I'll just sneak down this line of willows and get closer. You get mounted and take a wide route to the other side. You can ford the river down there below that riffle. Swing back around on the far bank. Keep a couple hundred yards between you and the birds until you're in line with where I'm hidden. Then you'll just turn toward the ducks and jog straight at them. They'll get up off the water when you're about fifty yards away and, with any luck, they'll fly into the wind and right over me, within range of this canon, as you call it."

Jeff smiled as he untied the mare. "All right, general, I've got my orders and will carry them out to the best of my ability." The girl stuck her tongue out at him, closed the gun, then turned to disappear into the screen of brush.

He rode downstream for about two hundred fifty yards, keeping his eye on the birds all the while. They seemed unconcerned. As instructed, he crossed the river at a shallow spot below the white water of the riffle, then rode in an oblique arc back upstream until he saw that he was in line with Maggie's horse. Turning toward the water, he put the mare into a slow trot and headed for the ducks. When he was within two hundred yards, they began to mill on the water a bit nervously. At a hundred they drifted toward the far bank, away from him. And, as promised, when he was within fifty yards, they launched up off the water, emitting a cacophony of indignant quacking. He stopped the mare to watch the show.

As if on strings, the ducks flew almost directly over the line of willows that grew down to the riverbank. At the last possible moment, just when it seemed they had gained too much altitude to still be in range, he saw two, quick puffs of white smoke erupt from the brush, straight up, and almost at the same instant was delighted to witness the two lead birds fold, one right after the other, dead in the air, and begin their fall, like dropped stones. Following were the tandem booms of the big gun, one ringing behind the other, not a half second apart.

He whooped and then laughed out loud, waving his hat in the air. The mare jumped a step ahead, spooked a little by his outburst. But, hell, she'd done it, by God! What a gal! Was there anything this girl wasn't good at?

Reseating his hat, he loped back the way he had come, splashed across the ford and came up to where the stallion was tied, just as Maggie emerged from the brush, the broken open shotgun in one hand, and two fat mallard drakes held proudly in the other. Jeff tied his horse and went to assist, taking the ducks and falling in beside her as she walked back to her own mount. She was a little flushed and breathless from the excitement. And she took *his* breath, too.

"I guess you really can use that canon, sure enough."

She gave him a dazzling smile. "It's deadly on geese, too, with coarse shot." She leaned the gun against a cottonwood trunk and untied the grub sack from her saddle.

"If you don't mind picking and dressing those birds, I'll get a fire going and heat up these potatoes and biscuits, and make some coffee. And there're pork chops if a duck doesn't fill you up. How's that sound?"

He set the ducks down and took out his pocketknife. "Sounds just fine. And I don't mind cleaning these birds. I guess I must'a gutted and picked about a jillion chickens for my mama, growing up. I expect I can still do a fair job."

She smiled up from her fire making. "I'll just bet you can."

• • • •

AS HORTENCIA had predicted, it turned out to be a mild, lovely afternoon. Jeff had stripped the tack from their horses and staked them out to graze while Maggie was cooking, and now, meal done, he leaned back on a saddle blanket and sucked on a leg bone from the duck that he had reduced to a polished skeleton. He had found it delectable. She poured him a third cup of coffee. "So what do you think of your first wild duck? You did say you've never had it before, right?"

He nodded, grinning at her slyly. "Oh, I reckon I didn't care for it. That's why I stopped before eatin' the bones, too."

She laughed. "Well, it's hard to beat a fat mallard roasted over a willow fire."

He nodded again. "I support that notion, ma'am."

She gave him a mock frown. "Why do you keep calling me ma'am all the time? Makes me feel old."

He tossed the bone into the coals. "Just my raisin' I guess. I was brought up to call any woman between the age of eighteen and eighty-five ma'am, and it's just hard to quit now."

She sat down on her own saddle blanket. "Well, I sure wish you could call me something else."

He took off his hat and laid it upside down on the ground, smiling at her. "Anything in particular?"

She scooted a little closer. "How about Maggie? It is my name, you know."

He couldn't stop himself from reaching out and brushing a stray lock of hair out of her eyes. "It's a pretty name, too. For a pretty girl."

She looked at him dead on and asked very directly, "Is there a girl in Pagosa?"

He held her look, couldn't turn away if he'd wanted to, and felt a little heat coming up in his neck. "No. Not any-more."

She kept him pinned with her eyes. "Does that mean there was?"

He managed to break eye contact, looked out over the river, but was drawn right back. "Nobody special. Just a lady who liked me a little bit. But that's done with."

She still had not taken her eyes off him. He felt his blood warming. "Is that right?" she asked.

He nodded. "Yep."

She raised an eyebrow. "Yep?"

He smiled. "Yep. Yes, ma'am. I mean, Maggie. It's over. Through."

She moved a wee bit closer. He felt her breath on his chin when she said, "Since when?"

He decided to just say it. "Since you."

Finally she took her eyes off him, picked up a napkin, and reached out and wiped his mustache. "What are you doin' that for?" he asked, his voice a little husky.

"Duck grease," she whispered, dropping the napkin and leaning in to kiss him very lightly on the lips.

When he leaned, too, toward her, she pulled back, breaking the kiss, and he looked at her with a question in his eyes. "Maggie..." he said, and his voice cracked a little, like a teenage boy, and then she was on him, pushing him to his back, and she kissed him harder than he'd ever been kissed in his life. It went on for what seemed like forever and he felt her tongue touch his, and he thought if she didn't get off him he'd explode, and then she was gone, back on her saddle blanket, breathing a little heavily, but in command of herself again.

He sat up in a few seconds, his breath coming fast, and he looked at her looking at him, and he wanted her so bad, feeling something that neither Inez Sullivan nor Addie Peach nor any other female in his life had ever made him feel. He moved toward her and she pulled back an equal distance. He stopped, just looking, and she looked back, with that unflinching gaze of hers, and he said, "Maggie...I", but before he could continue, she was there, half a foot away, reaching out and putting a finger to his lips.

"No! No, Jeff, don't say it. Don't say anything." She took her finger away from his mouth and reached up and ran her hand through his hair, then gently touched a fading bruise on his cheek.

He shook his head. "But I gotta tell you. I got money in the bank, in New Mexico."

She put her hand over his mouth. "No! Stop. Whatever you think you want to say to me now…you save it. Save it 'til you come back. Then, when you're here again, with your Pagosa life behind you, then you tell me. Tell me what you want to say right now. And tell me what you've been thinking while you've been away from me. Then, you can tell me everything. And I'll be ready to hear it. You just come back to me."

•   •   •   •

"YEH'RE MIGHTY quiet, lad." Sandy was adjusting the pack-saddle on his bay mule, puffing billows of rank smoke from his first pipe of the morning. Jeff had been only civilly conversant during breakfast, which was unattended by the girl, and since then had not said a word, aside from his farewells to Robert, Nacho, and a few others on the crew. After his and Maggie's picnic, he'd thrashed his way through a mostly sleepless night and now, moments from starting back for Pagosa Springs, he felt confused, tired, and in no mood for talk. Sandy would just have to hold up both ends of the conversation.

He and Maggie had said their goodbyes the night before, in the barn, after feeding their horses. "Today was just for us," she'd said. "I don't want a scene tomorrow morning. So you remember what I told you."

He nodded. "I will."

She took off her black hat. "You do that." And she put her arms around his neck and gave him a warm, slow kiss. Then, she turned and went up to the big house.

Now it was time to head out. Sandy had gotten to see his doted-upon niece, with whom he was delighted, and his younger brother, whom he loved, but who had been, as always, irritable as well as irritating. As for Jeff, he now found himself in new and very agreeable circumstances, and was eager to get to Pagosa Springs and close his old accounts, so to speak. He wished it was done, over with, and that he was already back, on the job, starting his new life. And that's what it felt like. A new start. A new chance. A new life.

And the girl. There was the girl. It has become all about the girl. She filled his head, made it light, made it float. It was all he could do to come down enough to concentrate on saddling the buckskin. Then he went through the motions of packing the mule and, if his hands hadn't known how to do it again, it wouldn't have gotten done by him.

All he could think about was the sight of her, sitting on a saddle blanket, smiling at him, leaning close to him, pushing his shoulders down and covering his body with hers. And the feel of her mouth on his, them breathing each other's breath, the taste of her, the weight of her pressing him into the blanket. And he caught himself staring down the long alley of the barn, the last place they'd spoken, and he tried to find her image again, the way she'd looked as she walked off after that last kiss. It was, of course, impossible. Having bridled the big gelding, he just stood there, looking out the barn doorway.

He jerked a little when Sandy touched him on the shoulder, a concerned look on his broken veined, bristle-bearded face. "Where are yeh, lad?"

Jeff reddened faintly. "Oh, no place, I guess. You ready?"

"I am that. And I'm thinkin' I'd like to take a little detour on the way back."

Jeff cocked an eyebrow. "Such as?"

Sandy knocked out his pipe on a post. "Just go a little south, down to Ignacio. Then swing back up the Piedra, come back on to the coach road at Chimney Rock. It'll add only a day to the trip."

Now that he was on a mission, Jeff felt loath to spend the extra time. "What's in Ignacio?"

Sandy was turning toward his horse as he answered. "An old Ute woman."

Jeff shook his head. "Damn, Sandy, I'd of thought you'd be done with that sort of thing at your age."

The old man scowled back, one foot in the stirrup. "Oh, for the love of St. Andrew! She makes moccasins, the most comfortable I've ever worn, and I'm in need of a couple new pairs. Got holes in me current models."

He swung up into the saddle and Jeff did likewise. "Well, let's skin out then. I got a job to start here and one to finish there. I'd as soon wrap the one up fast, so I can commence with the other."

Sandy ducked a bit as he rode out the barn door. "You were in no such hurry four or five days ago. But I understand fully. If I had what you have to come back to here, then I'd kill a string of good horses getting it done. Unfortunately, all we have is a horse and mule apiece, and must make them last. And, just for the record, my young friend, despite the years, I am a fully functional man, by God, and there's plenty o' venom left in this old stinger."

The sun was just breaking over the eastern peaks as they hit the trail that would connect them with the coach road to Pagosa Springs.

Sixteen

T HE BROTHERS Lucero pushed their empty plates toward the center of the greasy table and reared back in their chairs. Mano handed his brother one of two thin cheroots, put one in his own mouth, and lit both. They smoked for a few minutes in silent satisfaction, then Pepé said, "What good fortune for us to meet the blessed Reverend on the coach road today."

Mano smiled. "*Si, hermanito.* The Good Lord has provided. And the fat Reverend is cold tonight. Too bad for him. But now we have the means to live a little better than wolves, at least for a while. No more stringy elk meat. We'll get a room tonight and rest ourselves and our *caballos* tomorrow." Pepé nodded agreement as Mano signaled the barman. After their glasses were once more full, he said, "Little brother, we have been on this hunt a long time, no?"

Pepé nodded again. "We have, big brother. Seems like forever. How long has it been?"

Mano scratched his gritty neck. "*Quien sabé?* I don't know, exactly. A number of weeks. Long enough to become very tired of all of it."

Pepé drew in smoke and said, "I am tired, too. And cold. Here we sit by this stove, and still I am cold. I wish we could go back south, maybe down toward Socorro, or perhaps even as far as Las Cruces."

Mano frowned. "That is a very long ride, brother."

Pepé nodded. "I know, but it is warm down there, no?"

Mano said, "*Si*, Pepé. Warmer than here." He drained his glass and caught the barman's eye once more. "But there is a place much closer that is warm."

Pepé's eyes lit up. "Where is that, Mano?"

He paid for their re-fills and said, "I have heard of a place just north of here, a town in *Estado de Colorado*, called Pagosa Springs, on the *Rio San Juan*. It has hot water coming out of the ground, in streams and pools. The *gringos* go there to sit in this hot water. They say it cures them of their miseries."

Pepé looked fascinated. "Truly, brother, *verdad*?"

Mano nodded. "That is what I have heard, from more than one *viejo*. We could be there in two days."

Pepé smiled, but then took on a puzzled look. "But what about Jaimé's killer. Will we find him there?"

Mano stared into his drink. "Likely, no. We have done a lot of searching and not much finding. It may be that we are coming to the end of this hunt. It has been a long, cold trail, as you say. I see no good reason we should not ride up to these hot springs and spend a little time warming up. Besides, our poor *caballos* are showing their ribs. They need good feed, and a rest. And thanks to the fat, *gringo* preacher, we can afford a little side trip."

Pepé bobbed his head, grinning like a four year old. "*Bueno*, big brother. I would like to sit in hot water."

•   •   •   •

SANDY WRIGGLED his toes, a satisfied look on his face. "Now this is comfort. Yeh should get some made for yersel', lad."

Jeff shook his head impatiently. "No thanks, I don't have time."

The Scot sighed. "The haste of youth."

Jeff turned away to avoid looking at him. "It ain't that, goddamnit. It took the best part of two extra days to get here, not one, like you said, and then it took that old Ute gal another day and a half to make those slippers for you. Time we get back on the trail in the morning, we'll have spent four extra days just to get you re-shod."

Sandy tossed his old, perforated moccasins into the fire, producing an evil smelling smoke. "Sorry lad. She used to be quicker about her work."

•   •   •   •

THE BROTHERS could smell sulfur long before they made out any of the buildings of the town of Pagosa Springs, Colorado. It was as the old men had told Mano. Narrow rivulets of warm water bubbled out of the rocks along the banks of the San Juan, running down to mix with the icy river currents, sending up tall columns of steam. Pools of varying sizes dotted the level ground above the high water mark, lending their own plumes to the frigid air. Mano and Pepé grinned at each other like children and loped their horses through town to the livery barn.

It was early evening and after stabling their mounts they bought towels at a riverside mercantile and walked through the snow to a shallow pool screened from the road by a stand of willows. For all their crimes and excesses, they were self-conscious, modest men.

Hanging their filthy outer garments on convenient branches, but keeping on their long handles, the two of them eased into the wonderfully hot water. They slid down until they were chin deep, leaning their heads back against large, round rocks.

Pepé said, "Big brother, this is the first time I've not been cold since we rode out of Taos."

Mano ducked his head and came up sputtering. "*Si, hermanito*. It is heavenly, no?"

Pepé grunted. "Can we stay here until spring?"

His brother released a genuine, hearty laugh, such as was rarely heard from his mouth. "*Quien sabé*, Pepé? Who knows?"

•   •   •   •

THEY HAD PAID for two days board for their animals and on the third morning, after a post-breakfast soak, they strolled down to the barn to see the hostler about additional lodging for the horses. As Mano dug in his pocket for coins, Pepé gazed idly out one of the grimy windows. "It is so pleasant here. I wish we could give up this chase for the man who stole *la grulla* mare and stay until the weather warms."

He was, of course, speaking Spanish to his brother, but the livery man had picked up more than a little of that language in a town that was made up in large measure of old, land grant families. He paused in counting Mano's money and looked up at Pepé warily. His nervous expression was not lost on Mano. "What is it, *señor*?" He asked it in his heavily accented English.

The hostler turned from Pepé to Mano. "Huh?"

The older Lucero spoke more slowly. "I asked what is the matter, *amigo*. You look as if you see the ghost of your mother."

The thin, old man stood and shook his head. "Naw. Weren't nothin'."

Mano's instincts were shouting at him. He leaned toward the man. "*Amigo*, something is troubling you. I can see it plainly. Perhaps my little brother and I can be of some assistance." He said it with such unmasked menace that the hostler sat back down, the coins on the table forgotten.

"Well, I guess I savvy what you say a little. The young feller there said something about a mouse-colored horse?"

Every hair on Mano's body tingled with electricity. He took a deep breath and said very slowly, "You know of such a horse?"

The old man pulled a soiled bandana out of an overalls pocket and mopped his forehead. "That's a rare color, for a horse, that is."

Mano forced a mild expression. "You are correct, *viejo*, a rare color, indeed. And I ask you again, have you seen such a horse?" Any softness had left his voice.

The hostler was unable to meet his eyes. "Well, maybe."

The words were hardly out of his mouth when Mano's left hand shot across the table to seize the man's thin neck, and his right drew the long barrel revolver, cocked it, and pressed the muzzle against the sweating forehead. "Now, old man, I think you have more to tell us." He signaled to Pepé to watch the street. "It is drafty in your barn, my friend." He paused, looking around. And then continued, "Why don't we step over there, into that storeroom. I'm sure it is much warmer and then we can have a comfortable visit, no?"

•   •   •   •

THE COACH ROAD was in relatively good shape and by pushing the pace a little Jeff and Sandy arrived in Pagosa Springs after two more days. It was a mild afternoon.

As they approached the livery barn, they noticed two men dressed as *vaqueros*, and something about them caused a second look. Jeff took special note of their mounts. Fine-blooded animals, clean legged and tall, much better in quality than the run of the mill cow pony. As the two hard-looking riders passed them, going west, he studied the older of the pair and there seemed to be something familiar in the dead expression, something more than open menace, as though the features favored someone he'd seen in the past. Rather than crane his neck to follow them, he looked away. They rode on to the barn.

The hostler was nowhere to be seen, but Sandy suggested they occupy their usual stalls and return to settle up later. After unpacking and stabling their animals, the Scot elected to make an appearance at the hotel bar. Having had his share of his traveling companion's company for the time being, Jeff decided that he might as well look in on the Widow Peach.

No use putting off what was likely to be an uncomfortable interview, he thought. The sooner he had fulfilled his obligations to his former employer, the sooner he could head back to the Animas country and everything waiting for him there.

A five-minute walk brought him to the steps of the boarding house. All seemed as usual. The only difference was the presence of a young man in range clothes, lounging on a bench on the veranda in a small patch of sunlight by the entry. He slouched, his legs crossed at the ankles, hat pulled low over his face, a lit cigarette in one hand.

As Jeff mounted the steps, the sitting cowboy straightened up, paused a moment, rose to his feet and moved to block the doorway. Raising his hat brim enough to see well, he said, "You Cameron?"

Jeff stopped on the porch, two feet away from his inquisitor. "I know you?"

The man gave him an insolent grin. "Not yet, but you're fixin' to."

Jeff's face took on a perplexed look. "I don't believe we've met, mister, so if you don't mind moving, I got business inside."

Smiling with his mouth only, the man drew on his cigarette, tossed it past Jeff's shoulder into the street, and blew smoke just past his face. "That's where you're wrong, pard. I been keepin' an eye out for you. The Widow said you was due back. Looked for you to show up a few days ago, truth to tell." Jeff felt his face go dead and his whole body began to tense. The cowboy continued. "Anyway, fact is you don't need to bother going in there. No reason to."

When he spoke, Jeff's own voice sounded alien to him. "And how's that?"

The man grinned. "Well, thing is, you been replaced, pard."

Jeff nodded. "Is that a fact?"

The grin widened. "You don't have a job here no more. You don't have a room no more. I packed up your plunder and hauled it down to the livery. The hostler's got it in his storeroom."

Jeff's body felt made up only of nerve ends. "On whose say so'd you do all that?"

The cowboy leaned back against the doorjamb and hooked his thumbs in his belt. "Why, the Widow's. Who else? Like I said, you been replaced, pard. I'm doin' your chores now. *All* your chores. Day *and* night." The smile on his face was a sneer. He was enjoying this.

Jeff asked through clenched teeth, "Is that so?"

The man kept grinning. "Yessiree."

At that moment the front door opened and Jeff saw Addie Peach, looking good as ever, a neutral expression on her face. For several beats they took in each other, neither speaking. Then the insolent cowboy said, "I told him to move along, Miz Peach. I'uz jist fixin' to help 'im on his way." The sneer on his face went wider as he spoke. He made all this dirty.

With her eyes still on Jeff, Addie said, "Hush up, Sam. Sit back down and have another smoke."

The cowboy frowned. "But you said…"

She looked hard at him. "Sam!" The corners of the young man's mouth turned down, but he sat, like a good dog.

She had on a snug-fitting dress and no apron, and she looked fabulous. Jeff forced himself to keep his eyes on her face as she stepped aside, holding the door open.

"Please, come in," she said, her voice soft again, just above a whisper. Without waiting, she moved off past him toward the kitchen. Jeff followed, hearing a faint snicker behind him. "Easy," he whispered to himself. "Time for that later."

The kitchen was warm and she was pouring coffee into two cups as he came in. He stood awkwardly, twisting his hat brim while she brought the cups to the table. She sat and motioned him to the other chair. He complied. She lifted her

cup, he lifted his, and they both sipped. He was trying to
think of an opening when she set her coffee down and said,
"Long time no see."

He nodded, tried to hold her eyes. "Yeah. I guess so."
Reaching to touch a yellowed bruise on the side of his face he
said, "Had a bad horse wreck. Was laid up awhile." She stared
at him. He broke eye contact and drank more coffee.
"Christ," he thought. "This ain't much fun so far."

She crossed her legs and said, "That's it? You've been gone
close to a month and that's the whole story?"

Looking up again he said, "I sent a telegram."

She frowned. "*Sandy* sent a telegram. Which read something like, 'Jeff hurt. Stop. Back when he can ride. Stop. S.
MacTeague.' I understand that sending a wire costs money,
and Sandy may be a typically thrifty Scot, but that's not much
for me to go on. And that was ten days ago. Must have been
one hell of a wreck."

He worried his hat brim some more. "Yeah. I reckon."

She slapped her palms flat on the table, anger boiling
over. "You reckon? *You goddamn reckon?*" She was all but
vibrating.

He looked up, jolted. "Listen Addie." Time to tell all. "The
truth is…"

She cut him off with a chop of her hand. "Oh, for God's
sake, spare me. I don't expect to hear the truth from you or
that smelly old man, either, next time he comes creeping in
here." She fumed for ten seconds, then jerked to her feet,
snatched up their cups and stepped to the sink, slamming
them down against the porcelain bottom. He heard one
break.

He sat where he was, trying to think of something to say.
She stood where she was, forcing composure upon herself. At
length she turned around and leaned back against the drain
board. Her face was stiff. "It doesn't matter now, anyway. As
Sam said out on the porch, you've been replaced."

Jeff nodded, trying to keep the sarcasm out of his voice and failing. "He said he took over all my chores. Day *and* night."

She didn't even blink. "That is correct. Everything you used to do around here, he does now. *Everything!*"

"Well," he said, standing up and putting his hat on.

The look on her face softened just a little. "You left me too long, Jeff. You were needed here. I waited the two weeks, and a few days more. Then the wire came. I don't expect you got hurt on purpose, but by then it didn't matter. I needed a man. And you weren't here. And Sam was."

He shook his head. "You sure picked a fine specimen."

She flared hot again. "How dare you? You had responsibilities here. A commitment to me. You rode off for a holiday and found something you liked better. Don't deny it. Women know everything, you stupid boy. Do you think I've never heard of Sandy's niece? Don't make yourself a liar on top of everything else." She stopped to calm herself. After a while her eyes were soft again as she said, "You were special. That rounder out on the porch isn't. But he was here. And you weren't!"

What was left to say? Not one, good, goddamned thing. Looking past her, he made for the door into the parlor, but she moved to block his way, reached up and seized him by the bandana and pulled him down to her height, the same way she'd done at Christmas time under the sagebrush "mistletoe." He was stiff, but she pulled harder and put her mouth on his, kissing him fiercely. Just as he began to soften his lips she drew back, put both hands on his chest, and pushed away firmly. "So you don't forget," she murmured.

•   •   •   •

OUT ON THE PORCH again, and Sam, his replacement in all things concerning the Widow Peach, sat with his legs stretched out across Jeff's path. He forced himself to remain calm as he said, "I'd like to go on."

Sam uncoiled his lanky frame and stood up, still blocking the way. Taking the cigarette from his mouth he grinned, blowing smoke out, directly into Jeff's face. "Yeah, I just bet you would, pard. And I bet something else. I bet you're goin' to miss it around here. Three squares of hot chuck every day, not that much work, and a soft bed upstairs, with a visitor 'bout twice a week."

Using all the control he could muster, Jeff moved to step around the leering man, looking straight ahead. He was almost past when Sam added, "My favorite thing is when she bucks, farts, and bellers!"

A half second later, the new man was on his hands and knees, choking, blinded by a broken nose, and coughing and spraying blood. Jeff drew back his right fist, knuckles skinned, stepping quickly away from his replacement, trying to avoid getting blood on his jeans. "*Adios*, pard!" he said, touching his hat brim. Starting to turn, he was distracted by a movement in the corner of his eye.

A curtain in the window to the right of the door had been pulled aside and he saw Adelle Peach standing there, looking at him through the glass with an unreadable expression on her face. After a moment longer, he moved on.

•   •   •   •

IN THE BAR, Sandy was easy to find. Pulling out a chair next to him at the table closest to the stove, Jeff sat down heavily. Noting the blank look, his gristly friend asked, "Did yeh see the Widow, lad?"

He nodded slowly. "Yep."

Sandy's face was a question mark. "And?"

Taking out his makings and starting to roll a cigarette, he answered, "Well, about the best I can say is, I didn't get shot."

• • • •

AT THE EDGE of town, Mano spurred his horse into a long trot. Refreshed by two days of rest and plenty of oats and good hay, the eager animal surged ahead. Pepé's mount, equally full of vigor, picked up the pace to match his stable mate. Pulling up alongside his older brother, he spoke loud enough to be heard over eight, iron shod hooves. "I would have liked one more day to soak in the hot water, *hermano*."

Mano's face was grim. "*Yo tambien*, little brother. I enjoyed it also. But if what the man at the barn said is true, and I think he was too scared to lie, then we are closer now to Jaimé's killer than we have been so far. And we have a name. Jeff Cameron. And a description. Tall and young, with wide shoulders and light hair, a dark mustache, as the little boy in Chama told us. And the place he went. *El Rancho de los MacTeagues*, in the valley of *El Rio de las Animas Perdidas*, north of Durango."

Pepé's face showed admiration. "The old man told you everything, no?"

Mano's smile was a razor cut across his face. "With some coaxing."

Pepé pressed him further. "But what if he tells others about us? If he speaks to this Cameron's friends, he may be warned."

The elder brother's expression did not change. "You were watching the front door and did not hear our conversation, but he promised me he would say nothing about our visit."

Pepé was still concerned. "But brother, people break promises all the time."

Mano shook his head. "Not this man, *hermanito*. He will honor his promise, forever." The younger brother started to say more, but Mano raised a silencing hand. "*Basta*! Enough of questions. Durango is more than fifty miles to the west. But there has been no snow now for some time and the road is clear enough. These are the best horses we have ever stolen and they are fresh. Now we ride!"

•   •   •   •

AFTER AN HOUR of whiskey and observations regarding the unfathomable ways of women, Jeff and Sandy headed back to the livery. Once again, they found no one in attendance.

"Where the hell is old Eulis, I wonder? He's always here this time of day," said Sandy.

Jeff moved toward the storeroom. "Who cares? I just want to see what kind of shape my outfit's in." Swinging open the door and stepping through it, he stopped as if he'd hit a wall. "Aw, Jesus God! Son of a bitch!" Reaching out he grabbed the doorjamb, bracing himself.

Sandy was coming up behind him. "What is it, lad?"

Jeff fought his rolling stomach and said, "It's Eulis. His throat's cut!"

•   •   •   •

PAGOSA WAS in an uproar. Aside from card games gone bad and drunks shooting it out in the street, there had not been a sure enough murder in town for a couple of years. But the livery barn owner, one Eulis Foster, was very dead and from all indications had been murdered. The local undertaker, who doubled as coroner, said he thought the man had bled out more than an hour before being discovered by Jeff and Sandy. As to the identity of the knife wielder, no one had any ideas. And there seemed no apparent motive. There were coins lying loose on the desktop, so robbery seemed to be out. As well, the deceased was known as a straight dealer in his business affairs and, though considered somewhat irritable at times, seemed no grumpier than any other old man in town. He therefore had no known enemies likely to visit him with such violence.

The town marshal made a perfunctory investigation but, other than confirming the obvious fact that the deceased had been rendered lifeless by a knife wound that traversed his throat from ear to ear, he had little to add to the conclusions of the coroner. Jeff and Sandy were interviewed, but were able to shed no additional light on the matter.

After being questioned, they returned to the hotel bar for a nerve steadier. But the atmosphere in the barroom on that occasion proved less than conducive to relaxation.

As perhaps everywhere else in town that night, this location was rife with speculation as to who could commit such a foul and heinous deed. Theories tended to favor some unknown drifter. But the fact of the money left on the desk weakened that solution.

In the absence of logical suspects, one drunk loudly proposed suicide. This brought an angry dispute between those who supported that view, versus others who held that anyone fool enough to believe a man could cut his own throat was a certifiable moron. And so the debate continued.

Jeff and Sandy stood side by side, elbows on the bar. Jeff looked glumly into his glass, shaking his head slowly. Sandy stared at his reflection in the mirror behind the row of bottles. Neither spoke as controversy raged around them. Finally, the Scot broke the spell. "I knew Eulis for nigh onto ten years. While I canna' recall ever seeing him smile, I found him fair in all his dealings with me."

Jeff agreed. "Well, I hardly knew him a'tall, but he let me use that round pen for nothing and he always had top quality feed."

They sank into their own silence once again. Sandy bought another round and the friends sipped slowly. After an interval, he spoke a question. "So, lad. Now that yer arrangement up the street has been canceled, so to speak, where will you stay?"

Jeff took off his hat and set it upside down on the bar, ran his fingers through his matted hair, and then rubbed his bristly face. "I'm damned if I know. I guess tonight I'll bunk with my stock at the livery. It ain't that cold and I can make a good bed in the hay."

Sandy blanched. "Good God, son! A murder was committed down there scant hours ago. D'yeh imagine yeh can sleep in a place that reeks of such a foul deed just done?"

Jeff massaged his eyes with a thumb and forefinger. "Well, hell, what am I supposed to do? All my gear's down there, and my animals, 'cept for the blue mare. All of which reminds me, I got nothin' to hold me in this place any more. Thing to do is get some sleep and ride for your brother's in the morning."

Sandy shook his head. "You've been on the trail for the best part of a week, lad. Come out to the cabin with me. The snow is in retreat. Spring is on the way. Rest up a little. Robert does na' expect yeh for ten days at the earliest. Give yersel' time to sort things out. We'll have a hunt, rest up a bit."

Jeff gave it some consideration, briefly, but set his hat back on his head. "Nope. My life is back there now. This place has gone sour. I ain't back here half an hour and I got to break a son of a bitch's nose, and then I walk in on a dead man. And not just your average dead man. This one's had his head half cut off. No, sir. I believe I've about run out my string in this town."

Sandy hailed the barman, who had just resumed his post behind the counter after having stepped to the floor to referee a scuffle between opposing factions in the case of the murdered hostler. He barely had time to refill their glasses before needing to break up another argument that threatened to get violent.

Sandy took a sip from his drink, collecting his thoughts, and then said, "Very well. I know yeh enough not to waste me time arguing when yer head is set. Just tell me this. How much has yer haste to return to Robert's got to do with his fair daughter?"

Jeff turned on his elbow and looked the old man in the eye. "Everything."

SEVENTEEN

MANO HAD MADE no empty boast. They were mounted on the two best horses they had stolen in a long career as horse thieves. Riding at a long trot the rest of that day and through the night, except for a two-hour stop at the Piedra River to water and rest those horses, they were on the outskirts of Durango at first light. A brief investigation gained them directions to the MacTeague's. In the early afternoon, having fed their mounts and themselves, they took the coach road north, along the Animas. And at dusk, from a high outcrop of rimrock, they looked down upon headquarters for the Claymore brand.

• • • •

As THINGS turned out, it was all of a day and part of another before Jeff was ready to leave for the Animas. Among other matters, he had a bank account to close, and some minor bills to settle at places of business in town. He made time for a bath and a shave, of which he was in dire need. And the hours ticked by.

The next morning featured a farewell breakfast with Sandy at Shortstack's, over which he lingered, visiting with his friends. And then his world was stood on end. As he was saying his goodbyes, a young boy came flying into the eatery, blowing like a hard-ridden horse, with a piece of paper in his hand.

"Anybody in here know a Mr. Jeff Cameron?" he called out.

Jeff spun around. "That'd be me, kid."

The boy stepped up quickly with the paper. "Telegram for Mr. Jeff Cameron. Ten cents." Dime in hand, the boy fled as fast as he had come.

"Didn't know they delivered," Jeff said as he unfolded the paper. "Aw, goddamn!" he blurted, as he read,

```
TO JEFF CAMERON:
WILL GUNLOCK SHOT (STOP) MAY NOT LIVE
(STOP) BONNIE BLUE STOLEN (STOP) COME
AT ONCE (STOP) MAGGIE
```

•   •   •   •

WHILE JEFF had been settling his affairs in Pagosa, the brothers Lucero were keeping vigil from their lookout, high in the rocks above MacTeague's headquarters. They had built a small fire on the backside of a boulder, out of view of the ranch buildings below, but there had been a stiff wind and they'd spent a cold, sleepless night. Now, with the rising of the sun in a grey sky, they watched closely for activity around the barns and corrals.

Years before, down in Old Mexico, Mano had killed a captain of *Rurales* for the fine stallion that he rode. It was a rash act and he had been compelled to ride for his life. But the captain's horse was far superior to those of the rest of his command and the chase was brief. When he did have a chance to go through the captain's saddlebags, he'd found a high quality, European-made telescope, protected by a sturdy, leather case. It was the same optic he now employed to spy on MacTeague headquarters.

Before long, the brothers were rewarded by the sight of two men leading saddled horses from the big barn. As Mano strained at the eyepiece of the telescope, they mounted up and rode out of the yard. A middle-sized man in shotgun chaps and a woolen capote had mounted a tough-looking paint horse. The taller of the two was wide shouldered in a sheepskin coat and was riding a well-built animal with a luxurious black mane and tail. Its coat was a mousy color, a blue-grey. Like that of the crane. *La grulla*. They mounted and followed.

●   ●   ●   ●

WILL AND STOGIE jogged out of the ranch yard in high spirits. It wasn't often that Juan Loera assigned them to ride as a team. Friends that they were, they always looked forward to such days. On this occasion they were to ride up to one of the late winter pastures and check forage conditions. On their way back, they would inspect cattle they encountered for sickness or injuries that might need doctoring. At this time of year, with a threat of snow on the air, snow that might trap stock, it was an important job.

It was clear to the men that the pasture still contained a good amount of winter-cured grass, bent down from repeated snows, but no less nutritious. With that confirmed, the partners split up to work the country back down toward the main ranch. They had been separated for just under an hour when Will stopped on a low ridge to study a small valley close by. It was beginning to snow and he lingered, sitting Jeff's blue mare, watching the big flakes fly. The child in him was fascinated still by snowfall. He never heard the shot that spilled him from the saddle.

●   ●   ●   ●

"LA GRULLA is a good *caballa*," said Mano as he rose from his prone shooting position and brushed himself off. "See how she stands. She did not run even twenty feet." He slid his rifle back into the scabbard and swung up on his horse.

Pepé's mouth hung open. "*Jesu Cristo*! That was the longest shot you ever made, big brother."

Mano smiled. "No, *hermanito*, there have been longer ones. But now let us go down and make one more at close range. I want to finish this."

• • • •

JEFF PUSHED the telegram at Sandy, and dashed from the eatery toward the livery. Who would shoot Will? Who would steal the mare? Well, any cold-blooded horse thief, that's who. But he felt there was more. More to this than the telegram told, or perhaps the sender even knew.

He was done in this town, for sure, wrapped up. Nothing to keep him any longer. But there'd been too much traveling lately. He was fatigued. Having been in the saddle for days before returning to Pagosa, this interlude had been too brief. Another hard ride, a fast return to the MacTeague ranch, as he was called on to do now, was the last task he'd have set for himself. But Maggie had said come, that Will was shot and may be dying. That Bonnie Blue had been taken, and in God only knew what direction. And what would he do for a horse? It would be a long ride to MacTeague's, at a demanding pace. Buck had been too many miles already. He wasn't up to it.

Sandy arrived puffing just as Jeff was looking for answers. After a few moments of gasping, he managed to croak, "What'll you do, lad?"

Jeff shook his head. "I'm working on it. I can't take Buck. He's tired. Not broke down, but if I push him back to the Claymore at the speed I need to go, he will be."

Sandy said nothing but went to a stall in the far corner of the barn and came out leading a tall, grey gelding on the end of a halter rope. The horse stood close to seventeen hands and had lightening in its eye. His young friend broke into a surprised smile. "Why didn't I think of him. That's Iron Boy, ain't it? The thoroughbred Eulis tried to sell me last fall. The one the Chavez kid's been ridin'."

The Scot handed him the rope. "Aye, laddie, the self-same steed. And from the look of him, he's full of fire, well grained, and in peak condition."

But Jeff had ceased listening. Extending his arm, he led the horse in a circle, pivoting himself in the center. The gelding seemed built of spring steel, all coiled energy, tossing his head and bouncing at the end of the rope.

Sandy went on. "It's unclear at the moment if Eulis had heirs. So I suggest that while the matter is being looked into, yeh slap your rig on this great, grey beast and ride for Claymore headquarters, and don't spare the horseflesh, as the saying goes. If anyone questions yer taking him, I'll back you up."

Jeff looked in the animal's mouth. "He's no more'n six. I reckon he's prime, all right. But he ain't shod."

Sandy looked down. "Hmm. So he isn't. Well, let's be off to the smithy, then."

•   •   •   •

LUTHER POWELL looked up from his forge and was as surprised to see Jeff and Sandy as they were to see him. Sandy recovered first. "Well, Mr. Powell, I see yeh found yer way here in good order."

The broad face split in a big grin. "Yas, suh, I sho did. An' y'all know what? Dat man dat own dis place, he say he sick o' shoin' hosses and mules, an' he sell me his tools cheap, an' den he jes' walk off. Kin ya'll beat dat?"

In spite of his troubles, Jeff had to smile. The huge man's good nature was too infectious. "Glad for your good luck, Big'un. Now tell me, and I apologize for rushing you, but it's an emergency. How fast can you shoe this horse? And it don't have to be pretty. They just need to stay on."

Powell picked up one of the grey's forefeet and examined it. "Well, Mistuh Jeff, I got some blanks dat ought to fit. Look like a #2 in front and a #1 in back. De fo'ge is already hot. I 'spect I kin git iron on him in 'bout fotey minits."

Jeff nodded. "Do it!"

• • • •

MAYBE HE was a racehorse or maybe not, but he could run, and run. They left Pagosa Springs a little before ten o'clock that morning and for the first few miles the brim of Jeff's hat was flat against the crown, the horse devouring the road. Then they settled into alternating periods of an extended trot and canter. The gelding had a tremendous stride, and Jeff had never felt such raw power in a horse.

Thoroughbred blood, for sure. All, or nearly all. He had almost no handle on him, and probably couldn't turn around in five acres, but, goddamn, could he go!

They stopped twice. First at the Piedra River for an hour. The grey was holding up well, warm but not too hot, and his breathing recovered after ten or fifteen minutes. Toward the end of the hour, after he'd cooled, Jeff fed him a small amount of grain, balled up with a little molasses. He let him take some water. Then they were moving again.

The second stop was on the *Rio de los Piños*. Another hour break, with a bit of grain and water. Then back on the road once more. Just before full dark, they jogged into the stable yard at MacTeague's. Stogie Wilson was at his stirrup as he swung down, dead cigar in the corner of his mouth. He put out his hand and the two men shook.

"Jeff! By God, I'm glad to see you back so fast." His face was a mask of fatigue and worry.

"Will?" Jeff asked hopefully.

Stogie's expression did not change. "Hit hard. Nicked a lung. But he's still with us. Said he wants to see you soon as you show up."

Jeff gave Wilson's hand a final squeeze and released it. "Good. Now take this pony and treat him right. He's made a hell of a run since this morning."

Stogie took the reins. "You bet! I'll walk him cool and then rub his legs with bracer."

Jeff nodded approval. "Thanks. I never put a harder ride on a horse."

●   ●   ●   ●

"THERE HE IS!" Maggie said. She was at the big front window, having paced the living room for most of the evening, refusing supper, taking nothing but coffee, which only intensified her anxiety. At the sight of him, she flew out the door and off the porch, clearing the three steps in one bound, landing in the yard at a run.

Robert MacTeague watched from his office window as she closed the distance to a worn-out-looking Jeff Cameron, threw herself on him, wrapped her arms around his neck, and buried her face in his chest. "So that's how it is," Mac-Teague said to himself. "Did I see that coming? Should've, if I didn't. Maybe not so bad a thing. Seems a good, straight lad." Then he felt he was spying, and returned to his desk.

She breathed in his scent—tobacco, horse, and leather, along with something that was just him. He did likewise, smelling her hair and woman skin. After a half minute, they pulled back and regarded each other. Both had grave smiles on their faces.

"You made good time," she said.

"Yeah. Thank your uncle Sandy for that. He found me a good horse. Buck needed a rest."

They turned toward the big house and she took his hand, and he let her. Neither cared who saw or what they might think. Not anymore.

"How's Will?"

"Shot high in the lung, through the back. But it looks like he'll make it. An army surgeon, friend of Da's, came out from Ft. Lewis and did a wonderful job. Said it looked like a bullet from a Winchester, probably .44-40. Said it must have been a very long shot, because the slug was hardly deformed and barely had enough velocity to penetrate to the lung. All in all, Will is a very lucky cowboy."

Jeff frowned. "Yeah, if gettin' back shot is lucky."

Maggie looked up at his hard face. "I know."

Then they were in the house. Jeff hung up his coat and hat. "I want to see him."

Maggie took both his hands and shook her head. "Not yet."

He started to protest, but she put two fingers to his lips. "You need supper. Anyway, he's asleep right now. You could use some of that yourself."

He wanted to resist, but the look on the girl's face, added to the leaden feeling in his bones, gave her the argument. After beef stew and biscuits, washed down with sweetened coffee, which seemed to revive him not at all, he meekly allowed Maggie to lead him up to a spare room and put him to bed with a kiss on the forehead. She stepped to the window to draw the curtains, and he was asleep before she was out the door.

• • • •

BULLETS KICKED up snow at their horses' feet as Mano and Pepé spurred for the cover of the timber. Mano had *la grulla*, leading her by the reins, trying to keep her from running past and getting loose as the shots echoed down the little valley. Once in the shelter of the pines, he slowed his horse so his brother could come along side.

"*Jesu Cristo*! Who was that shooting at us?" shouted Pepé.

Mano yelled back, "*Quien sabé*?" He slowed his horse to a stop, pulling *la grulla's* head close to his knee.

"Perhaps the one who rode out with him from the barn this morning."

"Very likely, *hermanito*. Your thinking is *muy bueno* to-day."

The younger Lucero ducked his head. "Thank you for saying so, big brother."

"*Nada*," Mano replied distractedly. "But if it is more than just one man, we may be in trouble."

Pepé held in his excited horse. "Then we better ride, no?"

Mano cursed vehemently, then composed himself with some effort. "I would like to put one bullet in that *gringo's* head."

The little brother's tone was fearful. "But, Mano, he is probably dead already. You hit him *muy bueno. Mucho sangré.* The snow is red. Look, there is blood on *la grulla's* saddle."

It was true. Blood was freezing bright red in the cold air on the cantle. Mano turned his horse around and looked back the way they had come. "One more bullet, in the head, to make sure." He said it through gritted teeth.

Pepé's voice was rising with anxiety. "Big brother, we have *la grulla*, and the *gringo* is bleeding out in the snow, surely dead by now." His voice higher still, nearly shrieking, "What if there are a dozen of them? The bullets came so fast and so many. Too many for one shooter alone. We need to ride!" He was verging on panic.

Mano let out a string of profanity, such as Pepé had never heard, until he ran himself down. "Very well. *Vamanos!*" He spun his mount around, dallied the blue mare's reins to his saddle horn, and sunk the rowels of his spurs into horsehide.

•   •   •   •

MAGGIE BROUGHT coffee to Jeff just as the faintest hint of sunlight was coming through the space between the drawn curtains. He felt her in the room, rolled over, and looked up. "Morning, cowboy," she said, giving him a sweet smile, with just a hint of worry behind it.

He smiled back, rubbing his bristly face. "Reckon I could use some curryin.'"

She set the tray on the night table, then leaned over and kissed him lightly on the mouth.

"You look all right to me. A little scruffy, perhaps, like a mustang. Not a bad thing, really."

"What about Will?" he asked. She went to the door.

"Drink your coffee and wash your face. He's awake and feeling better. Wants to see you. Do you want to eat first?"

He shook his head. "Nope. Let me get into my britches and I'll be along." He started to throw the covers back and noticed her still in the doorframe, smiling at him.

He smiled back. "Git," he said. And she did.

"Damn," he thought. "She minded me."

•   •   •   •

"So, THERE I am," Will said, "layin' in a couple of inches of new snow and bleedin' like a stuck hog, an' this nasty-looking Mex is up over me on his horse, and he's got the reins to your mare dallied to his saddle horn, and a pistol look's long as your arm in his hand, an' he says to me, 'We meet at last, *Señor* Cameron, and now it is time for you to pay for our brother, Jaimé, or some such shit as that, and I'm trying to tell him that I ain't no such person, but my wind pipe's full'a blood, and I'm commencin' to have a coughin' fit. So he gives me this evil grin and thumbs back the hammer on that shooter, and I'm thinkin', well, hell, whatever this is about, I ain't findin' out now."

"But then, just as I'm figurin' I'm cashed in, good ol' Stogie opens up with his '73 from the ridge, and that thing holds about thirteen or fourteen rounds, and he's slinging 'em like he owns stock in a cartridge company." Will stopped to catch his breath while Jeff stood there by the bed, very still, as things fell into place.

Will continued. "Well, he ain't hittin' anything, but that's 'cause he don't want to hit me or Bonnie Blue. But it's close enough that this *cholo* and his pard forget about me and hustle for the tall uncut." He smiled at the thought of his friend. "Good ol' Stogie. He damn sure pulled my fat out of the fire this time."

He and Jeff were alone. Maggie had gone to the kitchen to ask Hortencia to fix some bacon and eggs. The two were quiet for a spell. Will, though much improved, was weak. As he lay back and breathed a shallow breath, Jeff framed his mind around what he knew he had to say. Setting his coffee on the windowsill, he pulled up the one chair and sat down beside the bed. Will sensed his friend's anxiety and turned, painfully, toward him. "You have my attention, pard."

Jeff nodded, briefly studying a water stain high on the wallpaper over the window. "Will, this here's a long story."

Will managed a weak smile. "I ain't goin' no place."

•   •   •   •

"So, YOU get it. You and me are about the same height and build, similar color hair and mustache. I guess he picked up my description somewhere along the trail, so when he sees you on that mare, why, he just naturally figures he's got his man and busts you."

Will settled back against his pillows, coughed weakly, shook his head. "Goddamn, pard, I ain't so sure it's a healthy thing to be *your* pard."

Jeff looked over from the spot on the wall, his eyes stricken with shame and worry. But his friend was smiling. "Relax," Will said, "This is the wild and wooly west. Everybody gets shot up a little now and then. It ain't my first time. It wears off."

There was relief in the laughter that followed, covering a faint knock on the door. Maggie let herself in, unbidden, looking a bit confused. "What could possibly be funny?"

They both glanced up sheepishly, lips tight, fighting the urge to laugh more, like school boys caught in a prank. "Well," she said, "Breakfast is ready. Yours is coming up, Will, and Jeff's is downstairs on the kitchen table."

Jeff smiled at her. "Thanks, Maggie. I'll be right there." She met his eyes, a puzzled look in hers, then closed the door behind her. He got his cup from the windowsill.

Will's eyes followed him. "What're you fixin' to do?"

"Go get my mare back."

"Well, you best git moving. You got trackin' snow, but maybe not for long."

"Yeah, I expect not." He reached for the doorknob, stopped, and turned. "You're shot on my account."

Will nodded. "True enough."

Jeff held his friend's look. "I wish that wasn't the way of it."

"I know it." After a pause, Will went on. "Could'a just as easy been the other way 'round. If I'd'a seen a sumbitch beatin' a sweet little mare like her, I expect I'd'a done same as you."

Jeff stood at the door and looked at him for another second. Then he grinned. "You get better, pard. We got horses to ride."

Will grinned back. "That we do, pard."

He was halfway out the door when his friend called after him. "Hey." Will's face was grim. "You be almighty careful, Jeff. That *hijo de la perra* is one bad *hombre*."

• • • •

OUT IN THE BARN again, him saddling the grey, her standing there in her father's heavy coat, holding his saddlebags in one hand, a full grub sack in the other. As he snugged the cinch, she said, "There's more to this than you're telling me."

He couldn't look at her as he answered, "Nothin' to tell. Will's shot and Bonnie Blue's taken. I've got to move while I got tracking snow. I'll be right back here once I catch up to 'em and get her back."

Dropping the bags, she reached out and grabbed his sleeve, pulling him around to face her. "You look at me, Jeff Cameron. Don't you dare ride out of here and not tell me what's going on."

He stared into bottomless, blue eyes and said, "Maggie, there's not time now. I got little enough chance as it is. But I promise you this. When I ride back in here it will be to stay, and I can't stay without cleaning up a mess that's been following me all winter, and I didn't even know it 'til this morning."

Her mouth fell open, then she said, "Well, if that isn't the most obscure, evasive load of horseshit I have ever heard. You're going off to maybe get killed and you don't intend to tell me more than that?"

He turned back to his horse. "There's no time for more now. I swear you'll hear it all when I get back."

She turned him around again. "*If* you get back. Will says there're two of them."

He nodded. "Yeah."

She was angry now. "Well, damn it, Jeff, improve the odds. Take Stogie and Johnny Blacktail to help you."

He shook his head. "Nope. I got one of your men shot already. 'Sides, they'd never keep up with this thoroughbred. And I'm bound to straighten this out myself."

She was bordering on furious as she said, "Well, for God's sake, take a fresh horse! Take my stallion."

He smiled and touched her hair. "Thanks, Maggie, but no thanks. Iron Boy here's had a night off and a good feed. He's a long way from used up. Besides, I might not be able to bring your horse back. And he's your foundation stud."

She blurted, "So are you, you dumb son of a bitch!" And she jerked off her hat and slapped him across the chest with it. Then she kissed him, hard.

EIGHTEEN

H E KNEW the ranch well enough by then to find where Will had been shot, based on his directions. There was still blood on the snow, frozen bright red amidst the confusion of horse tracks and boot prints. He dismounted and studied the sign carefully. The tracks of three running horses led off down the valley, toward the timber edge a hundred yards away. Turning to look back up country, he saw the high point where, based on Will's description, Stogie must have taken a position and fired with his Winchester. It had to be over four hundred yards away. He couldn't have hit much of anything even if he'd meant to.

Swinging up onto the racer, he felt the horse's energy coming up through the saddle. With no more than ten hours rest, following a hard ride of nearly sixty miles, the horse seemed fully recovered. "Wonder how much bottom you got, ol' son? Well, I expect we're goin' to find out." Jeff had no such energy. He felt only a little refreshed by the night's rest.

He found where the horse thieves had retreated into the trees. He saw no more blood and concluded that Stogie had managed to avoid hitting either animals or men. It meant, to that point at least, Bonnie Blue had been unharmed.

The trail continued down the little valley. It swung in a wide arc to the southeast, away from MacTeague headquarters, and connected with the coach road. There the tracks of the three horses were mixed with those of deer, elk, and even a few stray cattle, not to mention wheel ruts.

He sat the grey, letting him blow, and took the opportunity to build a smoke. He thought back on what Will had told him. The shooter had said he was paying him back for his brother, Jaimé. So, these men he was now tracking had been hunting him since sometime after the confrontation that left Bad Jimmy buried in the wash north of Taos. That made Taos his only clue, or as close as he could come to one.

Bad Jimmy had worked as a *vaquero* in the country thereabouts. Presumably, that's where his brothers were from, also. Or, if not exactly there, then at least northern New Mexico. Would they return the way they had come? He had to anticipate they would. It was country they knew. It was likely they had folks there to help them, that they could depend on.

His cigarette was down to a short butt. Flipping it into the road, he lifted the reins. The Luceros had close to a two day head start, and probably were not yet expecting pursuit. Likely they weren't pushing their pace too hard.

"So maybe we can catch 'em," he told the horse. "And the only way is to ride hard." Leaning over to rub the racer's neck, he said, "All right, Iron Boy. Let's see how much iron we got."

•   •   •   •

HOUR AFTER HOUR. Mile after mile. If one of them wound up killing the other, he didn't think it would be him killing the horse. There didn't seem to be a bottom to him. They made good time, despite the rutted, often treacherously muddy and icy winter road. Whatever he asked for, the horse gave him, and was eager to do it. Born for it.

That road, the most direct route to Taos from the Animas Valley, ran due east to Pagosa Springs and then southeast, more than two hundred miles. Perhaps, if the Luceros were not feeling hard pressed, he could catch them camped along the route. Possible, he thought, but unlikely. After all, they had shot and so far as they knew killed a man. And stolen a horse. More likely, there would be little stopping, and not for long, as they would want to continue putting distance between themselves and the scene of their crimes.

Upon reaching Chimney Rock, he checked at the small trading post for evidence of his quarry. He got no information about a blue mare or any desperate-looking *vaqueros* with hard-used horses. He rode on.

• • • •

HE PUSHED and the big horse did not falter. He'd bought more grain in Aspen Springs. He spent what time he believed he could spare in letting the animal rest and feed along their route. He noticed the horse had thinned, but he judged it from a general hardening, and not lack of feed. He felt a toughening in himself, as well—in body and mind. And while this was good, there was still the fact of his fatigue. Whatever the coming confrontation would require, he must be ready. He'd need his best judgment and quickest reflexes. He thought again of the ten-pound Winchester he'd left behind at MacTeague's to conserve weight. Any shooting required he'd have to handle with his Colt. He wished he was more skilled with it.

Mid-morning of the second day found Jeff and Iron Boy a short distance from Pagosa Springs. He considered whether the horse thieves would pass through town before turning south toward the New Mexico line. There was a shortcut that left the main road and angled southeast, missing the town proper and reconnecting with the main road to Chama a few miles below Pagosa. While Jeff was unaware that the men he pursued were the killers of the liveryman, Eulis Foster, he reasoned they would choose to avoid the town since they led a well-known horse, which could raise questions. Now a stolen horse.

"If I was them sonsabitches," he said out loud to the grey, "I believe I'd take roundance on the Springs."

A mile or so west of town he came to where the road turning southeast left the main one. It was marked by a small way station, which also served as a saloon, with a barn and a bunkhouse. Jeff decided to stop briefly to water and feed the racer, and to ask if anyone had seen the men he hunted. An old man sweeping the porch looked up and smiled in welcome.

"Mornin', son. I got bacon and fresh hen eggs if you're hungry. And some leftover biscuits, too."

Jeff smiled neutrally, but shook his head. "Thanks, dad, but I'm trailin' a pair of horse thieves, bandits heading Taos way. They dress like *vaqueros*, but they don't do any honest cowboy work. They back shot my pardner over on the Animas, and they're leading a nice mare of mine, colored kind of a slate-grey. You seen any such fellas?"

The old timer straightened his spine with effort, and a look of indignation grew on his leathery features. "I wish to hell I could say no, but it was likely them very scoundrels that come through here late, day before yesterday. Put their horses in the barn, fed 'em my hay and grain, acted like they meant to stay the night. Nobody else was here and I was pleased to get the business. I fried them bastards a couple of big beefsteaks, poured 'em whiskey, give 'em a couple of good seegars. And for all that I got this." Taking off his weathered hat, he bent slightly forward to reveal a large, angry-looking lump on his bald head.

"Pistol whipped me, did that no account rascal. Then they cleaned out the till and rode on."

Jeff's heart was pumping faster as the tale was told. He'd guessed correctly. He was on the right track. "Sorry to hear it, friend. And I expect you're lucky you ain't dead. Did you take notice of which direction they went?" The old man put his hat back on, pressed it down gingerly, and then turned and pointed with the end of his broom stick to the southeast.

"It was plumb dark by then, but what I couldn't see, I could still hear. They took the cutoff, the one here. It hooks up with the main road to Chama, about three miles yonder." The man leaned his broom against a post and turned back to face Jeff. "If you aim to run down that pair, you best get some grub down your neck. And that giraffe of a horse looks like he could use a feed."

Jeff decided to relent in the face of the old man's salesmanship, after all. "All right, dad, I reckon I got an hour. I'll toss this *giraffe* some hay while you cook." He stepped down off the horse and led it toward the barn.

The old timer called after him, "How you like yer eggs, son?"

Over his shoulder Jeff asked, "Can you flip an egg without breakin' it?"

Grinning, the man said, "Hell, yes."

Jeff called back, "Why, over easy then."

•   •   •   •

WITH A FULL STOMACH, and the confirmation of his hunch about the route of those he hunted, Jeff paid the combination saloon keeper, *café* cook, and livery man, then went to the barn to saddle the grey. He had stripped the gear from his sweaty back and rubbed him down with a gunny sack before going in to eat. It was his maxim. Take care of your ponies first, and they'll always take care of you.

•   •   •   •

TWENTY-FIVE MILES south of Pagosa on the road to Chama, New Mexico Territory, hard by the banks of the Navajo River, with a view of the spectacular Banded Peaks, sat the nearly non-existent settlement of Chromo, Colorado. More of a place than a town, it consisted of a saloon, a feed store, and a wagon yard with campsite for overnighting freighters to rest their teams and themselves before climbing the grade to the pass on their way to Pagosa Springs.

A tired rider on a still-energetic, grey gelding came down off that grade and into the tiny community of Chromo shortly after dark, and was astounded to see, by lantern light,

Bonnie Blue, tied to the hitch rack in front of the saloon. Next to her was a saddled mule, as well as the two fine-bred horses he had noticed the *vaqueros* riding as they passed him and Sandy some few days back in Pagosa. It was on the same day he'd found Eulis Foster with his throat cut. And so another piece of the puzzle seemed to fall into place.

He pulled up the grey and sat motionless in the street, a short distance from his mare and, he presumed, the men who had murdered Eulis and shot Will. Undoubtedly, they were inside. Feeling suddenly exposed in this position, he reined the grey into a nearby alley and stepped down. They were out of sight, and now he could think.

He'd hoped for luck and he'd found some. Here she was, in this tiny town. So far as he could tell, she seemed unharmed. Since they were no farther from the ranch than this, they must not have pushed too hard, at least not after their initial run. They must not be fearing pursuit.

He saw that Will's saddle was on her back, the bridle hanging from the horn. She was tied to the hitch rack by a neck rope, undoubtedly with a slipknot, as was commonly used by *vaqueros*. By simply jerking the tail of the lead rope, he could free his horse and be off with her. He could be gone with no one noticing, if they were sufficiently distracted inside.

So that was the plan. He would bide his time, wait for those *pistoleros* in there to soak up enough tequila to become loose and careless. And when he judged the time was right, he'd slip out from the alley, claim his horse, and be gone. Nothing to it. Maybe.

And so he did what there was to do, which meant waiting and watching. And being ready. He decided to give them two hours. If, on the other hand, they came out sooner, he would follow them. Not a complicated strategy.

It was cold. He grained the grey, and then rolled and lit a cigarette to calm his nerves. Hanging it in the corner of his mouth and cocking his head enough to keep the smoke out of his eyes, he shoved his hands deep into the pockets of his sheepskin, leaned against the warm body of the horse, and began his vigil. He had a good enough view.

• • • •

"GOOD THING we saved most of the Lord's money, eh, Mano?" Pepé could seem dim enough when sober. Drinking didn't improve him.

Mano looked at his younger brother through a growing tequila haze and said, "What?"

Pepé showed a childish grin. "The Lord's money, which the Reverend stole from him, which we stole from the Reverend. Remember?"

Mano laughed. "*Si, hermanito.* The Reverend. And it is true. If the old livery man had not mentioned *la grulla*, we might have spent all this money in Pagosa Springs, eating fine food, drinking fine wine, and soaking in the hot water."

Pepé smiled, a rhapsodic look appearing on his face. "Oh, *si*, big brother. *Agua caliente.* I loved that hot water."

Mano nodded. "*Yo tambien,* little brother. And it was *buena suerte* to get another fifty dollars at the cutoff from the *gringo viejo,* who fed us steaks and gave us fine cigars. Our luck is running well." Raising his glass toward his brother, who raised his in kind, Mano said, "*Salud!*"

They were celebrating the recovery of their brother's horse and the killing of his killer. And their good financial fortunes in crime. There was no one following them. They felt in the clear. And it seemed they could take their time in returning to Taos, where they could report the end of their hunt to *El Patron*, Don Espinoza. Finally, they could see to the end of their long, hard trail.

It was approaching ten o'clock and they had not thought of supper. As a result, the tequila had a good hold on them. So, at first they paid no attention to the man yelling on the boardwalk just outside the front door of the barroom.

• • • •

JEFF LOADED the chamber in the cylinder of the Colt that for safety usually remained empty under the hammer. Returning the pistol to its holster, he wiped his sweaty palms on the front of his sheepskin. It was time to act. His blue mare was still tied out front of the *cantina*, and the music and the laughter from inside had been rising steadily in volume.

"Well," he declared out loud to the grey, "our best chance is right now." He moved to the saddle, snugged the cinch, swung up, and eased the big horse into the street. There was no one else out. Everyone was either in the saloon or safe at home, he reckoned. "All right, let's git 'er done then."

In the small community of Chromo, no street lamps illuminated the dark. But for the glow of less than half a moon and a bit of light from two small lanterns, one on either side of the barroom door, all was dark around him. The high-strung racer felt his anxiety and was chafing at the bit, and he had to rein him in firmly. The grey jigged down the street until they were at the hitch rack in front of the barroom. Jeff saw no one at the door or windows. He eased the grey between the tied animals and reached for the rope that held his mare. It was nothing more than bad timing that caused the fat man with the pistol stuck behind his straining waistband to choose that moment to step outside for a breath of air.

Jeff had been right about the slipknot, and was backing his mare from her position at the rail, when light dimly broke from the just-opened door and seconds later a voice called, "Hey, *gringo*, *que´ pasa*?" He pretended not to hear and continued about his business.

"Hey, *gringo*! I ask you where you going with that horse?"

He looked up and smiled. "*No problema, amigo.* She is mine."

The fat man took another step forward from the doorway and called in a louder voice, "I don't think so." He was pulling his pistol. "And I ain't your *amigo*."

"Oh well, shit!" Jeff cursed and jerked his Colt, throwing a shot over the man's head with no intention of hitting him. It had the desired effect. The fat man back peddled into the bar, leaving the door wide open.

He considered for a moment shooting the two blooded horses of the *vaqueros*, as he knew he ought to, for the edge it would give him. But he could no more kill them than he could the old rental horse on which Bad Jimmy had followed him. Holstering his pistol, he pulled his belt knife, kneeing the grey in close enough to the Luceros' mounts to lean from the saddle and cut their reins. Sheathing the knife, he jerked his hat off and fanned it at the horses heads, crowding them hard and howling like a fiend. They both jerked back from the hitch rack and pounded down the street, headed west. Then he was out of time.

• • • •

A GUNSHOT can have a sobering effect, even on men as much in their cups as the brothers. At the report, Mano looked up to see the portly fellow backing through the doorway as quickly as his heavy body would move. He shook his head hard in an effort to dispel the alcohol fog in his brain. He was aware then of the voice of a madman screaming outside the entry. He rose from his chair and reached for his pistol. Pepé gave him a puzzled look, then caught on, too, and followed his brother to the door.

The scene before them took a moment to comprehend. Both of their horses were nowhere in sight. Gone, also, was *la grulla*. Only the fat man's saddled mule stood at that hitch rack, looking wild eyed at the end of her rope.

Mano was first to move from the boardwalk. Lurching into the street, he could barely see, partly because of the dark, but also as a result of his abrupt exit from the lit barroom. He stopped moving and cocked an ear. He heard departing hoof beats of at least a couple of horses going west down the road, and going east the sound of other running horses. Aiming east at the sounds in the dark, he got off five rounds from his pistol as fast as he could cock the hammer and pull the trigger. And then his ears were ringing from the first shot of Pepé's gun, fired close to his head. Turning in a fury, he snatched the piece from his brother and emptied it down the street to the west.

The fat man had come back out of the bar and into the street, and Mano, muttering "*Permiso, gordo*," untied the man's mule and swung up. Turning her into the street, he called to his brother. "*Hermanito*, run up the road to the east. Our *caballos* went one way or the other. If they are to the west, I will catch them and come for you."

•   •   •   •

JEFF WAS HIT. He'd never been shot before. High up in his right shoulder. Above the bone, he thought. It hurt, burned, but without the numb, shocked feeling he expected of a bullet through the shoulder blade. "Went on through," he figured, feeling warm blood running down the front of his chest. Must have cleared the collarbone, too, because he could move everything. But, "Boy howdy, it hurts!"

The horses were running freely, Bonnie Blue having no trouble keeping up with the grey. Jeff guessed they'd come two or three miles from Chromo. He could see almost nothing of the road. He was trusting the big gelding to find the way and, so far, it was working.

And then the first off-step, and after four more unbalanced strides Iron Boy was down, sunk on his knees, and then rolling over as the rider sprang off, keeping his feet.

It was on the right flank, about six inches behind the last rib, down low in the gut. Jeff had lit a match with his good hand, and it had gone out and he'd had to light two more before he found it. A neat, round hole that oozed dark blood. "Goddamn!" he cursed, "The dirty sons a bitches got both of us." He moved up to the gelding's head and drew his Colt, left handed, and then saw that he didn't need it. The tall, grey thoroughbred that was born and bred to race, that had carried him so gallantly and willingly, was dead. He holstered his revolver. Nodding down at the horse and taking in a tight breath, he paused and then let it out, and said, "Well. Well now, son. You did fine. Real fine. Never had more horse under me."

• • • •

MOUNTING AGAIN was difficult, not to mention painful, but he managed. Time to be moving. He settled himself, checked the tie-down on the hammer of his Colt. "Don't want to lose that," he told the mare. "Probably going to need it again before this thing's over. And I'm going to miss that saddle, genuine Visalia. But we've gotta fly now. Let's go, girl."

He touched a spur to her flank and asked for a slow, steady canter. A long trot would be too jarring. He pulled off his neckerchief as they loped down the road, stuffing it inside the front of his shirt against the wound. "Wish I could reach around and pack something in that goin' in hole. Guess it'll just have to leak. Man, this mare is smooth."

• • • •

MANO TOOK stock of his and Pepé's remaining funds. He found they had enough to hire a couple of men from the village to help in their hunt for the one who had taken *la grulla*, for the second time. It was also sufficient for the purchase of ammunition and provisions for the trail.

They had recovered quickly their long-legged mounts. At first light they set out, and in under half an hour came upon the grey gelding, stiff in death and still wearing Jeff's rig.

Mano stepped down and had one of the hirelings remove the saddle and hide it in a patch of brush. It was past sunup and things could be seen clearly. He found the animal's wound.

"All those shots in the dark were not wasted," he growled.

Pepé sat his horse, considered pointing out the fact that one of those shots in the dark had left a bullet burn on his own mount's hip, but then decided Mano would not receive well any such observation. Looking at the dead animal in the road, he asked, "Do you know that horse, big brother?"

Mano shook his head. "No, *hermanito*. But the fat man told me the one who took *la grulla* and ran off our *caballos* was a *gringo*, tall and broad, on a grey horse." Pepé's face remained blank.

"I think it was the man I shot in the little valley, when we recovered Jaimé's mare," Mano explained.

The younger brother's mouth dropped. "Surely not, Mano. You shot him *muerto*, no?"

The older man frowned as he remounted. "I do not believe it, little brother. But he must still be weak or else he would have hidden his saddle. He also must be tiring. We may find him soon. But we must push hard." Tuning his horse in the direction Jeff had ridden, he called to the hired gunmen, "An extra fifty *gringo* dollars if we catch him before dawn tomorrow!"

•   •   •   •

AN HOUR later, Pepé reined in and yelled to Mano up ahead, "Big brother, *aqui, pronto!*" Mano turned to see him off his horse with something in his hand. He rode over and his brother held up a horseshoe. He was grinning. "This is one of the shoes of *la grulla*. I would know it in my sleep."

Mano frowned. "How can you be sure?"

Pepé bobbed his head. "Oh, but I *am* sure. Since we got her back, I have been careful to clean her feet, as you instructed. I know her shoes. This one is from her near hind foot. See? It has a heel turned in and a bent toe calk. This is hers, brother. I swear it, on the Virgin!"

Mano crossed himself. "Careful what you swear to. But if you are right, this helps. She will be easy to track." Pepé stood there grinning. Mano granted him a smile and a nod. "Good eye, little brother. Good eye."

NINETEEN

COFFEE WITHOUT CREAM wasn't fit to drink. At least not in the view of John Jobson, United States Marshal, retired. That was half the reason he kept a cow, that and to feed the milk, which he did not care for, to a pair of shoats he was raising to butcher. But he stood by the cook stove this morning, steaming coffee mug in hand, staring at the small, empty cream can on the countertop, which that goddamned wild barn cat must have snuck in and knocked over. It was obvious that if he was going to enjoy his coffee, he had to go to the shed and milk the cow. In irritation, he dumped the coffee from his mug back into the pot.

Milking was a chore that he preferred to postpone until after breakfast, which he had not yet prepared for himself. No cream was inconvenience enough, but finding the cow gone, as he did upon reaching the shed, he considered a trial, and he said as much to his dog, an old pointer, who had seen his better days.

"I swear, Bob. This is a goddamned trial!" Bob thumped his tail against the barn floor and looked up at the old man as he saddled his horse and continued cursing. "I oughtn't to be subjected to shit such as this. Not so early in the mornin', and not at my age." Bob's tail stopped. "That damned old boss bitch is the worst milk cow I ever owned. Always lookin' for a chance to take a jaunt over the prairie. Serve her right if the wolves or a starvin' Jicarilla gits her."

It was obvious how she had made good her escape. She'd knocked down the same boards of her stall as the last time. And John Jobson figured he'd find her in the same place as last time, up at the mineral spring, half a mile above the cabin. She was fond of licking the deposits around the seeping pool, and he thought it pretty likely that's where she had returned.

The old lawman lived in the foothill country east of Chromo, Colorado, not too far from the south bank of the Navajo River, a couple of miles up Buckhammer Canyon. He was generally regarded as a good man, but of uneven temper. Two wives had agreed with that estimation. Now he lived alone, unless one counted the pointer, his saddle horse, a wandering milk cow, two weaner pigs, a few laying hens, and a barn cat.

He dropped a lead rope for the cow over his saddle horn and swung up. He was a big man for his day, close to six feet tall, and had been thickening through the body in recent years. But he could still sit a horse, and mounted with ease. Bob led the way as they jogged out of the yard.

Nearing the spring, the dog seemed to catch a whiff of something. Lifting his head and lengthening his stride, he loped on ahead. He disappeared into the brush that grew up around the water, and shortly Jobson heard him barking. The next thing he thought he'd see would be the cow coming out of the brush, full bag swinging. But having leaned over to duck a low limb, he straightened up and rode into the little clearing to a sight that stopped him cold.

There was the missing cow, as expected, but she had company. A well-built little mare stood on the other side of the pool. She was a smoky color, almost blue, saddled and bridled. But that was not what had the marshal's main attention. Lying next to the pool, one hand in the water, was the form of a man, face down, the back of his sheepskin coat stained in blood.

"Well, goddamn again!" swore Jobson out loud. "First no cream for my coffee, and now the spring is fouled by a corpse."

As the ex-lawman sat his horse fuming, the corpse raised itself enough to open an eye and croak, "I ain't dead yet, you grumpy, old bastard, but I'm close. How 'bout a hand?"

• • • •

JOBSON SHOOK his head. "That's one hell of a tale, son."

Jeff took another spoonful of soup, wiping his mouth on the sleeve of his long johns. "Well, I can guarantee I ain't making it up."

Jobson shook his head again. "No, I don't expect you are. If you could cook up a yarn like that, you'd be writin' dime novels, not punchin' cows and twistin' broncs."

His rescuer had put Jeff up on his own horse and led him to the cabin, careful to keep the wounded man from falling off. Bob, Bonnie Blue, and the cow had followed. As much as the cow enjoyed the salt lick, her bag was tight and she was ready to be milked. It was a chore that the Marshal had attended to as soon as he determined that the young man was not in imminent danger of death and had something to eat. Jobson had gotten him into a spare bunk and dressed his wound. And then he reheated his coffee and had a belated cup, with cream.

"Much obliged for the doctorin', Marshal. I expect I'd of been dead by dark."

Jobson smiled and said. "Nothin' to it son. I patched up many a man and corked many a bullet hole in thirty years of law work. Some of them holes I made myself." He went on, "And I ain't so sure you would of succumbed to that wound. You seem a tough critter and it weren't all that bad in the first place. Bullet passed through high, missed the bones, and closed up fairly quick. Your coat's a mess, but truth is, you didn't lose all that much blood. You're lucky."

Jeff frowned. "That damned Lucero's the lucky one, shooting in the dark and all, and me a hundred yards up the road by then."

The old man peered around from the stove. "You say Lucero?"

Jeff nodded. "That's right."

A dark look crossed Jobson's face. Then he nodded agreement. "Right. You said you took that mare away from Bad Jimmy. I forgot already. Don't get old son." Both were silent for an interval, but an uneasiness remained in Jobson. Jeff felt it.

"You know the Luceros?" he asked.

The marshal came back to the bunk, hooked a chair with his boot toe, pulled it over, sat down. "You got the makin's son? I'm slap out."

Jeff pointed to his shirt, hanging from a nail in the wall. "In the left pocket. Roll me one, too, if you don't mind."

When they both had cigarettes lit, Jobson returned to where they had left off. "No use trying to make less of it. I had dealin's with the Luceros years ago. Bad Jimmy's daddy weren't plumb rotten, but all his boys was no account. I credit their mamma for that. She was a *curandera,* a healer woman. I always figured her for more witch than anything else. And mean as hell. There was five boys, to start out. I had to shoot one up pretty good when he was drunk and terrorizin' a *cantina* south of here. Killed him. No choice. Sent another to territorial prison for cattle rustling. And if you got the one huntin' you that I think you do, then it's the worst pup in the litter."

Jeff sat up, grimacing. "That so?"

The marshal nodded. "The little brother's a mite slow. Got kicked in the head when he was ten or twelve, tryin' to shoe a mule. His name's Pepé. I caught him stealin' a horse when he was fourteen. His older brother put him up to it. He got convicted, but on account of his youth and low mentality, they not only didn't hang him, they let him go home after ninety days in county jail. The owner of the horse didn't press charges, had his horse back, and felt sorry for the kid. He probably wouldn't of turned out too bad, 'cept for that sumbitch Mano's bad influence."

Jeff drew on his smoke, let it out. "You think he's the one that shot my pardner. And probably me, too?"

Jobson leaned back in the chair. "That's right. He's the bad one. Emiliano. But everyone call's him Mano. He had a chance, at first. His daddy saw he was smart, sent him to a mission school for a few years. He learned to read good. Picked up English. Might of done all right, but that witchy mama come and got him and brought him home. Before long she'd poisoned his heart."

Taking a deep draw on his cigarette, he continued. "I chased him for a month one time. He killed a whiskey peddler down in Española just for his sample case. Was drunk when he did it, which made some folks think I should of gone a little easier on him than I did. But my position was, drunk or not, the man he shot was just as dead. Besides, I suspected him of robbing a federal paymaster the year before. Killed that man, too. Anyway, I run him to ground south of Deming. We gunned it out, but my aim was off that day. I just kinda' shot him up around the edges. He give me this." Jobson held up his left pinkie, which was missing down to the second joint.

"So he got across the border before I could finish the job. I haven't seen him since, but now and then I hear about some nasty piece of work that sounds like his doin's." He looked over at his guest. The food and warm bed had done their part on Jeff's tired body. He was nodding.

Jobson stubbed out his smoke in an empty saddle soap can, which now held sand and served as his ashtray. "Enough of my spook stories. I'm goin' out to check the stock. You get some sleep." Rising stiffly, he blew out the lamp and moved toward the front door. From the dark he added, "Sometimes old Bob gets to sleep inside, 'specially if it's cold, like tonight. But he's bad to get windy. I can't smell nothin' no more, so if he gets to stinkin' you out, just holler and I'll bring him in my room. Night son."

•　•　•　•

SHORTLY AFTER BREAKFAST, the ex-marshal came in from the barn with a full cream can in one hand and a grave look on his face. Jeff was up and dressed, sitting at the one table in the cabin, a cup of hot coffee in front of him and a cigarette resting over the edge of the ashtray. His right shoulder was sore, but otherwise he felt pretty good, if tired. Bob sat with his head on Jeff's knee, drawn to him as most animals were. The old man's sober mood was apparent, however.

Jeff spoke up. "What's on your mind, Marshal?"

Jobson poured himself a cup and laced it liberally with cream before answering. "That's a sweet little mare out there. She tried to pick my pockets while I was milkin' the ol' runaway."

Jeff smiled. "Yeah. I carry scraps of *tortilla* and cold biscuit for her. I guess I spoil her some."

Jobson came to the table and sat. "Did you know that she cast a hind shoe?"

Jeff's face clouded. "No, sir. I didn't."

He had left his makings by the ashtray and the marshal, frowning, reached over and helped himself. Lighting up and waving the match out, he took a deep pull and blew smoke up toward the ceiling. He smoothed his white mustache with a thumb and forefinger and looked at Jeff.

"So, if you didn't know she's lost one, then you sure don't know when she did it." This he said more to himself than to his guest. "And if you don't know when, then you don't know where. So we got to figure the worst."

Jeff was with him now. "Right. And the worst is that I've left those two killers a trail a blind man could follow."

Jobson looked over at him. "Yeah, that's about it."

They smoked for a time in silence, then Jeff stood up. "I better ride. I've likely brought 'em right to your door."

Jobson put up a hand. "Whoa, son. Sit down. You ain't in no shape to ride yet. And when you are, you're goin' to have to ride like hell. Which means that your mare needs all the rest and grain she can get first." He took a final draw on his cigarette and butted it out in the sand. Rising, he said, "Come 'ere."

Out on the porch, the old man pointed up toward a ridge to the southwest, about a quarter mile away. "Yonder is my summer night camp. Times when it's too hot to sleep in the cabin, I go up there for the breeze. I got a nice little set up. There's a cot under a ramada, and a sheepherder stove with a good slug of wood put by. It's all under a wagon sheet right now, and it's not so cold with spring comin' on that you couldn't lay up there a while, take that pony up there with you. We could haul some hay and grain up there for her, and a barrel of water. Take it in the wagon up the two track. Wouldn't look suspicious that way."

He was warming to the idea now. "And we could wrap her feet in gunny sackin', so she'd leave no trail if you rode her up from here. Could even sweep out whatever tracks she might make."

Jeff frowned. "That's putting you out too much. I guess I should just get on out of here."

Jobson turned to face him, and for the first time Jeff was treated to a small dose of the famous temper. "Goddamnit, boy, shut up for a minute! Just shut the hell up and listen to an old lawman." Jeff backed up a step, but said nothing. Jobson's face relaxed. "Okay, now look here. There's one of two things gonna' happen. One, these boys won't be able to unravel your trail, in which case, you can spend a few more days here 'til you and your horse are better fit to travel, and then be on your merry way." Jeff nodded, but still said nothing. Jobson went on. "But to call it like I see it, the chance of that happening is slim, as I expect you know."

Jeff nodded again. "Yeah, I reckon so."

The old man turned his gaze northwest and said, "Now, here's what I believe is more likely. The road between here and Chromo ain't much at best, and this time of year it's a mess. Likely ol' Mano and anyone along with him will have slow going, what with that road and the fact that they got to work out the mare's track from all the other sign there, even with a cast shoe. So I figure we got 'til sometime tomorrow, at the earliest, or if we're lucky, the next day, 'til we get a visit from the Lucero boys."

Jeff stood up straight. "All the more reason for me to travel now."

The frown was back on Jobson's face. "Yeah, and if you do, they'll catch you along the road to Pagosa, sitting on a played out horse, or laying in the road, looking like I found you up at the spring. No, son, here's what we're gonna do. We're gonna fix you up in my little night camp, you and your mare, and you can watch the road coming in. You can see it for most of a mile from up there. And when they come, and I figure it's when and not if, you'll be in good shape to drop off the backside of that ridge and make your run, with a head start on 'em."

Jeff detected a note of excitement in the old marshal's voice. "What about you, though?" he asked. "They're gonna follow that track right to your barn door. And I guess you'll just stand out here on the porch and say, "No, sir, Mr. Lucero. I don't believe I know any such *hombre* on any such horse." And Mano'll just say "Well, much obliged then, Marshal Jobson." And they'll turn their horses around and ride out peaceful."

The old man grinned at Jeff and hitched up his canvas pants. "Nope. I got it figured a little different. I'm plannin' a little party for Mano and whosoever he's got with him." He turned to look out over his yard and outbuildings. After a few seconds he said, "Son, I been stalled out on this place for close to ten years, drawin' a piddlin' interest on my savin's, huntin' and fishin', tendin' a sorry little garden, and milkin' a goddamned runaway cow. Now and then I ride into Chromo and have a drink, maybe sit in on a game. I thought I'd like it, and sometimes I do. The river's full of cutthroats and brookies, and the hills are spillin' over with deer and elk. I enjoy my days with rod and gun. But for thirty years I was a man of action. I helped tame this country. I shot it out with some of the bad ones and I'm here to tell the tale. Truth is, I'm bored. And I guess I'm a rough old cob, cause I never could get a woman to stick." Scratching his scalp through a thin patch of white hair he said, "Plus, I got no intention of pullin' my last breath in some goddamn rest home for wore out marshals." Shaking his head he said, "Nope, I'll not cash in like that."

Then he smiled again. "I'm going to enjoy this. Let the sumbitches come. They'll get a welcome they didn't count on. Now, I'm going to go slap a shoe on your mare." Standing up, he looked Jeff in the eye, holding up the hand with the abbreviated pinkie. "And besides," he said. "Mano and me's got some unfinished business."

•　•　•　•

THEY SPENT the rest of the day getting Jeff and Bonnie Blue's camp in order. When the hay was stacked and the grain stowed, the half barrel of water unloaded, and the canvas sheet that had covered the cot and firewood stretched over it all, the two men spent time shoveling the remaining snow into a barrier on the windward side of the ramada.

What with Jeff's sore shoulder, the marshal did most of the work. He seemed to glow with the effort. Surveying the results of their labors as the sun went down, Jobson said, "Not bad. Not bad a'tall. The wood's good and dry, so you can have a fire in the stove and not fret about smoke. There's feed for her and grub for you for a week. Our company ain't due to arrive 'til sometime tomorrow at the earliest, so I'd say we're set. We can go down now and you can stay in the cabin tonight. I'll lock your mare in the shed with my gelding and that damned cow. Even if they should get here early by some miracle, they won't try anything in the dark."

Jeff nodded. "You're the doctor, Marshal."

Jobson grinned. "I got a good appetite. Let's go have us a big venison steak, with some fried spuds and onions. Then I think we're gonna have another kind of party in a day or two."

As they rode the wagon down the slope toward the cabin, Jobson driving, the tall gelding between the traces, Jeff shook his head and smiled and thought to himself. "This old man's having fun."

• • • •

"LET'S GET one thing straight, son," said the marshal as he dried the last supper dish. "When you see them comin', you bail onto that pony and skedaddle. Don't hang around to watch the show. That makes all the risk I'm taking useless. When it starts, there won't be a damn thing you can do to help me. It'll all happen too fast. And if you was the greatest pistol shot on God's green earth, you couldn't hit no Luceros from up there if they was ten of 'em standin' in a huddle. You hear me?"

Jeff nodded agreement. "That don't mean I like ridin' off and leaving you to cover me alone."

Jobson frowned and shook his head. "You ain't hearin' me, boy! I'm the professional. Like as not you'd just get me killed if you was in it. When this thing's over, I'll wire you in Pagosa Springs and give you all the gory details."

Jeff's ears pricked up. "There's a telegraph office around here?"

Jobson nodded. "In Chromo. Not much else there, as you know. Just a bar and a wagon yard. You'd think the telegrapher would have his own little shack. But, no, he's in the saloon. If you find he ain't too drunk to do it, you might have him telegraph somebody in Pagosa that you're coming. And when you skin out of here, you should skip the main wagon road up the pass. Too exposed. And too muddy, rutted, and slow where it drops into a couple of drainages. Instead, from the saloon you could head cross country east a bit and then turn north, if you knew the territory."

Jeff brightened. "Well, I do, come to think on it. I do know some of that country. An old market hunter from Pagosa and me have worked a stretch from the San Juan to the Navajo, here on your end, hunting elk and deer. I expect I could find my way. That would keep me off the main road."

Jobson hung up the dishtowel and said, "That'd be the ticket, if you could. You'd be harder to catch over that broken country. I doubt them Luceros have ridden it a'tall. You'd have an advantage." He turned and went into his bedroom, and called back, "Hang on, son." He opened a trunk at the foot of his bed, dug around in it for a minute or so, and returned to the main room. "Here you go, take these." He handed him a pair of worn binoculars. "Won those off an army scout in a card game down in Albuquerque some years ago. They'll help you spot them rascals when they come."

• • • • •

AND THEM RASCALS were coming. It was late afternoon of the next day and Jeff had bacon frying in a small skillet on the sheepherder stove. Bonnie Blue was saddled, but with the cinch loose, the bridle hanging from the horn. While he waited on the bacon, he scanned the road with the field glasses. And just like that, there they were—four mounted men—just becoming visible as they crested a rise, coming at a long trot. All wore broad-brimmed sombreros. It had to be them. The brothers, plus two more. It appeared they had hired some help.

He swung the glasses back toward the cabin. No sign of the marshal. He was fearful for the old man, and considered a warning shot. Stupid! That would only give away his position. No, Jobson had stated it clearly. Just go, he'd said. And Jeff had given his word that he would.

Setting the skillet off the stove, he turned to the mare, snugged up the cinch, and bridled her. "Come on, Baby Blue. Time to ride."

•   •   •   •

JOHN JOBSON, United States Marshal, retired, had not survived more than thirty years as a lawman and many a gunfight without heeding his instincts. So when he got that familiar itch on the back of his neck, he looked out the front window. Four horsemen were just trotting into his yard. Bob, the pointer, was snoring behind the stove. "Lotta good you are," he said. He turned back to the window to see one man leave the others, ride to the barn, swing down, and step inside. His pulse was quickening. "Easy, old son," he told himself, "You don't do this just right, you'll never do nothin' else."

The others came steadily toward the house, Mano in the lead. He turned in the saddle to speak to those behind him. Jobson watched. "I ought to take you now, you rotten son of a bitch. I should crack the door, poke this shotgun out, and give it to you in the back, like you done for so many," Jobson said to himself. "That'd serve you right, and it'd take the starch out of the rest of 'em. Then I could fort up in here 'til the others lose interest." But in his entire career, that had never been his way. Every man who had gone down before his gun had gotten it in the front. Every man, no matter how bad, had his chance.

The rider who had split off to investigate the barn was back on his horse and had re-joined the others. Jobson had armed himself with a ten gauge, sawed-off shotgun. Cocking both hammers, he stuck a Colt pistol in the waistband of his pants for backup. Opening the front door just enough to get a commanding field of fire, he waited to greet his visitors. The dog was awake and pushed his nose past Jobson's leg as Mano and the others reined up at the porch. At first the bandit's face looked puzzled, and then it lit in a thin smile. The dog growled low in his chest.

"*Now* you tell me," the marshal muttered. The dog growled louder. "Shut up, Bob," he said.

"Marshal Jobson! I thought you was dead." Mano was grinning.

Jobson returned the grin. "Howdy, Mano. Whatever give you that notion?"

The killer laughed. "Well, you know. You are very old, and you never was too good of a shot, no?"

"So you figured somebody'd rub me out by now, huh?"

Mano nodded his head. "*Sí.* That's what I was hoping, anyway." His two hired guns were beginning to ease their horses to the flanks of the group. Jobson raised the double barrel a few inches. Keeping his eyes on Mano, he said, "Tell your boys to sit still."

Lucero's eyes stayed on the marshal as he said, "*Alto, muchachos.*" They held, and no one spoke for a quarter minute. Then Mano's grin returned as he thought of another way to needle the marshal.

"How's that little finger, Marshal?"

Jobson held it up slowly. "Still short. How 'bout them nicks I put in you? They heal up good?"

Mano tilted his head back, looking down his hawk nose at his old enemy. "Aye, you never touched me, *viejo.*" The smile was fading, and the marshal felt the strain increase.

He continued smiling. Through the smile he said, "Come on, *hombre.* I think we both know better than that."

Mano's smile was gone now. "Here's something else we both know," he growled. "You got something of mine hid out around here someplace. A little blue mare and the *gringo cabron* who rode in on her. Ain't that right, Marshal?"

Jobson shook his head carefully. "You lost me, *amigo.* All I got around here is a bay gelding over in the barn, which you know about, and a cow that likes to travel. Plus this old bird dog, and a couple of young hogs I'm fattenin' to butcher, and an old cat I don't hardly ever see. Oh, and six layin' hens. That's it. No mares or *gringos*."

Mano nodded slowly, a cool expression on his face. "Well, I tell you this, *amigo*. You are an old *mentiroso*. I think you lie."

It might have been that there was some prearranged signal in those last words of Mano's. Whether that was the case or not, the man who sat his horse to Jobson's right made a move for his pistol.

Instinctively, the old lawman swung his shotgun around, took a short step into the clear, and blew the man half out of the saddle with a full charge of #1 buckshot. A good part of the pattern hit the horse in the neck, causing the animal to take off pitching across the yard, slinging the corpse to the ground and continuing on into the sagebrush.

Sadly, the distraction gave Mano the time he needed to draw his own piece and get off two quick shots, one taking the marshal in the left ribs, the other in the neck. Jobson reeled back until his shoulders hit the cabin wall, then sat down hard, dropping the shotgun. Reaching feebly toward the revolver, he slid over to rest on his right shoulder. "Too slow," he whispered. He looked up at Mano and spat weakly. His last thought was to wonder who would milk the cow.

Bob came over, sniffed his master's corpse, and set up such a mournful howling that Mano, having no more regard for old bird dogs than retired lawmen, shot him, as well.

•   •   •   •   •

THE BLUE MARE seemed as strong as the grey racer. It was just before full dark when Jeff loped into Chromo. Turning the mare to look in the direction from which they had come, he saw nothing to cause alarm. No pursuing riders. No dust.

No startled flight of small birds. Nothing. "That old man's buying us time," he told Bonnie Blue.

As Marshal Jobson had promised, there was a telegrapher in the saloon, his key set up on a table by the window, wires running up the corner and out the building. The poles that held the wire followed the wagon road up the mountain. The telegrapher was reading a magazine and drinking from a cloudy glass. He did not seem drunk. Jeff went to the bar, bought two shots of whiskey, and sat down across from the man, placing one of the glasses in front of him. The man looked up, saw the whiskey, seized and lifted the glass in a toast. "Thank you, sir. You have my undivided attention."

He then tossed off the drink and returned his watery eyes to Jeff, who drank his own shot and then asked, "Can you get a message up to Pagosa Springs, right now?"

The man took a watch from his vest pocket and flipped it open. "Sure, son, if the wire's still up after that last storm. Hadn't sent nor received a thing since. But Phil ought to still be at his key."

Jeff grabbed the pad of paper and pencil that lay across the table, bent to it for some seconds, and then tore off the top sheet, shoving it under the telegrapher's nose. "How much to send this?"

The man scanned it quickly, then looked up. "Two more whiskeys."

Jeff rose and tossed the barman a coin on his way out the door. "Give that man a bottle!"

•   •   •   •

THE BROTHERS Lucero and the surviving hired gunman spent two hours in a fruitless effort to determine the direction of Jeff's retreat. By then the sun was low and the temperature dropping with it. Mano was furious. "I know that the *gringo cobarde* was here, and *la grulla* with him. I can feel them. But it is plain that none of us is up to this task. We need a *maestro* tracker for this work."

The surviving gunman spoke up timidly. *Con permiso, jefé,* but I have a *primo,* my cousin Raimundo, who is half Jicarilla. He can track a lizard across hardpan."

Mano's eyes widened, and then his jaw clenched in anger. "So for all this time you have kept silent while we wander around this cabin getting nowhere? I should take this quirt and beat you like a dog." Calming himself, he went on. "Where is this amazing *primo* of yours?"

The gunman, fearful now, said very carefully, "Raimundo rides the range between here and Dulce, but I saw him in Chromo two days ago. Perhaps he is there still. There is a woman he visits from time to time."

Mano reached in his vest and drew out a number of American greenbacks. "Ride now and get him. Tonight, even if you have to drag him from this woman's bed. Give him this money. Tell him there will be more. And if you are not back with him at first light, I will hunt you until I have you in my gun sights. *Comprendé?*" Taking the bills, the man nodded, turned his horse, and spurred for Chromo.

"Little brother, put our horses in the shed, unsaddle, and feed them. We will pass the night here. I am sure the marshal has left us something to eat. I will go look. But first, drag these dead men and that dog out of my sight."

• • • •

SANDY WAS SITTING with Shortstack in the hotel bar, nursing a sundown whiskey while his friend sipped a beer. Setting his glass down in its sweat ring on the table, the diminutive cook said, "So your niece rode all the way here from north of Durango in one day?"

Sandy nodded. "Aye. She always has a good horse. And a hardheaded lass is our Maggie. Wanted to know the whole story on the mysterious Mr. Cameron. She's lodged above our heads even now, on the second floor of this hotel."

Shortstack shook his head. "Must have a great interest in the man."

Sandy grinned and was set to comment further when the telegrapher's boy came pounding into the room, red as a beet and gasping for breath. "Mr. Sandy! Mr. Sandy!"

The Scot pulled his feet back from the stove. "Easy lad. Give me that."

The boy held the telegram against his chest. "I'm s'posed to git the dime first."

Sandy flipped him a quarter. "Keep it." The agile youngster caught the coin and handed him the paper, almost simultaneously, then ran out the door as fast as he'd come in. Sandy walked across the room to stand under an oil lamp, producing a pair of spectacles from inside his buckskin jacket. Shortstack stood at his elbow as he read,

```
TO S. MACTEAGUE:
IN CHROMO (STOP) COMING UP FROM NAVA-
JO RIVER (STOP) WILL LAY UP IN DAY-
LIGHT (STOP) RIDING HARD TOMORROW
NIGHT (STOP) MAKE P. SPRINGS SUNUP IF
MARE HOLDS UP (STOP) TRYING FOR FOS-
TER'S BARN (STOP) DEVIL ON MY COAT-
TAIL (STOP) JEFF
```

TWENTY

THERE WOULD BE some moon, close to a half. He had to figure that his pursuers would get past the marshal and find his tracks. Maybe they wouldn't. The mare's feet had been carefully wrapped in pieces of old burlap for her route from the cabin to the top of the lookout. Maybe his enemies were only average trackers. And maybe old Jobson could get them all. A lot of maybes. More likely, he was dead right now. Jeff had to figure it that way.

• • • •

SHORTSTACK LOOKED UP at Sandy when he had finished reading Jeff's message. Sandy glared down at him. "Well, little man, could yeh stand some excitement?"

Shortstack straightened to his full, if not formidable, height. "Do not call me *little*, you crippled up, Caledonian scarecrow!"

Sandy gripped his arm. "Aye, now that's the spirit, mon. Have yeh a more substantial weepon than that wee pimp's gun yeh shot the surly teamster with?"

Shortstack's face reddened further as he answered, "Yes, it so happens I own a Winchester '73, caliber .44-40, cut down to fit me and, yes, by God, I can *stand* all the excitement you can muster!"

Sandy nodded, smiling grimly at his fuming friend. "Excellent," he said, and strode across the bar room toward the hotel lobby. "Then let us consult Maggie, and gird our loins for war."

• • • •

FIRST LIGHT came with no sign of the surviving hired gun or his cousin Raimundo, the alleged miraculous tracker. Mano had roused his brother in the early morning dark to see to the horses while he prepared breakfast for them both. Now, done eating and champing at the bit to get started, he was on the edge of rage at the non-appearance of the men he had hired.

After another half hour of waiting, pacing, and fuming, he turned to his younger brother and barked, "This is impossible! Jaimé's killer is getting away in who knows what direction on *la grulla* while we stand around doing nothing. We should go back out and see if we can get lucky and find his trail."

Pepé shook his head warily. "I know you are anxious, big brother, but stop to think. The more we move around out there, the more chance we have of damaging whatever sign there is. We should wait for the tracker a little longer, no?"

Mano was taken aback at this logic from the lips of his usually slow-witted sibling. But this did not diminish his rising frustration. The anxiety was becoming unbearable.

"Very well, *hermanito*, your advice is *muy bueno.* But we must move now, do something. Go saddle our *caballos.* They must be done with their feed by now. We will ride to Chromo. Perhaps our man cannot locate his *primo*, or he may even think to take our money and run, in spite of our warning. Either way, we will learn something. I can stand idle no longer!"

• • • •

HIS TELEGRAM sent, Jeff mounted the mare and turned back east. The cross-country route to Pagosa would begin almost where he had started, near Jobson's cabin. His ride into Chromo had been solely to alert Sandy by telegram. Precious time spent, but worth it, he hoped. Crossing the Navajo river at a shallow ford just upstream from the village, he and the mare moved beyond sight of the road to the south, through brush and thin timber. Soon he could enter Cornish Gulch and begin his trek north, eventually to join his allies, if fate would have it, and deal once and for all with his enemies.

•   •   •   •

THE WAR COUNCIL was convened in the dining room of the hotel. Sandy, Maggie, and Shortstack sat down to thick steaks and black coffee. No more alcohol for now. And little agreement as they began. Sandy led and for once his words were strictly business. Gone from his face was any hint of wry humor.

"Yeh've both read his telegram. The route he's taking is long and arduous. The country is broken and difficult, but we've been over it together a number of times on our hunting forays, and I believe he knows it well enough. But it will be challenging, especially as he plans to ride at night."

Maggie's anxiety was obvious. She hardly touched her food. "Mightn't we ride that way, Uncle? Use the daylight tomorrow to good advantage, meet him partway along and help him make a stand against his pursuers?"

Sandy smiled at her gameness, but shook his head. "I fear not, lass. When he says he is coming by way of our hunting trail, that's more of a general than a specific thing. It's not a well-defined, single track, ya' see. More a ravel of game paths. He could be coming up along a half-mile-wide front, through broad swales and across wide saddles between ridges. We likely would miss him. And he'll be laid up during daylight, well hidden. No, my dear, I rather think we'd be bound to fail."

The girl's frown deepened. "But surely there is something we can do to help him!"

Around a mouthful of steak, her uncle responded. "Aye, there is much to be done. According to his plan, he'll come out upon the coach road about four miles southeast of town.

I know the precise spot to within fifty feet. It's where we always turn south, heading out on our hunts. There're great, huge pine trees round about, as well as shielding rocks and boulders. A perfect place for an engagement. Our pugnacious New Englander here can help me set up a cross fire that will be devastating to anyone chasing our young friend."

Shortstack nodded resolutely. "I look forward to it. My Winchester is oiled and loaded for bear!"

Now Maggie smiled a little, nodding, finally carving herself a bite of T-bone. "Sounds good. And I've my ten gauge and a full box of goose loads to join the action."

At this, Sandy knit his brow. The thought of risking his beloved niece in a pitched battle, as this plan was likely to become, was out of the question. He knew very well that should she be harmed he could never face his brother or, more importantly, live another day with himself. But knowing her as he did, he was just as aware that she would not tolerate anything that smacked of a ruse to keep her out of harm's way. Taking his most diplomatic tone, he asked her to listen.

"Cool yer blood a moment, girl. I've another assignment for you, if you'll hear me out."

She stiffened, with the forked chunk of steak halfway to her mouth. "If you're thinking to keep me safely out of this, you are very much mistaken. I'll not wait idly by in some secure corner doing nothing to help Jeff!"

Her uncle raised his hands in a gesture of peace. "I've no such notion, my dear. But I do know better than to put all our eggs in one basket. We absolutely must have a second line, a shooter in a reserve position, as it were. And that's your role. That would be you."

Maggie glared at him through suspicious eyes. "This smells of subterfuge, to me. I still think you intend to keep me safe, and I simply will not have it!" She clenched her steak knife like a weapon.

Sandy put his hands on the table and looked directly into her eyes. He spoke in a level voice. "Hear me now, niece. This sort of thing is meat and drink to me. Please recall my service to Her Majesty, Old Queen Vic, during the wars against the Mohammedan fanatics in Afghanistan, God curse that blighted country. I learned the lessons of wilderness warfare right enough. Saw many a good man die when unsound tactics were employed. And I want yeh to consider this. Suppose Shortstack and I are unable to fully deal with Jeff's tormenters. We don't yet know how many there are. Some few could get past us. We do know that our man intends to try to reach the safety of Foster's barn, to fort up for a standoff, if need be. What better position for you, then, than your hotel room, at the window, with perfect command of the street for fifty yards in either direction. He'll have to pass below that window to reach the barn, as will anyone following. That monstrous fowling piece of yours, choked so tight, will allow you at least four shots at any assailants as might still be a threat to him. It'll be rather like shooting driven grouse. A right and a left coming, two more going away. And I've seen you in a duck blind with that weepon. As quick as you're able to reload, likely you can get off more rounds than four. Think clearly, now, and without passion, and I'm sure you'll see the logic in it." He held his breath, and her hard gaze neither wavered nor softened, but she finally spoke.

"You are not fooling me for a second. This is a position of safety for me. But I cannot argue the wisdom of your strategy. There should be someone in reserve should you fail or, God forbid, be wounded or killed. And I am the choice for that assignment, without doubt. So I will not resist further. Let's have the rest."

•   •   •   •

THE LUCERO BROTHERS left Jobson's cabin and rode into Chromo a little before nine o'clock. They went first to the saloon to inquire as to the whereabouts of their hired gun, as well as the cousin—the master tracker. No one had seen them. In further rising anger, Mano led the way to the wagon yard. No luck there, either. By now he was virtually raging with wrath, but with no target upon which to vent it.

His brother fairly shook in his saddle, knowing the potential for mayhem. So it was with huge relief that he noticed, out to the west, two riders in tall sombreros approaching at a high lope. "Big brother! *Mira alla!* They come!"

Mano turned his horse and saw the men approaching. He said through clamped teeth, "You have eyes like *el gavilan, hermanito.* I should call you hawkeye. And I hope you are right. Let us ride to meet them. God help these men if they are not the ones we want."

But they were, and at the sight of Mano's grim face the hired gunman pulled up his horse roughly and called out from what he hoped was a safe distance. With a quaver in his voice, he said, "*Buenos tardes, jefé. Con su permiso.* I know we are very late, but my cousin was not at *la casa de la mujer.* But she directed me to him. He was in Lumberton, drinking and playing cards, and *muy boracho.* I had to pour *mucho café negro* into him before he recovered from his drunkenness enough to ride. But here we are, and he agrees to help you." The speech left the man breathless. The cousin looked wretched.

Mano's expression was black. The muscles in his jaw seemed hard as stone. "Ride closer, *muchachos,*" he said through clinched teeth. They walked their horses forward.

Mano looked them up and down. "Your *primo,* who you say can track a lizard across hardpan, looks useless. And those horses, they are ridden into the ground. *Maldito, maldito.*"

He glowered at them, and they turned their heads to avoid his gaze. Then he declared, "You two will have to do." Looking again critically at their mounts, he said, "But those animals will not." Ridicule in his tone, he went on, "We will go to the wagon yard and see what is available there. Later, we may find time to deal with your tardiness. But for now, we ride."

•   •   •   •

JEFF STOPPED the blue mare at the mouth of Cornish Gulch. The trip from Chromo and the telegrapher's key had been made in a hurry. He sat his horse a moment and wondered what had played out at Jobson's cabin. His instincts suggested a gunfight by now had occurred. He hoped for a good outcome. Hoped that somehow the old man had managed to defeat four, well-armed gunmen.

But logic said otherwise, that at best the marshal had gotten maybe one or two. Instead, he put his hopes on survivors having no success in finding the tracks of a horse with feet bound in burlap, searching with lanterns as darkness fell, hopefully damaging any sign with their own boot tracks.

In turning north, Jeff and the mare would be winding their way through a broken terrain of small valleys and bench lands, creek bottoms and ridges that made up Sandy's hunting grounds and lay between the San Juan and Navajo Rivers. If he pushed very hard he might make Foster's barn sometime mid-morning the next day. But he had said in the telegram that he intended to lay up the rest of that night and all the next day. It was a sound plan for two good reasons. He needed to rest and mend. The bullet wound in the flesh above his shoulder blade had opened and, while not leaking badly, was oozing more blood than he could afford to lose. As well, there was his concern for the horse. While not yet lame, there was heat in the tendon of the leg that had lost the shoe. He had felt it earlier in the day as he had given her the usual rub down. She needed rest, too.

As to his enemies, instinct told him they were not close, that he had some time. He felt it from his gambler's sense, something of a poker player's hunch. And he knew that he was in a game of high stakes, the highest he'd ever sat in on.

There was another consideration, as important in its own way. The fate of the marshal. Try as he might, he could not blindly honor his promise to ride on, to not look back. Likely the old man was dead. But what if he was wounded and still alive? Shot up and slowly bleeding out, unable to help himself? And what if Jeff could save him?

The mare fidgeted as he held her at the mouth of the gulch. The moon was not quite up. It was cold. Was Jobson lying on the frigid ground, his life slowly draining from him?

Time to decide, and he did. They could ride to the top of the same hill from which he'd first seen his pursuers. By the light of the near half-moon that would be clearing the eastern peaks soon, he could view the cabin and barnyard with the marshal's binoculars. If all was quiet, he could ease down and see to his friend's condition. Then at least he would have some answers.

His mind made up, but aware what a long a chance he was taking, he slacked the reins and gave the mare her head. Two miles farther east, he crossed the river again, turned up Buckhammer Canyon, and made for Jobson's place.

•   •   •   •

WHAT HE had in mind was relatively simple. He would come up the back side of the hill where the night camp stood, vacated in haste earlier in the day. With the aid of the moon, he'd have a view of the cabin below, and some sense of the state of things.

He judged the time to be past ten o'clock, by the position of the stars, as he tied the mare to a stunted oak just short of the hill's crest. On foot he reached the top and was able to see down to Jobson's yard, the small barn to one side and the cabin across from it.

With no real idea of what to expect, he still was surprised by what he saw below. It seemed quiet and peaceful. The yellow glow of lamp light from inside illuminated the two front windows. Could the marshal be there, unharmed, going about his evening business? Had he managed to beat all four gunmen? Jeff's hopes got the best of him for a moment. It was short lived, however, as next he saw the barn door open and a man step out, raised lantern in his hand, wearing a sombrero. Jeff lifted the glasses again and by the lantern light he could see clearly the man was dressed as a *vaquero*. The marshal had not won.

• • • •

HE BROUGHT the blue mare up and fed and watered her. In the short vigil of the night, he witnessed no further activity around the cabin.

What had happened there? What had occurred since he and his horse had dropped off the backside of their lookout the previous evening? He could see the marshal had not killed the four men. At least one, perhaps more, had survived. So it meant Jobson was either dead or held captive. After eating the bacon he had abandoned from the previous afternoon's cooking, he had rolled up in the wagon sheet and slept a short and fitful night.

By first light Jeff had been awake an hour. Now as the rising winter sun gradually gave light, he was in position with the binoculars to see more. He would watch and wait, and attempt to determine what had happened, and what would happen next.

• • • •

THE NEED to wait ended after only a half hour. Two men, who seemed vaguely familiar to Jeff, emerged from the cabin and moved back and forth, the taller of them gesturing vigorously and talking loudly. It was too far for Jeff to understand what was being said. But the man was agitated, that was apparent. After a few minutes, they separated, one to the barn and the other to the cabin. A short while later, the one returned from the barn leading two saddled horses. The other emerged from the cabin with saddlebags and bedrolls. Tying on their gear with haste, they mounted and rode out in the direction of Chromo.

Jeff waited half an hour for anyone else to appear. Having seen no sign of the marshal and with a sense of foreboding, he swung up on the mare and descended in a looping route through the sagebrush, obscuring the mare's tracks as much as possible. Coming around the cabin from the rear, he had his worst fears confirmed.

• • • •

FIRST WAS the body of a dead horse, a short distance from the cabin, beyond the dirt yard, in mixed tall sagebrush and weeds. It was stiff legged and swollen, with a large and bloody shotgun wound in the right side of its neck. Bonnie Blue shied at the smell of blood. From the tracks, Jeff could tell the horse had run there and collapsed, after having been hit in the yard.

There were drag marks as well, which led from the yard to a place fifty feet beyond the horse. And there, left unceremoniously exposed, were the bodies of two men and a dog.

Jeff sat the mare as his throat closed and his eyes filled. This was what he had feared, what he had to admit was virtually inevitable. But that made it no less difficult to take. His rescuer, his friend, had paid the highest possible price to buy him time. And as he looked down on the rugged features, frozen in cold death, he was proud of John Jobson, United States Marshal, retired. He had gone down fighting. It was his choice. And he'd taken toll on one of them who had come to his home to do murder. And he had done it with honor, head on, in his way.

• • • •

HE TOOK the short amount of time needed to bury the gallant, old lawman, where the ground was soft and sandy, along with Bob, his good friend to the end. They would rest in their long sleep, one with the other, sharing the single grave. He left the corpse of the invading gunman where he found it, to nourish the coyotes, magpies, and bugs, until someone else might come along who cared enough to put his remains under the ground. Jeff's work was done and he rode on, vowing to himself to return one day and place a stone.

• • • •

AN HOUR after he had left, the Luceros and their hired help rode back into Jobson's yard. It was just past ten o'clock in the morning. The fresh mounts had been grained and were eager. They had been obtained from a teamster at the wagon yard, a four-up hitch of well-matched, light coach horses, also broke to ride. The teamster initially was loath to part with them, but was convinced to deal by the offer of good money, the trade of their well-bred but jaded mounts, and the air of malevolence that radiated from Mano like heat from a stove.

Raimundo Rosa, the tracker, while apparently recovered from his earlier night of excess, had his work cut out for him. The three other men waited on the porch of the cabin, smoking and fretting, under instructions to stay out of the way, lest they damage the sign. It took the cousin an hour to work out the track up to the lookout. The mare's feet had been unbound there. He signaled the others with a pistol shot, and they all gathered at the top.

"See, *jefé*. The horse's feet were wrapped. The tracks have been swept, also. But up here the wrappings were removed. And we see the mare has a new shoe. On the near side hind. Look how the track is sharper than the others. But this is still confusing. They go off the back side, toward Chromo. But tracks come up, also, from that direction. They seem to be made at about the same time."

Mano was seething again. "So what do you suggest, *maestro?*

Raimundo squatted on his heels, removed his sombrero, and scratched his head. "I think this may be an attempt to fool us. I think we should follow these tracks that go off the backside. I believe he ran to Chromo. It may be that he has friends there to help him. Or he may take the wagon road to Pagosa. Or he may even have some hideout nearby. But here he is trying to run us in circles. We should back trail him and see if we can unravel these tracks."

Mano's jaw was tight. "And while we ride back and forth, wearing out these new horses, he is getting away."

The tracker shrugged. "But, *jefé*, if we do not work out this puzzle, we have no idea the way he went, and we will never find him, no?"

Mano scrubbed his stubbly face with a rough hand. "*Si.* Lead on, then. But make no mistakes."

• • • •

AS THE LUCEROS and their retainers headed once more in the direction of Chromo, Jeff and Bonnie Blue were well up Cornish Gulch, past Tater Mountain and looking for a good place to lay up until dark. They crossed the Little Navajo River and when in another three miles they came to Spring Creek, they entered the water and rode downstream for half a mile. On the northwest bank, high above the creek, Jeff saw a deep overhang, reminding him of the one that held the ancient ruin on the heights above Claymore headquarters. Leaving the water by way of a shelf of slickrock, they made their way carefully up the bluff to the opening.

It seemed ideal for them, this alcove. Here they could hide from view as they rested out the day until sundown. It gave them considerable command of the ground below, as well. If overtaken, here he could make a stand. And here Sandy might find and rescue them, if they were unable to appear where described in the telegram.

After leading the mare through the opening, Jeff stripped off her tack, moved her to the rear of the alcove, and hobbled her. She had watered in the creek, and he gave her grain in the *morral*. The tendon was warm, but not hot.

He spread the saddle blanket where he could see back down the creek. Then he retrieved a box of cartridges for the Colt from the saddlebags, laid out a handful on the blanket before him, placed the revolver within easy reach, and stretched out and closed his eyes.

• • • •

PARTWAY TO CHROMO from the marshal's cabin, Raimundo played his own hunch. He turned north for sign and found prints of the blue mare returning from the direction of the village. He signaled Mano and the rest. "*Mira, jefé*. The tracks of *la grulla* coming back. It is as I thought. But he is not fooling us now. I believe these tracks are fresher. See here, in the weeds and sagebrush, the moisture still in the edges of the hoof prints? I think he is behind us now. Follow me!"

Without waiting, the tracker wheeled his horse and spurred away. Mano, a black look on his face, said nothing, but fell in behind. There was nothing else to do. But *los santos* preserve this man if he was wrong.

• • • •

AS HE APPROACHED the base of the hill near the marshal's cabin yet again, the tracker found the sign swinging wide in a broad arc, passing behind the cabin and into tall sagebrush. Having not been present for the shootout, he was puzzled by the body of the horse, the dead gunman, and the freshly turned earth. This was the first time that tracks led him to the rear of the cabin.

He called to Mano. *"Jefé, que esto es?"*

Mano drew rein and sat beside Raimundo, his mouth partway open. After a few seconds he said, "This *gringo* is bold, indeed. He has returned to bury his friend, *el viejo* Marshal Jobson, while we were gone. We did not notice, so hard did we work to find the trail in front of the cabin. He is still making fools of us." Reaching across the space between their horses, Mano grabbed the bandana of the tracker and yanked the man toward his face. "And of you!"

The tracker felt Mano's fist at the base of his throat, his windpipe tight with fear, and he croaked. "But, *jefé*! This means he cannot be far!"

Mano released his hold. *"Verdad, maestro.* That is true. So find the way he left from this place. We have two good hours of daylight left. We can catch him tonight. We *will* catch him tonight!"

●   ●   ●   ●

AS THE LUCEROS sat and watched the tracker puzzle over the way ahead, Pepé turned to his older brother. "This *gringo* we hunt, he's pretty good, no?"

Mano looked at him and frowned. "How do you mean *good, hermanito?"*

Pepé's face looked worried. "Well, you shot him off *la grulla* back in the Animas country, and he bled *mucho*, and I would have sworn he was dead. But then he comes to Chromo and steals the mare back. Then you shoot his grey horse out from under him and he jumps on *la grulla* and keeps going. And he comes here to the house of *el viejo* Marshal Jobson, and the marshal gives his life for him, to buy him time, and also kills one of the men you hired to help us. And here we are, where we have been before. And he toys with us, and before long it will be dark and cold, and still this *gringo* stays ahead."

Mano frowned. "So, what are you saying, *hermanito*?"

Pepé shook his head and looked down at his hands, holding the reins. "I don't know, Mano. But I think this *gringo* is very good, or very lucky. Perhaps both. And I begin to wonder if we will catch him at all. And then I remember what the old saddle maker in Taos said to you."

Mano was ready enough for Pepé to be done with this, but he kept his voice neutral as he asked, "And what did he say?"

Pepé wanted to cross himself, but resisted the urge. Instead he answered, simply. "He said that if we caught this *gringo*, we might wind up like our brother."

•   •   •   •

THE BLUE MARE nickered and stomped a forefoot, and Jeff was stirred awake. But in the first moments of wakefulness he was confused. Where was he? What was happening? What had alarmed the horse? What time of day was it? What did he need to be doing?

Not the panicky sort, with slow, deep breaths he began to collect his thoughts and take stock of the situation. He was under the rim of a deep rock outcrop, he and Bonnie Blue. There was nothing happening except the sun going down, the light fading, and the temperature dropping. There was no wind. As to what might have caused her movement, he couldn't tell.

Rising quietly, he moved to the edge of the overhang's mouth. There he stayed motionless, utterly silent, as he looked and listened. He could detect nothing that seemed to suggest a threat. Maybe the horse was telling him it was time to go. As to what he needed to do, that would be to pay attention to her.

There was a good hour of daylight yet. There was no evidence his enemies were close. Bonnie Blue was ready, she had told him so. She seemed to understand the game he had dealt them into. He stepped to her, removed the hobbles, and saddled her. Before mounting, he felt the swollen tendon. Cooler now. Barely warm. That would have to be good enough. Time now to swing up and ride.

• • • •

RAIMUNDO ROSA, the master tracker, now displayed that mastery. He had worked out Jeff's route of retreat, and he and his *compañeros* were at the banks of Spring Creek as the sun rode just above the western peaks. He stopped his horse at the point where Jeff had put the blue mare into the water. The creek was shallow in winter volume, less than twenty feet across and a foot deep.

Turning in the saddle he addressed Mano and the others. "*Amigos*, if you will permit me. I would like to cross this creek and determine what the *gringo* did, his path from here. There will be less chance of making a mess of the tracks if the three of you wait. I will not take long. *Con su permiso.*"

Considering permission granted, not waiting for the word, he pushed his mount into the water. Mano said nothing, less agitated now that they seemed to be making progress. Let the man earn his pesos. Now let him show his genius.

• • • •

SANDY AND SHORTSTACK sat at a table in the hotel bar, nursing drinks. Just one apiece. Sandy's orders. There would be no swollen heads in the morning. This was serious business. The most serious imaginable. Killing business.

They had shared their plans with no one. The town marshal, well known for his untimely disappearances, was off on an elk hunt, according to the barman. Just as well, thought

Sandy. The lawman had no great reputation as a fighter. Likely he and his deputy would be a distraction, and possibly interference, trying to take charge, which could make a hash of things. Or he could forbid the action altogether. No, much better to keep it among the three of them. If Jeff could be helped at all, they were the ones to do it.

Sandy regarded his abbreviated friend, a firm look on his face. "So, Mr. Brakefield. Your thoughts on possibilities for the morrow?"

"Well, I believe I'm up to it, whatever it might bring."

"Killin' is what it's likely to bring. Have you studied on that?"

Shortstack put his elbows on the table and tented his fingers, looking his tall friend directly in the eyes. After a brief pause he said, "As far as you know, I've shot a rude lout through the foot, and that's it. Well, the fact is I served with the 4th Vermont Regulars during the war of rebellion. I was eighteen years of age, qualified expert with the Springfield rifled musket, and could climb a tree like a cat. So they made a sniper of me. Even had a telescopic sight on my piece. I would venture to say I've killed three men to your one, should we compare our records, which I'd prefer not to. So, to answer you. Yes. I've studied killing and proved an apt pupil. Any further questions?"

Sandy sat back in his chair, showing surprise and admiration on his face. Raising his glass in a salute to his friend, he said, "No. No further questions. I believe you'll more than do."

• • • •

THE *MAESTRO* TRACKER had ridden the bank of Spring Creek for a half mile in both directions, quickly but carefully, and now re-crossed the water to the silent, scowling men who had been waiting on his judgment. Dipping his hat brim deferentially, he addressed Mano. "*Jefé*, the *gringo* has not left the creek in either direction. I believe he has taken to the water to mask his trail. And I believe he has gone downstream."

Mano nodded slightly. "And how are you able to determine that, Rosa?"

"Because I think this *gringo* is smart. And I think he knows that if he goes upstream and we arrive soon after him, that we might see the cloudiness of the disturbed creek bed, the muddy water drifting down to us. But if he rides downstream, all that dirty water is taken away below him, showing us nothing. That is my thought."

Mano nodded again. "All right, seems reasonable. What do you suggest we do now, *maestro*?"

"I will ride swiftly as I can and with what light remains try to find the place he leaves the water. You three follow me on the bank, so as not to muddy the water that flows past me. When I find the spot he leaves the creek bed, I will wait on you."

Mano almost smiled. "I am gratified by the confidence with which you say 'When I find the spot.' Lead on, *maestro*."

•   •   •   •

IN THE HOUR of daylight that remained, Jeff and Bonnie Blue rode hard, crossing Coyote Creek and Benson Creek. They arrived at the confluence of Rio Blanco and Big Branch as darkness came down around them. A faint glow behind the peaks to the east told Jeff the waxing moon soon would be lending them all the aid she could. He decided to rest the mare for the short wait that the moonlight would require. As yet he had no evidence that his pursuers were close, or even that he was still hunted at all. But in this game he knew he had to play a scared hand. To become over confident was likely to die.

They had rested half an hour, Jeff beside his horse, when the mare's ears swiveled back the way they had come.

Simultaneously, the hair on the back of his neck prickled. He could hear nothing, but his insides now screamed for them to move. He stepped into the saddle, slackened the reins, and she needed no further urging. At a lope, she carried him north.

• • • •

IRON-SHOD HOOVES left plainly visible scars on the slickrock shelf where Jeff and the blue mare had climbed out of Spring Creek. By the last of the fading light, Raimundo had found them. And just as readily, he tracked them to the overhang where they had rested away the afternoon. The other men gathered at the mouth of the alcove as the tracker unraveled the story. Moving from place to place, pointing out the sign, he told the tale.

"He hobbled his horse there, at the rear. He fed her grain from a *morral*. There is some spilled on the ground. Then over here at the mouth of the overhang, where he could see his back trail, he spread his blanket and rested. Perhaps he even slept. I am guessing they spent at least four hours here. Then he rose and saddled his mare and left this place."

As he stooped and moved and talked, he carried a lit candle, a tool of the trade he was never without. Then he led his mount as he worked his way down from the alcove and onto the lower ground to the north. The others followed.

"Here they take the game trail again. Now we can make better time. And soon we have *la media luna*."

• • • •

THE AFTERNOON LAYUP had helped, but it could not erase the rigors of many days in the saddle and the problem of the slowly bleeding wound in his shoulder. Jeff was tired. In spite of his best attempt at a makeshift bandage, the hole from the bullet continued to seep. His body felt heavy, as though it was transforming, muscles becoming lead, bones becoming stone. He knew Bonnie Blue was suffering, too. He had no idea how much she had been pushed by the Luceros from Claymore range to Chromo, where he had recovered her. But he knew since then that she had been ridden hard, steadily, by him, with little rest, but for a respite at the marshal's.

One thing, and a positive factor. She was now on familiar ground. On his hunts with Sandy, they had taken game in this area. He had ridden the blue mare through here, several times. It felt to him that she may know the way home, so confidently did she travel now. So he decided to trust her. There was some moon, but not enough for him to see the trail. He could determine the profiles of ridges, and the general lay of the land felt right to him. It seemed they were where they belonged. And, as in a poker game, he was going as much on instinct as evidence.

The way was steeper again, but she continued without hesitation. He didn't need to push her. If anything, he had to restrain her, make her stop to blow for short intervals on the flat spots. She was pushing herself. Somehow, she knew they were hunted. And the warning of hair standing up on the back of his neck had not left him. And so their pauses were brief. On the trail, he let her set the pace. They were back there, those killers. He knew it. And so did she.

•　•　•　•

THE MOON was close to half, and it was a help to Raimundo Rosa as it climbed. Only occasionally now did he need to dismount and lead his horse, bent over the ground with the lit candle in hand. He believed the tracks to be fresher, believed they were gaining. Now and then he asked his companions to be still so he could listen. He didn't want to run right up the *gringo's* backside and catch a bullet. By first light, he would have them. He felt confident that if he could kill the *gringo* himself, there would be praise for him, his skills, and, most importantly, a substantial reward of money.

•   •   •   •

IT WAS up to her now. The trail was steep and rocky. There was snow, but not enough to block the way. His pursuers were well mounted. He recalled his decision to spare the two long-legged mounts of the brothers. It was going to come down to who had the best horse.

"Wish I was meaner," he told himself. "Mean enough to put down two good, sound horses. Animals with the bad luck to be ridden by horse thieves and killers. Not their fault. It ain't ever the horse's fault. And this blue mare, with the hard luck of being owned by that son of a bitch, Bad Jimmy. And the worse luck of being rescued by me. Hard luck horse, packin' a hard luck man." Had he known about the fresh mounts of his pursuers, his heart would have sunk lower still.

They would scramble for a hundred yards, then he would stop to let her blow. Then go another hundred, maybe hundred fifty yards, and stop for another catching of wind. There were places that were dangerously steep, where they had to take detours from the main trail, due to drifts and deadfall timber, and Jeff would have to dismount, grab her tail, and swat her on the hip with his hat for her to pull him along. And she did it, as if she knew that both their lives depended on it.

On through the dim moonlight she carried him. They were both approaching exhaustion. The mare had gone beyond anything he had ever asked a horse to do. He had pushed himself as far as he ever had. The switchbacks seemed endless. There were stretches through timber where the moonlight failed to penetrate. He could see nothing, had to trust her, and he did, and she advanced unerringly, whether by scent, sight, or instinct. She never hesitated. No doubt about it, he told himself. She seemed to know this was a run for their lives.

He was approaching the limits of his endurance. The wound in his shoulder throbbed, and though he was not bleeding badly he was still losing blood, which he could ill afford. He knew it was weakening him. The cold gnawed at him, too. He got off and led her and, as he struggled along as fast as he could, he tried to form a plan. Should he try to ambush their enemies?

That would be foolish. His location would be known at once from his first shot. Even if he were expert with a sidearm, which he was not, he was exhausted and could not be assured of a steady aim. And three-to-one odds sounded long to the gambler in him. He was grateful that Jobson had been able to improve those odds. He did not, of course, know of the tracker Raimundo Rosa.

He thought of the half-drunk telegrapher and knew there was no guarantee his wire had reached Sandy. And even if it had, what could one man do? Form a posse and come to his rescue? Unlikely. And did the Scot understand by which route they were coming? Hopefully. Probably. Maybe.

Even if Sandy did muster help, he might guess wrong. And if he did, by only a few hundred yards, he and every armed man in town would be of scant assistance. "No," he told himself, as he mounted up, having difficulty making his legs obey him. "It's our show, hers and mine. To the end. Whatever that end turns out to be."

He sat a moment. His head was tired, like his body. "Let you blow a spell, honey. We don't even know for certain sure that they're comin'. Might of fooled 'em with those tow sacks on your feet. Last time we saw 'em, they were headed in the wrong direction." But he didn't believe it. He knew that it was fatigue and weakness talking, and dangerous talk to listen to. So he stopped listening, and rode.

• • • •

THEY TRAVELED upstream along the Rio Blanco, no longer trying to obscure their tracks. Now it was a run for the money. But it wasn't about money. It was about living.

Five miles farther they cut northwest and rode through the saddle between Square Top Mountain and Blue Mountain to the southwest, and crossed Sheep Cabin Creek. He stopped the mare for a brief rest, dismounted, and ran his hand down the suspect leg. The tendon was the warmest it had been yet. But she had not been limping. Bones of iron, tendons and ligaments of steel cable. Heart of a lion. No quit in her. There would be no quitting for him, either.

•   •   •   •

THE PURSUERS' HORSES, fresh that morning, were beginning to tire. Handsome bays, well matched, with blazed faces and white stockings. Good for pulling light coaches over decent roads. Not for bearing relentless men over rough trails up and down mountains. Their riders showed them little compassion. These men would be happy to ride them to death in the chase for the murdering *gringo*, if it meant they could catch him.

The tracker, pushing his mount, used his quirt more often as the moon rose higher and he sensed the distance narrowing between them and their prize. Mano and the others applied their quirts, as well, eager for the kill.

•   •   •   •

THEY WERE on the banks of the Rita Blanco, well north of the Rio Blanco, a stream they had crossed hours before. Two streams with names enough alike to confuse travelers not familiar with this country.

The mare was flagging. Jeff knew he must ration what horse he still had. And thinking over how much she had already done, it amazed him that he had any horse left at all. He concluded that it was her heart. It was bigger and deeper than in any horse he'd ever known. Beyond even the grey thoroughbred. That Spanish blood. None to match it. And her mind. An attitude that seemed to declare, "No, I will not quit. Will not be beaten. I will win. We will win. This man and I."

But they had to rest where they could. So they were stopped for fifteen minutes, him out of the saddle, the mare with her head down, catching her breath. It was dead calm but for the low murmur of the stream, barely audible under a thin cover of ice. And the steady sound of Bonnie Blue's breathing.

Quiet enough that when he first heard it, there was no mistake. Iron on stone, horseshoes on rocks. She heard it too, had heard it before him, head up, ears turned. Not close, not yet. Maybe a half mile back. But they were coming. No doubt about it now.

"Now what?" he said out loud. Well, hell, just keep going, what else? The horserace was on. Mounting the mare, he took her across the icy creek and then they were on solid ground, running for their lives.

•   •   •   •

THEY DROPPED into Echo Canyon and scrambled out. It was a brutal climb. Crossing a mile-broad divide, they stopped long enough for a look from the rim of Spruce Canyon. Three miles down this defile and they would strike Mill Creek Road, where he expected to meet Sandy, if the gristly Scot was coming at all. It was the perfect place for an ambush, if that was Sandy's plan.

There was light now in the east. The moon was still up, but daylight was coming on. He heard hoof beats from the direction they had come, and the faint voices of men speaking in Spanish. The blue mare stepped off the rim for the run down Spruce Canyon, with her rider hoping there were friends at the road.

•   •   •   •

ONLY FIFTEEN MINUTES later, Raimundo stopped his horse at
the same spot where Jeff had sat the blue mare. In the
growing light, he could see their tracks dropping off the rim,
digging up the snow and muddy ground in a steep descent.
There was no further effort on their part to hide the trail.
They were running for it. Raimundo reasoned that they had
a destination in mind, were not just trying to escape pursuit.
He should take particular care in this chase now. But still he
must make the catch, the kill. He wanted to be the one.
Turning in the saddle, he made sure the others were close
enough to see him as he rode into the canyon. Now, let them
follow.

· · · ·

DOWN IN THE TIMBERED CANYON, they were below the edge
of daylight. It was dark again. They were side hilling as they
angled for the bottom. Descending the slope was easier on
the mare's lungs than climbing, but harder on the swollen
tendon. She did not let it slow her.

There were areas of deadfall timber strewn like jack-
straws, and she picked routes through with no direction
from Jeff. What she couldn't step across or go around, she
jumped. Her progress was sure and steady. Her rider's heart
swelled with pride. The road was not too far ahead now.

· · · ·

THE MOUTH of Spruce Canyon gave onto Mill Creek Road in
a scattering of great Ponderosa pines and granite boulders.
Two unlikely-looking friends, one well over six feet tall, the
other one less than five, had stationed themselves there,
about four miles from town. It was seven o'clock in the
morning and they had been at their posts since first light.
Their horses were tied a hundred fifty yards back in the
timber. Sandy had been to and from the Navajo River valley

for years, and several times with Jeff. This was where Jeff would come onto the road. He had said so.

The .54 Hawken was loaded and capped, leaning against the trunk of the enormous pine that hid him. A long barrel Colt revolver was stuck behind his belt, next to his Green River knife. Across the road, Shortstack kept vigil behind a boulder, the cut-down Winchester across his knees. Each had a clear view of the trail. They were ready.

• • • •

JEFF AND THE MARE were nearly through the canyon now, about half a mile from the road. He was standing beside her, his shoulder still throbbing. The horse was lathered and steaming, but her breathing was more even. She wasn't used up yet.

He was shaking. His legs felt like India rubber, his feet were numb with cold. The nerve ends in his body seemed to be singing, or misfiring. He was exhausted. But the mare was still game. It would be a near thing.

He took a deep breath and tried to stop his legs from vibrating. Could they have come so far, gone through so much together, only to lose now, in the home stretch? He uncinched the saddle and dumped it in the snow. And then she lifted her head, swiveled her ears toward their back trail. "You hear 'em, don't you, little sister? I can't, but you can. I trust you. I've been trusting you. My life is on your back. Both our lives are on your back, in your lungs and legs, carried in your heart." He struggled up onto her, bareback now, and asked her to move.

• • • •

RAIMUNDO ROSA had his eyes on the tracks before him. They were sharp and fresh. There was plenty of light now. Then, raising his eyes above the ground, he was astonished to see the object of his chase, no more than two hundred yards ahead, struggling along on the jaded, blue mare. He whooped in triumph, and the cousin who had now ridden up beside him hollered, too. Mano and his brother were bringing up the rear.

"It is him, *jefé*. We will kill him for you!" Not waiting for a word or a sign from Lucero, the men cut their horses with their quirts and rushed on. But these horses were flagging, too, their freshness taken from them by the difficult terrain, and they had no great speed left. Mano swung his own quirt, eager to be in on the finish, wanting the kill for himself. Pepé came last, hoping to draw some of the gringo's blood, as well.

• • • •

DESPITE THE YEARS and the many empty jugs, Sandy was still a hunter. And he was on the hunt now. Stone cold sober. It was full daylight and clear, the sun climbing, glancing off the snow, and making the air bright. When he heard the sound of a running horse, he waved to Shortstack and took up his rifle. And then there was Jeff on the blue mare, and it was obvious they were near the end of their endurance. He stepped out beside the trail when they were fifty feet away. His young friend's face was a mask of fatigue. Jeff called out, "They're right behind me!"

"Get to the barn," Sandy responded, as horse and rider labored past, sweeping his arm in that direction as if it could help push them there. Sandy cocked his old mountain rifle. He chanced a look across the coach road to Shortstack's hide and saw the scrappy Vermonter's head above the boulder. Nothing else was moving on the trail from the direction Jeff had come and he called to his friend, "Don't know how many, but soon. Shoot to kill!"

Shortstack raised his Winchester above his head. "Only way I do this sort of work."

Sandy returned to cover. And then they could hear them, and then they saw them. The range was dead certain, and as the tracker closed to twenty-five yards, Sandy eased around the tree trunk, shouldered the Hawken, and shot the man through the upper chest, hurling him backwards off his horse. Shortstack fired at the same time, and the single shot struck the cousin below his hat brim, dropping him to the ground, as well.

Mano saw his eager employees spilled from their saddles as the report of the guns reached his ears. Reining toward the timber, he rode hard for cover. Pepé followed. More shots came in their wake.

• • • •

SANDY JUMPED from cover as the Luceros rode past, drawing his revolver and thumbing the hammer rapidly, throwing six shots at the retreating brothers. Neither man fell. He fumed in frustration as they disappeared into the trees. Shortstack came from behind his boulder, joining his comrade in arms.

Raimundo Rosa lay on his back in the trail, staring sightlessly up through pine branches. His dead cousin lay no more than fifteen feet away, a bullet hole in the center of his forehead. Sandy looked down at Shortstack and quickly extended his hand. They shook grimly.

"Fine shooting, my cool headed friend. But why only the one shot?"

"Damned gun jammed as I worked the lever, or I'd have got the other two, as well."

Sandy nodded, glancing briefly in the direction of the road. "I doubt it not. I'm no master with a side arm. Expect I hit neither of them. Too bad your piece failed."

Returning his attention for a moment to the bodies in the road, he frowned once more. "First man I've killed in twenty years," he said. "Hoped there'd never be another."

Shortstack reached out and touched his friend's arm. "You did it for Jeff, same as I did."

The Scot smiled soberly, still deeply concerned. "Aye. For Jeff. And dear Maggie. Now let's ride and help him finish this."

TWENTY-ONE

THEY HAD MADE town. People in the street got out of the way as they labored past, the mare's strides faltering, her lungs working like bellows. A bullet snapped past Jeff's head. And then another, on the other side, kicking up snow ahead of him. He asked the horse for more. But she seemed, finally, to have no more to give. His enemies were close enough now for him to hear hoof beats bearing down from the hard-packed street behind them. Squeezing the barebacked horse with all the strength left in his legs and taking a deeper hold in her mane, with his other hand he drew his Colt and swung it to the rear. Over its front sight he could see two riders pursuing, one with a raised rifle, the other, a pistol. He snapped a shot, without apparent effect. Two more did no better.

Looking ahead again, he could see the blacksmith shop fifty yards before him, the front door open. Trails of smoke curled out of the doorway and from under the eaves. Luther must be working at his forge. Cover, and maybe even help from the giant. But why should this man he'd known only briefly risk his life getting mixed in this scrape? Did he have a right to ask it?

Beyond was the livery barn, another forty yards past the blacksmith shop, on the same side of the main street, with its big sliding door half open. Leaning farther over the mare's neck, his mouth almost in her ear, Jeff cried out, "Come on, Baby Blue! There's the barn! Let's go home!"

She had already seen it. He spurred her harder than he'd ever done before, hating himself for it. And she answered. She reached down, all the way down, to her very bottom, and from somewhere there, some well of endurance never called on before, she pulled up the very last she had.

He felt a surge, felt her power rise through his seat. She seemed to swell under him, and his heart nearly burst in his chest. And he felt he was flying.

The blacksmith shop was coming up fast. And now here it was, with no more time to ponder bringing Luther into his fight. Jeff threw himself from her back, landing on his wounded shoulder at the smithy door in a pile of snow shoveled off the boardwalk. The impact and pain took his breath. A slug slammed into the shop's front wall, above his head, and then another scattered snow beside him. Fighting down panic, he scrambled sideways through the doorway. The mare continued down the street.

Staggering inside, past the glowing coals of the forge, he was aware of a great, hulking figure, standing partially in shadow. "I heard de' shootin'!"

Jeff didn't stop, but blurted, "Trouble! Big'un." Glancing back through the entry, he lunged for the back door, which gave out onto the alley.

•   •   •   •

PEPÉ HAD GAINED the lead. He swung off the running horse as they reached the blacksmith shop. He was hit, too, but not bad. A round from Sandy's Colt had pierced the fleshy part of his upper left arm, but he hardly felt it now.

He was resolute. The *gringo* was in there. He'd seen him duck inside. Jaimé's killer was seconds from justice. Pepé cocked his pistol and entered the shop in time to see his target plunging through the back door. He fired hastily, missing. Cocking the piece and pulling the trigger again, he heard the hammer fall on a spent primer. He had to reload. How proud his big brother would be if he were able to kill this troublesome *gringo*. Perhaps he'd never be angry with him again. Flipping open the loading gate of his revolver, he heard a voice erupt behind him.

"Hey, you!"

He turned and caught the working face of a four-pound, shaping hammer on the crown of his head. It was swung with all the force that two hundred and eighty pounds of Luther Powell could put into it. Pepé fell like a dropped anvil.

Jeff heard the shot that missed him, as well as Luther's bellow of rage. But there was no time to view the results. He was moving down the alley as fast as his exhausted legs could carry him, toward the livery barn.

Now Mano was there, on the walkway in front of the blacksmith shop. Sandy had hit him, as well, ironically in the same spot he'd shot the old marshal. The stub of his left, little finger was stinging and bleeding, but he ignored it. There was another, lesser wound, in the loose flesh just above his belt on his right side, and he disregarded that, also. His horse had been hit, too, and was now down and dying in the street outside the shop.

He was put on his guard by the heavy silence following Pepé's gunshot. With a porch post between himself and the smithy's front doorway, he called out, "*Hermanito! Que pasa?*"

For several seconds there was silence, then an unfamiliar voice called back, "Welcome, stranguh. Yo' friend is right heyah, on de flo', restin' up. O'cose he don't look too good. His haid be shaped some diffunt den when he come in!"

It sounded like gibberish to Mano, some foreign language. Then there was quiet again. His instincts said stay away, stay out. Whoever the strange speaker was, he sounded dangerous.

He stepped from behind the post and moved warily along the side wall of the smithy, not wanting to walk into a bullet. At the corner he stopped and peered up the alley toward the livery. And there he saw him, maybe thirty-five yards away, the *cobarde* Cameron, scrambling toward the safety of the barn.

Aiming his rifle and squeezing the trigger, he felt the hammer fall on an empty chamber. More ammunition was in his saddlebags, on a dead horse somewhere behind him. Dropping the carbine, he drew his revolver. He took a two-hand hold, settled his front sight, and squeezed. The gun bucked up out of his line of vision and he saw his target go down at the corner of the barn. Mano gave a fleeting thought to his brother, but dismissed him for the present. Now, to finish. It should be easy, but his instincts told him to go cautiously. This man had shown himself to be clever, as well as deadly, and very hard to kill.

TWENTY-TWO

JEFF FELT a heavy blow to his right hip. He went down, and then scrambled on hands and knees, along the barn wall, toward the front door. He felt no pain from the new wound. Just numbness.

Fighting to regain his feet, he managed a shambling run to the entry. Inside, there was a vague feeling of shelter. It was dim, but as he made his crippled way along the main aisle, he could see that Bonnie Blue had gotten to her usual stall. But she was down. No time to check on her now, though.

He had no doubt that at least one bandit, maybe two, still pursued him. What he needed was a place to fort up. Scanning the interior in desperation, he could barely get his mind to serve him. Between loss of blood and the fatigue of over a week in the saddle, covering more than two hundred miles, the last of it at a desperate pace, his brain seemed to be shutting down.

At the end of the aisle, next to Foster's office door, was a stack of unopened grain bags, fifteen or twenty, with room enough behind them for a man to hide. They made a waist-high wall where they'd been offloaded. Jeff hoped that fifty pounds of oats would stop a bullet. Either way, it would have to do.

He limped and hopped along as fast as he could, but it was maddeningly slow. After what seemed forever, with the last of his energy, he threw himself over the top row of bags, just as a slug thudded into the office wall. He rolled into a sitting position. His hip wound was bleeding freely, soaking the floor where he sat. The bullet hole in his shoulder had re-opened and was bleeding, as well. But he felt almost nothing.

Drawing the Colt again, he got up on his knees and peered over the stack of bags. And there he was, Mano Lucero, ten feet inside the front door. Jeff cocked his pistol, and Mano, hearing the metallic clicks, made a dive for an empty stall to one side. Jeff threw a hasty shot at the moving figure from behind his makeshift fortress. "Missed! God-damnit," he said out loud, his brain foggy and dull. "I'm gonna have to practice up with this thing one day."

He could see movement between the slats of the stall where Mano had disappeared, and aimed again. But when he pulled the trigger, rather than another sharp report, he heard the flat, sickening clack of a firing pin falling on a dead primer. Four more pulls with the same result and he knew his gun was empty. He couldn't remember doing so much shooting. Then he recalled the shots from horseback, during the run into town.

It was all mixed up in his worn-out brain. He sank back and let his head rest against the wall. His shot-up, exhausted body was drifting away. It seemed he was floating. Trying to retrieve more rounds from his cartridge belt, he was disappointed to feel them slip through his disobedient fingers.

If *he* knew his revolver was empty from the dead falls of the hammer, then his enemy knew it, too. He must have heard it. And sure enough, there was the sound of boots approaching, jingle bobs ringing against the steel rowels of his spurs. Jeff was slipping from consciousness, struggling to stay awake, aware that the musical footfalls were nearly upon him. Soon, it would be over. "Made a good run," he thought. "That little horse and me. Hell of a horse. Not her fault. I weakened, not her. God bless her."

He didn't realize his eyes were closed until he heard the voice. "Surely you are not dead, *cabron*?" His lids fluttered open to see a figure above him in a tall crowned sombrero above a sharp, brown face, black eyes burning.

And then those eyes registered dismay. "*Qué esto es?*" The face leaned forward. "But you are not the man I shot off *la grulla* in the canyon, the man I saw before me on the ground."

Jeff croaked, "My pardner. Ridin' my horse. You back shot him, you sorry son of a bitch." And that was all the breath he had for talk.

Mano nodded. "Yes, it must be so. You could be *hermanos*, the two of you, looking so alike." His right hand came into view, the revolver in it. "But that is nothing now. And I have to say, you are one tough *hombre. Muy duro.* But now your run is over. Even your assassins along the road could not stop us."

He stared down at Jeff with hatred, his full torso looming above the grain sacks, gun in hand. "You risked much to steal the mare. You stole her twice. Once from my brother, Jaimé, and again from me. She must mean much to you. As much, perhaps, as my brother meant to me."

Jeff was played out, his arms to his sides, his empty pistol loose in his right hand, and cartridges from his belt lying on his lap and next to him in the blood-soaked dirt. Though strength was gone, his spirit burned. "Go on. Get it done, you bastard *chingadero*," he said. Or had he just thought it? His chin on his chest now, eyes half closed.

But Mano had more to say. "Such a shame that the thing you killed for, murdered Jaimé for, and are about to die for, lies dead herself, in that stall." Jeff barely heard him. "But no matter now, *Señor* Cameron. Time for you to pay for your rash behavior. And for our brother." Mano lifted the revolver. "*Vaya al Diablo!*"

Funny how much thinking a man could do in the last seconds of his life. Thoughts of Maggie, how she'd take this hard. Thoughts of what they might have done together. He hated to miss all that.

And then he heard a shout. Mano swung halfway around and saw a backlit figure in the barn aisle, twenty feet away, redirecting his weapon as he turned.

The blast, like the report of a twelve-pounder canon, split the air in the barn, and Mano's sombrero disappeared in a cloud of shredded felt and dust. Jeff's eyes opened again, and he felt his face and chest splattered. Something was wrong with the head of his enemy. From the jaws up, it seemed mostly to be gone. And then the man dropped from sight, below the wall of grain bags.

What did this mean? Had the revolver blown up in the killer's hand? That made no sense. "So, I ought to be dead," he thought. "Surely, I am. And what's this mess all over me? More blood? Mine?"

His confusion deepened as another hat appeared above his fortress wall. But beneath that hat was a beautiful, flushed face, teeth clenched in a firm jaw. Looking down at him—a worn-out, blood-spattered figure on the barn floor—she broke open the goose gun and extracted the spent shell. White smoke curled up from the empty chamber.

"Howdy, Maggie," he whispered, grinning weakly. "You really can use that thing."

•   •   •   •

SHE WAS SIPPING her forth cup of coffee, watching from her lookout. Her stomach was too tight to tolerate breakfast. The ten gauge hammer gun lay across the bed, loaded with #3 goose shot. There were more such rounds in her coat pockets. And she had just turned and set her cup down on the washstand when she heard the first gunshot. Springing to the window, she could see nothing at first. And then two more shots cracked in the winter air. She threw the sash up and leaned out to her waist, and here they came, Jeff and Bonnie Blue, and she saw he was riding bareback, and her throat clutched at the sight of them.

The mare was lathered as if on a day in August. Her belly was drawn and her coat was soaked. But she was running like a horse possessed. Jeff looked like a ghost rider, hat gone, no coat, and his face an ashen grey. Maggie started to yell, but then got her first glimpse of his pursuers, only fifty yards behind. Some instinct held her voice, and in the next instant she saw Jeff throw himself from the mare's back, to pile up in the snow in front of the blacksmith shop. She saw him crab his way through the front door, and drew herself inside the window. Enough watching. Time to get in the game. In spite of Sandy's instructions to stay at the window, she turned toward the bed. Snatching up the shotgun, she jerked open the door and pounded down the hall to the head of the stairs.

•   •   •   •

SHE WAS ALMOST to the smithy door when she heard a single pistol shot from inside the livery. The action was now there. Mending her course, she ran down the rutted street, trying to stay in the softer, quieter snow, the heavy weapon across her breast at port arms. Stopping at the entry, she caught her breath and tried to see inside, but she was blinded by sun on snow and could make out nothing in the dim interior. She could hear a harsh, unfamiliar voice, with a heavy Spanish accent. She pulled both hammers back to full cock.

With all the stalking skill her uncle had taught her, she eased into the barn, hugging the row of stalls, cat footing toward the sound of the voice at the end of the aisle. As her eyes adjusted, she made out a tall figure in a black sombrero, leaning over what appeared to be a stack of grain bags. A long barrel revolver hung in his right hand, loose at his side. As she closed the distance to twenty feet, she saw the pistol come up and heard the man say, "Senor Cameron." With no hesitation she planted her feet and mounted the shotgun. As the butt snugged into her shoulder, she cried, "Nooo!" The man pivoted, bringing his gun around to bear. But Maggie's sights had found those terrible eyes. She fired.

•   •   •   •

SHE AVOIDED looking down at the mangled corpse on the barn floor in front of the barricade. And she feared what she would see behind those grain bags. Her heart was in her mouth as she forced herself to lean over the wall. And then his eyes looked up out of red sockets, and his dry lips formed the words, "Howdy, Maggie, you really can use that thing." She nearly fainted in relief.

•   •   •   •

HE COULD HEAR voices. They annoyed him. His hip hurt. His shoulder throbbed. He wanted just to sleep. "And where is here, anyway? It ain't heaven, that's plain. Angels wouldn't talk so much. And, if I was dead, I wouldn't be hurtin' this much? Guess I'm not dead then. Unless it's the other place. Oh, hell! Could be."

Then he was sure he did hear an angel's voice, warm and sweet. And familiar. "Better see about this," he thought. He cracked an eye open and there was Maggie, still in riding clothes, hair loose, her brow furrowed. So he opened the other eye, too, for here was a sight worth seeing. And now that frown turned into a blinding smile, and his heart beat a little faster, and the hip hurt not so much.

She stepped out of his view and was replaced by that old drunk of a doctor, who seemed sober enough just now. Then she was back in the picture, talking to the doc, but about what he couldn't tell. Too much effort. Back to sleep.

•   •   •   •

"HE'S DRIFTED off again," Maggie was saying, with concern in her voice. Doc Maynard put a hand to Jeff's forehead, left it a few seconds, took it away.

"It's the laudanum, and pure exhaustion. There's no fever, and I don't expect any later. Sleep's what he needs now. He's lost some blood, but it doesn't appear to be too much. We're lucky that bullet didn't hit the femoral artery on the way through. And it's good I got down to that barn so fast."

Maggie smiled. "I appreciate your quick response, Doctor."

He smiled back. "A pretty girl waving a ten gauge always gets my attention." They both laughed. Looking down at his patient, the doctor went on. "No, I don't think you have much to worry about. I got all the fabric and bone chips and dirt out of the wound, I believe. The hipbone was nicked, but not shattered. He'll have a bit of a limp for a while, but he'll get over it. Now, when he's my age, it might aggravate him some, but that's a long ways off. And that hole in the shoulder, above the clavicle, is nothing of concern. It's several days old, and whoever tended to it knew a little about patching bullet wounds. He'll be fine."

She smiled down at the face she loved and then turned back to the doctor. Her expression had clouded. "Will he ride again?"

Doc looked up from closing his bag. "Oh, hell yes. It'll hurt some, at first, but I got an idea he'll just grit his teeth and saddle up anyway. This here jaybird's tough, honey. But I expect you know that."

She reached down and smoothed Jeff's hair. "Yes. I do know that."

•   •   •   •

VOICES AGAIN. Low and murmuring. One was gritty and harsh. He opened an eye and saw the town marshal peering down at him.

"How you feelin', son?"

Jeff licked his lips. "Been better, marshal. How's yourself?"

The marshal smiled. "Fine, son, just fine. I don't mean to bother you, but there's a heap of dead *banditos* stacked up on the boardwalk in front of the hardware store, so when you're up to it, I can use your help in doin' my report. Nothin' to worry about, though. By all accounts I've gotten so far, everything happened on the square. I guess I picked the wrong time to take a huntin' trip. Sorry I missed that little fracas." Jeff nodded weakly as the door opened. Out of his line of sight he heard a voice he did not recognize.

"What do you want me to do about them bodies, marshal? It's gonna be a warm afternoon."

"Well, what do you suppose, Frank? You're the dern undertaker."

"All right, but who's gonna...?"

"The town'll pay, dammit. Plant 'em!"

•   •   •   •

FLOATING TO THE SURFACE, again. And opening his eyes to see Maggie beside him, her hair up now, lovely in her dark velvet vest and long dress. Three more figures, down at the foot of the bed, almost comical in their contrast. A small head and part of a torso showing above the footboard, sharp eyes over a neatly trimmed goatee. Next to him, a towering, broad mass of a man, face dark as old saddle leather, grinning brightly. And then the tallest of them, in buckskin and plaid, bristling white beard, bright blue eyes. All smiling now to see their friend awake.

Maggie leaned over and put her lips to his forehead. "Hello, cowboy." Her voice was warm, like those lips.

"Howdy, Maggie." Maybe he had died and gone to heaven after all, for surely, here was that angel again. Then he looked back at his friends. "Nope. Guess not."

"Don't I git a kiss from ya'll, too?" he asked. The three laughed.

"I don't like you *that* much," said Shortstack.

Luther shook his head. "An' I don't nevah kiss no mens!"

Sandy smiled. "Pairhaps after yeh've bathed and shaved, lad."

They all went on laughing, more from relief than any real humor in the absurd request.

He looked around the room. Plain, neat, and orderly. One picture on the wall to his left. A painting of a maple tree, regal in fall colors. "What place is this?" he asked.

Shortstack made a sweeping gesture. "Welcome to Hotel Brakefield. You're in my bedroom, back of the eatery."

Jeff grinned wide. "I thought this bed was a mite short." All laughed at that, too. "And I smell bacon."

Maggie touched his cheek. "Hungry?"

He looked up. "Starved. I could eat a green cowhide. Hair on." More chuckles.

"I'll get busy," said Shortstack, turning toward the kitchen.

Luther's eyes followed him. "I 'spect I could eat, too."

Over his shoulder, Shortstack called back, "Well, come on then. I'll just cook up that dead horse Sandy shot out from under the bandit chief. Should hold you 'til supper time."

Sandy fell in behind Luther. "Aye, Big'un. With me around, we'll never lack for meat. Scotland is a legendary hotbed of horse eaters," he teased, as they filed on out.

Maggie shut the door behind them and returned to Jeff's bedside. Reaching out, she took one of his hands. "You're looking better."

He smiled up at her. "This is gettin' to be a habit with us."

She cocked her head. "How's that?"

"Well," he said, "me layin' in bed and you looking after me."

She smiled back. "I suppose. But this time, you took on more than one old, Spanish bull."

"Yeah," he mused. "I s'pose I need to take up a more peaceful career."

Still smiling, she said, "I'd advise it."

They looked at each other for a few seconds. Then he said, "But I'm kinda' hazy on a few things. I guess I'm a little shot up."

She nodded. "A little. Two holes. One high in the right shoulder, the other in the left hip. Good news is both bullets went clean through. The hipbone is nicked, but not broken, says Doc. Does it hurt much?"

"Some. Not too bad right now. Helps to see you."

Her smile widened. "Doc did a good job," she said, "with just enough whiskey to steady his hand."

He frowned. "What about ridin'?"

She heard a hint of apprehension in the question. "I thought you might fret about that. But don't. Doc said it might be painful at first, but that you can ride as soon as you've been on your feet awhile."

There was relief in his face. "That's good. If I couldn't ride…well."

She nodded. "I know."

He ran a hand over his face. He was remembering some of it now. Looking in her eyes. "There must have been five of 'em altogether. I saw what happened to the one that almost did for me, at the barn. The one you got with the goose gun."

Maggie said nothing.

"Thanks," he said.

She only nodded.

"What about the others?"

She pulled up the one chair in the room and sat. "Only two made it to town," she answered.

Jeff smiled faintly. "Old Jobson got one."

Maggie looked puzzled. "Who?"

He shook his head. "A fellow along the trail who helped me. Tell you about him later."

She nodded. "Well, anyway, Uncle Sandy and Shortstack were waiting, where the mouth of Spruce Canyon hits the road."

"Yeah," Jeff said, "now I remember going by Sandy. Shortstack was there, too?"

"He was, behind a boulder. You yelled as you rode by that they were right behind. Uncle shot the first man dead. Shortstack killed another and then his gun jammed. Then Uncle emptied his revolver at the others as they went past. It seems he hit at least one of them, perhaps both, but not fatally. He hit one of their horses, too. It made it to town and then collapsed near Luther's."

Jeff whistled. "The friends I got."

She smoothed his hair again. "More than you know. Do you remember leaping off Bonnie Blue and taking cover in Luther's shop?"

He knit his brow for a few seconds, then nodded. "Right. One of 'em was breathin' down my neck. Took a shot at me inside the shop, but missed."

Maggie smiled. "That's right. The younger one. Unfortunately for him, that was the last round in his pistol. He was trying to reload when Luther hit him."

Jeff said, "Luther hit him?"

Maggie nodded. "Indeed. With his blacksmith hammer, on the head."

Jeff winced. "Ouch!"

Maggie went on. "Luther doesn't want to talk about it, but Doc says he must have swung that hammer with his last ounce. The bandit's head is completely caved in. They had trouble getting his hat off."

He winced again.

"Don't feel sorry for that bastard," she said.

His eyes widened. "Why, Miss MacTeague. Such language."

She blushed. "Well," she said, "It doesn't pay to mess with my man!"

He seemed still confused. "But how come you to be here?"

She scooted the chair closer, putting on a mild frown. "When you rode out of Claymore headquarters, I was furious."

He grinned sheepishly. "So I noticed."

She went on. "I knew there was more to this story than you had said. And I recalled you telling me that the great, grey horse had come from Uncle Sandy, that he had arranged it. So I did some fast thinking and came up with a plan, which was to ride to Pagosa and force that cantankerous old man to tell me everything he knew about you. Because frankly, Jeff, I was having some serious doubts."

He swallowed as he said, "Everything, huh?"

She nodded. "Everything."

He couldn't hold her eyes. "And?"

She leaned back. "I had a troublesome first night, but the next day Uncle sat me down and told me a few more things, foremost of which is that everyone in this country has a past. And I decided he's right. And I decided that you are a good man and, whatever you did in your past, before we met, short of mayhem and murder, is none of my business."

He raised his eyes back to her face. "Some might say I did murder."

She shook her head emphatically. "You killed, but both times in self-defense. That's different."

He wondered, "But if I'd'a minded my own business, two men would still be breathing."

"Correct," she said. "Two bastards who would have gone on abusing horses and terrorizing young women. Too bad it was you but, if not, the job would have fallen to another."

Voice breaking, he said, "But I got that young girl killed." He rubbed an eye with the heel of his hand.

Maggie squeezed the other one. "Jeff. Listen to me. You made an honorable attempt to liberate a young woman from a bad man's tyranny. A girl you felt deeply for. The fact of her death is tragic, but it was simply a case of horribly bad luck. Not your fault. Not her fault. The blame lies with the gambler. His bullets killed her. And think on this. As the saying goes, 'The only thing required for the triumph of evil is for good men to do nothing.' And you *are* a good man. And you didn't just stand by and do nothing. Not with Bad Jimmy, and not with Surratt."

It was quite a speech, and it got to him. Some of his guilt lifted in those moments. The way she put it, things didn't sound quite so bad. But he had more questions. "All right. But I guess you stayed in Pagosa after your talk with Sandy?"

She smiled again, and with that look of determination that was a MacTeague trait, explained, "Uncle Sandy tried to make me go home, but was unsuccessful. And it seemed logical you'd return here first, rather than bring trouble to the ranch. And then your wire came. I was in the hotel at the time. Uncle Sandy, Shortstack, and I held a war council. I wanted to join them at the canyon mouth, but they convinced me to take a reserve position here in town. It was good that I did."

Jeff frowned. "And before all that, you rode here from headquarters, alone?"

"Right. I knew if I asked Da' or told anyone, it would just cost me time and aggravation. So I left a note and rode."

"Who'd you ride?"

"The Spanish stallion, of course."

"Hard ride on a four year old."

"Nonsense. He was splendid. Still had plenty of horse under me when I got here."

"And the barn? How'd you show up there?"

"I saw you come in with the last two on your heels. I was watching from the second floor of the hotel, from my room. By the time I got down to the street, you were in the livery."

"And you just happened to bring that cannon?"

With a thin smile she answered. "A girl never knows when she's going hunting."

•   •   •   •

AFTER A HEAPING PLATE of bacon, eggs, and pancakes, he should have felt better, but she noticed sadness had come across his face.

"What is it, Jeff?"

He looked out the window, in the direction of the livery barn. "I guess I rode Bonnie Blue to death."

She grinned, ready with good news. "Oh, no! She's alive! Joe Barr is here and he's taking care of her."

He was relieved, elated. Then puzzled. "If Joe's here…I can't imagine he packed up and rode all this way lugging his horse doctoring gear. How long would that take? How long have I been out?"

She took his hand again. "Four days. In and out of consciousness. Doc says he's rarely seen such exhaustion. And, of course, you'd lost some blood. You needed a good sleep."

"I'll be damned."

"And Joe took the stage. The road's open again, at least enough for a light coach and a six-up hitch. He brought his veterinarian supplies. I wired Da'. He chartered the coach for a special run."

Jeff nodded. "There's a man I owe."

Maggie smiled. "Don't worry about it. He says he'll work it out of you."

"All right. But what about the mare?"

"I waited 'til Doc Maynard said you were out of danger, and then went down and got her on her feet. And now Joe's been with her just about every minute since he arrived. Has his meals brought to the barn. Says she's got a bowed tendon, but not the worst he's seen. Near hind leg. And she's wheezing a bit, but he's having her breathe steam with eucalyptus and camphor. And she's dehydrated, but willing to drink. Doesn't have much appetite, but she's taking a little warm, bran mash."

Jeff nodded, face still grave. "What's he think?"

Maggie's smile widened. "Joe says she's going to make it. Says he stakes his reputation on it." Her face sobered. "But she's got no more runs in her. He says she'll be fine for easy rides, but nothing too hard."

He nodded. "I hate what I did to her."

She squeezed his hand. "That little mare saved your life. If you hadn't ridden her like you did, you'd be the dead one, instead of those killers."

He blinked at the thought of what he owed the horse, what he owed them all. "Yeah," was all he could say.

"And, Jeff, we can breed her now. With my stallion. She's proved herself, and more. Now we can concentrate on combining those bloodlines."

He brightened. "You're right." Pausing, he gazed at her.

She grew uncomfortable. "What?" she asked.

He took on a serious look. "A minute ago you said something about it don't pay to mess with your man."

"That's what I said."

"Does that mean me?"

She cocked her head, warm eyes on his face. "Who else?"

He raised himself in the bed, propped up on elbows. "Are you my girl?"

She leaned in close. Now her look was serious. "Aye, I am that. As long as we ride side by side, as equals. I'll neither ride nor walk so much as half a step behind. Not for you or for any other man. Never!"

He responded with his best smile back at her. "I wouldn't expect anything else, Maggie, nor want it any other way."

She beamed at him. "Good. So does that mean you're my man?"

He nodded, his throat tightening as he declared, "From the crown of my hat to the heel of my boot."

She kissed him lightly on the lips. "Again, *good.*" She kissed him once more. This time, long and deep.

"Well," he said, a little breathless, "that being the case, I'd like to raise the possibility of startin' another bloodline."

Maggie beamed, her eyes shining. "Start talkin', cowboy."

EPILOGUE

IT HAD BEEN more than a year since Jeff had taken a bullet in the hip in his final showdown with the Lucero brothers. His limp had become almost unnoticeable. There was still occasional pain, but time spent in the saddle had seemed to help. He felt a twinge now as he stooped to set two cups of coffee on the new cabin's front porch. Maggie sat on the top step, her back against a support post, her nightgown open to admit the eager nursing of the baby in her arms. She collected a cup. "Thanks, Hon," she said, sipping, careful not to spill any on her child.

He stood beside the pair. He'd never seen anything so beautiful as the morning sun lighting the faces of his wife and son. Drinking from his own cup and thinking momentarily of the previous year, he almost had to pinch himself to confirm he was here and living this sweet dream.

Across the yard, Bonnie Blue fed from the hay bunk in the corral. Her foal, a sturdy filly, already showing strong signs of her Spanish blood, was nursing greedily. The sire, Maggie's dun stallion, his head out the top door of his stall in the small new barn, looked on. Jeff was struck by the picture of these two, beginning families. Two fathers, two mothers, two nursing babies. "Looks like breakfast time for young'uns, down on the farm," he said, grinning at Maggie.

She turned her face up and favored him with a smile so bright that he felt his breath nearly leave him. "Yep," she said, "A couple of good ol' brood mares serving their progeny. 'Course, some credit's due you two randy studs. But not too much."

He chuckled. "You're startin' to sound like me now, like a cowhand."

She looked down at her child, smoothing his fine, blonde hair. "Well," she said, "I'm just thankful I still have you to listen to. The Luceros nearly shut you up for good."

Jeff's face clouded. "That's past. I don't care to recall it."

She smiled back up at him. "All right." After a moment of shared silence she said, "I love our little cabin. But I think you worked yourself too hard on it, still mending as you are."

He shook his head. "I was building a dream house for my dream girl." She looked up again, with an even brighter smile. He chuckled. "Well, it ain't much more than a stout shack right now, but I'll be adding on a little later, once the gather and brandin' are done."

Looking away from him, out across the yard, she said, "Well, no hurry, there being just the three of us."

He grew a sly grin she didn't see. "That's a situation liable to change."

She reddened a bit, which he couldn't see. "I'll hold you to that, Mister. But let's be frugal. You've already spent too much on the land. Dad wanted to give us these two sections as a wedding present. You didn't have to pay him."

Jeff frowned mildly. "We've been down this trail before, Sweetie. I told you when I proposed I had my own money. I didn't show up here to woo the boss's daughter and collect a patch of free ground. Besides, I paid for only one section. The other was his gift to you.

She looked dismayed. "But he wanted to do it. It was his gift to you as well. He felt insulted."

Jeff shook his head. "No such thing. He respects me for it, I know he does. And I'd say fifty head of cows, two good bulls, and a dozen fine brood mares was wedding present enough." She said no more about it. Her silence was all the accommodation he was going to get on the matter and he knew it. So, he let it go.

Sitting down next to her and looking out over the little valley, seeing the narrow creek winding its way through the notch in the low hills that hid the main ranch from view, he solemnly promised himself never to take any of this for granted. He retrieved tobacco and papers from his pocket, paused, and then put them back. No smoking around the boy. Mama's rules. "That's all right," he thought. "Ought to give it up anyway." She'd promised more kisses if he did. Pretty good trade.

A little breeze came up, lifting puffs of dust and leaf litter from the yard. Bobby slept, his belly full, his small mouth still locked to his mother's breast. She disconnected him carefully, standing up. He didn't stir. Looking at her young husband she said, "Don't forget we're going to Da's for Sunday dinner." He nodded. "You don't mind shaving do you?"

He peered up at her, grinning. "Sure, Sweetpea." Again, he found himself taken with the sight of her above him, hair down loose, the breeze lifting the hem of her nightgown and revealing her strong, rider's legs. Tossing the last of his coffee into the yard, he rose to his feet. "I'll bring the buckboard around once I get cleaned up. I expect it's too soon for our son and heir to be up in the saddle with you."

Maggie, smiling, but in her decisive fashion said, "On the contrary, my dear. I believe it's high time this young man got horseback!"

—El Fin—

GLOSSARY

Armitas – chaps cut in the Spanish style.

Amansadore – master horse trainer.

Banderas – banners.

Bosal – braided rawhide noseband, part of the Mexican hackamore bridle.

Bosalito – a small diameter bosal, typically used in conjunction with a bit.

Buena suerte – good luck.

Caballero – horseman, gentleman.

Caballa, caballo – female horse, male horse.

Cabeza – head.

Cabrío – goat.

Cabron – bastard.

Cantle – dish-shaped part of the saddle directly behind the rider's seat.

Cobarde – coward.

Cocina – kitchen.

Cocinero – cook, chef.

Copper cricket roller – single roller, made of copper, centered in the mouthpiece of a bridal bit, which makes a sound like a cricket chirping when the horse rolls it on its tongue.

Comida – food.

Git down rope – light rope tied around a horse's neck, behind the jaw, and run out through the bosal or bosalito to tie the horse when the rider *gits down*.

Hermano, hermanito – brother, little brother.

Hijo de la perra – son of a bitch.

Honda – small loop in the end of a lariat through which the tail of the rope passes to form the loop.

Hostler – one who tends horses, liveryman.

Jefé – chief, boss.

Latigo – leather strap connecting the saddle to the nearside cinch ring.

Maestro – term of respect used in addressing a man, usually older; one who is accomplished, a master of his trade.

Maguey rope – a rope braided from fibers of the maguey plant.

Mesteños – feral horses, mustangs.

Mecaté – set of reins braided from the mane hair of a horse.

Mi'ijo – my son.

Morral – feedbag hung on a horse's head, from which it eats grain.

Muchacho – boy.

Mulo – mule.

Panniers – canvas or leather bags that hang on both sides of a pack saddle for carrying food or equipment.

Patron – male head of a ranch or family; term of respect.

Peligroso – dangerous.

Pobrecita, pobrecito – poor little thing, referring to a girl, boy.

Ramuda – herd of horses from which ranch hands select their mount.

Raton – mouse.

Reata – rope braided from rawhide splits.

Romal – length of braided rawhide with leather poppers on one end, the other end connected to rawhide bridle reins.

Roundance – to go around or avoid.

Santa Barbara bit – an ornately engraved and frequently silver mounted bit in the Spanish style, usually with a spade or half-breed mouthpiece, developed in the 1800's on the southern California cattle range.

Segundo – second in command; term of respect.

Tienda – store or mercantile.

Vaquero – Mexican cowboy.

Viejo – old man.

Zócalo – village square.

AUTHOR'S NOTE

FOR HALF MY LIFE, I have wanted to write a story about an incredible endurance ride, testing one horse and one man to their absolute limits. Well, finally, here it is.

I suppose I should issue the usual disclaimer about my characters, all being fictitious, none of them resembling persons living or dead. For the most part that's true, with the exception of Joe Barr, the old Anglo cowboy who appears about halfway through this story.

I knew the real Joe briefly, during my stay in southern California. He was ninety-two years old at the time. He helped me with an off-the-track thoroughbred gelding, and I learned more from Joe in one hour than I could have figured out on my own in a year. Joe was a true, old time California *vaquero*. He was the real deal, and I consider knowing him a remarkable privilege. I have a bridle of his, and it's one of my most prized possessions.

The geography of this story is real. The creeks and rivers, mountain peaks and valleys are all there. I have ridden through a lot of that country. And hope to ride the rest, if I live long enough. You can find most of it marked on any good map. It is fine country, worth a look. Maybe I'll see you out there.

John R. Wright
Mancos, CO

ACKNOWLEDGMENTS

NO ONE ever writes a novel and gets published without plenty of help. I am no exception. I am graciously indebted to the following:

Paul Berkowitz, author of *The Case of the Indian Trader: Billy Malone and the National Park Service Investigation at Hubbell Trading Post* and *U.S. Rangers: The Law of the Land*, former neighbor, and a great friend, for his early proofreading, as well as sponsorship and good counsel.

Karen Blaine, a woman so tough she fights badgers (with a shovel), for her gentle reading and good ideas, as well as staunch friendship.

Kathleen Steele, PhD, A.K.A., Sweetpea, for her love and support during the early stages of the writing process.

The Absolute Bakery in Mancos, Colorado, and all who work there, for providing sustenance that kept body and soul together when eatin' money was hard to come by.

My editor-publisher and dear friend Raymond Rose, PhD, who goes to the head of this list. He took a messy manuscript and turned it into a book. Without his indefatigable efforts, there would be no *La Grulla*.

DEDICATION

THIS BOOK is dedicated to my father, Captain Thomas R. Wright, U.S. Army Air Corps. Recipient of the Bronze Star for distinguished service in the Korean Conflict. Daddy loved going to Western movies and he always took me with him.

ABOUT THE AUTHOR

JOHN R. WRIGHT is a life-long horseman. He moved west from Tennessee as a young man, working as a ranch hand, packer, hunting guide, and horse trainer. Much of the country portrayed in this story he has ridden. He lives in southwest Colorado in the shadow of the mighty San Juans, beside Mesa Verde National Park, with a Labrador Retriever, a Tennessee Walking Horse, and various transient cats. His other published works include *Trout on a Stick* from Willow Creek Press, and numerous articles appearing in *Ducks Unlimited* magazine, *Gun Dog* magazine, the *Retriever Journal*, and several anthologies.